Discover how it all be

Reflections of Toddsville

by

Hollie Van Horne

A time-travel novel unlike any other you will ever read!

America's best selling historic romance writer, Trudy Johnson, has just one problem—her love life! The only man she's taken to bed in five years is the photo of a Victorian man taken in 1891 that she keeps on her bedside table. Writing five novels in five years has been grueling work, and her agent, Jennifer, thinks she needs a break. So she pays for Trudy to take her summer vacation in a rustic cabin by a peaceful lake in Richfield Springs—just outside Cooperstown, New York. Trudy's research detective, Bruce Wainwright, thinks it's a bad idea—unless she takes him along. The two brothers who own the cabins, Sam and Jim Cooper, are friendly but talk in weird riddles. Nevertheless, she finds peace and serenity in this idyllic forest—until everything goes wrong! On June 21, 1997, she falls asleep in her Richfield Spring's cabin only to awaken in the same bed one hundred years in the past—and not alone! The man from the photo is right beside her. His name is Cuyler Carr, and he's not happy about his fishing trip, or his reputation, being ruined by her arrival. Looks like Trudy's love life is starting to pick up!

From the author of *When We Do Meet Again*

The first novel in the Time Travelers, Incorporated series

Somewhere in time Trudy Johnson will meet the man of her dreams. Will time also separate them?

I was dreaming and rolled over in the bed. I felt something in the bed with me. No, I felt *someone* in the bed. It couldn't be. Another cautious touch. A warm masculine smell touched my nostrils. This was no dream. It was real. I raised my body from the mattress just a bit hoping to see in the blackness if it were alive or dead. It moved. I screamed. Loudly, and for a long time, I screamed bloody murder as I wrapped myself in the bed cover.

It screamed too. Loudly, and for a long time, it screamed bloody murder as it wrapped itself in one of the sheets.

Silence.

"Who...who...who are you?" I said, straining to see the shape of my adversary.

"I dare say, I could ask you the same question."

Reflections of Toddsville
by
Hollie Van Horne

This book is a work of fiction. Names, characters, places, and incidents are either the products of the author's imagination or are used fictitiously.

An original publication of Time Travelers LLC

Time Travelers
Columbiana, Ohio
44408
www.timetravelersinc.org

ISBN: 0-9674552-6-X
Library of Congress catalog card number: 00 090257
First printing June 2000

Printed in the U.S.A.

* The photos on the front and back cover of the paperback version of Reflections of Toddsville are from 1890 and were produced by the Smith and Telfer Studio, Copperstown, New York. The New York State Historical Association in Cooperstown has graciously granted permission for their use on both covers of the book.

Reflections of Toddsville

Hollie Van Horne

Time Travelers Inc. Book One

This novel has been written as a loving

memorial to the beloved storyteller of

Toddsville

Cuyler E. Carr

So long as men can breathe, or eyes can see,
So long lives this, and this gives life to thee.
William Shakespeare

Acknowledgements:

The stories of Cuyler E. Carr which have been printed in *The Freeman's Journal* and *The Otsego Farmer* and in Lawrence William Gardner's (data from Cuyler's personal scrapbook now owned by Mrs. Martha Kinney's descendants) book *Recollections of an Early Mill Town Toddsville*
The stories of Samuel Street Todd as told to James Fenimore Cooper for his book *The Legends of a Northern County* chapter entitled "Toddsville"
Clarence L. Peaslee
Lawrence William Gardner
Lance Gardner
New York State Historical Association's entire staff
The Huntington Library--Oneonta
The Cooper Inn
The Inn at Cooperstown
Tunnicliff Inn and the unnamed waitress who hummed the theme song from "Somewhere in Time"
The Smith and Telfer Photographic Collection-New York State Historical Association who gave permission for the cover and back photos of Cuyler to be used for this book
Jim Havner
David Petri
Barbara Green
Rodney Ingalls's data on the Ingalls family
Loretta Bush's genealogical research on the Carr families
David Carr's genealogical data on the Carr families

The many people of Otsego County who pointed the way and took the time to help, not just the people from 1997, but those departed souls whose names are mentioned in this work of fiction and whose lives and stories give us a clearer look through the "window of time."

And last but not least—Cuyler E. Carr who took me on my first trip through the time tunnel!

Other books by Hollie Van Horne:

Wild Roses for Miss Jane(Book two)
McKnight's Revenge (Book three)
When We Do Meet Again (Book four)
The Diary of Jean-Jacques Coupier (Book five)
Portrait of Lydia (Book six)
Beneath the Wings of Isis (Book seven)
Speak of the Dead (Mystery)

Coming soon:

The Serpent and The Rose (Book eight)

'Once you met Cuyler you never forgot him. He always took the conversation in hand. Cuyler was reserved, aristocratic, proper, and always well-dressed. He was eccentric though... as if he didn't belong in his own time period. He was in a different world from everyone else.'

As stated to Hollie Van Horne by
Rodney Ingalls 'Cuyler's mother's great- grand-nephew'
on June 22, 1997
in Hartwick Seminary

Chapter One

My name is Gertrude Johnson. You may have read some of my romance novels. This isn't a romance novel. It's my true story whether you believe it or not. It's a story about love, but the most unusual one you'll ever read. When I'm finished writing this, it will be June, and I'll go back to him. To Cuyler. To Toddsville. It will be 1898, and we have plans for a wonderful future. Because, this time, I'm not coming back.

It all began when my agent, Jennifer Rosenblum, gave me a book of Victorian photos she had found on her summer travels. The photos came from a collection by Smith and Telfer who took photos in and around Cooperstown, New York in the 1890s. You see, I use photos, dolls, and nearly anything I can get my hands on, for inspiration when creating a character for one of my romance novels.

One photo of a Victorian man intrigued me so that I folded the book to the page and rested it above my Macintosh Performa 6116 CD. Later, I found the beautiful face of my innocent heroine, placed it beside the man's photo, and my Victorian romance novel was on its way to my fans.

One year later, Jennifer and I celebrated the novel's publishing contract with dinner at a small restaurant in Brooklyn. She paid.

"You're going to rest after this one. My orders," Jennifer said.

"Why should I stop now? I'm on a roll," I said, as I sipped my usual rum and Coke.

"Inspiration—perspiration. You need a break. You've stopped answering my phone calls. You haven't seen a hairdresser in months. You buy all your clothes from catalogues. And Wainwright told me that the two of you haven't pillaged a library in months. The movie video on your kitchen table is overdue by three months, Trudy. I haven't seen the dust on your coffee table change shape for six. Look at you. You used to wear makeup—curl your hair. And there was a mischievous twinkle in your eye whenever a nice looking man with cute buns walked by. Three have cruised our way, and you haven't so much as glanced at them. And they're our age. Something's very wrong, Trudy, and I'm worried about you."

I fingered the linen napkin—so soft. How nice to have real linen and not paper. How elegant it must have been in the Victorian time period about which I had just written. Sometimes, I became too engrossed in the past when I wrote. "Maybe you're right," I said.

"Not to change the subject, but here's your first check and a special bonus from me," she said, handing me one of her stylish, self-addressed envelopes. I peeked inside. There was a check for twenty-thousand dollars and something else.

"What's this?" I said, my head starting to swirl from the drink. Inside was another envelope. It wasn't sealed. I slipped it open with my fingernail—what was left of my fingernail, that is. Typing destroyed my manicures.

It was a gift certificate for a three month stay at a private cottage in Richfield Springs, New York.

I scowled. "Isn't this place some sort of health resort—on a lake—where people fish?" I hate fish.

"I'm surprised you've heard of it," she said, sipping her Martinis. How could she drink those things?

"It was mentioned in the book of photos you gave me. It's near Cooperstown, New York—Baseball Hall of Fame—and..."

I wasn't born yesterday. "And it's where you and Syd traveled last summer, isn't it?"

"Right you are. I thought about you, pal, and reserved the cabin for you. Syd and I stayed in a motel. You know Sydney. Not the camper type."

I was incredulous. "You're sending me to a bug-infested campground?" The rum was white, Bacardi, and the drink was loaded with the stuff. I was becoming loud, and she hushed me by placing her finger to her lips.

"It's a beautiful place. The grounds are covered with trees, flowers, birds, chipmunks, squirrels..."

I didn't let her finish. "And mosquitoes, smelly fish, ants, campers, and little kids screaming."

"You can take your computer, your FAX, and your telephone so that you and Wainwright can *buzz* each other." She had an interesting way with verbs. It must come with the publishing business. "You know the New York State Historical Association is located in Cooperstown," she said, in a manner which resembled seduction.

I realized how ungrateful I was sounding. After all, the trip probably cost more for three months' rent in this isolated cabin than my whole check. Plus, she was thinking of my well-being.

"I'll think about it," I said. "I'll check and see if *Chadwick's of Boston* is having a sale on mosquito-netted jumpsuits."

That was how it began. The photo, the novel completed, the cabin by the lake, the man. It seems so easy to write it like that. One sentence to explain everything. But, this will be the hardest story of my whole career to write.

We devoured a delicious meal. I don't eat much when I'm writing a book. A banana, three to four cups of coffee, and many cans of ginger ale seemed to sustain me through my creative stage. I consumed a medium-well cooked prime rib, a baked potato with butter—not sour cream—a huge salad with honey-mustard dressing, something which appeared to be fresh, steamed vegetables cut up into those interesting flower designs, a shared bottle of champagne, a piece of Turtle cheesecake, and hot, black coffee. My anatomy applauded.

She drove me to my condo. I promised her I'd think about the trip when I thanked her for the meal and the solace. I checked my handbag to make sure I had the gift certificate and the check.

When I unlocked the door to my condo, I faced darkness. I had forgotten to leave any lights on in my house, which I hate doing because I've seen too many slasher movies. They invariably spring to mind the moment I open the door. I just knew someone with a major mental deficiency was lurking in my shower.

He wasn't. I walked over to my phone and replayed the messages. There were three. The first was from my mother reminding me of my third cousin's wedding. Sorry Mom, I'm going to miss this one. The second was from a company terrified that the windows on my house were old and needed replacing. That was an interesting one since I live in a condominium complex that takes care of such things. The third was from Bruce Wainwright, my research analyst.

I looked at the clock, saw that it was one o'clock in the morning, and decided to be cruel. I was rewarded with a sleepy voice.

"Hello. Who the hell is this?" he said.

I had a vague erotic thought of what he might be sleeping in—if anything—or with whom he might be sleeping.

"Did I wake you? It's me, Trudy. You said on the message to

call as soon as I got in," I said, as sweetly as I knew how.

"Oh, Trudy." His vocal tone rose, making its quality ring with sudden interest.

"I was celebrating with Jennifer. I sold the book. What did you want?"

"Congratulations on the book. Have you been drinking?" he said.

"Yes, why?"

"Your voice sounds low, nebulous."

"I sound like a cloud?"

He laughed. "I should know better than to banter words with a writer. Anyway, I was wondering if you were going to need me in the next three months."

"Well, I don't need you now because I have no ideas. But, Jennifer gave me a reservation for a three months' stay somewhere near Cooperstown, New York, and who knows what I may come up with there. I understand it's loaded with natural inspirations," I said.

"Black snakes, eh? I've seen ads for cabins for writers in *Writer's Digest* magazine. Is it like that? You need to get away to write?" Wainwright said. I got the impression that he had another idea for how I might be cured.

"How could I become more of an ascetic than I am? Actually, writing is only her second motive. She thinks I look like shit and need some time off before I have some sort of nervous breakdown or something."

"The Cooperstown area is loaded with Victorian structures, and I know the research director of NYSHA."

"Is there a librarian anywhere in the world you don't know?"

"Perhaps in some distant clime like—Tibet maybe," he said.

"What were you going to do for three months if I didn't need you?"

"Well...I had the same idea Jennifer had. I was thinking of visiting some friends in Europe and was wondering if you would like to join me." He clarified. "Not because you need a break—which you do—but because I thought it would be fun."

"You think I look like shit too?"

Let's face it, I hadn't had a sex life since I graduated from Harvard five years ago and wrote my first novel. The only time I left Brooklyn was to do historical research or attend romance writers' conventions. I never met any interesting men there! I *had* harbored the thought of going to a mystery writers' convention just to see whether the crime and suspense authors were more *intriguing.* I could think of a few detectives I wouldn't mind dating. If their masculine authors looked anything like them...well.

There. Now you see the problem. I can't escape living in a fantasy world my father always argued I enjoyed more than real life.

"You know I think you look adorable," said Wainwright.

I'd asked for the line, and he'd delivered. Good boy.

He continued, "Wouldn't you rather travel the countries of Europe rather than kill mosquitoes at some *lake*? I have an interesting way of traveling that I'd like to..."

"Yes, as a matter of fact, I would," I said, interrupting him.

But, it was the possibility of romance with Bruce that concerned me.

Actually, the story of Wainwright and my meeting *is* entertaining. I met Wainwright in New York City where I stumbled into him—literally—in the history section of the New York Public Library. We found the situation so amusing, we decided to go to my hotel's bar, share stories, and get tipsy.

He told me that he was a research-for-hire detective who helped college professors and overworked, underpaid journalists. He worked for anyone who wanted to spend more time at their computer writing and less time at the library researching.

I told him that I liked doing my own research, but admitted that it would be easier to have someone do the leg work for me. He loved history and enjoyed playing literary detective as much as I did. I asked his fee and hired him on the spot.

He returned to Brooklyn with me, where we purchased a wealth of computer equipment and communication devises, then installed them in my condo. I went on-line, and we've been e-mailing each other ever since. When he acquires any data, he Faxes copies to me. It's quite convenient to have things shipped to you from libraries all over the world. I pay his airfare; he pays for his hotel room.

"I'm afraid if I vacation with you, I'll hurt Jennifer's feelings. She spent a lot of money on the reservation, and I don't expect she can get her money refunded. If you want to go to Europe just keep in touch. I'm taking all my equipment to the cabin with me. Don't worry I'll include the manuals when I pack. There isn't any reason why you shouldn't take a vacation between novels. You need a break as much as I do," I said.

His voice changed again, but this time to a soft, low, masculine tone which sent shivers up my spine. "I *could* come along. I'll bring a three month supply of Raid, a fly swatter, and a snake bite kit. Do North American snakes, indigenous to New York State, have poisonous venom?" he asked.

"I don't think so. *I don't know.* I'll get some books. Thanks for the offer of help." I had to admit the idea had merit. "Come on, Wainwright, you know romance writers have no sex life. We write about it, but we don't live it."

His voice retained a sensuousness which made my body yearn to be touched. "I promise never to tell. Perhaps you need to spice up your own sex life so that your next heroine has an even better time than the last one. I'm a good actor. I'll play the role of your next hero. I could even help you with the dialogue."

My body is saying, "Go, Trudy, go." My mind is saying, "Say goodbye to the nice man." Instead, I said, "Really?"

See! That's what gets me about Wainwright. He's tall, dark, and handsome and has the cutest blue eyes. He's very intelligent, actually looks cuter when he's wearing his silver-rimmed glasses, and he's my age. He's available and has never spoken for or against commitment. He doesn't make advances while we're working, but always gives the impression he's restraining his passion for me. Bruce dates, I guess, on occasion but seems to be keeping his love life open for me to take control if I show any interest. He likes women and thinks I'm attractive. I haven't had sex for five years, and he has a nice body. He believes that research should be matched with physical exercise so that one did not become fat, or a *computer potato*— as he calls it.

He's moral but never talks religion or politics. He has an intelligence which surpasses mine but couldn't write a clear paragraph if it killed him. He's even-tempered, good-natured, and we never argue or even debate anything. Furthermore, he has no qualms about having a woman boss. He loves every word I write, and thinks I'm a genius.

So, what's the problem you're probably asking yourself right now?

If I knew the answer to that one, I would be heading for Europe instead of Richfield Springs!

"Well, I'm not leaving until the end of June," he said, interrupting my thoughts. "I could drive you to the campground and install your equipment, provided they have electricity in this rustic cabin."

"I'm sure Jennifer would never send me to a place that rustic."

I was praying for her definition of the word "rustic" to be a fireplace, kitchen, log cabin exterior, comfortable furniture, microwave, coffee maker, and a decent sized bed. After all, she did say I could take the equipment with me.

"I'll think about it, Wainwright. But, not right now. It's late and I've awakened you."

"All right. You know my number." He sounded disappointed.

I'd think about it? Ha! I liked being alone. Of course, I didn't fancy the long, lonely drive north. I dropped the phone onto its base. Goodnight, Wainwright. Sorry.

I stripped and put on my negligee. I looked pretty in my frilly satin despite Jennifer's comments that I looked like shit. I decided to reconnoiter the damage. I went to my dresser and stared at my reflection in the mirror.

My eyes looked smokey like someone who stares at a computer screen eight hours at a time. I lifted my gown. My legs were firm from running up and down the stairs between the kitchen and the computer room. My stomach was flat, and my breasts were large and firm as they had been for as long as I could remember. My face was pale, though, and my skin splotchy. There were dark circles under my eyes. My hair, which normally looks brown with blonde sunlight washed through it, looked like dishwater. Its style was a short haircut gone bad parted on the side. It needed shape, a perm, something. I'd make an appointment tomorrow if I could remember the beautician's name.

I needed a shopping trip before this vacation too: cosmetics, soaps, creams, new clothes, and casual clothes to wear where mosquitoes dine heartily on human blood. Despite the fact that I was going into the wilderness, I wanted feminine lingerie and several new bras, as well as the ever-practical warm socks and waterproof shoes.

I wanted to purchase a new camera, lots of film, office supplies, and several notebooks.

My compact Beretta would have to haul everything, so I had better service the car, check the tires, and clean out the trunk—finally bringing in the Christmas gifts from my last trip to my folks.

I slipped into my comfy bed and removed my nightgown. Nothing felt better on naked skin than cool cotton sheets. For no apparent reason that I could think of, I began to cry. Maybe it was the conversation about my looking like shit, maybe it was my indecisive feelings about Wainwright, maybe it was finishing the novel and saying goodbye to my characters, maybe it was PMS.

The moon was bright, and its light fell upon the desk where I still had the two pictures of the leading characters from my last novel. The man's face was reflected in a shimmering silver mist.

Now why couldn't I meet someone like *him*?

The next day I made an appointment for my hair and went shopping. I was amazed at what I found. I purchased all sorts of jumpsuits, jeans, belts, socks, solid and comfortable shoes, and two denim skirts. I found an array of durable and carefree blouses. After all, I might have to beat them with soap on a rock to wash them. I indulged in some feminine and sexy items, as well. I bought lingerie as if I were going to Europe with Wainwright. Then I ate dinner alone in one of the department store restaurants and drank a glass or two of wine.

When I got home, I decided I might as well tell my mother where I was going and give her my address and all the information the retreat's brochure had as to emergency numbers and such.

She thought I was crazy and would be killed by psychotics or bears. My father, on the other hand, surprised me. He told me to have a good time and relax. He said it was about time I got out of Brooklyn for a nature-filled retreat. He added that I was starting to look like shit, and if I kept up the loner act, I would have a nervous breakdown.

I called Jennifer and told her that I was complying with her wishes and would keep in touch. I asked her to watch my condo and collect my mail. I wanted her to send all of it to my cabin's address. I still had to pay bills, after all.

I could place my checks in my account with my bank card. I

made sure I had plenty of checks in my checkbook and planned to live by Mastercard as much as possible. Would you believe that I had very little on that bill? I used cash or travelers' checks when I traveled. Other than purchases from catalogues, which were minimal, I hadn't many items on my Mastercard bill, and hadn't come close to my credit line. If this area of New York was as quaint as Wainwright said, I might pick up some Victorian antiques and add some digits onto that account.

The next day, I went to the hairdresser and told Wendy—I finally recalled her name—that I was headed for an adventure into the wilderness and needed a style to match. We chose a short style and permed it with a light curl. The highlights in my hair bounced into view. It wasn't too short, was feminine around the sides retaining some length in the back— enough to make a small ponytail. Wendy promised that the style would last a while without another trim. I purchased eighty dollars worth of shampoo, conditioner, and styling gels. I also picked out a new blow dryer and one of those traveling curling irons.

With my new "do," and my face made-up with my department store cosmetics—which were designed to make you look natural but pretty—I surveyed my visage in my car's mirror. What a difference! Nothing like a little self-indulgence to perk up a girl's attitude.

I returned the movie to the video rental store. I owed more in late charges than the movie was worth if I'd bought it. The sad thing was that I couldn't remember what the movie was about or even if I'd watched it.

On the way home, I stopped and purchased more luggage since I'd have to lug my whole household to Richfield Springs. When I started thinking about detergent and soap, I stopped. It wasn't as if I were going to a foreign country. I mean, they have stores in Richfield Springs. Don't they?

That evening, I dismembered the business equipment and put it in the car. I took the manuals just as I had promised Wainwright. One of my neighbors was watering his flowers, and I decided to tell him where I was going and for how long. He lived on the other side of my apartment, and he would keep an eye on my place. I warned him about Jennifer's trips so that he wouldn't call the police when she picked up my mail.

The night before I left, I panicked. There was a fearful moment when I almost called Wainwright to ask if he would come along after all. I restrained the impulse by reminding myself that I could find a computer store that would have someone who could help me with the installation. I further realized that if I took Wainwright along, I could ruin our perfect working relationship by either sleeping with him or not. I suppose I could fall madly in love with him, and we could have a married partnership for the rest of our lives, but that sort of ending was for my books, not for real life.

Okay, let's just stop right there for a minute. I know what you're thinking. You're probably wondering why this hostility towards a subject I use daily to earn my living. I was in love once—in college—sure that old story. I was burned by a jerk who liked to drink too much, party hardy, and smack women around when they disagreed with him. He's a lawyer now. He married some poor woman who looks about as assertive as a cheese Danish nuked.

Needless to say, I'm not ready to take the plunge into wedded bliss, and I haven't had any nurturing urges to cuddle a cute baby to my breast. That doesn't mean I don't get passionate urges on Saturday nights when I'm done writing for the evening. It's especially hard to fight off the desire to have a physical affair with a cute male just after my heroine succumbs to the embraces of her true love. My heart beats a smidgen faster during those paragraphs, and there are times when I finish the page in tears.

What I'm trying to say is, I'm twenty-six, healthy, looking for love in my computer, but not in any of the right places. My acquaintances don't find dates for me when there are publishing parties. I take Wainwright with me as often as possible because he works as hard as I do. We travel together when we do certain kinds of research and sleep in separate hotel rooms. I've no need to buy contraceptive devices or pills because I don't sleep around. If and when love strikes, it better be for good, because I've had my heart broken before, and I have no intention of letting it happen again.

Chapter Two

I don't own a pet so there was no sobbing goodbye to Rover when I took off for 'my cabin in the sky' at five the next morning. My plan was to leave early enough and beat the rush hour traffic. I was correct and breezed onto 278 North that runs into 87 North. It was clear sailing for some time. Of course, I hit some construction on the way, but fate was on my side—the workers hadn't started yet and there were no lengthy backups. It was almost surreal for a car trip. *As if something supernatural were pulling me towards my destination.*

At Ardsley, I went across Coopertraw Bay where the route becomes 287 at Montebello. Once again, I was back on 87 and cruising through the Schunemunk Mountains. They were breathtaking. I stopped the car at one of the rest stops and just breathed deeply, feeling the peace springtime brings to the mountains. I was headed into the land of Cooper, Mohicans, and Washington Irving. Perhaps, the magic spell of the Catskills and the Appalachians would overpower me, as well.

Highways can become boring rather quickly, and I stopped for lunch just to stifle my yawns with some coffee and a sandwich. Then I returned to the road. By now I knew the license plates of all my fellow travelers and continued on 87 North putting the car on cruise control.

When I reached Albany, I went west on 90. The view became intoxicating, and I slowed to the speed limit to see it all. This angered a truck driver who almost ran me off the road. I was justified later when I saw a patrolman pull him over and give him a speeding ticket.

I went through the Palatine Bridge thruway and turned south at Mohawk. It was late afternoon, and I was almost there. I had some trouble finding 20 and missed a turn twice.

Then I saw the sign for Richfield Springs just outside a small town called Van Hornesville.

I pulled off the road for a minute. I needed Jennifer's reservation certificate and the brochure with its map because this cabin was high in the mountains supposedly overlooking Canadarago Lake. I couldn't see any side roads after traveling back and forth on it twice.

I noticed two, small motels and then saw the rough road that led to the old, but supposedly redone, cabins. There was a crude, hand-painted sign on the *right* side of the path—go figure—which explained where the cabins were and how to get to them. I had to leave the car and walk around to the other side of the Beretta to read it.

This was a restricted campground, and only those with reservations were allowed onto the road. When I attempted to follow their directions, I wondered why they'd bothered. And despite the warning, there was no security guard to validate my intrusion. I had to hand it to Jennifer. She didn't want to lose me as a client. Isolated? No one could have seen this place from the main road. It was buried in the mountains and covered with trees. My Beretta sighed and hurled itself over the rocks and crevices on the "road."

It was beautiful country. There were only a few cabins, and they were so far apart from each other that privacy was guaranteed. It was exactly as I'd dreamed it would be.

I found the office, and a cheerful fellow greeted me. His name was Sam Cooper, and I got the impression that his family had lived in this area for years. One look into his eyes told me that he would have more stories to tell than Mother Goose, and I couldn't wait to hear them. I liked him.

The cabins were rustic, but modern electricity and conveyances were coverered by an antique setting.

Sam didn't ask for my reservation. Well, why would he? No one would be up here unless they had one.

"You going to stay the whole three months?" he asked.

"Probably."

He started to help take the equipment into my cabin. "I thought you were vacationing," he said. "This looks like work." He smiled and meant no insult.

"I'm a writer. I don't go anywhere without this stuff," I said.

As soon as I saw my new home, I knew I would stay the duration. It was a log cabin, but old stone masonry and new cedar planks only made it more outstanding if less historic. It had a front porch with several rocking chairs, and a flower garden neatly weeded around its perimeter. There were beautiful trees and a trimmed lawn.

The interior of the cabin looked inviting. I found the great room served as living room, dining room, and kitchen. Lace curtains, which looked Dutch, covered the small windows. There was a rounded archway which led to the good-sized bedroom that had just enough closet space for all my things. I checked the new electrical outlets. There was a large, old fireplace which looked as if it had been built in the early 1800s. It still had the iron handle for a black cooking kettle.

"I sure hope you know how to install this," Sam said, planting the last of the equipment on the floor by the couch.

"Well," I laughed, "I don't really. Is there a computer store nearby?"

"I'm sure we have one near Cooperstown, but my brother knows how to install this stuff. He wouldn't charge you either."

I smiled my gratitude, moved my luggage into the bedroom, and opened the fridge.

Sam noticed. "You hungry? I was heading into town to get groceries. If you don't mind my pickup truck, you're welcome to join me."

I loved the idea. Tomorrow, I'd be too busy unpacking. The sun hadn't set, so there was still time to sightsee. I couldn't drive down that road again, but relished the idea of being the passenger. I might not get a chance like this again. "All right, let me get my purse and lock up. Are there any other guests?" I said.

He grinned, and it was a weird sort of expression. "Not yet. I usually get more the later part of July...all through August," he said. Something told me that I was being scrutinized from head to toe. It made me feel uneasy, and I didn't know why. "I've never met a writer before," he continued. "What sort of books do you write?"

"Historical fiction-romance," I said, leaping into the passenger's seat of the pickup truck. I was amazed how high above the road we were. I felt powerful, as if I could run over anything.

"Did you come here for inspiration? I've heard writers do that sometimes," he said. The truck needed a few turns of the ignition before starting.

"Actually, I just finished a novel, and my agent thought it might be good for me to relax. If I get inspired—so much the better. I always bring the equipment just in case. Does your brother live far from here?"

"He owns an antique store in Milford that's not far from here.

He redoes furniture—stuff like that."

"I'd like to see his store. I collect antiques," I said.

"I tell you what, when you get settled into your cabin, how about I take you on a tour of the area. James Fenimore Cooper wrote all of his books here. The place has many stories to tell. The mountains have their own mysteries too as Washington Irving recalled in his short stories. My family has lived here for generations." He looked at me from the corner of his right eye and winked. "You couldn't get a better guide." Then he smiled. Otsego charm? I could get used to this.

He pulled the truck into a Ma and Pa style restaurant which must have been there for a hundred years. He helped me from the truck. No one had done that for me in ages.

"I hope you don't mind home cooking," he said.

There wasn't much ambience to the place, but the food was great. I ordered a cheeseburger, fries, and a chocolate milkshake. I watched the old woman make it in a blender with real ice cream, sundae sauce, and whole milk. She even sold baked goods. I purchased two-dozen sweet rolls for tomorrow's breakfast and gave one of the bags to Sam.

"What's this for?" he said.

"For being so nice and welcoming me," I said with a smile —my charm—all right, I was flirting. I think he was too.

We drove to a small shop which looked like a general store from by-gone days. I bought so many items we filled the bed of his truck with the boxes.

We must have hit every bump on the return trip to the cabins. In the Beretta, it had been hell; but, in the truck, it was rather thrilling.

I climbed out of the truck myself this time. I froze. I moved slowly to my cabin. I knew Sam was watching. His eyes were burning holes into my back. Before me, was the most glorious sunset I'd ever witnessed. From my front porch, I could see streaks of orange and mauve stream like ribbons from a lady's hat across a pale, magenta sky. No artist could have painted it. And I wasn't poetic enough to attempt to put it into a stanza. A light blue haze poured through the white of the clouds making the horizon resemble a wedding bouquet.

I think the magic of the mountains cast its spell over me right then. Every night of my vacation, I'd have this magnificent view to watch from my front porch. I'd be able to dream my dreams in the shade of these huge trees whose large limbs and strong trunks would keep me from walking off the mountain and into the lake. The invigorating smell of pine would tickle my nostrils, and a barely distinguishable smell of cedar would lull me to sleep each night. Rhythmic sounds of frogs or crickets, or whatever they were, would sing their twilight lullaby. And the spirit of the majestic pines, as they pressed their arms together, would make a protective dome, cathedral-like, to insure I was protected from all evil. I was not afraid of the forest now. I did not mind being without Wainwright. I was not alone anymore.

Sam coughed and said, "Now you know why I stay here. Even in the winter— and Lord knows we get some mighty awful winters—I've never moved. I don't worry about advertising this place. It sells itself. One visit and they're back the following year. I don't want to be a pest, Miss, I can see you have a lot to do. But, I'll be over in the office if you need me."

I said nothing in response and could feel his smile on my back as he retreated.

While I was gazing at the sunset, he had moved all my packages into the cabin. I had to put everything away before it spoiled.

The dusk became black with night. Unlike other hotels, there was almost no outside lighting in front of my cabin. I noticed some Tiki lamps that I would light if I needed to. When I was finished with the groceries, I found some matches in the kitchen and lit all of them.

I felt primitive. I was Natty Bumppo. Brave, self-sufficient, I could live off the land. Nothing frightened me. I would sleep beneath the trees, in God's country, far from the maddening crowd, far from the humorless city, from the stoic restaurants, from the evil video rental places, from the unending turnpike, from the heartless interstate. I heard something like an owl hoot in a nearby tree. Perhaps I could appreciate nature better from *inside* the cabin.

I have to admit I did feel lonely after sunset. I had a T.V. and a radio in the cabin. I decided to listen to a local station. I found nothing but static after searching the varied channels. The television hummed to life with a friendly old sitcom. I let its patter befriend me as I unpacked.

While putting all of my personal items in the drawers and hanging my clothes in the mirrored cabinet, it crossed my mind that the place was certainly old enough to have existed at the time of my last historic novel—1896. Imagine, someone put their clothes in this closet a century ago, someone stared over the lake from this porch just as I was doing, and someone sighed at how empty and sad it was to be on vacation by yourself.

When the place was beginning to look like a livable possibility, I took a Diet Coke from the fridge and turned off the T.V. I extinguished all the lights and stood by the window to watch the moon as she regarded her reflection in the lake. Dimpled, dotted, diamonds sparkling like quivering fairy wings flickered across the water.

I was wearing one of my satin floral negligees. The one with the matching robe. I pulled the satin sash tightly around my waist. I was exhausted. It was time to find out if the bed was as comfortable as it looked.

I slept like a dead woman that first night. A train could have come right through the house, and I wouldn't have noticed.

Chapter Three

The sun's rays woke me the next day. I went out to the porch to make sure I hadn't dreamed the cabin into existence. The lake and the fantastic view were still there. I was famished and needed coffee.

I made a simple breakfast of two of the rolls I had purchased at the restaurant the night before and a mug of black coffee. I took them onto the porch to enjoy. I rocked a while on the old, wooden rocker. I was only in my robe but who cared.

I had my first "Snow White" encounter then. The birds came down to the lower branches of the trees and inspected their new guest with curiosity. A squirrel performed stunts for my entertainment. I could see the "critters" were used to guests giving them food. I obliged. I went into the cabin and found another roll. I had no seeds or whatever woodland animals expect from humans.

I threw the food to the ground after ripping it into bite-sized pieces. I could not believe it. They went for it without a second's thought. They must have thought I looked *normal*. They trusted me!

I watched the sunrise while sipping my lukewarm coffee. A new day—a new beginning. Then I remembered—I had to install the equipment.

I tried plugging the wires into the back of the computer and knew right away I was in trouble. I gave up quickly because I didn't want to damage anything.

I went into the bathroom, which was behind the bedroom, and showered in the tiny trickle of tepid water which issued from the shower nozzle.

I dusted my limbs with my Johnson and Johnson's baby powder and made myself presentable. In other words, I wanted to impress Sam Cooper. I would need his brother after all. Plus, he *had* promised a ride into Cooperstown, hadn't he?

He was already up and planting something in his garden. He smiled and lectured me on the Latin name for the flowers, but as far as I could see, they were purple daisies. He had already had breakfast and thanked me again for the rolls.

I leaped into the truck as if I had done it all my life. We started the tour as soon as we hit the highway.

I realized, when we toured Cooperstown, that I would need a day or two in this city. I wanted to see the Fenimore House and look into the adjacent library that housed the New York State Historical Association. I remembered that Wainwright knew the research director there. Wainwright! If I did not hook up the equipment soon, I would never hear from him again.

We traveled through Toddsville, a sleepy hamlet I hardly noticed at first. I was astonished that anyone could find such a tiny place.

We zipped through Hartwick and sailed passed Fly Creek. He brought me through Oneonta, which actually looked like an antique dealer's idea of a sexual fantasy, and then we came to Milford.

I remembered the photo book Jennifer had given me while Sam lectured like a tour guide. This was the county Smith and Telfer had photographed. Here was the street where the annual Fourth of July parade began. The torn down depot of a once popular railroad station was over there. The old Victorian edifice to my right was the church where the Victorian couple laughed and ran through the rice. This century home looked exactly like the one with the unusual balcony from which the young bride threw her wedding bouquet to her friends below.

Those homes were still standing and being lovingly cared for. But, they had been new when Smith took his camera out of his new studio for his first photo session.

This was the campground where that one family played with their children. There were several shots of that family. They must have been important members of the community. We passed what *looked* like the farmhouse where sixty-some people had been photographed dining in their backyard: sharing corn on the cob as they sat at long, picnic tables hastily erected for this year's family reunion. A large American flag had been draped like a canopy above their heads. And, this empty pasture lot might have been used for the fair ground where that white horse leaped into a tub of water. The photographers had taken many shots of that spectacle. Poor horse.

How the streets had changed. Mud roads had been replaced with asphalt. The people, living here now, had enough pride in their history to hold onto their landmarks. Most everything I saw was more than a century old, but it looked new.

On our short tour, I saw men hanging outside the buildings' windows and over the roofs, painting the Victorian structures with their original colors. I fell in love with everything. The citizens of this county had allowed me my chance to travel back in time.

Travel back in time.

We stopped about a block from Milford's main street—close to some railroad tracks—and a real engine being used as a museum. We were greeted by Sam's brother, Jim. He was every bit as tall as his brother—over five feet seven inches. He had long, sable hair pulled back with a rubber band, and when he stopped working to talk, he adjusted it.

He was refurbishing an old oak table but did not seem to mind stopping to chat with us. He told his brother that he would have some free time later in the day and would drive back to the cabin after his dinner to help me. The azure blue of his eyes seemed intensely intelligent, sensitive, concerned. Different, in a certain way, from his brother's.

He mentioned some wires, and plugs we might purchase before he tried to install the computer. Apparently, the shops in Cooperstown were overrun with tourists in the summer, and he wanted me to get everything before he started to work on the equipment. I mentioned that I thought I had brought everything I needed from home, but he reminded me, gently, that I might need specialized wiring to hook all the equipment to a country cabin's electrical system. He told Sam and me that another trip to Cooperstown for a small plug wouldn't be much fun at six o'clock in the evening. Sam then informed me that the roads were very dark and windy, and that driving was a pain any time of the year. I laughed and asked where the nearest store was, and what I should purchase.

We stayed about twenty minutes and when we left, Jim warned me not to believe every story Sam told me. I giggled and told him that a writer didn't mind fiction.

I wondered why the two brothers didn't maintain the cabins together. I asked Sam on the way home, but he seemed evasive on the subject. That was odd because he had chatted endlessly the entire day. The moment I asked a personal question, he was as tight-lipped as a secret service agent. He changed my subject back to his history of the towns. I listened and took mental notes of all the stories, but I was suffering from exhaustion.

We made one quick stop—to purchase the wires and plugs—and then headed homeward.

I gave a last quick look at Cooperstown and deciphered how long I would need to inspect everthing. I had all summer but wanted to start tomorrow on my historic trek.

I decided to take a walk in the woods as soon as we returned to the cabins. The trees stood like proud kings all around me, and the silence was spiritual. I'm not into meditation, but I did shut my eyes and lean against a tree. I felt a heaviness—a sadness—creeping deep into my chest. My heart felt as though it were swelling, doubling its size. My hands and fingers started to tingle as if the blood were boiling in my veins. For no reason, tears came to my eyes. I took a deep breath, suddenly aware that I had stopped breathing. Had I really worked so hard? Was I so close to a breakdown that this peace was too perfect for me to bear? I sensed an odd presence, as if an unseen visitor were calling to me. It must have been the natural surroundings; the eerie sensation that came with complete tranquility.

I returned to my cabin and unpacked more of the equipment, setting it where I thought it would be easiest to use. Then I made a sandwich, opened a can of Diet Coke, and ate, letting my mind wander while rocking slowly in the old chair on my porch.

I didn't realize I'd fallen asleep until Jim tickled my cheek with a green leaf.

"Hey, enough of this resting. We've work to do," he said.

"Oh, sorry, I didn't realize how late it was. I must have fallen asleep," I said.

"That's okay. Let's take a look at that equipment." He turned the computer and its partners upside down moving them away from all the neat spots I had planned for them. It took him no time at all to hook everything to the electrical outlets.

"Here, you can take this back to the store. I didn't need it. They'll refund your money. I even hooked it up to the Internet for you. When you want to leave, just give me a call, and I'll help you tear it down. It's nice machinery," Jim said.

"I'll try to e-mail my friends tonight. Check out how it's working. How can I ever thank you?" I said.

"Got a beer?"

I told him I had rum and Coke, and he agreed to sharing a

drink on the porch with me. I wondered why Sam didn't come over.

We sat in the rockers and watched the start of the sunset. I felt as comfortable with him as I did his brother. It was nice having someone to talk to.

"You've lived here all your life?" I said.

"Yep, as depressing as that sounds," he said and laughed.

"Why do you say that? I think it's pretty here."

"You arrived on a sunny day. Most of the time it's rainy and cloudy. As a matter of fact, most people who move into these parts from other states mention a change in mood when they've been here for a while."

I said, "Maybe the trees shade the land too much."

"That and we get terrible winters here. Lake effect snow which can really bog us down," Jim said.

"Has your family always lived here and owned the cabins?"

"My family goes all the way back to the 1700s. We owned this land, and my great-great-great grandfather built a homestead here and tried to farm. Don't know too much about him though. As years went on, we built the cabins for our own use. Eventually, we made them into summer cabins for rent," he said.

"Well, you're lucky. It's a beautiful spot."

"Sort of surprised Sam let you have *this* cabin."

"Why?" I said.

"This is the oldest cabin and Sam's special favorite. He very rarely rents it to anyone. 'Course he said you were staying for three months; that's probably why."

"Don't you ever come to Richfield Springs and help him?" I said.

"Oh, I'll be here soon enough." He smiled, chuckled at some private joke, and asked for another rum and Coke.

I hurried to refresh my guest's drink. "Want some chips?" I said.

"Sure."

"When will you be here?" I handed him his drink desperate to discover more.

"June 21."

I thought that was mighty specific.

"Why is your brother so closed-mouth about the cabins?"

"He's real proud of his historic knowledge of the county. As a matter of fact, you can believe anything he tells you. I was just teasing you before about not listening to his stories. You said you write historic fiction? Well, you've got a gold mine with my brother. There's nothing he doesn't know about the late 1800s. He's a walking library," Jim said. "He travels..." He stopped abruptly.

After a small pause to see if he'd continue, I said, "Well, I guess I came to the right place."

He took his drink and a handful of chips from the soup bowl in which I'd placed them.

"Miss, the citizens in this county *pride* themselves on knowing as much as they can about the area. We restore it just like I restore old furniture. Take a look around. The houses are kept exactly as they were in 1890." There was an odd twinkle in his blue eyes.

"We're like the Indians who used to live here. Down through the ages, we tell our history to our young so that the memories live forever," Jim said.

"That's beautiful." I was entranced with his words.

"And so are you," Jim said.

I quickly looked at him to see what was meant by the remark. There was nothing hidden behind the words. "What?" Maybe I hadn't heard him correctly.

"Don't get excited, I'm not making a pass. I mean, there's something inside you, a respect for times gone by, a wonder and interest in what people tell you, a desire to connect to something you've found but haven't identified. Somewhere, behind those eyes, is the mind of a searcher. Inside your heart, you're motivated to seek forever until you remember what it was you found," he said.

"*What* are you talking about?"

"I can see it in your eyes while you're watching the sunset. You said a friend gave you the reservation. Well, it must be destiny. Sam must have seen it too—the first moment he saw you. That's why he gave you his special cabin. It's the oldest one we have. Goes back to 1720."

"I'm from Brooklyn, friend," I said, swallowing my second drink a little faster than the first. "You'll have to spell this one out for me."

"I've never seen someone with it quite so strong—except Sam.

He wanted it and found it—and so will you."

Before I had time to collect my thoughts on what he had just said, he was leaving. Jim found his keys on the kitchen table and came back to the porch.

"Don't worry, though. I'll be here from June 21 through September. If you need anything just call," he said.

"Wait a minute," I gasped, not wanting him to leave until he had explained his comments. "What are you talking about? What is it I'll find? How will I find it? Is it in the library at Cooperstown? NYSHA?"

His smile looked like one right out of a James Bond movie—sideways, knowing, secretive, mysterious, old and wise.

"I've got to get back to Milford. Like we told you, the roads are dark at night, and it's hard enough to manage some of those curves when you're sober let alone filled with rum and Coke." He tapped my nose with his index finger and smiled.

I'm not sure why I said this, and I swear I could hear Jennifer saying, "Why did you *say* that?" the moment I remarked, "You *will* come back and visit, won't you? I don't know anyone but Sam and you. I've got a feeling it gets mighty lonely here after a while."

That James Bond wicked smirk again. "Trudy, you don't mind if I call you Trudy, do you?" he said. I shook my head no. "You aren't going to be lonely." His head rocked backwards, and he laughed outloud. "But, I'll check in on you, I promise."

I tracked him down the path to his truck and waved goodbye as he backed his old sedan out of the parking lot. When I turned to go back to the cabin, I perused the area for Sam. He was nowhere.

I remembered that I was on-line now. I ran back to the computer and clicked her into gear. If I were lucky, I'd still be able to contact Wainwright.

It took some doing, but soon he was on-line.

"How do you like your woodland home?" he said.

"Just call me 'Snow White' from now on," I said.

"Okay, 'Snow White', just call me 'Prince Charming'." What can I do for you?"

"*Talk to me* and remind me what reality is like."

"I get the idea you've been transcendentalized," Wainwright said.

"If that's a word, I suppose I am. When are you leaving for Europe?"

"I was shipping out June 21. Why? Have you changed your mind about a visit from Prince Charming? After all, it can be *lonely* with only furry bunnies and dwarves to talk to."

"How do you know I'm lonely?" I said. "I've met one man who's a walking encyclopedia on the history of the area, and another man who installed my computer equipment for me."

"I told you you wouldn't be able to hook it up with just the manuals."

"You were right, Wainwright." I flipped him off. I hated the assumption that he *should* have come along to check out my equipment—*all of my equipment.*

"These men, how old are they?" he said.

I smirked. "One of them is 64 and the other is a lot younger—at least 59. They're old geysers with long gray hair and matching beards. They look like dwarves—just as you thought." If I told him about the two brothers who were only slightly older than myself, and were very attractive, he'd be up here in three hours.

"Are you sure they aren't those mountain men Rip Van Winkle played nine pins with?" he said.

"They may well be. So far they haven't asked me to climb any mountains or take any long naps."

"You know, I was thinking I might just take a ride up there and check things out. I could use a fresh dip in a cool lake before I head for Europe," he said.

"Well, there isn't much room Wainwright, old pal. I was planning on doing some research on my own tomorrow. I still don't have any ideas for the next book."

I didn't know what to say to him. After all, there was no reason a friend couldn't come by for a quick visit. He had somewhere else to go and wouldn't stay long—maybe. What if he decided to ditch the friendly trip to Europe in lieu of a summer retreat with me? I had to think fast. I didn't want to hurt our friendship by insinuating his suggestion was lecherous.

"Actually, Wainwright, I'm trying to make friends here and these people are very helpful because they think I'm alone, trying to write a book. They don't seem to be as open-minded as we are back in Brooklyn. If you showed up right now, it could dampen my relationships for the whole summer. Maybe, when you get back, and they've gotten to know me better, a man sleeping in my cottage might not cause any waves," I said.

"Why do you care what they think? You know our relationship is friendly and businesslike. Who cares what those yokels think?"

"I guess I do, Bruce. Sorry, please don't be angry. I still want to keep contacting you."

"Every night. If you fail to communicate one night, I'm going to rush up there, from wherever I am, and make sure you're safe. I don't trust Rip Van Winkle."

"Thanks, you're a love for caring. I won't miss a night, I swear."

I heard something move outside the cabin. "I've got to go now, Bruce," I said. "I'm going to call Jennifer tonight so she knows I made it."

"Okay, Trudy. Keep safe, friend."

I felt like a creep when he said that last comment. He really cared about me. I went to the cabin door. Cautiously, I opened the door and stared into the darkness. If something were there, I couldn't see it. I went inside and phoned Jennifer.

"Oh, it's you, Trudy. Do you love the place or what?" Jennifer said.

"I love it! How did you ever find it?"

"Syd and I were traveling and stayed at the little motel down the road from the cottages. We ate in a restaurant close to the motel the next day, and the woman told us about it. So, the ever-adventurous Sydney, drove up the mountain, and we looked over the cottages and the view. I talked to the man there, and he suggested the reservation. I told him about you. He seemed fascinated that you were a writer in need of escape. He told me that they get repeat visitors, and, since they didn't have many cottages, I should reserve a year in advance."

"You talked to Sam Cooper?" I said.

"I don't think that was his name. Cooper is correct, but I think it was Jim," she said.

"When were you here?"

"The middle of July—just after the Fourth. Isn't he there? There wasn't any trouble, was there?"

"No trouble. A man named Sam runs the place until June 21

when Jim takes over."

"That's odd. Did you get your equipment hooked up?" she said.

"As a matter of fact I did, with Jim's help. He lives in Milford and has an antique store," I said.

"I think he mentioned it. Well, I hope you're having fun and relaxing. We may start the book tour mid-December."

"We'll publish that soon?" I said.

"The fish are biting, pal."

"You said the 'F' word."

"Oh, sorry. Well, Sydney's having another theater party at our place tomorrow evening, and I have to help, so I'd better go."

"Gee, I'm sorry I'll miss that one," I said sarcastically, and she laughed.

"Maybe, I should come up there and miss it myself. Have fun and call often. Reverse the charges. I don't want them to bill you so much you aren't allowed to leave at the end of August," said Jennifer.

End of August? Could I make it *that* long? Or would I become so attached to this place I couldn't leave?

It was ten o'clock, and it was time to call it a day. I admit I felt much better now that all the communication devices were working.

When I snuggled into my bed, I noticed the moon. It wasn't a full moon, just a sliver, but its powerful beam came through my window.

Smack! A mosquito? So soon? I would ask Sam for something to ward off the miniature vampires.

Chapter Four

The next morning, I decided to treat myself to breakfast at the Ma and Pa restaurant where Sam and I had eaten that first night. I dressed for town wearing a denim skirt and a short-sleeved denim blouse. I fixed my hair, and added makeup, and slipped on my summer, leather sandals. I took my notebook, business cards, two pencils, and two pens. I rearranged my new purse, with all the credit cards I thought I might need and some cash for purchases.

I looked for Sam to give him a cheery good morning, but he was nowhere.

The Beretta coughed to life as if it were telling me I had left it far too long. We bumped our way down the old path.

I found the restaurant easily, congratulating myself on remembering the way.

The older woman smiled and asked me if I were ready for a big breakfast. I said I was famished, and we made the usual conversation about fresh air and a hearty appetite. I ordered three pancakes, scrambled eggs, bacon, buttered toast, and hot black coffee. It was delicious. Since there was no one else in the restaurant, she continued our conversation as she wiped away the crumbs from the counter.

"Ever been to Cooperstown before?" she said.

"No, never," I said.

She refilled my coffee cup for the third time. "Do you like it?"

"I like the area very much. I write historic fiction, and this area is full of history."

"You know the New York State Historical Association can be a real help," she said. I was beginning to think maybe NYSHA trained people to advertise for them.

I took a chance and said, "I hear Sam Cooper, the man I came in with the first night, is a real history whiz."

A devlish smile crossed her face. "He sure is." She sat down and poured herself a cup of coffee. "Spend an afternoon with him, and you won't need to do any more research."

"Then I'll speak with him a lot this summer," I said, coaxing the answers from her.

"I don't think he's here much in the summer. Jim takes over

sometime in June."

"Why is that?" Now I was on a roll. I would play the detective. Who needs Wainwright?

"I don't know. I guess he goes on holiday and lets Jim take over," she said. Well...that really helped.

I pushed it. "Does he ever mention where he goes? It's just that I thought his information might come in handy. I'm starting a new book." The new story routine always worked.

"I've no idea where he goes. It's very mysterious. His brother is pretty knowledgeable about the area though. Maybe he can help you."

Dead end!

I told her I'd be back, paid for my breakfast, and gave her a big tip. She said she'd be happy to see me again—anytime. I guess she didn't get many customers.

I took Route 28 and parked on the main street of Cooperstown. I considered myself lucky to find a place for the Beretta. The sidewalks looked as if they'd never changed from the day they were placed in the city. The buildings were restored Victorian shops of all styles, and I was going to have a wonderful time. My Visa and Mastercard were close at hand.

Disappointment set in instantly when I realized that the only antiques I would see in these stores were baseball memorabilia. I went ahead and sauntered through the streets and viewed the old houses anyway.

Then I walked to the dock at Otsego Lake. There was an array of lovely boats, and I fantasized about riding in one. I saw a pretty sailboat and a man easing it westward—away from the beach. I could tell he had dark hair for the wind blew it into the breeze. His head was tilted towards the sun as he smiled into his sails. The young man looked serenly content, and I envied him.

The car was anxious to leave—something to do with the tree it was parked under dripping sap on its front window. I continued passed the Otesaga Hotel and found myself at the Fenimore House. I decided to forego the family-style, historic farm across the street and went into the house. You had to buy a ticket, and after I overheard two women talking about what they had viewed in the rooms, I decided I'd visit the gift shop instead.

I perused the small store until I spotted some photo books. I saw the one Jennifer had purchased for me. The Smith and Telfer book was not expensive, so I decided to buy another copy now that I was here and wanted to match the locales to the photos. Beats me why I didn't bring my copy. I could give this one to Wainwright when I returned to Brooklyn.

As I was waiting in line to make my purchase, I flipped through the pages to the picture of the Victorian man I had used for my hero in the last book I had written. There he was. I laughed with delight for the picture had that effect on me.

When I gave the girl the money for the book, she smiled and asked me what was so funny. I showed her the picture. "Oh," she said, "there's another one just like it in the library next store. It isn't the same pose, but it's actually a better picture. Ask Beth to show you the whole collection. What sort of books do you write?"

I told her and mentioned some of the more popular titles. She had read them all. Her visage changed immeasurably. "I'm sure she'll be *pleased* to help *you*, Miss Johnson," she said.

Fame sometimes has its rewards.

As soon as I walked into the library, every one of my intellectual nerve-endings twitched to life. The woman at the desk looked up at me and smiled. I mentioned what I wanted, my name, and asked for Beth. She stopped reading instantly and hurried to the back room. I waited no more than three minutes. Beth greeted me with a radiant face and twinkling eyes.

We climbed three flights of stairs. Then she slipped a special card through a computer lock and ushered me into their private archives. She pointed to several file cabinets and told me that I was free to help myself to any of the folders. I was to call her if I needed anything. Then she pulled out one specific drawer that held photos of men in various poses from the time period I wanted. I thanked her and began to flip through them. One folder was marked: photos with special props. Since the man had two props in that one photo, I might find him here.

There he was! The man had taken a second photo the same day. The background, the rattan chair, the suit, the cigar, the mustache, and the newspaper in his lap-all the same. *The attitude was the same.* But, most wondrous of all, was that in this photo I could see the man's face. In the other photo, the man's head was down as if he were reading something in the paper.

And oh, what a handsome face it was! Even in black and white his eyes hypnotized me. Big brown, soulful eyes, which were covered by long dark lashes. His hat sat jauntily atop his dark brown hair. His face—oval shaped—and his long sideburns and perfect ears had been the visage incarnate of Charles Hemingway, the wealthy heir to Hemingway Estates back in 1896 New York.

Hemingway had been the hero in my romance novel. He had swept the lovely Penelope Chaucer off her feet at the climax of my story.

I was so excited that I began to chatter uncontrollably to Beth. I told her about the new book that would be on the stands by Christmas, and she smiled with enthusiasm. She didn't understand about photos and dolls, but she liked my books, so whatever worked, I guess.

Beth told me how I might obtain a copy of the photo. For a fee, they could reproduce the 8x10 black and white for me. It would take a few weeks to do, but for a famous writer, they could do a rush order. I filled out the form and gave her the cottage's address and phone number. I told her I'd be there for three months and that there was no rush. However, I paid with my Mastercard and told her to Federal Express it to me as I sometimes didn't leave my computer for weeks when I got an idea for a new story. Beth said she understood and made a note on my order.

"By the way, you don't happen to know who this dashing fellow is by any chance?" I said. I assumed the answer would be a sad smile to the negative.

"Oh, Miss Johnson, I'll call the historian in charge of the Telfer and Smith photo collection," she said. "Just let me write down the photo's I.D. number." She did, and then she was gone.

As easy as that? Wainwright was correct about the people in the library being helpful.

I tried to look at the other photos in the various folders, but I kept coming back to HIM. "Okay, you handsome enigma," I said like a fool to this picture. "I'm going to find you. Don't try to hide. It's no use. I'm good at this."

I could have sworn the photo said, "Really?" in reply.

Beth was back in no time. "His name is Cuyler E. Carr, and he lived in Toddsville, Milford, and other areas of Cooperstown. We might have some more information on him, or you can check for yourself. If we can be of any assistance, Miss Johnson," she said.

I took my credit card and my receipt planning to depart. I didn't want to leave the photo behind in that folder. "When do you think I can have my picture?"

"We'll process it right away. We could have it to you in two weeks."

"That'll be wonderful." I looked at that face one last time as she closed the folder. Good-bye, Cuyler. Nice name. Nice man.

I said farewell to the people at the front desk and autographed someone's dog-eared paperback copy of *Twilight's Last Kiss* and grinned. "I'm sure I'll be back before I return to Brooklyn in August," I said.

I traveled for some time down the road before I realized where I was going. I was heading for Toddsville. I thought about what Beth had said and tried to find the town. Despite Sam's fantastic tour, I couldn't discover a single road that led to the small hamlet. I kept landing in Hartwick.

I stopped the car and walked around the main street of Hartwick. There wasn't much. I snapped some photos: one of a church, and one of a nice hundred-year-old house. I returned to the Beretta and gave up the chase.

I was almost to Milford and decided I'd stop and say hello to Jim. He was working outside. "I've just come back from a very informative trip to Cooperstown," I said.

"Oh, yeah?" he said, throwing down the tool he was using. "What did you find?"

I told him about the photo and the whole story of how I had used it for my novel. I asked him whether he knew enough history of Milford to know anything about Cuyler. It appeared that, until I had more detailed information, he couldn't help me. After all, it was just a name of someone who died before Jim was born. I asked him how his head felt after our "party."

"I made it home all right. A little rum won't hurt me. Want something to drink?"

"No, oh, by the way, the equipment works fine," I said. I told him about calling Wainwright and Jennifer.

"This Wainwright sounds too interested in your vacation." His eyebrows raised. "Thought you said he was just a research analyst who worked for you."

"He is, but we work very closely, and you know what that's like," I said.

"Sure. Did you see Sam today?" he said.

"No. Is there something wrong?" I sensed authentic concern in his voice.

"Oh, no, he gets a little edgy when he's leaving. Sometimes goes into the mountains for a while, or fishes in his boat to deal with it," he said.

"Deal with what?"

We were going to have to bring out our decoders once again boys and girls. Cooper coded message coming through.

"Leaving," Jim said.

"If it bothers him so, why does he leave?"

"You wouldn't understand."

"Try me."

"Sorry, you'll have to solve this puzzle by yourself. I'm not divulging any more information." He waved both his hands back and forth in front of his stomach to rid himself of any guilt. "Ask Sam."

We talked a while longer, and then I drove home. I looked for Sam as soon as I stepped from my car. I saw him walking up the mountain path to his cabin. I would stop him and make him talk.

"Well, hello. You disappeared," I said.

"Got to freshen the old hunting and fishing skills," Sam said. He swung the fish in front of my eyes. "Want some?"

"Ugh, no way. I hate fish."

"Too bad, these beauts will be tasty when I fry them."

I thought I would vomit on the spot. I persevered.

"By the way, your brother said you were leaving for the summer. Is that correct?"

There was the familiar Cooper brothers' smile again. "He told you that, huh?" he said.

"He said he would be handling the campgrounds while you were away. Is this true? I thought you were going to be my faithful guide all summer," I said.

Then he said something odd. "You'll have a guide. It just won't be me."

"In English, por favor?" I said, resting my hands on my hips.

"I leave during the summer solstice. The first day of summer I'm gone, and the first day of autumn, I return. Remember that. It could be more important than you realize."

"I must have stayed in Brooklyn too much of my life because I don't understand half of what you and your brother are saying."

He put the fish down on the grass and touched my shoulder lovingly with his hand. "I won't be here after June 21 this year," he said. "I'll be back in September. We'll talk then, okay? Don't try to figure it out now. It'll all make sense soon."

I smiled as if I got the joke when I hadn't. I wasn't staying until September. Maybe he meant we'd talk by phone.

"Hope that Wainwright guy doesn't show." He picked up the fish and left me with my tongue swelling in my mouth, and my words tangled. I had never mentioned Wainwright to him. Not his name anyway. "Curiouser and curiouser said Alice," I said to myself.

I returned to my cabin, changed into my swimsuit, and walked the path to the lake. There were fish in there, and they'd probably nibble at my toes while I was swimming, so I made a big splash in the water when I dove in to scare them away.

I swam around the lake and regarded the old boats tied there. One cute, little-faded red boat appeared to have a name on it. You could just barely detect a five letter name. Weather had ruined the wood and original paint, so I couldn't read it. Maybe I could row it around the lake. I examined it only to find that it had too many holes in its underbelly, and the wood was all rotten. It was still a wonderful discovery, anyhow.

I made my perfunctory exchange to Wainwright, but I did not call Jennifer because of the party she had mentioned. Besides, she wanted me to relax, not call her every night as if she were my mother. My mother! I hadn't phoned to tell her I was alive.

I made my dinner and called her after five. She was pleased I was having such a nice time. She informed me not to swim in the lake because I might catch some disease and to watch out for the mosquitoes because they carried killing viruses. Oh, well, you don't have to tell your mother everything, do you?

I had forgotten to find an ointment for the biting mosquitoes. I noticed the time and date on the digital clock on my bedstand. June 18. Wainwright and Sam would be gone soon. At least I knew where Wainwright was going. June 21. Didn't he say June 21? So had Sam!

I have to admit the days grew tiresome. I still had no idea for a story, but I had to keep my writing skills sharpened. I sat at the computer and began writing anything that came to my head. I wrote character sketches of Sam and his brother Jim. I wrote the lady who owned the restaurant into my sketch-saver too. I wrote a humorous selection on: *Places you don't want to visit in America*, and then deleted it. I wrote a poem about the sunset. It wasn't bad, so I wrote one about swimming in the lake. Then I wrote one about the man in the photo:

Oh, face from the past,
What a spell you've cast.
Oh, man from history,
My enigma—my mystery.
Touching my mind from the start,
Awakening life in a lonely heart.

Well, Shakespeare would have a few more stress-free good nights in his tomb unhindered by worry over competition from me. I'd never been good at writing poetry. This was why I stayed with prose. Still, the little stanza was my own creation. So, I put: TO CUYLER E. CARR FROM GERTRUDE JOHNSON above the first line and saved it on my hard drive. Then I printed the poem onto clean white paper. I took it into the bedroom and placed it on the nightstand.

It was silly to become attached to a photo of a man you'd never meet. Wait a minute. I'd meet him some day. I asked the Almighty that, when my day came to travel to the great beyond, I'd meet Cuyler in person.

The next day I actually bought a ticket and went through the Baseball Hall of Fame. I never realized how far back in time the game of baseball went. They had baseball equipment which went back to the mid 1800s in the museum. And I discovered that there was a women's baseball team in 1891. I bought a postcard with the picture of that team on it, as well as a big tee-shirt with the same photo on it, in the gift shop. I wrote on the back of the postcard and mailed it to Jennifer.

I treated myself to lunch at the Otesaga Hotel and marveled at the Smith and Telfer photos on the walls. They had a huge version of that family reunion I had seen in the photo book. I strolled through the older hotels and restaurants which I remembered seeing in my photo book also. Still, no story idea came to me.

Chapter Five

On the twentieth, I watched Jim drive up the long hill to the cabins. He didn't seem to be in any mood to chat. He and Sam scurried like ants around the place checking and rechecking the reservation books, the lake equipment, and the cabins. I stayed out of their way and out of trouble.

However, Jim came by my cabin before it turned nighttime. "Just a reminder," he said. "This is the night of the summer solstice. I just wanted you to know in case you're frightened by the supernatural. City folks don't always understand these things. You might want to turn-in early and keep a light on."

"Is Sam going now?" There was a childlike quality in my question.

No smile this time. I saw only a concerned face. "Sure. Don't feel awkward about it. I told you I'd be here if you needed me." The smile returned.

"Well, you go ahead and do whatever you have to do. Don't worry about me. I'm becoming quite the little traveler," I said and chuckled.

His eyes widened, and he looked over his shoulder at me. "What? What did you say?" He was in earnest.

I fidgeted like a person under an interrogation spotlight. "I just meant, I'm learning how to fend for myself."

He shook his head and continued on his way.

Some people can get so touchy when they're under stress.

Jim was correct. It was creepy that night. I felt apprehensive, as I always do in the dark. I left all the lights on and didn't sit on the porch and drink my usual rum and Coke. My heart was beating rapidly. Why was I so worked up? I would miss Sam, naturally, but I liked Jim so it'd be all right.

I spoke with Wainwright for the last time before his trip. He had an early flight the next morning, so I didn't keep him on-line long.

I reduced the voltage except for the living room lamp. I found my floral nightgown and snuggled into the cool cotton sheets. I decided that my nudity act was fine for my condo, but stayed in my nightgown in the cabin just in case I needed to race out of there in the middle of the night. Of course, I heard all those noises that you hear when you're scared. I was sure snakes, and mosquitoes were plotting to take me away. At the very least, the psychotic killer would-at last-reveal himself. Eventually, I fell asleep.

It must have been two in the morning. I was dreaming and rolled over in the bed. I felt something in the bed with me. No, I felt *someone* in the bed. It couldn't be. Another cautious touch. A warm masculine smell touched my nostrils. This was no dream. It was real. I raised my body from the mattress just a bit hoping to see in the blackness if it were alive or dead. It moved. I screamed. Loudly, and for a long time, I screamed bloody murder as I wrapped myself in the bed cover.

It screamed too. Loudly, and for a long time, it screamed bloody murder as it wrapped itself in one of the sheets.

Silence.

"Who...who...who are you?" I said, straining to see the shape of my adversary.

"I dare say, I could ask you the same question." The voice was frightened too. It didn't sound like the voice of a killer. As a matter of fact, it was a nice voice.

"What're you doing in *my* cabin?" I said.

"*Your* cabin! This is *my* cabin," the voice said.

"There must be *some* mistake. I've been in this cabin since the beginning of June."

"*So have I*," he said.

"Well, you must be sleepwalking or something because I've been in cabin 1 all month. It was reserved by a friend of mine. It was a gift."

"Really. Well, my family has been vacationing in cabin 1 for as long as *I* can remember."

"Look, maybe we should both go into the great room and talk this out."

"Quite reasonable suggestion." Just like that the shape moved with dignity, in its sheet, towards the archway.

The two of us edged tenuously towards the lit space of the open room. I could barely distinguish him from the shadows. It was a man, all right, and he was wrapped in a cotton sheet. But, what I saw in the cabin paralyzed me with fear.

The only light burning in the living room was an oil one—*a nice, heirloom, oil lamp from the Victorian time period.* Everything in the cabin had been changed. No computer, no phone, no FAX, no printer, no refrigerator, no electricity, no micro-wave, and a pump at the sink.

I screamed loudly and for a long time before I started to cry. Hysterical sobbing issued from every one of my pores. I'd done it this time! Worked myself into a nervous breakdown.

The man seemed uneasy, unsure of how to handle a sobbing female.

"Good heavens, Woman, if you want the cabin so much, I'll move to another," he said.

I examined him as sanely as I could. The hair, the mustache, the long eyebrows, the perfect ears, the soulful, brown eyes—it was Cuyler Carr. I screamed again, but my voice was wearing out. I clutched the bed cover for security and found a modicum of comfort from it until I realized it was someone else's quilt.

The coverlet dropped. "Here," he said, retrieving it from the floor, "put this around you. That floral thing, well, it's not proper for me to see you in such a thin, frail..." His voice faltered.

"I know who you are," I said.

"Do you?" His right eyebrow rose, and his mustache twitched. "Well, it's clear you've the upper hand."

"I think you'd better sit down. Do you drink?" I said. I was going to offer him a rum and Coke.

"No, I do *not*. There are *no* liquors of any sort in my cabin," he said.

"Well, there was a little bottle of rum in mine."

"I keep telling you, Miss, this is *not* your cabin."

"It is but it isn't," I said.

"That makes no sense at all. You must be out of your mind."

"That too. What year is it?" I said.

"1897, of course." He tried to remain dignified as best he could wearing a cotton sheet around his body.

"Well, when I went to sleep in *this* cabin last night it was 1997."

He pulled at the edges of his mustache with his fingers. Some sort of male cognition stimulator, I think.

"That's ridiculous."

"When were you born?" I said.

"August 27, 1869, in Toddsville, at the Carr homestead." He stated it as if it were proof that he existed, and I did not.

"Well, I was born in 1970, in Brooklyn, in a nice hospital," I responded with authority.

"Perhaps, you should lie down. This whole thing is upsetting your mind," he said.

His long, lean fingers reached for me, and I did finally sit beside him on the 'couch.' His hands were strong, and I found myself staring at them for no reason.

"My name is Gertrude Johnson," I stammered. "My friends call me Trudy. I write historic-fiction—romance novels."

"Dime novels? You'll forgive me for saying so, but they are trashy examples of literature," he said.

"I don't write dime novels. I write books: 100,000 words, and 400 pages of pure prose. I write very little erotica, Mr. Carr."

He eyed me suspiciously. "How do you know my name?"

Now I had him.

"When I write my books, I sometimes use photos of interesting people to 'portray' my characters."

"Are you saying that you have a photo of me?"

"It's a photo you took some time ago, I guess, by two photographers named Smith and Telfer. In the picture, you're wearing a nice suit and hat. You have a pocket watch in your vest's side pocket and a cigar hanging from your mouth. There are two photos, actually, and in both of them you're reading a newspaper," I said.

"Oh, that one. I put it away a long time ago. Had it taken when I came home from business college. My mother insisted. So, I wore my new suit and hat, my father's pocket watch, and took along two props I felt sure every business man in New York City needed to be a success: a copy of the Stock Market report, and a cigar. I never lit the thing. How on earth did you see it?"

"My agent and her husband were traveling through Cooperstown last summer and purchased a book of the photographers' favorite prints. You were in the book. Then, when I sold my last novel, Jennifer—that's my agent—gave me a three month vacation for these cabins. A few days ago, I was looking at some photos in the New York State Historical Association's archives, and I saw your other picture. I think the one where you're looking out is nicer. I ordered a copy of the photo."

"Why?" He seemed incredulous about everything I said.

"I liked it. I liked the picture." I smiled and looked innocent.

We needed a moment to reflect.

"So you say you're from 1997. *That's absurd.*"

"Tell me about it," I said.

He eyed me suspiciously.

"And you're staying in the same cabin I'm in only at a different time?"

"For three months or longer." I toyed with the lace on my negligee, and he noticed then turned away. I pulled the quilt around my shoulders.

"How can you possibly expect me to believe such a story?"

"How do you think I'm dealing with it?" I said. "You think I like to awaken in 'Back to the Future Land.' *Your life* has changed very little. We're still in *your* time period! What's the worst that can happen to you, huh? You have to change cottages—life goes on. But, what about me? Here, I stand in a floral nightgown in front of a man who is one-hundred years older than I am, and all of my clothes are in the closet I left behind in 1997. Women aren't even liberated yet." I started to cry again.

"Now, now, Gertrude, don't cry. I'm sure this is some sort of dream. There's a *logical* explanation."

"How can there be a *logical* explanation? You people haven't put H.G. Wells' book, *The Time Machine,* in the local drugstores yet." I continued to cry as befitting my sex.

He walked. He paced. He pulled at his mustache. He went into the bedroom and returned with a hanky. In gentlemanly fashion, he offered it to me. A Victorian version of Julius Caesar in a cotton sheet.

"I'll put on my clothes, move to the next cabin, and when I wake tomorrow, *you* will be gone." So it has been written by Cuyler E. Carr—so it shall be done.

I have never in my life used my baby blue eyes to gain an advantage over men, but they had a mind of their own. They rolled up to meet his. Direct eye contact. Tears. "You don't believe me. You think I'm a drifter with no money and no roof over my head," I said.

"Well, it explains things, doesn't it?" he said.

"I wouldn't lie to you. I'm a writer like James Fenimore Cooper. I came here for inspiration for a new book. When I arrived, I met the Cooper brothers, Jim and Sam, and everything about this place turned mysterious." I remembered Sam and his trip. So that was what it was all about. Sam knew this would happen because he said he would talk to me when he returned. And Jim told me the cabin was special and normally never rented to anyone. Where was Sam? Why was I here?

"Very well, you're a writer. Name the *title* of one of your books." Point—game—Cuyler wins. I could hear the Jeopardy music playing in the background. Think fast, Trudy.

"*Twilight's Last Kiss,*" I said. My eyes were wide and trusting—innocent.

"I pride myself on having read all the current novels, but I've never heard of that one."

Well, I guess I wasn't going to get the play-at-home version of this game. You could just see how confident he was on breaking my story.

"Have you any idea how I feel right now?" I said. I stopped playing with the lace, and my hands flew into the air as I told my story. "I have no money, no clothes, no identification, no Visa or Mastercard, and the only people who can identify me are back in Brooklyn, *and none of them have been born yet.* I'm telling you the truth. I'm from 1997, and I have somehow traveled through time and landed precisely where I was before, only with one difference, one hundred years difference. I know who you are, but aside from that, I know no one."

There should have been melodramatic violins strumming around us. I continued, "I have no way to buy clothes, and sooner or later whoever owns these cabins will want to know who I am and where my reservation is. They'll kick me out of the only housing I have and send me to jail for vagrancy. There I will stand, in the middle of the court house in Cooperstown, in a floral negligee. They'll probably send me to some insane asylum for the mentally deranged, where I'll be attacked and raped by some unfeeling thugs who work there and think I'm an easy victim. I have no idea how long this whole thing will last, but I do remember Sam Cooper saying something about the summer and autumn whatevers—oh yeah, solstice. If you leave me now—I'll be *abandoned* by the only person I know."

Tears streamed from my eyes. I knew the story was pathetic, but what choice did I have. He couldn't leave me now. I was desperate. His eyes showed pity.

I gathered the tulip quilt around me. I was beginning to shiver uncontrollably.

"Let's just say that I believe you," he said. "I'm not saying that I do, mind you. But, let us look at the longitude and the latitude of your story. I've been here all summer, and when I went to bed last night there was no moon, and you were not beside me."

"Correct."

"It's now past two o'clock by my pocket watch..." He listened to it as though it might not be working correctly. "And suddenly, out of nowhere, you have arrived."

"Correct!"

He sat down beside me again. "Even though most men would not mind waking to an unusually beautiful woman slumbering beside him, I do have my reputation and the good name of my family to consider. Thankfully, no one but myself is inhabiting these cottages at the present moment, and Isaac Cooper, who owns these cabins, has been summoned to Morris for a family funeral. There is no one here but the two of us. I could see my way clear to lending you some money for some clothes."

I groaned—another Cooper to meet.

"Gee, thanks, Cuyler," I said, but my voice was sarcastic. "How am I supposed to manage this? Do you want me to walk through the muddy streets of Cooperstown in my nightie and shop for a nice shirt waist, skirt, belt, and lace-up boots?"

"Good heavens, no."

"I could hide way up here in your cottage. You could find me some clothes, and then...and then..." I was stumped. You really must understand how surreal this was to me.

He walked. He paced. He pulled at his mustache.

"Let's just say I believe you," he said.

Here we go again.

"You must understand the circumstances could destroy my reputation. I can see the next issue of *The Freeman's Journal: Cuyler E. Carr is enjoying a visit from a certain Gertrude Johnson, a writer, who has come all the way from Brooklyn circa 1997 to sleep with him in his cottage in Richfield Springs.* My mother would be livid."

It occurred to me that I wasn't being very understanding. After all, it was just as much of a shock to him as it had been to me.

At least I could comprehend a time traveling scenario. I'd been educated in books and movies which depicted such situations. I'd read Einstein's theories. Cuyler didn't even know who the scientist was. He'd never even seen *Star Trek.* He had no education in such things, and his culture was being threatened.

"Well, I see your point," I said. "The whole thing is a real mess. Maybe, I should go up into the mountains and hide in a cave until it blows over. Maybe, I should just go down the hill and drown myself in that lake." My feminine side was just pouring out all over his floor.

"No, I'm sure there's a way to solve the problem. There's no point in saying we're related. My family is well known. Every cousin is accounted for in the family Bible," Cuyler said.

"That's sweet." I cuddled into his side. I was exhausted from the ordeal and the emotion. I've never felt so completely helpless in my life. For some reason, I trusted Cuyler Carr to straighten the whole thing out. Before I knew it, I was sleeping with my head in his lap. I'd never known such peace. The last thing I remembered was Cuyler's long fingers fondling my short brown hair.

Chapter Six

I woke in his lap and ascertained my surroundings quickly. Cuyler's head was lying straight back on the top of the couch, and he was sleeping soundly. I had a chance to survey my new home.

I cautiously moved from the couch so as to not awaken him. I went into his room and found *our* closet. Inside was a man's robe. I hastily donned the warm garment. It smelled of his cologne—whatever that was. I'd become accustomed to it already.

I returned to the great room and tiptoed to the front door. I said a silent prayer and opened it. The woods looked exactly as they had in 1997. The sunrise could still be seen by sitting in the *new* rocker on the porch. The boats in the lake were freshly painted—just built. The birds flew to the lower branches of the same tree and asked me whether I had any sweet rolls for them. The squirrels raced to greet me and earnestly chattered good-morning. I smiled and then silently wept. Would I ever see the "critters" by Sam's cottage again? What about my mother and father? Jennifer might have to find another writer, and Wainwright would have to find another employer—one who *would* sleep with him. Oh, hell!

I curled my body into a ball at the base of the tree and cried with all my heart. Hadn't I always dreamed of being in the time period of one of my stories? Didn't I collect antiques from this era and scatter them around my condo to sense the history? I had willed this to happen. In some perverted way, I was living my own whimsical fantasy. Jim Cooper had said that I was searching for something I'd already found. Now I understood what he meant.

Cuyler came from nowhere and stood behind me. Bending over me, he touched my shoulder in the same loving way Sam Cooper had. The next thing I knew I was in his arms and holding onto him for my very life.

"Oh, I'm so sorry, Cuyler," I said. "I've ruined your summer and probably the rest of your life. I'd drown myself in the lake to ease your suffering, but they'd probably have you up on murder charges when my hideous bloated corpse rose to the surface amid the vacationers' fun. I've no idea why this has happened, but I feel just awful that it's affected you, your family, and your reputation."

"I believe you," he said.

"What?" I looked up at him.

"I said I believe you. No one could have said all that if she weren't a writer of high melodrama. And my father always said you could tell when someone was lying to you because they won't look you in the eye. You're not lying. You mean every word even if you are a mental case."

He was smiling, and there was merriment dancing in his eyes. Everything would be fine—sort of.

"But, I don't understand. How will you explain me to your friends, your family? What if I suddenly disappear with no trace? How will you explain that? You won't *leave* me will you? I don't think I could survive if you left me. Will we stay here?"

"It shan't be easy, but I have a plan. I won't lie to anyone, Gertrude. I'm a moral man and lying is not in my nature. However, stretching the truth just a wee bit is in the realm of possibility. We may have to fib. I'm not sure the residents of Otsego County are ready for the truth."

"They'll think I'm a witch and burn me at the stake?" I asked.

"Not in this century. There's only one way you can live under my protection, so that I may help you pretend to be born in 1870. And, as I see it, there's only one way you can stay in this cottage, or even in this county, with me." He had a way with high drama himself and a natural way of telling a story which made you breathless with anticipation.

"Okay, Mr. Carr, I'm waiting for your plan."

He pulled away and regarded me at arm's length.

"You will have to marry me immediately," he said.

"What?" This was his terrific idea?

"As I see it, there's no other solution," he said. "We'll say you were vacationing at the resort. Cooper's gone, so we have no one who'll say you didn't come here to rent a cabin *after* he left. We'll say I let you have cabin 2. That way your virtue and my reputation will remain intact. I'll tell them you're from Brooklyn, but I can't tell them you're a writer. As you said, you might suddenly disappear just as you arrived. If you were a writer, there'd be questions about your recent books, which you cannot produce. You'd have to write in a different style than you're used to, and you'd have to be published by a company you know nothing about, but are supposed to, as you are saying you're a famous writer. Furthermore, there would be no earthly reason for you to leave the area, as I can see it, since we have a tremendous heritage for storytelling here. I shall simply tell them you're visiting your sister in Brooklyn—if you disappear. If this situation should happen repeatedly, I'll make up some other occupation for you and say you have to go to Brooklyn to manage it."

"You've got this all mapped out, don't you?" I said. "What if I don't show up again? What if I never time travel again?"

"If you don't show, I'll continue with the same usual line until I reach a ripe old age. Then I shall tell everyone that you died. We'll bury you in the family plot. I'll put you right beside me."

His plan was touching even in its absurdity.

"Wait a minute. We just met, and, though I've already spent one night with you, you can't seriously mean that you're willing to forgo your future happiness to help me explain a strange situation. You might meet some nice girl, fall in love, and want to settle down with her."

"But, you're compromised. As you yourself just stated, we've spent the night together."

"Nothing happened. You were a perfect gentleman. I can't let you throw your life away. In my time, a man and a woman live together before they are ready to tie the knot."

"How silly and vulgar," Cuyler said.

"Marrying someone you don't love sounds rather odd to me too," I said.

"It isn't odd in *this* era. Can you think of any other way to solve the problem?"

Given the historic period, I had to agree with him. There was no other solution. "Okay," I said, "I'll marry you."

"That a girl," he said, as if I had just agreed to play another game of croquet. "Now, we need some ground rules for our masquerade."

It was my turn to be suspicious. "What sort of ground rules?"

"First, you must never converse freely on your personal history lest you give away some of the truth accidentally," he said.

"Agreed."

"Until you know your way around, you will remain by my side night and day."

"Agreed."

"I've noticed a tendency towards speaking your mind, and I like it a great deal; however, it doesn't suit a woman in 1897. You'll attract attention if you don't mind your husband."

"So, you want me to be submissive in front of your pals," I said.

"Look. You're the one needing a helping hand," he said.

"Agreed."

"I'll take care of you completely. You'll live with me, be kind to my family, entertain my friends, go to church with me, cook my meals, clean my house, and attend all functions I find interesting."

"Whoa. This is as far as I go. Women gained equal rights. My grandmother and mother didn't raise me to grovel at the feet of a male chauvinist."

"The chief problem being?" He really was flabbergasted.

"Men in *your* time period want a female slave, and I wasn't raised that way. I don't think I can pretend I like jumping every time my husband clicks his fingers. I understand about not speaking my mind, and how everyone will notice if I don't behave like a Victorian miss; but you're asking too much if you want to change me completely. You've devised a plan which sounds more like a prison sentence," I said.

"Men in your time period don't act this way, huh?" he said.

"They try. They want to go back to the way it used to be, but it'll never happen."

"Oh? Why?"

"Neither women nor men should be controlling a marriage. It should be a *shared* experience, a partnership type of union based on mutual respect, friendship, and love."

"I see. Well, how about this—in public you are submissive and in private we do the best we can."

I grinned at him. "Agreed." What a thoroughly congenial and open-minded man he was.

"Also, I shall respect the unusual circumstances of our marriage and not come to you in the nighttime," he said.

"Say that again," I said.

"We shall sleep in separate quarters. Under the circumstances, it would not be proper to force myself upon you simply because we are legally married."

I was amazed. "No, it would not be proper." This man truly was my enigma—my man of history—and very much like the hero I had made him in my last novel.

"I think we should start immediately," he said. "First things first though. I'm famished. This cabin is an antique and has a wood burning stove. I have some food in the icebox. If I start a fire in the oven, would you cook us breakfast while I try to find some clothes for you?"

"Where can you find clothes here?"

We started walking back to the cabin.

"As I've told you, my family and others vacation here frequently. Some of the people leave clothes in their cabins. It's worth a try."

We entered our cabin, and I surveyed the kitchen: a wood burning stove, a small icebox, a kitchen table and four chairs, a sink with a pump. Over the counter of the sink were a few shelves lined with tins of flour, salt, and other baking goods. I could do this. It occurred to me that Cuyler probably could too, so I'd better do a complete job.

I went to the icebox. I found an uncut slab of bacon, a bowl filled with eggs, a smaller bowl which held what appeared to be real butter, and a loaf of homebaked bread which had been cut once. There was also a jar of some sort of homemade jam. It was strawberry. It must be his favorite and probably preserved by his mother. I took everything out of the icebox and laid it on the counter.

He lit the stove for me. He had placed wood inside the belly of it the night before. He pointed to a cupboard which held the china and some glasses. Inside a drawer, on the counter next to the sink, was the silverware. I smiled courageously. "No problem." He grinned in reply and went into his bedroom to change from his sheet.

I regarded the stove much the way David must have eyed Goliath. Don't pick up the burner lid without a towel! I looked for one. When I found a linen cloth, I cautiously raised one of the lids. FIRE! Okay, so we cook *on* the lid. I looked for a frying pan and found a huge black iron one. Cooking utensils? Someone had made little hooks for the bigger ones. I found a spatula.

Coffee? I found the pot and the tin of coffee on the shelf. When I opened it, I saw that he had only beans and that I would have to grind them first. I remembered seeing one of those old grinders in an antique store. I deciphered the only possible way it could be used and smashed the beans into a chunky powder. I ground enough to make six cups. Success! I had a passion for fresh coffee. I opened the kettle then looked to the pump. Defeat!

I hesitated for only a moment then went to the pump. I jerked its handle a few times and water poured into the sink. I rushed for the coffee pot. When I got back to the sink, the water was gone. I pumped again. This time I filled the pot, slid the cylinder into it, adjusted the strainer, took a spoon and scooped six tablespoons of coffee into it, and put the lid on top. Just then Cuyler reappeared.

"How's it going?" he asked. "Need any help?" He was dressed in a pair of pants with suspenders instead of a belt, a clean white long-sleeved shirt opened at the top so that you could see his undershirt, and he wore black socks and leather toe-crunching, lace-up boots. His hair was combed back from his face, and his mustache had been brushed also. I detected the smell of his special cologne; he had shaved.

"If you want to freshen up before breakfast, you can use the basin and pitcher in my room. I left a towel for you. You can use the pump in here to get water and take it into the room with the pitcher. It'll be cold unless you heat some in a pan first. Soaps in there too. If you need to use the Necessary—it's outside—anywhere you want," he said grinning.

"Well, I do have to use the 'Necessary,' but I'll make our breakfast before I attempt a bath," I said.

"Are you *sure* you can handle the cooking?" He slipped on a vest that he had left on a peg in the wall of the great room, but did not button it.

My feminine nature was bruised. "Of course, I can make breakfast."

"All right, I'll be back in about fifteen minutes."

I waited until he left and then hustled to the nearest bush for relief.

I adjusted myself as best I could and arranged the dishes and cups on the table. Then I placed the coffee pot on the stove. I took the big skillet and put some butter in it. I didn't know how Cuyler liked his eggs. Best to scramble them. My mother would be so proud to see how I managed the eggs—fluffy, and not overcooked, because the skillet had not heated so much as to dry them. I saw a warming tile by the stove and placed it on a burner. I placed the eggs in a china bowl I found. I covered them with a towel to keep them warm.

I took a large knife and sliced thin pieces of bacon on a cutting board I found near the sink. I fried this to a crispy perfection. I put the slices on a large meat plate and pushed them to the side.

Then I took the same knife and sliced the bread. I couldn't make thinner slices. This would have to do. I buttered the skillet—think of the cholesterol—and placed the bread on the sizzling fat. I found a meat fork for turning the bread. The coffee was perking energetically and smelled delicious. I turned the toast once. With the towel around the warming tile, I withdrew it from the stove and placed it in a wooden basket. It fit. The toast was golden brown and looked like grilled cheese sandwiches because the bread was cut so thickly. I put the toast on the plate with the bacon. Then I put the plate on the warming tile.

I went to the sink, found a stopper, and started to pump a sinkful of water into it. No, this won't do. It has to be hot water. I found a pan, filled it with water, and put it on the stove. There was some soap, and I placed it at the bottom of the sink.

The coffee was ready. How did he like his coffee? Black or sugared, for there was no cream in the icebox. *The jam.* I put all the extra supplies back into the icebox and took the jam and placed it on the table. I found the sugar, salt and pepper, and put these on the table too.

Just then Cuyler walked through the door with a bundle in his hands. He looked shocked. Hey, I couldn't help the way I looked in the morning.

"I found some things for you," he said. He was mesmerized by my full table.

Urgently I said, "That can wait, your breakfast will get cold."

He sauntered towards the table while I poured the coffee. I placed the meat plate in front of his seat and retrieved the bowl of eggs placing them on the table before his plate.

I waited.

He put a hearty portion on his plate and so did I. He tenuously bit into a forkful of egg. He took one of the slices of bacon and slipped it delicately into his mouth. A spoonful of strawberry jam was then spread on my golden toast slices. One teaspoon of sugar went into his coffee, and then he stirred it into the black liquid. He sipped carefully so as not to burn his lips. Well, I said to myself, say something!

"Gertrude."

"Yes." I just looked at him quizzically and waited.

"Not only are you intelligent, and beautiful, but you can cook better than my mother. I'm beginning to think I shall be a very lucky man, indeed, to have such a wife."

At that moment in my life, the day I received my first pay-check for my writing suddenly paled in comparison with what Cuyler E. Carr had just said to me.

I tasted my own home-cooked breakfast and thought how wonderful eating in the great outdoors could be.

"Do you think we could take our coffee onto the porch and sit in the rockers to drink it?" I asked. I wanted to feel as close to my experience in Sam Cooper's cottage as I could. We were finished eating, so I placed the dirty dishes into the boiled water and soap on the sink. I let them soak.

"But of course, Gertrude. If that's what you would like," he said.

"I haven't had time to freshen-up yet. Did you find some clothes for me?"

We went to the porch, and I sat in one of the rockers. He put his coffee cup on a small wooden table. "Let me show you what I've found."

He went back for the bundle. I was frightened. What if they were too small? After all, I'd seen clothes from the Victorian period in antique stores and marveled at the teeny sizes.

He held up a skirt. "I found this in cabin 2." It looked as though it might fit.

Then he held up a lacy, long-sleeved blouse, with a high Bertha collar. "I found this in cabin 3."

A three inch wide, woman's, black belt was next. "I found this in cabin 4."

I was excited because I felt confident that I could manage everything. Then he held up a pair of moccasins which were small, probably size 4 or 5. "I found this in cabin 6." *Moccasins!*

"Oh, Cuyler, moccasins. Won't I look odd? I'll look like a lacy version of Natty Bumppo"

"I doubted I'd find shoes. Boots are very personal items and rarely left behind. The skirt is long enough to cover them, and we'll tell anyone, who is rude enough to ask, that your shoes fell into the lake and shrank when they dried. As a matter of fact, we'll say that all of your clothes were damaged in the rainstorm we had the other day. Bad roof or something."

"Very well. I probably can manage soft, leather, Indian slippers for a while."

"That a girl. Why don't you try them on?"

"I have to wash first."

"I'm not going anywhere. Thought I'd feed the critters what's left of the toast." He crumpled the toast and threw it to the ground where the birds and animals scurried to retrieve it. I remembered thinking that the animals at my cabin had acted secure when I fed them—as if someone had done it before. They trusted Cuyler, too.

I went into the cabin and took what was left of the boiling pan of water to the bedroom, poured it into the porcelain basin, and returned the empty pan to the sink. The lukewarm water was just right. I closed the door and gave myself a sponge bath then toweled myself dry. As an afterthought, I put some of *his* cologne—which was sitting in an opened wooden case on his dresser—behind each ear.

I inspected the new clothes on *our* made bed. We had a problem. Cuyler hadn't found one stitch of lady's undergarments. I would be bare-ass naked under these frilly clothes. A lace blouse could be embarrassing to wear without a camisole. I decided to leave my long nightgown on under the outfit. The nightgown was tinted with soft, pastel shades in a floral print, the background was a creamy ivory. It would do until we found a lingerie shop. All of a sudden, I was brimming with excitement. I was going shopping in 1897. Furthermore, Cuyler was paying for everything. Cuyler—*my fiance'*—was paying for everything.

I tried the skirt first. It was large, but I would rather have it so than the alternative. The belt would help. I had some trouble buttoning the blouse in the back, and it was snug across my breasts but passable. I secured the belt and slipped into my moccasins. I looked at my reflection in his shaving mirror. My hair. No woman in 1897 would have short, permed, and layer-cut hair. I would cause a scandal. On second inspection, I realized the high-collar was perfect for my long neck and suited my face. The creamy lace made my complexion glow.

I looked pretty.

I went to the porch, cleared my throat, and when he turned to look at me I swirled around for his inspection. The look on his face told volumes. "Gertrude, my word, you have become a Gibson girl before my very eyes," he said.

"I'm sorry about the floral slip. I'm afraid it will have to do until I can buy some lady's undergarments," I said.

He blushed and sipped the last portion of coffee in his cup. We went into the kitchen. Together, we washed, dried, and put away the dishes. He was whistling, and I could swear the birds were following his lead.

"How long have you rented this cottage?" I asked him.

"Like I said, my family rents the cottage for the whole summer. We take turns using it. Generally, I'm the only one who comes here. Why?"

"I was wondering if we might come back. I'm actually enjoying myself. It's funny too. I didn't think I would. I told everyone how I would hate living in a rustic setting."

"Everyone being who exactly?" Cuyler said. The space between his long, dark brows narrowed.

"Look. We do need to fill each other in on our *other* lives. I tell you what. I assume we're traveling in some sort of tea cart, and your horse is somewhere in the vicinity. Why don't you saddle up the rig—or whatever you call it—and I'll close and tidy the cabin. Then we can talk."

"Agreed," he said. We laughed because we were starting to exchange expressions.

We were on our way to Cooperstown. The Victorian couple on a day trip.

"All right, Cuyler, my life and times. I was born in Brooklyn, and I have a mother, Loretta and a father, Thomas. I have no brothers and sisters, but umpteen million cousins. One of my cousins is getting married this very weekend. Guess, I'll miss that one for sure. I did well in school, was moderately popular with a select group, and wrote extensively even as a child. I never drank at parties or lived the wild life in college. My boyfriend did, however. For one weak moment in my life, I was seriously attached to a jerk. Victorian definition: imbecile. He was more interested in partying than studying, and when he got drunk or high, he smacked me around when I disagreed with him."

"Gertrude! The cad. I *am* sorry."

"I went to Harvard and received my degree with high marks," I continued. "A friend of mine, Jennifer Stein, strayed from our aesthetic pursuits and became an agent for writers. This worked perfectly for me, as I did not have to wait like most writers, to get published. She made real headway when she married Sydney Rosenblum who owned his own prestigious agency. They've been happily married for four years. He's a little older than she. Jennifer is the lady who gave me the reservation to the cottage. I, on the other hand, swore off romance in a personal way, and decided to write historic romance novels rather than the great American novel. It pays better. Especially if someone makes a movie out of it."

"Movie?" he said. I smiled and touched his hand when he said that.

"Not everything on one day, Cuyler. Let's take it slowly on the future stuff. I've lived the life of a recluse for five years. I've had no romantic adventures. I hired a research analyst named Bruce Wainwright, and he does all my leg work, so that I can write. I pay him for the service. Sometimes, we travel together and hunt through libraries and museums just for fun. He wants to make a bigger deal out of the relationship, but I'm not ready for it. I don't want to end a beautiful working relationship if it, like the one in college, goes sour."

"Then you're not married in your time."

"Good heavens," I said mimicking him, "no. I wouldn't agree to this union with you if I were married." I looked at him. "If you have anymore questions about my personal life, now's the time."

"I should say what you've told me is satisfactory for the moment."

"Okay, shoot," I said.

"I beg your pardon."

"It's *your turn* to tell all."

"Oh! I was born at the Carr family homestead in Toddsville on August 27, 1869. I'm the son of Chester Holbrook Carr and Olive Burlingham Ingalls. I'm their only child. My paternal grandfather was Ephraim Carr, and his wife was Sally Todd. My paternal great-grandfather was Robert Carr who was born in Connecticut, and his wife was Prudence Wheeler. Robert's father came from Scotland. Anyway, there's more to come on the family history, but I don't want you too confused. I attended the district school in Fork Shop as a child, graduated, and then went to Hartwick Seminary. When I graduated from there, I attended and graduated from the Newark Business College in Newark, New Jersey. As a matter of fact, my hobby is history. I enjoy researching the local history wholeheartedly. I write sometimes too."

I was impressed.

"I have been entertaining the notion of opening a store in Milford where I might sell hardware goods, feed, and other supplies," he said. "It has also crossed my mind to open my own coal dealership. I have a wagon and a team, and there is a clear need for my product. But, I have been in a quandry about what to do. My father passed last year."

"I'm sorry, Cuyler." I could see the grief in his eyes.

"Thank you for the sentiment, Gertrude. His death has left me the sole manager of our farm. It has also made me painfully aware of how fleeting one's life upon this earth can be. I've been eying a building that just went up in Milford. It has living space above it, and its location is ideal. A banking firm is already established there, as well. I know the men who own the bank, and they have mentioned that I should consider joining the board of directors."

"I think it all sounds wonderful but you're leaving out something."

"What?"

"Have you had any affairs of the heart?" I said.

"Oh, no. I'm rather pleased with single life. I've never thought about obtaining a domestic existence until my father died. I planned to continue to live in Toddsville, at the homestead, with my mother." He smiled and touched my hand. "Now that's all changed, hasn't it? Perhaps I'll make a bid on that shop after all."

I was guilt-tripping myself. "Cuyler, are you *sure* you want to do this? I mean, there could be another way of handling the situation, if you want to remain single and live with your mother."

"You may not believe this, Gertrude, but in an odd way, you have suddenly become the answer to my prayer."

We were coming to the main street of Cooperstown. The buildings looked similar to what I had seen in 1997. The present folks living in Otsego County had researched their town thoroughly and insisted on authenticity when they restored the buildings. Of course, many buildings which I saw now, were not there and vice versa. The hotels were just as beautiful as the ones still standing a century later. One, a majestic brick structure, was breathtaking. I felt certain that I would have noticed it when I drove through Cooperstown on my shopping trip. It was almost an entire block long and four stories high. I counted ten windows on each level. And every window had its own private awning. Three tall and majestic spires grew from the center and corners of this massive building. A lengthy awning, spanning one whole side of the hotel, covered the carriages by the sidewalk entrance.

I held my breath and enjoyed the excitement. I was physically stimulated and could sense this in the rapid pounding of my heart. I held onto Cuyler's arm for support. He touched my hand with his. This wasn't going to be the piece of cake I hoped it might be. I had entertained the tenet, that I would simply role play one of my Victorian heroines. After all, I did write her dialogue for her. But, Cuyler E. Carr was no shadow figure in the town.

There were "Hello, Cuyler's"; and, "Back so soon from your fishing trip, Cuyler?"; and, "Caught a big one this time, didn't ya, Cuyler ha-ha-ha?" I contemplated flipping that one off. All men. Standing on the corner, gawking at us, and joking with Cuyler as he drove his rig to a hitching post. He stepped from the rig. One old fellow, with a scraggly mustache, came up to Cuyler with this Cheshire Cat grin on his face.

"Hello, Cuyler." The old man spat tobacco juice into the dirt.

"Hello, Mr. Chambers." Cuyler looked at me and winked.

"Pretty girl, Cuyler, you gonna introduce us, or are you just gonna keep her to yourself?" he said.

Cuyler came to my side of the tea cart and offered his assistance as I genteelly made my way to the street.

"Miss Johnson, I would like to present to you Mr. Hezekiah Chambers. Mr. Chambers, I would like you to meet my fiancé,

Gertrude Johnson."

Mr. Chambers removed his hat, took my hand and kissed it, and then returned his hat to his bald, little head. "Fiancé?" he said. "Why, Cuyler, what a surprise."

Cuyler said softly under his breath, "I'm sure it won't be once you put it in the paper."

How would Penelope Chauncer reply? "I'm charmed to make your acquaintance, Mr. Chambers." Not bad. "My fiancé has spoken highly of you." An open-eyed, amused look from Cuyler. Keep going, kid, you're on a roll. "Don't you think the weather is unusually hot for late June?" Bingo! I had it made. All I had to do was think of writing dialogue for Penelope, and I was home free.

"Where did you find this lovely angel, Cuyler?" Mr. Chambers said.

"She came to the Cooper Cottages for her vacation. She's from Brooklyn. Now, if you don't mind. Gertrude needs some clothes. There was a nasty gap in the roof of cabin 2, and many of her dresses were ruined in that bad storm we had several days ago. By the way, my mother doesn't know yet, so please refrain from telling the whole town before I've told her the good news," Cuyler said.

We walked away from Mr. Chambers. Cuyler whispered, "The old fellow will tell half of Cooperstown in the next half of an hour. Come on. We need to stop at the bank first. I'd better obtain a hefty amount of cash since you have virtually nothing. Then we'll head for the first shop on the other side of the street. Lady's undergarments. Now, don't be alarmed if I leave you then. Men don't usually frequent such places. However, I shall attend to you at the shoe store and the dress shop. I'm afraid you'll have to do the best you can in lingerie. By the way..."

"Yes, Cuyler," I said.

"Good job with Hezekiah."

"Thank you."

We walked to Cuyler's bank. The building seemed out of place with the other architecture in town. It had a gray stone frame instead of the usual red. Rust colored paint identified the arches on the door and front window. They had also painted faux arched windows into the stone of what seemed to be the second floor. It had a New Mexican look to it.

We entered. Silence. Every eye was watching us. Several ladies, in the lines, glared at me. We went to the first available teller. I stayed glued to Cuyler's side. The clerk regarded us from under his shade, then glared at me over his rimmed glasses while Cuyler wrote out some sort of withdrawal form. The man looked at the paper. "I'll get that for you right away, Mr. Carr," he said.

"Thank you."

I felt like the prize cow at the county fair being shown to the buyers.

The money was counted out to Cuyler, and we left. I had no purse in which to keep the cash he wanted to give me for buying lingerie. We found a small accessory shop and purchased an embroidered handbag. I put his money inside.

"Do you see the men on the corner?" said Cuyler. He pointed to a group of men standing in front of an old light brick building which must have been built in the early 1700s. It had a large white door with a curved stone arch above it. On both sides of the door were three windows each in its own column, placed lengthwise on the pillars which supported the arch. The windows were old and trimmed white with an American flag protruding from the one over the door. Above the stone frame was a wooden second floor painted blue with white trim. There was an old stone fence in front and a porch. I could see a brass plague on the door but could not make out the words. I later learned that this was the notorious men's club known as the *Mohican Club*.

"Yes, Cuyler," I said.

"I'm going over to visit with them and smoke a cigar while you're finding what you need. When you're finished come and find me. This is very important. I'll have said a great deal to them as they are close associates of mine. So, don't say anything but hello and smile prettily when I introduce you. Follow whatever story line I'm on presently and agree excessively."

I giggled, something I rarely did at home. "Yes, Cuyler." He regarded my expression and then smiled his relief.

I went into the ladies' lingerie shop. Victoria's Secret of the 1890s, or rather Victorians' Secrets 1897. The lady was quick to come to my aid. I wanted to say, "Give me the works," but instead I demurely commented on the destruction, by rain, of most of my clothes. I needed to start with the basics.

"Yes, Ma'm. What size?" she said.

Size? Shit. Now what? Do you say size six panty and a thirty-six double D bra in 1897? Probably not. "You know, I have lost some weight recently, and perhaps this would be a splendid opportunity to reevaluate my sizes." I had said the right words and made the lady's day.

"Oh, yes, Ma'm. I'll find my measuring tape."

Whew. Nice save.

While she was gone, I quickly eyed the stock. I want ten of these pant looking things. I'll need a corset. That wasn't a pleasant thought.

The lady returned and measured me. "Now, would madam like a full corset, or one of the newer models which cannot break at the waistline. Will you be wanting to hold up your stockings?"

I took a deep breath and forged ahead. "Let me try both." She handed me two corsets. One, a Chicago waist with little straps for stockings; the other, a Cresco flexible style. Then she ushered me to the back room. Before I went naked, I needed pants. "Could I have ten of these, and one to try?" I pointed to a size—which looked correct—of Root's underpants. She agreed, and I could see **"BIG SALE"** flash across her eyes.

As I tried to figure out what to do with the corsets, and she hooked me into them, she gave her advertisement. "I chose the ladies, long waisted model for you as you have large breasts. This model is made in Chicago, and we have black, drab, and white. You may have a clasp or button front. It is made of the finest sateen and is our most popular style."

I gathered that bit of information about it being made in Chicago was critical. And what color was drab? Sounded like white underthings which were thrown into the wash with a dark colored garment.

She went on. "It is called the G-D, and many of my customers think they are *the* most comfortable of the waist corsets." Many of her customers weren't from 1997 either. Did they not breathe in 1897?

I have to admit I thought it would be worse. I told her I would take it, and she went for stockings. When she returned she asked, "Would madam like to try the other corset?"

Sure, why not. "Oh, of course, thank you." To my surprise this one was even more comfortable than the first.

"This is the new Cresco corset. Its principle selling feature is that it cannot break at the waist because it is disconnected in the front. It has elastic gores on the side which insures comfort and a snug fit. Many find the smooth adjustment indispensable for handsome grooming with the latest fashions. It comes in long, short, or medium lengths, and we have it in white or drab. It is manufactured by The Michigan Corset Company in Jackson, Michigan." Ah-ha! Not a Chicago corset!

I wondered if those little stocking garters could be attached to this one. Probably not. "I'll take both in white." The lady was catching onto the necessity of needing everything, so she showed me the store.

The slips came in the following colors: Black, Yale Blue, Purple, Violet, Heliotrope, Lavender, Cardinal, Cerise, and Maroon. I bought one of each of the four styles in black, yale blue, lavender, and cerise. She measured me for the length, and we mixed and matched styles: A, AA, B, and C.

I purchased ten pairs of style 106 stockings from the Racine Hosiery company in the only color-*black*. I thought the ones I picked were sexy. She smiled and added five pairs of OMO dress shields to the final items. I decided to forget the bustle attachment thing she showed me. After all, I had to save something for another shopping day.

I had one nightgown to my name. I looked at the beautiful white, lace nightgown in the window.

"Oh, Miss, that is our trousseau gown," she said.

I bought it. After all, I was marrying Cuyler E. Carr. Nothing but the best since he was paying. I found a silk kimono and purchased it as well. I must admit, with the undergarments, the slips—I was wearing two of them—the full-waist corset, and the sexy black stockings hooked to my garters; I felt like a new woman.

I started to worry. What if I did not have enough money? Cuyler might not know how much lady's undergarments cost.

"Will that be all, Ma'm?" she said.

"Yes, thank you. Will you wrap it up for me?"

"We'll give you one of our *exclusive* boxes. And I'll just slip some catalogs of our corsets and slips in the box for madam to peruse." She grinned with joy. *Catalogs.* Well, I'd made one friend in Cooperstown.

When she had the bill totaled, it came to $40.00. I couldn't believe it. I looked at the itemized bill, reached into my handbag, and found Cuyler had given me fifty dollars. He knew.

I paid, and she gave me my change while her associate wrapped my items in a lovely box, and tied a beautiful ribbon around it. I had paid half the total of this bill for one bra on my shopping trip in 1997. I had a feeling I was in for the culture shock of my life. The corsets had been a dollar each.

Now, for the real test of endurance. I took my package, walked out of the door, waved a cheery goodbye to the clerk who replied that I could come back anytime, and looked down the street for Cuyler and his pals. I would have to cross the street as they were still chatting in front of the Mohican Club which was right next to that grand hotel I'd noticed earlier. It was called the Fenimore Hotel.

"Ah, there's Gertrude now," I heard him say. I approached the men.

"Miss Johnson, may I present you to my friends: Jim Wheeler, Clifton Clark, Robert Stiffler, and Joseph Laurence."

They all said good-day and tipped their hats.

"Good-day, gentlemen. Fine hot weather we're having for late June, don't you think?"

Jim said, "Yes, indeed." His eyes never left my face.

Clif said, "Just so." This man's gaze was lower.

Robert said, "It might rain though." He stared directly into my eyes.

Joseph said, "It was similar weather last year at this time." Joe looked heavenward pretending to examine the sky for rain clouds and thus change his first glance which was at my breasts. The smaller blouse was causing an enlargement of my bodice in this new corset.

Oh, I was in for one intellectual discussion after another with these gents. I could see that I must have been lucky enough to have zapped into the bed of the only *intelligent conversationalist* in Cooperstown.

Cuyler said, "Did you find everything you needed, dearest?" I could see his eyes quickly appraising my new look—relieved the corset was in place. My skirt flared also from the petticoats. My moccasins fit better with the new, black stockings I was wearing.

"Cuyler tells us you'll be wed soon. Is that so, Miss Johnson?" Jim said.

"Yes," was my demure reply with lowered eyes. I am almost certain I blushed.

"Are you a member of the Presbyterian religion, then?" Robert said.

"Yes," was my wide-eyed, 'what-else could-I-be' reply.

"Cuyler said you two might purchase a store in Milford and live above it. Do you like the idea of not living at the homestead then?" Joe said.

"Yes," was my 'whatever-my-husband-wants-is-fine-with-me reply.'

"You'll have to tell us some day how Cuyler won your affections, and how he persuaded you to be his," nosy Clif said. *I bet you'd like to know.*

"Well, my dear, you have far too much shopping to do to waste time with these ruffians," said Cuyler good humoredly. Everyone laughed. Rescued by my hero again.

He took my arm and escorted me to the dress shop, which was—thankfully—adjacent to the shoe store which was within close proximity to the hat shop.

"How'd I do?" I was anxious for my test scores.

"Splendidly. Have you any money left?" Cuyler said.

"Ten dollars. Is that all right?" I was responding like a wife already.

"You buy whatever you need, Gertrude. I'm not worried about the price. Keep your money in your purse, so that you'll have cash in case you need it. I'll pay from now on."

That would solve the problem of being unclear about the prices and money of the times.

We entered the dress shop. "Oh, Cuyler. Look, Sally, it's Cuyler and his fiancé."

He looked at me, shook his head, and smiled. News travels fast in a small town, I guess.

"Yes, Mrs. Sloat. This is Gertrude," he said.

"Oh, look, Sally," I liked the chubby, maternal woman. "Isn't she pretty? Well, you've picked a pretty rose, Cuyler," said Mrs. Sloat.

"Her hair's cut," said Sally, who wrinkled her nose in distaste. I didn't like *her* at all.

"My, yes, dear. Such a short cut. What happened?" The older woman was embarrassed by the comment and tried to cover the girl's rudeness.

I was about to tell her something when Cuyler cut in. "She was in a terrible fire at her home in Brooklyn. That's why she's vacationing at the cottages while they rebuild. Her hair was singed, and she decided it might just as well be cut off entirely. It may never grow back."

I looked at him with wide-eyed astonishment. Where did he come up with this stuff?

"Oh, how awful for you, dearie," Mrs. Sloat said.

"And what few clothes she had were ruined the other night by rain dripping into her cabin. I'll have to tell Cooper, when he returns from Morris, that he's got a bad crack in the roof of that cabin," Cuyler said.

"Poor dear. It is just like Cuyler to do the Christian thing and help you with the expense of new clothing. But, Cuyler, you can't stay here. We've got to show her some wedding gowns." The woman giggled. Sally did not.

"Well, couldn't I stick around until then?" Cuyler said.

"Oh, look, he can't bear to be away from her for even a second. How sweet! They are so much in love, Sally," she said.

"Real quick, isn't it?" Sally said. "I mean, you hardly know each other." *Sally is jealous.*

I looked to Cuyler and let my lashes drop over my eyes in shy- idolatrous worship of my hero. Penelope did that when she met the heir of Hemingway estates. "I would not want to choose a dress of which Cuyler did not approve." Even Cuyler blushed on that one. Those long dark lashes waved over his big brown eyes.

"Oh, all right, you can stay, but you have to leave when we bring out the pretty gowns. A bridegroom must not see his bride's dress until the wedding day," she said. "It's bad luck."

Sally flirted. "When is the big day, Cuyler?"

"First, we must catch our breath and speak with both my mother and Reverend McBride," he said.

"Then I'll see you both at *church* on Sunday?" Sally said.

"I wouldn't miss church for anything," I said, realizing I would have to beg forgiveness on judgment day for that lie.

"Well," said the older woman, "let's get started."

She showed us skirts, blouses, suits, and dresses. I tried on all of them. Apparently, if it did not fit snugly, it would be tailored, for she measured all the ones we liked. I knew I was larger than the average Victorian lady.

We bought a Taffeta shirt waist which was made with narrow tucks across the yoke, and above the belt it had three box-plaits also covered with tucks which extended from shoulder to the waist in the back as well as in the front. I liked it particularly and planned to wear it the rest of the day with the dark blue skirt.

It was just the start.

We bought a dressy, evening shirt waist blouse made of satin over which chiffon was softly draped. It had an oddly shaped Bertha—or high—collar which formed a yoke in the back and was made with a crepe de chine cloth. Cuyler chose a Cheviot walking suit for me which had to be tailored slightly and would be done tomorrow for Sunday church. It had a jacket fastened plainly with frogs, and the lapels turned back broadly over the sleeves. The front was cut long and rounded. The upper skirt was cut in deep blocks over a shaped ruffle. It had a plain linen standing collar, and it also had a vest of lace and a collar of chiffon. I liked the little tie at the base of the neck.

We chose two house gowns. One was a cloth frock the skirt of which was made with an attached flounce. A silk braid ran the top of the bodice and along the skirt above the flounce. The part of the dress I liked especially was the yoke, which was made of cream white lace and ran all the way to my elbows. The collar band was a pale, yellow satin, and pieces of the same yellow satin were cut and basted here and there under the most prominent patterns of the lace on the yoke but not on the sleeves.

The second gown was the older woman's favorite for me. It was all black, as if it were meant as a mourning dress, but it looked striking on me. It was made with black cashmere which was combined with steel-blue gros grain. Silk formed the waistband, the skirt, and the collar-band. A white material was pulled over the collar and made-what she called-a chemisette. Bands of *passementerie* edged the top of the front panel and extended to a point at the back of the skirt on each side. Straps of black, velvet ribbon trimmed the waist and the upper part of the skirt. It fit perfectly and displayed my figure beautifully in my new corset. I saw Cuyler's eyes light up.

Cuyler was then told to go out on the street and smoke a cigar while I tried on one of the wedding gowns. He smiled and left, but tried to peek in the window I noticed-worried I'd be in trouble with Sally.

I didn't know then that the first gown I tried on would be the one I would wear on my wedding day. It was a proper, Victorian gown in every way. It had leg-of-mutton sleeves and a scalloped Bertha collar. The chapel-length train had a scalloped hem and an additional hem of scalloped lace. The all satin gown was exquisite with knife pleats at the top of the scalloped lace hem and the Bertha collar. The bodice had a cut at the waistline which made the waist look as if it were going downward right in the center of the gown. They placed a headdress, which was a crown of rosettes, in the palest shade of pink, around my head. The matron of the shop said it needed little tailoring. She promised to do some altering to it by adding tiny ribbons of pink on the scalloped hem of the dress because Cuyler was her favorite person in all Cooperstown.

"Your mother will be proud to see you in such a beautiful dress," she said. That did it. Looking at myself in the mirror, with this beautiful gown for a mock wedding, brought tears to my eyes. When she mentioned my mother, who wouldn't receive her usual Sunday evening call from her reclusive daughter, I sobbed.

"Oh dear, what have I said? Fetch a handkerchief, Sally." She helped me from the gown and quickly buttoned me into my new blouse and skirt. Then she ran for Cuyler.

"Come quickly, Cuyler. Your new bride to be is crying her heart out."

Cuyler threw his cigar into the street and rushed into the shop.

"What did you say to disturb her so?"

I couldn't tell him what was wrong; I was unleashing quantities of water and stress.

"I mentioned her mother. Has she passed?" Sally said, with true concern.

Pure drama from a non-actor. "Yes, I'm afraid so," he said. "Died in the fire at their home."

"Oh, dearie, I'm so sorry," she said hugging my shoulders.

Sally ran to me and threw her arms around me. "I know how you feel, Gertrude. My mother passed last year," she said. We both started crying like fools.

The owner of the shop placed my old and new clothes in several boxes, and Cuyler paid the fee for all, including the wedding dress and the veil I hadn't even tried on.

"Wait till you see her in that gown, Cuyler. It's heavenly."

My fiancé took the elegant boxes and leaned down to comfort me. "There, there, my darling. Let's get you outside where you can manage some fresh air," he said. I shook my head in assent.

I heard the woman say as we exited the store, "Isn't she the most precious baby doll you've ever seen?" I'd try to be more chipper when we came back for my suit tomorrow. I didn't want the whole town thinking that I was a manic-depressant or something.

"What was that all about?" Cuyler said. He put all the boxes into the carriage, so that we no longer had to lug them around.

"I don't know what got into me, Cuyler. I saw the wedding dress, and I looked so much like a bride; then I remembered that it was just a sham, and I lost it. She mentioned my mother seeing me in the dress, and I thought of my own mother back in Brooklyn 1997, who I may never see again, and the tears just gushed. You'll have to forgive me. I'm under a lot of stress, you know," I said. He gave me his hanky again, and I dried my eyes.

His eyes were sated with pity. "I know what will perk you up." He nodded towards the hat shop.

"Very well, if I must—I must."

This was actually fun. I tried on quatities of hats. I bought a pretty hat with an upturned brim. It had ribbons and flowers on the top and was not ostentatious at all. I also bought a round hat which was for shopping, and had a ribboned band and a feather. They put the one hat in a hat box; I wore the shopping hat.

Before I left the shop the lady said, "Don't forget the other box for *that* hat, Miss." Apparently, you kept your hats clean by preserving them in their original boxes. Our great-grandmothers must have felt as I did when I walked downtown in my new hat.

The shoes were the easiest things to purchase. I did not have to know my size. They measured my foot, and I chose two Ultra black leather lace up shoes for $3.50 each. Good-bye moccasins.

"When do I meet Mom?"

"Mom? I've been thinking about that," he said.

I was frightened by the hesitant tone in his voice.

"It might be a good idea if I warmed her to the idea with you nowhere in sight. First, the shock of seeing *me* could be rough as I am supposed to be at the cottage. She'll assume something terrible has happened. If I walk into the homestead, promptly thrust my new fiancé into her parlor, then tell her we need to marry immediately—well, she would have a fit, assuming even more terrible things. I would like to broach the subject to her in a gentler manner. It might be easier for her to accept you. Remember, she just lost her husband last year, and I am her only child."

"Sensible, sensitive, and above all wise," I said. "What do I do? Do you want to take me back to the cabin?"

"I hope you don't think that I would leave a defenseless woman alone in a cabin by herself."

"Oh, Cuyler, I can take care of myself. I live in Brooklyn."

"No, I promised to never leave your side, and I must compensate for the fact that I have to for a few hours. We'll spend some time here in Cooperstown shopping. Then we'll have a late lunch at the Fenimore Hotel. I wanted you to stay at the Carr Hotel, but my uncle said it was full. I must apologize. I had wanted you to stay with family; but, it's summer, and his hotel—which sports a small saloon—is a popular spot. So, I'll get you a room at the Fenimore for one night. I'll go home and talk with my mother. If she is agreeable; I'll bring her to the hotel at noon, and we'll have lunch together. I'm hoping she will be the grand hostess and invite you to stay with us at the homestead. It would be like her to do that. You could go to the dress shop and pick up your suit tomorrow. We'll gather your luggage and bring you home Saturday evening. All three of us will go to church Sunday morning together. We belong to the Presbyterian Church of Cooperstown. You and I will talk to Reverend McBride about our matrimonial plans. Mother can begin the wedding arrangements. I'd say we'll be married by early August or late July. How does it all sound?" He was talking as easily as a man planning a buggy ride and picnic.

"You are amazing," I said.

He smiled the first boyish grin I'd seen on his face since we met. "Really? Do you think so?" A twinkle of joy gleamed in his eyes.

"Not only are you intelligent, and handsome, but you are more practical than my father. Cuyler E. Carr, I'm beginning to think I shall be a very lucky woman, indeed, to have such a husband." I tilted my head flirtatiously and smiled.

We strolled down the main street of Cooperstown. I looked into every store hungry for information. After our constitutional, we went to lunch at the Fenimore Hotel. The dining room was elaborately decorated, but I was becoming used to the overdone Victorian designed rooms.

I had no trouble with the menu and ordered a chicken breast dinner with potatoes and carrots. Cuyler ordered a steak, well-done. We had ice cream for dessert. The prices, again, were minimal, but I reminded myself of the depressed nature of the economy of their time. People made only a dollar a day or less. No wonder the women had been so happy with my purchases that day.

I could tell he was nervous about finding a room for me. I signed the hotel registry and made a mental notation that, if I ever returned to my time, I wanted to see whether my signature was still in the books stored in one of the libraries in Cooperstown.

"Gertrude, I cannot come to your room," Cuyler said. "I'll retrieve your new purchases from the carriage, and you will need a bellhop to take them to your room. I'm sorry, but it isn't proper for a man to be inside a lady's hotel room even if he does plan on marrying her."

I smiled. "Don't worry. I'm catching on to things quickly, and I can take care of myself. In fact, I might stick around the lobby a while and check out the action—ah—watch the people. I won't talk to strangers or take any wooden nickels. I won't discuss my past or our future. It will be all right."

I was intrigued with the appearance of panic on his face. Either he did not want to go home to mother, or he did not want to leave me for any number of reasons. He left me long enough to bring my packages to the lobby. He motioned to a bellhop to take the packages to my room and told him to bring the key back to me. It was my turn to panic.

I didn't want him to leave either, and it had nothing to do with fear of flying alone. What if he came back with bad news? What if he and his mother were not in the restaurant by noon the next day? The same emotion I had experienced when I watched Beth close the file book with his photo inside came upon me. If you don't come back, what will I do? Find a job. I'd have to live in this hotel with ten dollars to my name until I found work. How would a stranger find work in this town? Could I write for the newspaper? What would I say were my qualifications if they asked?

The bellhop returned, and Cuyler tipped him when the boy handed my room key to me.

"Well." He took my hands in his and smiled like a man being brave before heading into battle. "I'm off to the homestead. It isn't far away." His hands were shaking.

"Cuyler, it will be all right no matter what happens. Everything will be fine even if she throws a maternal fit. I can take care of myself. I've been on my own for five years. We can still be friends no matter what. I'll even see you in church Sunday if you don't come tomorrow." I squeezed his hands affectionately and chuckled. "I have no idea where it is, but I'll find it and wear my new suit and my matching hat. Thank you for all your help. Really. I'll be fine."

He leaned down and kissed my cheek in a brotherly fashion. "Everything will be fine, Gertrude. You meet me at the restaurant tomorrow at noon for lunch. Whether she comes with me tomorrow or not; I'll be there."

"Very well, until tomorrow." I smiled. He turned and exited the hotel. I was alone in Cooperstown, and it was 1897. *Oh God, Cuyler, don't leave me!*

I decided to view my new hotel room. I climbed the stairs to the second floor, walked down the white-attractively painted-hallway, found the right room number, and opened the door. I slipped the key into my embroidered handbag. The room was painted pale blue. The floors were wood with several fancy but small tapestry rugs. There were three windows, as I had a corner room, which had white shades and ivory, ruffled, colonial, tie-back curtains made of cotton. Two, deep blue chairs with floral throw pillows sat beside the windows. A small, cherry table was between them. The bed was big enough for two and had a white embroidered spread and blue ruffled throw pillows on it. There was a small cherry table next to the bed with a fancy crystal gas lamp waiting to bring light to the room. The room had a cherry dresser that held a white, china pitcher, basin, and an attached mirror. My suite was decorated in a feminine and comfortable manner, and I couldn't wait to make it home.

My packages were on one of the blue chairs by the window. I unpinned my hat from my head and placed it carefully in its empty hat box. Well, what could a girl do with herself before curfew for unmarried ladies? I flopped on the soft bed and regarded the sky blue of the ceiling. Go to the library? Old Wainwright would salivate at the idea.

I would take the risk of being molested and go to the library. Could I take notes? If I purchased a pencil and a tablet at the drugstore, I could. Could I take them to 1997 when I returned? When I returned? *If I returned.*

I sashayed my little behind past the leering gentlemen reading newspapers in the lobby and exited to the sidewalk. I inspected the path both left and right. I thought I had seen a building which looked like a library far down the street on my hotel's side of the street. I walked past the Mohican Club heading towards the center of town. I noticed a sign on an attractive white building next to the men's club. Photograph Gallery. And under the big sign, a smaller one which said: W.G. Smith. *Smith and Telfer's Cooperstown Studio.* Cuyler's photo had been taken here.

I wasted no time and entered the building. No one waited on me. I saw no one around. So I decided I'd snoop. Just as I was about to draw the curtains and peek into the gallery, a man came rushing into the shop from the street. He was carrying camera equipment and was short in stature, cute, and wore a handlebar mustache on his round face.

"So sorry to keep you waiting, Miss," said the man. "Been down at the docks getting a few shots of the new statue." He placed the equipment behind the curtain. "Have you seen it yet?"

"Ah, no." Keep monosyllabic, Trudy.

"The Indian Hunter? Cooper would be so proud. Just placed it on the yard today. Everyone in town is down there. You should go and see it."

"I shall."

"Oh, sorry. You wanted something?" he said.

"Why, yes, indeed. I was wondering if I might have a photo taken by one of the photographers. I'm new in town and about to be married. My fiancé and I would like them to take wedding photos, too."

The man wiped his hands on a cloth and said, "Really. Well, I'm Arthur Telfer, but folks around here call me Putt."

I could feel my heart pounding again with excitement. "Putt?"

He smiled. "I got the name because it's the sound my motorboat makes." He chuckled. "And your name, Miss?"

"My name is Gertrude Johnson. I'm from Brooklyn. Here for a holiday at the cottages in Richfield Springs."

"Do I know your fiancé?" Putt said.

"Assuredly, you took his photo some time ago. Well, actually you took two photos of him." I was so thrilled at meeting this man I threw caution to the wind.

"Really? Who might that be, Miss?"

"Cuyler Carr."

He started laughing so hard I thought he might fall down. I wondered why he thought Cuyler was so amusing.

"*Cuyler Carr.* He told all of us he'd never settle down with a wife. Well, how about that." He paused and turned reflective. "You know the photo wasn't his idea it was his mother's. He went to New Jersey and graduated from a business college there. When he came home, his mother and father were so proud of him. Although, I think his father wanted him to run the dairy farm for him, to be honest with you. But, little Cuyler always had a mind of his own about things. In fact, it almost seemed as if he went opposite his father on everything just to make his own stand. Here, do you want your photo today?" Putt said.

Why not. I might not be here at the next full moon. "I just purchased new clothes and would like you to take it today. If you have the time."

"I'll *make* the time. Come with me into the studio, and while I setup for the photo, I'll tell you how I know Cuyler Carr."

We went through the curtain and lit a few lamps. Putt rearranged the backdrop to be the one Cuyler had in his. Then he motioned for me to sit in a cherry chair. "Putt, could I use the rattan couch Cuyler sat on?"

"Sure." He went to find the chair. He wasn't long. "Say, how did you see that picture?"

Ah-oh. "Cuyler showed it to me," I said my voice shaking.

"Did he now? Well, then he *must* like you because he swore

he'd hide it until the day he died. Wiggled and squirmed so much I took two, one while he was pretending to read the Stock Market report, because I figured it was the only one I'd get that day. I thought I had the only copy of that one, but I guess I must have given him one if you saw it."

From now on Trudy keeps her mouth shut.

"How'd you lose your hair?" Putt said. "If you don't mind my asking?"

"I was almost killed in a house fire. My hair was singed so much it seemed cutting it short was the only remedy."

He posed me. "I'm sorry to hear that, Miss Johnson. Anyway, Cuyler would not look at the stick in my hand long enough for me to get a proper picture. His mother thought he needed a graduation picture, and apparently he did not. Refused to take the cigar out of his mouth. I finally convinced him with history. I told him he would travel through the annals of time if a good photo were taken."

How right he was.

"On the final try, he just glared through the long ordeal of staying perfectly still to make a nice photo."

I thanked heaven Cuyler had obliged Putt. Putt was ready for my photo ordeal and stared through the lens at me.

"You are a pretty girl, and this will be a terrific photo."

"Thank you, Putt."

"I remember Cuyler from Hartwick, Miss. He was nearly ten when I was thinking about leaving Hartwick. I remember him playing with his pals. He would always stop to talk to me, though. I think he liked my photo equipment best. He was a curious little fellow. And, boy, does he love to talk. You'll find Cuyler stops to chat with everybody. I can remember his father and mother would come driving their rig through town on their way to church on Sunday. The poor little fellow would have this look—well, the one in the photo you saw—like that wool suit he was wearing was pure torture. The look on his face was abject irritation. No sooner had they hit the homestead after church than he was upstairs like a flash of lightning, changed into his dirty clothes, and running out the kitchen door flying towards that short cut of his like the devil was chasing him. If they wanted to catch him, they hadn't a prayer. He'd run the few short miles over the hills and be in Hartwick with his friends causing mischief by noon."

It was difficult to see Cuyler as a boy of ten.

"You need to hold still for a long time now, Miss. Just relax and look natural. Focus your eyes on the stick. That's right."

I wanted this picture to be perfect because I wanted Cuyler to keep it forever. I also wondered if it would be in the NYSHA archives with the others in the Smith and Telfer photo collection.

When the session had concluded, he told me to wait in the foyer of the studio.

"Putt, do you have a journal? Do you mark down everything about your photo sessions?"

"Yes. Why do you ask?"

"You take so many wonderful pictures. As you told Cuyler, they will last forever and always chronicle the history of Otsego County. Take good care of them. They will be invaluable to future generations," I said.

He looked at me. "I see why you and Cuyler hit it off. You both respect the past. He has a strong desire to chronicle the history of this area, but you'll discover that soon enough. I hope you like it in Cooperstown, Gertrude. Watch out for the winters. They can be nasty." He started to go back through the curtains and then turned suddenly to say, "You must be something extraordinary to catch a dedicated bachelor like Cuyler."

If he only knew.

"Your pictures will be ready in a few weeks. Stop in to see the proofs. Pick the one you like, and I'll give you the photo and the bill then."

"Thank you, Putt. Thanks for the information about Cuyler, too."

He laughed. "Any time."

It was a beautiful summer's evening, and I did not want to return to the hotel. I remembered from my 1997 walk through town that there was a dock by the lake. I wanted to see the Indian Hunter statue. It wasn't far from Main Street. I sauntered down an alleyway, across a tree-lined street and strolled down a lush, green parkway shaded by pine trees. There were some lovely, old houses scattered by the park, and I could see the statue of the muscular Indian crouching next to his dog ahead of me.

That was not what was taking my breath away, however. It was the lake. Shimmering crystal like a mirror, it reflected the boats and the birds soaring above it. There were three docks that stretched from the stony beach. A small lighthouse stood proudly at the head of the middle one. There were benches next to the stone walls which surrounded the boats. Small fishing boats and sail boats beckoned to their owners. The whole lake was encased with a coastline of mountains and trees. The water was as serene as the wind caressing my hair. There were few people nearby, and the solitude was soothing.

I decided to sit on a bench by the boats and let the invigorating aroma of the water send me back to the cabin in Richfield Springs. The sunset stretched its long talons across the azure sky. How odd. It seemed like only yesterday that I had walked these same streets. I was beginning to believe the cliché about the more things change—the more they stay the same.

The seagulls screamed their warning, but I was too deep into my thoughts to notice. I had not learned their language, or how to listen to nature when it speaks.

So, I was unaware of the tall man who had been lurking behind my bench. He was of average height. You could see a gap between his two front teeth when he smiled. He wore a waxy little mustache above his fish lips. He had a face that resembled a tortured toad, and an aromatic smell of mosquito repellant encircled his whole body.

"Mind if I sit here beside you on the bench, Miss?" he said. His voice was low, assertive, and far too intimate. I didn't like it one bit.

"As a matter of fact, I do." Cuyler was not present and my modern demeanor would emerge sooner or later, but I had made a promise to him.

The man laughed. "I don't see a ring on that pretty finger, Miss." The low and creepy voice again. "You're *new* in town, aren't you?"

"Yes, I am. Now if you don't mind leaving. My mother told me never to talk to strangers, and you're about as strange as they come."

The man laughed. "Well...I have some mints here," he said. He opened a bag of chocolate covered mints and thrust it under my nose. "Would you like one?"

"What I would *like* is for you to leave me alone," I said.

The man laughed. I wasn't getting through to this oily weasel.

He decided to sit down beside me anyway. He put his arm around the back of the bench and accidentally-on-purpose touched me.

"You're a pretty little thing. I could go for a real sweet baby doll like you. You got a show girl figure, if you don't mind my saying so. Ever done any vaudeville?" When he grinned the gap between his teeth widened.

I turned my body so that I could whisper what I had to say to him. "Look you horney little bastard. I was sitting here enjoying the sunset when you forced your attentions on me. I don't like you, and I don't like your unwelcome advances. If you don't leave immediately, I shall summon a constable. If he doesn't come fast enough, I'm going to take my knee and slam it into a place that'll really hurt. Do you get my drift, *sir* ?"

He coughed. "Obviously, this is not the convenient time, Miss," he said. He removed his arm, stood, and tipped his hat. Then he moved from the bench in haste. "Some other time, some other place." The bag of mints disappeared inside his jacket.

I stood by the bench and glared at him. "Not in *this* lifetime, not in *any* lifetime." I liked my own personal twist to the axiom.

He left rapidly. A young man painting his fishing boat had been watching the altercation. When I glared at him, he worked more diligently but couldn't refrain from grinning. The gent whistled a popular tune, tried to repress a chuckle, shook his head, then doubled over with laughter.

I iced him with a stare. "Why are you snickering, young man?"

"Nothing, Miss. Nothing at all," he said. "It's just that, I've never seen a woman do that before."

"Well, it's high time you did," I said, coldly first but then I softened. After all, I wasn't angry with him. He seemed harmless, so I walked over to him. "This your boat?"

"Yes, Ma'm. My *fishing* boat. I have a sailboat too. Do you want to see her?"

I agreed to go with him for his eyes conveyed an honest merriment hard to resist.

It wasn't far. The boat was magnificent. "You're Cuyler Carr's fiancé, aren't you?" he asked.

"Word gets around in Cooperstown."

"Want to go out on the lake?" he said, bashfully lowering his head as if he expected to be rejected.

Would I! "I don't know whether I should," I said, innocence and purity oozing from every pore.

"Look, I don't want any of my body parts injured," he said. There was that boyish grin. "I won't hurt you. It's only a lake." I wanted to know if he had a life jacket, but he handed me something to wear, and I stepped into the boat. "My name is Daniel Watson. I live here in Cooperstown. Cuyler and I have known each other for some time. He wouldn't mind my taking you for a boat ride."

He was a masterful sailor, and soon the wind filled the sails. I could watch the sunset kiss the lake good night.

What I liked about Daniel was that he was quiet. He was enjoying the wind in his hair and the streaks of white and blue in the sky as much as I was. I rested my head on one of his pillows, relaxed, and closed my eyes.

"You won't get angry if I say something nice, will ya?" he said. His lips suppressed a simpering grin.

"What?"

"I think Cuyler's made a wise decision. He used to tell me how he would never marry. He said he didn't want a woman running his life. I think it might have had something to do with his mother. He loves her, but you know how it is when you're the only child."

"Yes." I could have said that I knew how Cuyler felt because I was an only child too, but then I remembered how Cuyler was going to create a sister for me, so I decided that I'd better heed my closed-mouth motto.

"When I saw you light into old Ellis back there, I knew why Cuyler chose you. There isn't another woman like you in all of Cooperstown."

You can say that again, Danny boy. I was already bonding with this charmer.

"And there is no other man quite like Cuyler, is there?" I said.

He grinned. "You've got that right." He lifted his head and inspected the wind in the trees.

"What is it really like here, Daniel?" I said.

"Well, the summers are fantastic. You can swim, sail, fish. We've got county fairs and parades. All sorts of things to entertain you. Hot air balloon races. People come from miles around to vacation here. But, the winters are bad. Old folks can't handle them. More colds, bronchitis, pneumonia, than you'll want to know about. Our newspapers run every personal item they can because, unless you go to church regularly, you might not see some people for months in the winter. Come spring you might find out that one of your friends died in January. We do a lot of dairy farming—cattle, horses. We don't plant anything unless we're going to eat it or feed it to the livestock. Grounds too hilly for much else. Lately, we've been having a depression. Nobody has much. Farms are going bankrupt all around Otsego County. The orphanage is full of kids. Parents die or leave them to get jobs elsewhere. Men leave their women and children never to be seen again. Women have it hard then. Men like Ellis," he said, tossing his thick, black headful of hair towards the bench, "feed on their helplessness. He's in the banking business. You know what that means. If he wants a woman, and she's behind in her rent—well, there's always a way to pay Ellis, if you know what I mean. He'll see to it that the slate is *never* washed clean. She'll use the money she gets from selling milk and eggs to buy bread for her little ones, but there's never any left to match Ellis's figures in the account books. Even when she's made enough to pay him, somehow the ledger shows she owes more. Once he's hooked her; she's trapped."

The thought of that horrible, ugly man putting his hands on some helpless woman made me ill. I thought of Cuyler handing me all that cash. Revenue he could not afford to spend just to help a stranger. If I had to work in this town myself, I'd pay Cuyler back.

"Cuyler is telling folks he's going to open a store in Milford. Is that so?" Daniel said.

He'd said the right thing at the right moment. I knew how I'd help my savior. I could work in his store, write advertisements for him, help him with the books. I'd clean the house, or cook his meals, whatever he wanted me to do. He had spent over a hundred dollars on me today, more than that if you counted the hotel room. He had never made reference to the expense. "Buy what you need," he'd said. With a farm and a widowed mother to take care of, he couldn't afford the sudden extravagance of aiding a time traveler or, for that matter, a sudden wedding. He had not mentioned it, and, of course, I'd not realized anything because of the shock of my situation. To top it off, I'd had my picture taken today, and that would cost him, too. Well, I *had* to do that. I didn't want him to forget me if I suddenly disappeared. I would repay him. Somehow.

I thought of all the money I'd made from my best sellers. How I wish I had it with me now. I would give him the money and help him start the business he wanted so much.

"It's getting cool, think I'll head for the dock," Daniel said, and maneuvered the boat towards town.

"I appreciate the ride, Daniel, and the conversation."

I stepped from the sailboat. "I valued the company, Miss." I could have sworn he blushed.

"You can call me Gertrude, or Trudy, if you want," I said.

He grinned and squinted into the last rays of the sun while scraping his foot on the dock to dry his boot. "Well, thanks. Hope to see you in town sometime, *Trudy*."

As I walked to my hotel, I thought about all the young man and Putt had said. I wished I *had* kneed that old slimy bastard. Imagine taking advantage of poor, helpless women like that. Jerk. What was the word Cuyler had used? *Cad*.

I found the hotel with no problem. In a light hearted moment, I fantasized an AAA brochure for time travelers. Each section would be dedicated to a different time period, then subdivided into locales. Each city, that harbored a starred hotel, would be mentioned. Prices would be highlighted, and they might tell you how to convert them to our dollar value. The areas weather and the clothing to take would have to be in the front of the book. A map of each world view, for that particular time period, would be at the start of every section. Phraseology, etiquette, customs, and entertainment would have to be told to the traveler. You'd be given special discounts if you were an AAA member. Well, so much for the flight of fantasy. Obviously the creative juices were still alive. I'd have to obtain a pencil and pad tomorrow morning and start writing. Maybe I could remember that silly poem I wrote to Cuyler.

I was ready to enter my room when a shadow fell across my path. It was Ellis.

"So *this* is where Cuyler keeps his girly while he heads to the homestead and mother," he said.

"I told you to leave me alone."

The man laughed. "You'll change your tune soon enough," he said, blocking the small hallway door with his back and folded his arms across his chest. "Cuyler wants to rent that little store in Milford, doesn't he? He keeps his accounts in my bank. He'll probably make his rent payments to me. His family trusts me. I could make it very difficult for him to make good on the rent or outright buy that little piece of property in Milford before he has a chance to pick up the lease option on the store. It's for sale, you know. Bankers can move finances quickly when they want to, my dear. But..." He moved towards me, pressing me against the wall. "If his new honey were just a little nicer to me; I could see he has a reasonable rental agreement. What do you say? How about I come into your room, and we can discuss it? Hmmm?" His fingers grazed my cheek and trailed through the curls in my hair. A cold shiver ran through my spine. My mouth was too dry to scream.

I was in a tough spot. If I made this man angry, he could make things difficult for Cuyler. On the other hand, to be seen with this slime-ball would ruin my reputation, and Cuyler would never be able to marry me. I wasn't even considering how horrendous such a prospect as being nice to this guy would be.

I took a deep breath and forged ahead. "Listen, you weasel," I said. "You *do not* threaten me or my fiancé. Do you hear me? I will tell Cuyler what you just said as soon as I see him tomorrow. I meant what I said at the docks. My fiancé will take care of this matter. Now leave me alone." I turned away from him, placed my key into the door's keyhole, and turned the doorknob.

He placed his hand on my shoulder. I turned, lifted my petticoats for maximum mobility, and smashed my knee into the softest anatomical place of his body. He bent over in pain.

"I *warned* you. Don't you *ever* bother a member of the Carr family again."

He uttered something that sounded like, "Aarrgghh."

Spoken like a true Carr? Actually, I was just giving Ellis some Johnson pride with a lot of Brooklyn attitude mixed into the bargain. I was beginning to see why Cuyler was nervous about leaving me. I entered my room and locked the door. Then I stood by the door and listened to Ellis's painful retreat. I hoped I'd not made things awful for Cuyler. I wouldn't hurt him for the world, but I certainly would not let Ellis win. There had to be one woman who had the balls to tell him off.

I was alone in my own room at last. I searched for my nightgown, which I'd hidden with the lingerie when the store clerk wasn't looking. I didn't want to wear the pretty honeymoon one until the day of my wedding. Call me sentimental. Though the wedding was a marriage of convenience, and Cuyler would never see me in it, *I* would know it had been saved for a special occasion. The poor, old, 1997 nightgown was showing the need for a washing, but I wore it anyway.

I pondered many things my first night in 1897. Would I still be here tomorrow morning was the first? Was I doing the right thing in marrying a man I might never see again? Why did all this happen to me? Did it happen to everyone who vacationed at the cottages? Where was Sam? Was Jim still protecting my equipment back home? Would I find the answers to these questions at the end of summer? What if I wanted to stay here? Wasn't there some literary rule about not changing the past—not intruding so much that you dismantle what will happen naturally? What would Cuyler's mother think when she met me tomorrow? What hell was he going through right now for my sake? I envisioned it in my mind before I fell asleep.

There was a powerful storm that night. I'd slept for only a few hours when I was awakened by loud thunder and explosions of lightning. It wasn't that I was afraid of storms, but something frightening happened during this one.

I went blind. I felt dizzy and nauseous. The more intense the fury of the storm, the more intense my discomfort.

When the storm subsided, I retained my balance. I was apprehensive that this business was some sort of jet lag which paralleled my time traveling, but who was I going to ask? I could not call in a physician and have him say, "Take two aspirins, and if you don't feel better we'll have to send you back to 1997." I wondered if I should mention it to Cuyler.

I was in fine spirits the next morning, however. I was singing whatever song Cuyler had been whistling yesterday at the cabin as I washed my face in a real bathroom sink and bathed in a real tub—after waiting my turn. I needed some toiletries and writing supplies, so I decided to find a drugstore after breakfast. Then I would go to the dress shop and retrieve my suit for Sunday church. By that time, I hoped to meet Cuyler and his mother for lunch. If all went well, I would have a home by this evening.

I had a memory flash of last night's incident with Ellis when I sauntered into the hallway. I locked the door to my room behind me. As I walked downstairs and entered the restaurant, I wondered if my good spirits had more to do with the storm, the comfortable bed, or the fact that I was tickled to be in 1897.

I found a table with a street-side, window view. It was a beautiful, sun-filled day in Cooperstown, and everyone was on Main Street enjoying it. My waitress came to my table and filled my cup with coffee and placed a large glass of orange juice by my plate. "Oh, Miss, I didn't order juice," I said.

She smiled and winked. "Compliments of the house," she said.

How nice. I drank the fresh squeezed orange juice. When my waitress returned, I ordered oatmeal with brown sugar and two buttered slices of cinnamon toast.

"Yes, Miss Johnson. Right away." How did she know my name?

One by one, each business man who walked by me, greeted me by name and tipped his hat. People were sure friendly around here.

I finished my breakfast—which was delicious—paid the bill, and left a tip.

With my new hat jauntily adjusted on my head, I walked to the nearest drugstore. Again, everyone greeted me by name. I gathered soap, rose water cologne, toothpaste, and a toothbrush. I chose five tablets, pencils, ink pens, and a bottle of ink.

When I checked my items with the cashier, she smiled and exclaimed, "Here, Miss Johnson. Try this cologne. It's new, and we're having a special price on it today. *You* can have it as a gift, because you're new in town, and we want to welcome you. Do you want some cosmetics? Let me show you some Lablache face powder. Women love it."

The young woman radiated such warmth that I purchased face powder, a brush, comb, and hand mirror. This was getting expensive, but I needed supplies. Cuyler's homestead was a farm in Toddsville, far from Cooperstown by carriage, and who knew how far away it was? I might not see Cooperstown for some time to come.

The bill wasn't extravagant. I still had some money in my purse when I headed to the dress shop. I prayed I wasn't too early.

"Good-morning, Mrs. Sloat," I said. "I hope I'm not rushing you. I can come back if you're not ready. Good-morning, Sally." I was cheery and trying hard to convince them of my good-humored nature.

They both *screamed* good-morning to me in what could be conceived as idol worship. Even Sally was overjoyed to see me. They rushed about like hens finding the finished suit. I tried it on, and it fit perfectly.

Okay what gives?

"Oh, dearie, I want you to have this blouse," Mrs. Sloat said. "You can't have one blouse to your name. The formal one you purchased won't do for daytime, and you simply can't wear that one every day."

"I don't think I can purchase anything more, Mrs. Sloat," I said.

"Who said anything about buying? Sally and I want you to have it because of your recent triple loss: the fire, your mother, and the ruined clothes after the storm. No one should be put upon so mightily. It's a Christian's job to help someone in need."

When she scampered away to find a veil for my wedding gown, and show me the ribbons she'd placed on it, I had a chance to find out what had happened to make me so damn popular.

"Is it my imagination, Sally, or is everyone unusually nice today?"

She giggled. "It's you. Everyone is talking about it," she said. "What you did to Ellis last night."

I blushed to think that everyone knew such personal business. "How would anyone know about that?"

"Everyone knows that Ellis has only one thing on his mind. You were new in town, and he would have to introduce himself. He didn't know you were Cuyler's girlfriend at first. Well, the men in the lobby of the Fenimore Hotel saw him ask the desk clerk who you were and what room you had. Every man sitting there saw him walk up to your room, and every man watched as you went upstairs. They waited behind their newspapers. I guess when old Ellis came down unable to walk, with his hand over his crotch, the men hid behind their newspapers to hide their laughter. That story was spread faster than cake icing on a hot day," Sally said.

"Is that good?" Had I ruined myself forever in this town?

"Good? Are you kidding? The whole town's been waiting for the first woman to do exactly that. It gave every woman hope that they might be bold enough to do the same. Oily villain."

"Will what I did to Ellis hurt Cuyler?"

"No, Cuyler's homestead isn't under any mortgage. His great-grandfather had that paid off a long time ago. The land has been Carr property for some time. Actually, I think the family is in good shape financially. Of course, this is personal Carr business, and I don't know everything about it. Ellis is a villain, and I would be careful about him. You needn't worry about Cuyler and the Carr-Todd faction. They can take care of the likes of Ellis. You really *do* belong with them. You've a lot of spirit to smack old Ellis where it'd hurt. If he ever tries touching me again, I'm going to try it myself," she said.

Oh, Lord, I've created my own women's militia. This was why all the ladies of the town had been so sweet to me all morning. I was the one to confront old Ellis. One small step for Trudy, one giant step for womankind.

"I'm sorry for the mean way I acted when you came in for your clothes yesterday, Gertrude," Sally said.

"Don't worry about it," I said.

"You belong with him—with Cuyler. *You're the same.* I've known him for some time. I can tell how he cares for you."

This touched my heart: first, her apology was sincere; and second, she was the fourth person to mention how Cuyler and I belonged together. If they only knew the truth. I hoped his mother would find me equally charming.

"Are you meeting his mother today?" Sally said.

"Yes, for lunch. I hope she likes me."

"She'll be rough at first. You just be yourself, and she'll like you. I threw in a lace hanky for you when I wrapped your suit in the box. It's hidden under the suit so look for it. I'll see you in church tomorrow." She went back to the sewing room.

Mrs. Sloat showed me the gown, and the ribbons on the hem were adorable. The veil added the final touch. "Any idea when the wedding will be?" Mrs. Sloat said.

"I think late July, or early August. Provided all goes well with Mrs. Carr."

"You don't worry about Mrs. Carr. She'll love you. Besides,

she wants Cuyler to be happy. Just show her that, and he'll have his mother's blessings. Anyway, she's not losing a son, she's gaining a daughter."

"Thank you for everything, Mrs. Sloat. I'll be back in town for the gown when it's ready. And thanks for the advice."

I left the shop and regarded the rig and horse beside the hotel. They belonged to Cuyler. How quickly could I inform him about last night before someone else did? I walked across the street as fast as my booted feet could go. I put my new packages in his carriage, and searched for him in the hotel lobby.

It was only eleven o'clock by the big clock on the wall. Had something gone wrong? He had come to tell me I was on my own. His mother wasn't here so disaster must have struck. I found him sitting on a leather arm chair reading a local newspaper. I rushed to his side.

"Cuyler, what's wrong?"

"Good-morning, as well, Gertrude," he said. "Why don't we go somewhere less public to talk?" The words of doom. Goodbye warm bed—hello cave.

We walked to the side of the lobby to talk behind a huge, green fern in a large, white vase that covered us rather well. I could feel the tears gathering in my eyes, and I could not swallow because of the lump in my throat.

"Oh, Cuyler, she told you to send me packing, didn't she?" I said.

"Calm yourself, Gertrude," he said, nervously looking around to see if anyone was watching me cry behind a fern. "She's here. We just came early so that she could make some purchases for the house. She's not wild about the idea of my marrying a total stranger, but she's willing to meet you. She'll be on time for lunch; I assure you. Now what has you in such a state?" I saw his comforting smile and relaxed a bit.

"Oh, I've had such a night. I had some weird physical side effects because of the storm last night. As the storm intensified, I became dizzy, nauseous, and everything went black."

"Are you all right now?" He put his arms on my shoulders.

"I have never felt better in my life. But, Cuyler, I have to tell you about something else that happened last night."

He looked away from me, and I got the feeling that I was losing him. "Yes, of course, but, mother is here." He waved to a tall, attractive woman in the lobby. "I'm afraid it will have to wait."

I took a deep breath and forged ahead. Keep your mouth shut, Trudy. Smile and be pleasant, Trudy. Don't show her that she's upset you. And above all, don't show any temper. Be agreeable.

"Mother, I do hope you have found whatever it is you needed. This is Gertrude."

I thought Mrs. Carr was pretty, and I could see where Cuyler had inherited his good looks. "Good to meet you, Mrs. Carr. I'm Gertrude Johnson."

The waiter motioned to us to take an empty table. The attentions from the citizens of Cooperstown began anew. Every businessman having lunch in the restaurant tipped his hat to me and said, "Good day, Miss Johnson," and smiled. The waitress I'd had in the morning smirked and waved and said she was glad to see me again. If that wasn't enough, Daniel came breezing through, dressed in a suit, looking quite unlike he had the night before when we sailed together. "Howdy, Cuyler. Nice to see you again, *Trudy*."

I wondered if the egg on my face was visible. Cuyler looked at me, and I could read the '*Trudy*? I guess you do have a lot to tell me,' look on his face. I grinned sheepishly at him.

He helped his mother into her chair and then his bride-to-be.

"Well. She has only been in town one night, and *everyone* knows her. She's a friendly one, isn't she?" she said. Her lips were persed.

The waitress came to our table. His mother ordered a sandwich; Cuyler ordered chicken; and I ordered a luncheon plate with egg and tuna salad and fruit. The waitress winked again at me and smiled.

"I can see you've made *quite* a few friends, my dear," Mother said.

I smiled. To myself I said, "Yes, and one major enemy."

"Cuyler tells me you are vacationing here?"

"Yes, Mrs. Carr." My hands were wet with perspiration.

"Seems you've had quite a time of it lately. No money, no home, *no hair*," she said.

That last one was leveled at my back.

"I explained that to you, Mother," said Cuyler.

"Quite so. However, as a mother of a son, my dear, I'm used to Cuyler's stories. The wilder they get; the less truth there is in them."

Cuyler stared at his napkin.

She continued, "He said you're from Brooklyn, is that true?"

"Yes, Mrs. Carr." I could just see myself in a James Bond movie with Mrs. Carr playing Goldfinger, and me tied to the restaurants table with the laser beam inches from my personals. "*I don't expect you to talk, Trudy, I expect you to die and leave my son alone.*"

"Your family is from Brooklyn then, Miss Johnson?"

Cuyler said, "I told you that her mother is dead, and only her sister is alive after the fire. Her father abandoned them." He was filling me in, and I envisioned myself onstage in a play I knew nothing about with a role I was unprepared for, and everyone in the cast was improvising me through it.

"I asked *her* the question, Cuyler," Mother said. I was beginning to see what his home life was like.

"What Cuyler said is correct, Mrs. Carr."

"He informed me that you lost all your clothes when a storm tore shingles from the roof of your cabin, and rain destroyed what was left of your clothes."

"You know what they say—it never rains but it pours," I said.

Cuyler gave me a quick look of panic. I just smiled at him. If she were going to entertain this game of hers; I would play a bit myself.

Our food arrived, and the now familiar waitress remarked, "Cuyler, did your fiancé tell you what she did last night to old Ellis?"

My egg salad was going to be hard to digest. Two curious pairs of eyes glanced my way.

"No, we haven't had time to discuss last night yet," he said.

"Well, every woman in town knows." She hummed as she walked away. That's it, no tip!

I ate lunch waiting for the other shoe to fall. When Mrs. Carr finished her sandwich and drank a few sips of her cooled coffee, the bright spotlight of interrogation hit my face again.

"If every woman has heard the story, pray, I'd like to hear it myself," she said.

I felt Cuyler's hand on mine under the table. He squeezed it reassuring me that he was still on my side no matter what. After all, I'd tried to tell him in the lobby, and he hadn't given me a chance. The touch of his hand was all I needed.

"I decided to take a walk last night," I said brightly. "It was still quite early when I arrived at the hotel; so I went to the Smith and Telfer studio to have my photo taken. I met Putt."

"Well, well, another bill for us, Cuyler."

I ignored the comment, but I could feel my stomach muscles tighten. "Then I decided to take a walk to the docks."

"A young woman should not walk to the docks of Cooperstown unescorted in the early evening. Perhaps that is *common* practice in Brooklyn."

Cut off again. "Correct, Mother Carr. Some man named Ellis pestered me. Daniel Watson, who saw the whole thing, offered me a ride in his sailboat, and we had a lovely view of the sunset. We also had a nice conversation."

"Flirting with *younger* men. A boat ride? Indeed. How charming."

Cuyler looked like a man drowning in a maelstrom. My temper was moving to its threshold of tolerance.

"When this man, Ellis, tried to purchase my attention with a mint. I told him to leave me alone in a not-so-nice way."

"Why should he think you are the type to be *purchased*, dear?" she said.

I felt my checks burn with anger. "After I rejected him the first time, he apparently searched until he uncovered my name, my fiancé's name, my hotel, and my room number." Blessed silence and all eyes on me this time.

"He was waiting in the hallway outside my room and threatened me. He said if I did not allow him in my room for a more *intimate* chat, he would ruin Cuyler's chances of obtaining the store in Milford. He said he would buy the property outright." I was speaking fast and emotionally. "If Cuyler wanted to rent from him, he would see that the rent was so high, the only way Cuyler could afford to pay it was if *I* let him have his way with me. A helpless situation with only one inevitable solution," I said.

Cuyler interjected, "*He couldn't do that.* The property belongs to my friends, who own the bank next to it. I only have a small account with Ellis. I would be paying rent to the bank in Milford. After what you've just told me, I'll withdraw all my funds from his bank and move them to the one in Milford. The cad! How dare he say such things to you! I've heard stories about him. Now I know they're true. To think he could use such blackmail on a Carr."

"That's exactly what I told him, dear. But, you must understand. Since I'm new in town, and you and I have just met, he supposed I'd not know that. And, let's face it, Cuyler, I didn't."

"What did you say to the villain, Gertrude?" Mrs. Carr said all ears now. I could tell my very life depended on what I said next.

"I told him I would inform my fiancé of his advances, and that Cuyler and I would not tolerate him threatening any member of the Carr family from this day hence forth."

She said, "Assuming you become a Carr."

Okay, Mrs. Carr, why don't we just take this outside. It's high noon. I remained cool. "He continued to bother me, placing his hand on my shoulder, and wanting in my room, etcetera."

"And you let him?" she said.

"No, Ma'm. I kneed him in the crotch. Then I went into my room, alone, locked myself inside, and listened as he stumbled down the hallway."

I thought Cuyler would fall off his chair with laughter. I tried to look as innocent as possible and managed a 'did-I-saysomething funny?' expression on my face.

Mrs. Carr rested her coffee cup in its saucer, contemplated only a second, and then spoke, "Cuyler, you cannot leave your fiancé alone in this hotel anymore. What were you thinking, Son? It's far too dangerous for an innocent woman to be left with no protection in Cooperstown. I can see that now. I insist you bring her to the homestead this very day. After we finish our coffee, find a bellhop, and bring her new purchases to the carriage. I think Gertrude has had more than her share of troubles for one month. Don't you?" She patted my hand.

Cuyler wiped away his tears of laughter with his linen napkin. "Yes, Mother. It was only out of respect for you that I detained her in town."

"I'm aware of your manners, Cuyler; I taught them to you. I know this Ellis, and I'll talk to both the Carrs and the Todds about him. You just see if he stops you from buying that lovely store in Milford."

Cuyler looked shocked. I gathered from his expression that

this was a complete reversal of her original feelings about his business venture.

"Imagine. That villain blackmailing favors from an innocent young woman; a stranger he knew was betrothed to my son. After I speak my mind in this town, he'll be lucky to own a *piggy bank*."

I let those baby blues of mine flash a margin of helplessness, and I felt Cuyler's touch on the hand I had under the table again. Now he knew the danger I had been in, and why Daniel Watson had intervened. I sipped the last of my delicious coffee.

"Welcome to the Carr family, my dear," Mother said. She smiled into my eyes. "No question in my mind you belong with us"

Hallelujah!

"There is another question, however, I have to ask you, dear," she said.

I was relieved and opened myself up for anything she wanted to ask.

"Do you love my son? Marriage is a sacred institution and should never be entered quickly or taken lightly." Her focus was frozen on my visage.

There was a pause while I thought. She had us that time. We were planning a sham.

I didn't look at Cuyler; I looked into her eyes. With an assurance I meant, I said, "Yes, Mrs. Carr. I fell in love with Cuyler the very moment I laid eyes on him." It was the truth. Just as Jim had said. I'd been searching for that which I had already found. I did love Cuyler, even though I knew he couldn't answer his mother in like manner towards me. How could he? We'd just met. I squeezed his hand and looked over to see his reaction to my statement. He was staring at his linen napkin. I had embarrassed him. Linen napkin. *How nice it would be to live in a time where they had linen and not paper napkins.*

Cuyler helped us from the restaurant, paid and tipped the waitress, and then summoned a bellhop. He told the bellhop to take my luggage from my room to his rig. I went with the young man to arrange my packages and place them in the carriage. Then I had to check out of the hotel and leave my key at the desk. I had a new home.

He and his mother were headed for Ellis's bank. I was not to follow. I assumed it was something like the Carr-Todd version of the gunfight at the O.K. Corral. They were going to withdraw their money from his bank.

When I had all my luggage in the carriage, I gave the young boy a quarter. That gesture finished my money.

I sat in the rig. Daniel sailed by and spoke, "How'd it go with his mother?"

"Just as you might have guessed. Once I informed them of Ellis's plans for my future, everything went smoothly. You don't know this, but Ellis was at my hotel door last night, Daniel. I kneed him in the crotch."

Daniel chuckled as he had the night before.

"Young man," I said, in an affected manner that imitated my former response, "what are you snickering at?" Then we both laughed.

"I shall have a surprise for you and Cuyler. It's my own idea for a wedding gift. I hope you like it." He motioned to me that Mrs. Carr and Cuyler were coming across the street. The expression on her profile could kill. "I'd better go now. See ya around." I waved goodbye, and he vanished.

I tried to read Cuyler's mood, but it was far too masculine for me to comprehend. I decided I'd wait like a good, little, Victorian miss until he was ready to tell me what had happened at the bank.

"We'll take Gertrude home, Mother, and help her unpack. After our meal tonight, I'd like to drive her to Milford to see the store. Do you want to come along, Mother?"

"Not tonight. Some other time. You two need time to plan your wedding."

The ride home was quiet.

The homestead was a photo from my dreams. It was a two-story, stone, Federalist-style home. The stone used was quite unusual. It wasn't like the normal brick—large, chunky, square and round cuttings that you might have seen on old houses. It was made of flat stones, like the sort you see in a creek, stacked together perfectly. Cuyler told me that the stones had been brought from a quarry owned by Abram Van Horne in Van Hornesville. The house had been built by Ephraim Carr in 1825. It was aristocratic. He pointed out the stone marker that bore the name Carr and had 1825 written underneath it. There were four windows on the top floor with green shutters, and three windows with the same shutters on the ground floor. Cuyler pointed to an unusual glass circle between two of the second floor windows. He said, "That bottle of whiskey, and the glass underneath it, were placed there by the masons who built this house. A large barrel of whiskey was placed in the cellar of the house so that the masons could drink while they worked. Supposedly, one of the masons wanted to be sure that Ephraim Carr always had whiskey in his house, so he filled the bottle and cemented it into the wall."

There was a small, white, painted porch with fancy bric-a-brac pillars and a rectangular roof just above it. Four steps led to the front door. The porch wasn't in the center of the house as you might have expected it to be, but off to the left side of the house. There was one huge chimney in the back of the house. I was to discover this large chimney led to the kitchen. There was an adorable white picket fence with green posts which surrounded the yard and the house. There was another porch on the left side of the house against what appeared to be the door to the kitchen and its pantry.

"That wing frame off to the side of the house is the original frame home of the Carrs not just a wing and porch. Ephraim brought it over after he built the stone house and attached it to the back," Cuyler said.

"Two homes for the price of one?" I said, and Cuyler laughed.

Before we unloaded the packages, I was given a tour of the outside the house. Cuyler was anxious to show me his mother's flowers in the garden to the right of the house. There was a carriage house across the street from the front porch. The animal barn was next to the carriage house and a smaller barn sat next to it.

He lived high enough on the hill to be able to see the mountains and the valleys. It was a splendid view. There was a lot of farm land here. I remembered how the hills of pine trees ringed Otsego Lake. Their lush pasture land was shaded by the same trees, and I noticed a dirt road which led into the higher terrain. How enchanting it all was! I could see why Cuyler's grandparents bought the acreage from Judge Cooper. Robert Carr and his family had broken their backs tilling the soil to make it flat, smooth, and beautiful. A country home saturated with the history of one family. My family. My home. Not some condo-a real home.

I followed him into the large barn and watched while Cuyler urged the horse—whose name I soon learned was Samuel—into his stall. Wouldn't Sam Cooper just die to learn that my new tour guide was a Samuel, too? While we were there, he showed me his team of horses, and the other wing of the barn that housed the dairy cows. The barn had fresh hay strewn around the stalls, and Samuel grasped it with his big mouth and threw it into the air around his head while he ate. I noticed how good-natured Cuyler was with the animals. His voice was soft as he soothed each animal.

We then went to the carriage house where he showed me his prize. "This is the grandest carriage you will ever see, Gertrude, and once belonged to Governor Dix." It was ornate, very old, and in great shape. He showed me a variety of carriages and tack that were stored in the small barn.

Grasping my hand, he hurried me into his home. The rooms were decorated with heavy cherry furnishings. The first room was a parlor with chairs, a couch, and a piano. I eyed him curiously. He assured me that he did not play. Then I was ushered into the dining room that had a cherry dining table that sat twelve, and matching china cabinets that guarded Mother Carr's precious crystal and plates.

The stairs to the second floor were in the middle of the house, and we flew up them. I noticed a sudden lightening in his spirit. He smiled and pointed to the guest bedroom, his room, his parent's master bedroom, and another smaller room. Doors connected each room to the other. I placed my new hat and purse in the guest bedroom.

We darted down a back servant's stairway that led to a huge kitchen and pantry. The gas stove was a modern addition and sat next to the old stone fireplace. The black kettle sat uselessly on its iron ring. The pantry had cupboards with glass on the tiny doors. Next to this area was a washroom. I took a moment to look out of the kitchen window and saw an outhouse behind the house.

He and I managed to bring all my new items up the stairs and into my room while his mother made tea for us.

We were alone now. I was exhausted and reclined on my comfy bed.

"You are phenomenal," he said, catching his breath and resting his back against the door frame.

I sat up and looked at him. "What do you mean?"

"My mother had already decided against the marriage, but I begged her to at least meet you. I didn't want to tell you that before lunch." He crossed the room. "She has hated the idea of my opening a store and living away from Toddsville, but now she is as happy as a lark about the idea." He sat next to me on the patchwork quilt sewn with pink and rose shades.

Cuyler became serious and said, "She and I will deposit our individual accounts in the bank at Milford. Ellis will never harm you again. He has nothing with which to threaten us."

"Did you see him when you went to withdraw your funds?" I asked.

"No, but I hit him where it will hurt him the most. A little higher than yours, however. In the wallet."

I faced him. "I don't suppose it was proper of me to knee him." I scrutinized his face. "I don't suppose a Victorian miss would do that, huh?"

"No, a Victorian miss would not." He lounged on the bed resting his sore back. "I think that's why I enjoyed the fact that you did. You won mother over because you refused to be intimidated by a bully. You fought back and saved your pride, your reputation, your virtue, and the family name, as well. You also proved you supported her son no matter the odds. I would not have expected a stranger to do that."

He sat up, propped himself up on his right elbow, and said, "Living with you shall be one adventure after another, I can see that." I gave him a serious look. "I'm immensely grateful that you landed in my bed the other night." Sentiment veiled his eyes.

"Are you sure of that?" I said. My voice held a softer more ladylike tone.

He stood up from the bed, walked to the door and closed it, pulled me by my arm from the bed with his strong, right arm while grabbing me around the waist with the left, and gathered me into his arms. I was shocked. "More than I can ever say," he said. He kissed me. His kiss conveyed what was in his heart. I thought I might just faint. The kiss surprised me, and I pulled away from him for a moment to look into his eyes. I didn't leave the crease of his embrace and sensed he wouldn't let me go anyway. I saw happiness replace the loneliness that once lay behind those beautiful brown ovals. My own eyes must have been twinkling with delight. I smiled and offered my lips with tender affection.

"I wouldn't have done that, Gertrude, if you hadn't said what you did at lunch. It didn't sound like a falsehood to me. Was it?" Cuyler showed courage and vulnerability in asking the question.

"Look into my eyes." He searched for the truth inside the blueness. My emotions swept me away, and I kissed his lips with abandon.

"How could this be?" I said. "We've just met." I held his face between my palms while kissing his cheeks—coveting my newfound love.

"I've never met anyone like you." He laughed. "I don't think I could have met anyone like you in my own time. You're an angel, I suppose. For some reason, you've come from heaven to arrange my life. You've helped me attain something I was unaware I needed until you arrived. I find that overwhelming and amusing. I gather you find your dream when you aren't looking for it. You'd think you'd know your own heart, though. I wanted to open that store, but I'd made no move to reach for my dream. I'm not sure I ever would have if you hadn't entered my life."

I stared at him. It wasn't a comment two people could have simultaneously created. For it seemed as if Cuyler had taken the distinctively phrased philosophy right out of Jim's mouth.

The memory of Jim Cooper reminded me of something which had, for at least a few hours, flown from my thoughts. *1997.* Returning! The tenet was a knife in my heart. How could I return? Would I depart the same way I'd arrived? Poof, a mist, some smoke, and I'm gone. I touched his handle bar mustache with a feminine stroke of my finger. I could *never* leave him, Cooperstown, or Toddsville. For I'd frozen my heart for five years, denying anyone access, and Cuyler Carr had just melted it with a word and a kiss. This was no idle affection.

I'd often informed Jennifer that I'd have to *really* be in love before I offered my heart completely to a new lover. Only a few hours prior to this moment, I had. For Life. For Eternity. The Fates could not be so cruel as to tear us apart. I had finally found the man of my dreams. Would I lose him?

I sensed he was reading my mind. "I know," he said. "I've been pondering that, as well. Let's not think about it now. We have some time if what you've been told is true." I saw the emotion in his eyes. "Let's not waste one minute of it thinking about its possible conclusion. I love you, Gertrude. I wasn't planning on feeling this way about anyone. Then suddenly you were there—sleeping in my lap—and it felt right somehow." He snickered. "I always told my friends I'd never marry. That was because I'd never met a woman I could love, who made me laugh, made me think, made me want to be the greatest business man Otsego County has ever seen. I knew I'd never find her here. My heart was safe. Then this incredible woman from one hundred years after my time drops into my cabin."

He held me tightly against his chest and whispered into my ear, "You've crawled deep inside my heart, Lady. And there you shall remain for all eternity. However long we have together, let us cherish it. Then we'll have no regrets if it should end."

I held him close for fear of losing him, and closed my eyes to fight my tears.

No jokes, no clever lines, no wise remarks. Not now. I wanted him to cradle me in his arms and keep the strange reality of the time traveling at a distance. I had journeyed so far to find where I belonged. I wanted to remain here in Cuyler Carr's arms. Marrying him, loving him, and being the best wife I could be for him, for as long as I could. I gave him a long, languorous kiss and felt the gentle beating of his heart against my breasts. I whispered into his ear, "Can you hear the rhythm of *my* heart?"

He answered, cuddling his kisses into my neck, "Yes."

"From now on our hearts beat as one. No matter where I am or where you are—always remember that." Our lips met, and a fire began to smolder inside my body. A happy sensation I hadn't sensed in years. My desires began to overpower my reasoning. "I think we'd better go downstairs," I said. "Your mother is going to become suspicious." I smiled. "Now that we will be married, I think I can wait." I left his embrace.

He sighed and said, "I think we'll send those invitations out Monday morning if I have to hand write them and stamp them myself."

"Maybe I can help you. I could lick a few envelopes myself."

His arms caught me around my waist again. "You keep talking like that and mother will wait for tea." Another kiss—another moment to speak of love.

We took to the stairs and joined his mother in the parlor

where tea and cake were waiting. It was hard to disguise the giddiness we felt.

Mrs. Carr had a cook—a rotund, cheerful woman named Johanna. This unmarried woman had cooked for the Carr's since their marriage in May 1866. She would have many tales of Cuyler's childhood, and I couldn't wait to hear them. She agreed to tell me anything I wanted to know and winked at the frown on Cuyler's face. She whispered for me to come to the kitchen early in the morning when she did her baking. Coffee and conversation in the Carr's kitchen would be heaven to an author of historical romances. As a matter of fact, when we had finished our meatloaf dinner, I ran to my room and fetched my writing pad and two pencils. I had an idea for a story.

Chapter Seven

Cuyler hitched Samuel to the small carriage and told his mother not to expect us for several hours. We were traveling to Milford to look at the future business site of Mr. and Mrs. C.E. Carr.

As soon as we were in the carriage, our privacy overwhelmed us. Since the ride from the cabins to Cooperstown yesterday, we'd had no time to talk.

"I hope you aren't angry about the photo. I wanted you to have a picture of me, just in case."

He laughed. "How could I ever be angry with anything you did?" he said. "I'm glad you did it. I must tell you how sorry I am about the incident with Ellis. I should never have left you alone. I broke my promise to stay by your side, and you paid the price for it."

"You were right in doing so. You couldn't thrust a total stranger on your mother."

"My mother was harsh with you yesterday. I'm sorry," he said.

"If I had a son as wonderful as you, I would be dubious of a woman who purchased half of Cooperstown with his money too," I said.

He changed the subject. "I promised a history lesson, and it's a long ride to Milford. I'm afraid you're stuck with listening to my stories unless you want to walk."

I flipped the cover of my tablet to the first page. "I'm all ears."

He seemed astonished by my secretarial pretense. "Are you going to take notes?"

"Will it bother you?"

A satisfied smile creased his cheeks. "Not in the least." The sun was in the three o'clock position, and Cuyler was doing what he loved best—telling the history of Toddsville.

"About 1788 Samuel Tubbs purchased a tract of about 350 acres of land from Judge William Cooper. This land was bounded by the Daniel Wheeler farm on the north, and by a farm now owned by Arthur E. Stevens on the south, and by a farm owned by the late Deforest Carr and James Carr on the west, and by a ridge of eastern hills on the eastern side. Tubbs erected a log house near the drive leading to what we call the 'Dr. Almy house' and a grist mill on the Hartwick side of the stream. The little town was known as 'Tubbs Mill' at the time. I have to assume that this was the only grist mill for miles where the settlers could get their grain ground. New settlers from the Unadilla Valley would bring grists to Tubbs Mill. I assume they came down the Unadilla River to the junction of that stream and the Susquehanna a few miles south of Sidney. Then they would have had to travel up the river to the place where Oaks Creek meets the Susquehanna and then to Tubbs place."

My pencil had to flow as fast as a stream in a flood to keep up with him.

"This must have been a long and tiresome trip—taking days of wading some of that stream at times. I suppose the trails, and paths were not well marked in those days, or they surely would have chosen a better route. The settlers, from Burlington and other settlements north of here, came with bags of grain on horseback to Tubbs Mill."

He looked at me and smiled. "Are you getting all this down?"

I flipped my sixth page. "No problem."

"I like that phrase,'No problem.' Shall I continue?" he said.

"I hang on your every word," I said.

He laughed again. "On or about 1794, or1795, Tubbs built the first frame building. This is the oldest house in Toddsville. Samuel Tubbs died soon after and gave part of the acreage to his daughter in his will. Her name was Mrs. Sally Story. The other part of the Tubbs Patent, including flow rights, he gave to Judge William Cooper. I shall have to assume this was the case because the Todd title came from Judge Cooper. About 1796, a century ago, Gertrude, Jehiel Todd and his family—which then consisted of Lemuel, Ira, Caleb, Asabel, Bethel, Sally, and Polly—came to the area."

"Sally Todd was your grandmother," I said.

"You do listen, don't you? Anyway, they came from Wallingford, Connecticut, and purchased the south half of the Tubbs Patent from Cooper. The Todds enlarged the grist mill, built a woolen factory on the Hartwick side of the stream, later a saw mill, and lastly a paper mill on the Otsego side of the Tubbs Patent. After the death of Tubbs, the name of our town seems to have been changed to 'Todds Ville' which, of course, led to the name

Toddsville."

I wrote until I thought my hand would break. His demeanor was natural and intellectual, as if he could tell this story in his sleep. I was missing some of the scenery, but since it was mostly farm land, I could only be missing a cow or two. The road became familiar a few miles from Cooperstown. Though it was only a dirt path now, it was the road Sam and I had traveled in his truck the day we went to speak with Jim.

"In the '80s, a man by the name of Samuel M. Shaw succeeded in having the name changed to 'Seymour' in memory of the late Horatio Seymour, governor of New York," Cuyler said.

I chuckled so much that my pencil slipped from my hand. "Oh come on, Cuyler. *Seymourville*?" I searched and retrieved the pencil.

He smirked but remained serious. "The citizens drew up a petition, and the name of the town was speedily restored to Toddsville. Did you write it all?"

"I have my history lesson down on my tablet. I'll be able to answer any question you may quiz me on later."

He stopped the rig just before we entered Milford. "The only quiz question you need answer is this." He kissed me and held me until I thought I could not breathe. "Do you love me, Gertrude?" he said.

I held my breath and straightened my hat. "Yes."

He slapped Samuel's rear with the reins. "You pass with honors."

I no longer was as intent on Cuyler for I was mesmerized by Milford. Except for concrete roads and reconstructed sidewalks, restored buildings, and *modern* advertisements on the walls of the stores, not much was different. We stopped the rig in front of what I would call a plaza.

The store was facing the major intersection, so our business location was excellent. The front door was only inches from the street. There were two front windows on the double story building which had two roof lines. The one roof line ended in a dormer arch over the front door. This would be where we would hang our business logo. There were two pillars which lifted the arch giving some shade to our customers as they entered our store. A fresh coat of white paint covered the newly-built edifice. We walked inside the building. "Are you sure your friends won't mind our peeking?" I said.

"No." He held the door open for me. "There is nothing in here yet."

He preceded to show me where the bins for nails would be, where the cash register would sit, where the balance for weighing items would be placed, and where he would place the office desk.

"I will stand here," I said, and pointed to the desk spot near the cash register.

"You're not working, Gertrude."

"I want to help. Please. I owe you."

"You owe me nothing." Then he softened. "But, I suppose working side by side on our own business might be fun. I could help the customers, and you could tally their order and take their money. All right."

We closed the door on our business, then walked to the right side of the front door. There were steps to the second level and an awning over a small porch. I noticed a large coal bin. We climbed to the second floor. He opened this door. There were four windows and plenty of space. Normally this would be a storage floor, but it was going to be our temporary apartment.

"You don't mind, do you? It's just until I plan a house for us," Cuyler said.

"Once I put some curtains on the windows, some furnishings in this room, make a bedroom here, we'll be quite cozy. Someone might need an emergency hammer in the middle of the night, and you'll be the one they'll come running to because you live right above your store. It's just fine, Cuyler." He held me close, chuckled, then kissed me on the nose.

"Come on, I want to show you the bank."

That wasn't difficult. All we had to do was walk down the stairs, go past the door of our store, and keep walking. There was another section built onto the plaza. The front and first roof line, which shielded the pedestrians, was connected to another with five white pillars. This section had two stories also with apartment or office space above. I noticed that the roof was higher than the one in which Cuyler and I would live. Some wooden attachments accented the roof line as well as securing it in typical Victorian style. There was a dormer arch over the windowed door to the bank. I looked inside and saw that-though new-it was already doing business. Of course, it was closed now, so we would have to speak with the bank manager Monday to deposit the money. We continued walking south on the street until we passed a beautiful home and a Presbyterian church. I hesitated when I saw a cemetery up ahead. It occurred to me that this cemetery, in my lifetime, might be where all whom I had just met in 1897 were buried. My head felt dizzy again.

"May we go home? I'm suddenly very tired."

"Of course. This must be quite a strain on you." He regarded my visage for signs of illness.

"Cuyler," I said, looking into his eyes. "I was in Milford only a few days before I traveled through time." I pointed to the west end of town, to the large, newly-built home, which in 1997 was Jim's big, gray house. "That large building was still standing when I visited Milford. The man who owned the cabins brother lives there now. He restores old furniture. The train station," I pointed to the beautiful structure where a woman was reading a book while she waited for a train, "is no longer the way you see it now. The train tracks are still there, but a small museum stands where you see the engine. There's no need for it now. Transportation in your county has changed. You see, Cuyler, I was here only two days ago, but it was 1997. I'm fascinated to see how it all looks today. I wish I had my camera so that I could take pictures and show them to Jim. But, it's also the oddest experience. You love history so much. Let's say you traveled to 1797 and could see Toddsville in Jehiel Todd's day. It would be thrilling, at first, but you would not be able to stop yourself from comparing it to the way Toddsville looks in 1897. It's wonderful, frightening, and sometimes too much for a person to deal with. I suppose over the next few days I'll get used to it, but, right now, I think I'd like to go home. Your real home. Our home."

He supported my body by slipping his arm under mine. He helped me as I lifted myself into the carriage. He sat quietly beside me, then he lifted the reins, pulled them backwards until the horse could maneuver the rig around and head homeward. He slapped the horse's rear to make him move.

After a minute or two he spoke, "I told you I believed your story, as difficult as it was to comprehend, when I first met you at the cabins. However, just now, when you mentioned what it might be like to return to 1797, I fully understood your predicament. I wonder why it happened. Is this some cruel joke, or the answer to your prayer to see history from a personal viewpoint? I can't believe God would hurt us."

I placed my head on his shoulder and closed my eyes. I could almost see his mind working on the problem. "It's a blessing, Cuyler, and let's always think of it that way." I placed my hand on his cheek reminding him of my love.

I sighed and let my hand slide and then rest on his chest. "For without this experience," I said, "I'd never have met you. I'd never have known love."

We meditated upon the setting sun as he drove the rig slowly back to Toddsville. The sky was pomegranate—hot—scarlet.

Tomorrow was Sunday, and I would meet all of Cuyler's friends at his church. I haven't been to church since my high school graduation. I'm Methodist not Presbyterian, but I didn't feel there was much difference. I'd know how to behave. I might even know some of the hymns. I was looking forward to speaking with the reverend about our wedding.

I was hoping that domestic life might take a slackened pace now— drinking morning coffee with Johanna in the kitchen, and watching his mother tend her flowers in the garden. Peaceful.

Well, Jennifer had told me to stop and smell the roses. She just didn't mean the roses in another century.

Chapter Eight

I awoke the next morning with the sun shining its face through the lacy curtains of my new bedroom. The sun's joy at the Sabbath morn also renewed my happy mood. As I said before, the clouds and trees shaded most of Otsego County from the warm rays of the sun. This was not the case at the Carr Homestead. The house and its full, flat acreage was bathed by the heat of the sun.

I made my way to the stairway to get a pitcher of boiling hot water for washing but bumped into Cuyler who was bringing one to my room. He had a tiny bit of leftover shaving soap on his chin. "Good morning, Beautiful," he said, on the landing outside my bedroom door. "Sleep well?"

I took the pitcher of warm water, walked into my room, and placed it on the dresser; then, with a towel, I wiped the soap from his chin. I noticed that he nudged the door half closed with his foot when he followed me into the guest bedroom.

How could he think I looked beautiful? One quick glance in my mirror told me my hair was pulled in more ways than a punk rocker's. I finger combed it into place. Still half-asleep, I mumbled something to him and returned the towel to my dresser.

He wrapped me in a bear hug. My body, naked under the nightgown, warmed to his sudden closeness.

"I'm going to enjoy waking to you every morning," he said. "It's a good thing we're going to live above my shop. I've an idea that I shall lie in my bed for some time before I'm able to leave this Venus I now hold in my arms."

"Are you sure you're not a writer?" I said, as I played with his bushy mustache, curling the tips that had already been groomed.

"I write quite a bit, just never published it. Why?"

"Because you sure do have an artsy way with words." He kissed the side of my long neck. I giggled then sighed in response. "I can't wait. Please." Passion made me forget where we were, and what day it was. His mother came out of the master bedroom, dressed in her suit for church and regarded us from the landing. One look from her broke us apart.

"We certainly cannot lay abed all day, Gertrude. Hurry to breakfast, dear, or we shall be late for service." Her shoes clicked down the stairs.

"Did you mean what you just said?" Cuyler said.

My kisses smothered his lips in reply. "We have to wait until we're married," he said, trying to remain sensible.

I held him at arms' length. I was flirting with him, wiggling my finger, beckoning shamelessly, and it was unfair. His manhood was telling him to close the door completely, but his Victorian mind was telling him to go to his own room and dress for church.

"I can't stay in here. What will mother think?" he said.

I was unhindered by any moral dictates of *his* time period. Shamlessly I curled my body into his.

"This is indecent. This is my *home.* We've not exchanged vows."

"But, we will, won't we? I don't suppose you'll change your mind on that score, will you?"

"I'm not going to keep you from making breakfast on time; I won't make you late." I guided his arms around me and kissed him. "Hold me. Just hold me. Then you can go, and I'll wash and dress for church. I promise. You're the only man I'll ever marry; I already think of you as my husband."

The look in his eye was husbandly, as if we had done this from the dawn of time. We both closed our eyes. "Oh, I want you, alright," he said. "The moment I saw you standing in the middle of the cabin—so much a stranger, so beautiful in your flimsy, floral gown. I think I knew right then that I'd met my wife. That's why I suggested the false marriage, never imagining it would turn out to be true. When you were crying in the shop about the wedding being a sham, something told me then that it wasn't going to be."

"We need to send those invitations," I said. "I won't tease you anymore." His eyes glowed with desire for me.

"I have an idea, Gertrude." He pulled away from me to talk.

"Ohhhh...why does that not surprise me?"

"Why don't we go back to the cabin for our first night?" he said.

"That's a wonderful idea. Since you have the cabin for the summer, no one will mind if we stay there as long as we want. Will you need to tell Isaac Cooper?"

"Only in the sense that he should ignore us completely," he

said. He pulled me close again. His kiss was lethal.

"You'd better go now," I said. "We'll talk later. I don't want your mother to be angry with me; although, you're living proof that she understands what we're going through."

"Gertrude!" He smacked my posterior good-humoredly, winked, and whistled as he left my room.

I sponge bathed quickly and combed my hair after washing it in the tiny basin of warm water. The brownish-blonde curls burst from the perm Wendy had set them in way back on Thursday, June 1997. I shaped them into a Gibson-girl style. The front of my hair did justice to that fashion, and once I put my new hat on, maybe no one would notice the short length.

I snickered when I remembered my conversation with Wendy. If she only knew that I would be going into "no-blow-dryer-or-gel land."

I took a quick peek into his room. Cuyler had already gone to breakfast. I took my new suit from the closet. I slipped into the corset. The stockings I rolled up my legs and pinned to the garters. I wore two slips. I put on my beautiful new suit, buttoned up the frog closings, and laced up my shoes. I was ready for Reverend McBride's inspection, as well as the entire congregation's.

I grabbed my pencil and pad. I wasn't going anywhere without them. I ran down the back stairs and hurried into the dining room. There were eggs, bacon, and toast on the sideboard. I found a china plate, filled it, then sat next to Cuyler and listened to the conversation. Johanna poured my coffee for me, and I thanked her.

"Good morning, Mother Carr," I said.

"Good morning, Gertrude. I trust you slept well?"

"Yes, indeed, thank you. And you?"

"Quite well." She grinned, and I noticed how pretty she was when she was pleasant. "Cuyler and you will speak to Reverend McBride after church. I'm going to speak with the Ingalls and Mr. Carr's relatives about the wedding. We'll hold the reception here. Johanna will cook the wedding feast. We'll decorate the house ourselves. Of course, there must be music and dancing. Have the two of you thought about a wedding vacation?"

"Yes," Cuyler said, letting me eat. "We want to return to the cabin for a week or two. It's where we met, after all. Then I'll move my bride to Milford, above the store I'm going to lease from my friends."

"You're your own man now, Cuyler, and I won't tell you that I shan't miss you at the homestead, but a couple cannot become domestic with their mother underfoot. If you need anything, you'll come to me, I hope," she said.

I was overwhelmed. This was the woman who had frightened me so at lunch yesterday. I leaned over and kissed her cheek. "Thank you, Mother Carr."

She reached for her handkerchief. "Now don't start with sentiment, dear, or I'll start crying. I think we need to see how soon you two can share your vows. It's clear that nature will take its course if we don't."

"Mother!"

"Don't think you're fooling anyone, Cuyler E., with that innocent look. This is your mother, after all. I can see the love you two share. It's plainly written right there." She pointed her finger to his nose.

He leaned over to kiss his mother, and she hugged him. "I *am* happy for you two. When the good Lord wants two people together, who am I to keep them apart. Now we better get to church before the sermon starts ahead of us. I want everyone to see my beautiful new daughter-in-law in her lovely new suit and hat."

Cuyler had another carriage—more like a surrey—for Sunday. He took Samuel from his stall, hooked him into the harness, and we eased our way into the seats. His mother sat behind us, and I rode next to Cuyler. My purse held three items inside: the lace hanky Sally had given to me, my pencil, and my paper pad.

I noted every detail of each tree and house as we rode into Cooperstown. The birds were singing, there was hardly a breeze, everyone was going to church. Not one citizen appeared to be working in a garden or tending to farm animals. All the carriages were polished and ready. One by one the citizens of the various hamlets came out of their homes in their finest clothes.

I saw a grand and mysterious house at the foot of one of the hills and pointed to it. It seemed austere, as if someone important once lived there.

"Oh, that's the 'red house,'" he said.

"Not big on fancy titles around here, are you?" I said. "I'd have called it rose with white trim, unpainted for at least ten years, and run down looking."

He laughed. "No, that's just what we call it. It's *haunted*."

I don't want you to think that I believe in that nonsense, but ever since I was a little girl growing up in Brooklyn, I'd always felt a chill in my back when anyone talked about supernatural things like ghosts and haunted houses. When I shivered, Cuyler noticed and his eyes ignited. With almost sadistic joy, he told the story.

"It has been said that a peddler was murdered in one of the upstairs rooms, and one can go up there any time and pick pennies out of the cracks in the floor. One time, when I was driving home alone in the evening hours, late from an overly-long chat with my friends, I heard strange noises issuing from the edifice," he said. I moved closer to him on the seat. It seemed that the quarter horse was slowing for me to get a closer look at the house.

"I heard a sound like two men wrestling, but it might have been the wind," he said, darting a quick look my way. "Then I heard a low, growling, gasping noise: the sort a man makes when someone is *squeezing* the life from his throat."

I gasped.

"The noise and the tussle kept up for some time until I heard what appeared to be a man's dying gasp. Then I heard a thud. After a bit of silence, I detected despicable laughter."

I slipped my arm into his for comfort, but his rendition of the tale hypnotized me.

"On another occasion," he said, examining the effect his story was having on me, "when I came home from a week in the cabin, about this time in the summer, as a matter of fact; I heard what appeared to be digging noises. I slowed my rig until I could just barely make out the sound. Sure enough, the sound was that of someone in the backyard of the house with a shovel—digging the dead man's grave. I could hear the groaning the large man made while completing his laborious task. Then I heard the man's feet, padding on the soft dirt, as he entered the house through the kitchen door. There." He pointed to the spot.

Pauses and hushed words helped him interpret the tale. He continued, "I listened and soon heard the murderer's footsteps: one, two, three, and so on. He was headed for *that* room upstairs—there Gertrude. See the corner window on the second floor? Above the roof line? He was going to retrieve the corpse. Remove every clue of his cold-blooded crime. I listened further, until I heard the heavy steps and thumps as the villain brought the lifeless weight of his innocent victim—the murdered peddler—down the inside stairway, into the kitchen, and finally to his eternal resting place in the backyard. He would bury the deceased under the flower bed—right over there. You can still see it from the road. There." He pointed to it.

I gasped. It *did* look like a grave.

"Then I heard him try to fit the cadaver into the earth," he continued. "The fiend swore a horrid word, which I dare not repeat in front of you, Gertrude. Apparently, the tall peddler would not fit into the prepared grave. The demon incarnate went to the kitchen to find a butcher knife. I heard him say, 'I'll have to cut you down to size then.'"

I buried my head in his shoulder.

"Cuyler E. Carr," interrupted his mother, "I forbid you to speak such wickedness on the Sabbath. How dare you fill the girl's head with such terror before a holy sermon!"

I looked at him to see whether it was all true or just a Halloween story.

"It's true, Gertrude." He smiled. "If you like, I'll bring you around the place after dark, and you can hear the sounds yourself."

I had the feeling he was setting the record straight for my flirtations this morning. "*Oh no, Cuyler.* I believe you. We don't have to come here."

His mother's hand flew over the back of the leather seats and gave him a gentle smack on his arm. "I should never have let you read that Edgar Allan Poe book your uncle bought you for your ninth birthday."

In broad daylight, he had frightened me to the very core of my being.

I was still shaking from his story when we arrived at his church. He helped his mother and me from the carriage and waved to his friends across the front yard. They were the young men I had met Friday.

The First Presbyterian Church of Cooperstown was a white colonial structure which had been erected in 1805. It had the most interesting cylindrical, stained glass windows. The chapel was connected to a smaller rectory by way of a pretty, triple arched walkway. All the doors were curved at the top and painted glossy black.

When I first looked at the church, I did not notice the steeple, which crowned the roof line like a medieval lady's hat. Nor did I see the four black faced, brass numbered clocks, which greeted you from every direction, for they were covered by the foliage of the trees which graced the walkway.

He told me to go into the sanctuary with his mother so that he could speak with his friends. This gave me an excellent chance to meet the relatives, view the congregation, and inspect the interior of the church.

I could tell the Carr men, uncles and cousins of Cuyler's, were no nonsense types. Their wives and Cuyler's aunts greeted me, but the men kept their distance until we were introduced. I wondered which one gave the book to Cuyler. Perhaps the stern looking one about thirty who was pulling on his mustache and examining me with a keen eye. I was introduced as Cuyler's fiancé, and their demeanor changed quickly. My hand was taken, kissed, shaken, one man gave me a bear hug, and the women made comments about it being about time.

Someone made a remark about Cuyler's father, and how they were glad the son was not following in his father's footsteps. Apparently, Cuyler's father, Chester, had not taken a wife until late in life. He had been forty-one years old when Cuyler was born.

I also met the Todd clan, who made comments about my attractive appearance, and how I'd make Cuyler a pretty wife. The Ingalls arrived later, and the family reunion was complete. I prayed for Cuyler's return. He walked into the sanctuary and joined us.

The moment the family saw Cuyler take my hand, they beamed with pleasure. The men smacked him on the back congratulating him on a splendid choice. The older aunts pinched his cheeks and told him he was a devil for not telling anyone he had a girlfriend. He explained the circumstances. All the personal problems I'd gone through in Brooklyn and in the cabin were mentioned. He beckoned to the Carr men to join him at the side aisle. I'm not sure, but I think he told them about Ellis. I regarded their expressions. I wouldn't want to get those Scotsmen angry. Fire burned in each man's eyes. Suddenly, they burst into laughter, in the same manner Cuyler had when I told him what I had done to Ellis.

One by one, the men and women of my new family took their places in their designated pews. I was aware that I'd been situated inside the circle of relatives. The uncles dried their eyes from the tears of laughter as they took their seats, but renewed giggling was suppressed every time their eyes met mine. Poor Reverend McBride. This wasn't the way to start his sermon.

After sitting only a few minutes in the pews, I became acutely aware of the seat's hardness and stiff back. The fullness of my suit cushioned my tush from the discomfort.

I noticed the oddest woman in the front pew. It was the same woman I had seen in the church yard when we arrived. She stood out because she was knitting. I mean, she didn't stop! She greeted her friends with a quick look to their face, and then resumed knitting one and pearling two. When the reverend started his sermon, she quietly placed her yarn work and needles in her lap and smiled. I whispered a question to Cuyler.

"That's Mrs. Johanna Perry. She knits for everyone in town for so much a knot of yarn. She knits for my mother too. She's quite good. I was kept warm many an Otsego winter because I wore her socks and mittens. She even walks through the streets while knitting. She takes it everywhere she goes and only stops her work during Sabbath service. She's a reverent soul and has been married three times," Cuyler said.

"Three times? What happened?" I said.

"She was married to a peace officer named Patton F. Sholes, but he died. Then she married a man named Gibson, but he died, too. Then she married a Reverend John Perry who's a minister from Schoharie County. He spends a good deal of his life smoking, fishing, and permitting his wife to support him."

"Well, that doesn't seem very nice for a reverend." Speaking of reverends, ours was about to address us.

Cuyler said into my ear, "When speaking of her matrimonial career, she tells anyone who asks that she has had a devil, a drunkard, and an angel for a husband."

I giggled at a silent moment in the reverend's sermon, and the Carr men turned in their seats and regarded me with interesting looks. The one uncle chuckled, still unable to comprehend me kneeing Ellis. I looked at Cuyler who feigned innocence; he was astonished by my feminine reaction in such a sacred place. Speaking of being married to an angel, I could see the little halo circling his head right now.

I wasn't sure if I wanted to kick him or kiss him. Kicking seemed more appropriate, so I attacked his shin with my booted foot. He jumped and made a pain inflicted gasp. When he looked at me, his former expression was written all over *my* face—innocent bewilderment. Perhaps a bee had stung him? I examined the air around me searching for the little beast with a perplexed expression on my face. The Carr men turned again and scrutinized Cuyler with annoyance.

The sermon of the day was patience—patience was a virtue. Christians needed to exercise self-control in all things. It appeared to the reverend that rushing matters the Lord had planned for us, which took time to unfold in a Christian way, was a sin. How did he know about this morning?

There was a long moment of silence for us to pray for anything we were inclined to discuss with the Lord. I took this opportunity to tell Him I was sorry about my behavior that morning. I told him I loved Cuyler and was happy. *I also asked him what was going on!* I waited for an answer. None. Then a tranquil aura blessed my soul. I swear I could hear some tiny voice say, "PATIENCE." I held Cuyler's hand with a total disregard for etiquette. He placed his hand over mine, and we looked at each other while everyone else had their eyes closed in prayer.

We sang several hymns and then prayed one last time. The service ended. I met many citizens from Cooperstown as we left. Charming and sociable, everyone smiled their approval of our wedding and told us they would attend. Mrs. Sloat was in attendance. Sally was there also with a young man on her arm. I already felt apart of this whole family who made up Cuyler's life in Otsego County.

The young men, who were his friends, bragged to the others that they were the first to be introduced to me on Friday. The women jabbered about how wonderful it was that Cuyler had finally found a woman to love, and what a wonderful time summer was in which to marry. No one spoke of the haste.

Mother Carr told us to greet the reverend with our news and

ask to speak with him. When we shook hands with him at the church door, Cuyler introduced me as his future wife.

The reverend smiled, and this time I blushed. We asked to speak with him immediately. He motioned to his wife. When she came over to him, he told her that he would be late for dinner as he had to speak with this new couple. He motioned that we should follow him into the rectory.

We entered his office and sat in two comfortable red, leather, high-back chairs. He sat across from us at his big desk.

"So you two want to get married, eh?" he said.

This was Cuyler's story, and he spoke solo. "Yes, sir. We would like to marry soon."

"Why the sudden haste?" he said.

"She may have to return to Brooklyn. Her family is all gone save her sister. Her father departed a while back, and her mother died in the house fire that harmed Gertrude's hair."

Imagine, I thought, shamelessly telling *fibs* to a preacher. Well, what would *you* say?

"Have you spoken with your mother?" Reverend McBride said.

"Yes, sir. She approves and has welcomed Gertrude into our home."

"Gertrude, what have you to say about this rush to marry?"

"I love Cuyler, and I want to make him happy for all his *days,"* I said. Did you happen to notice that I said *days*?

"Splendid. There isn't really very much more to marriage than that, is there?" His grin cut his chubby face in two. "As long as two people are in love, and are willing to suffer the pains, the torments, the disappointments, the hardship with money, the children and their *many* problems, the doubts, and the frustration through sickness and in health till death do they part, then they should be holy wed."

What a cheery look at marital bliss. I couldn't wait. I wondered what Cuyler thought. Probably how fast he could send me packing.

"When would you two like to share your vows?"

"As soon as you can find room on your schedule," Cuyler said.

"My, my, Cuyler. When you finally make up your mind about something, there's no stopping you, is there?" He looked at his ledger. "I have the third week in July free on Saturday. That would be roughly four weeks from now. Does that suit you?" he said.

"You have nothing sooner, sir?" Cuyler said.

"Well, I have the second week in July free, as well. Will that give your mother enough time?"

"Plenty of time, yes, sir."

I looked at the calendar in his schedule book and gasped.

It was noticeable, and Cuyler said, "Is something wrong, Gertrude?"

I felt teardrops again. "It's my birthday." How interesting I thought? I would get married on my birthday in a year seventy-some years before I was born.

"Well, isn't that perfect." The reverend smiled. "A sign from the Almighty. I'll reserve the church, and you can speak with housekeeping, as soon as you can, about decorations. Will the reception be at the Carr homestead?"

"Yes, sir."

"Well, I guess you have plenty to do to get ready, to be sure. I won't hold you and your mother up with discussion today. However, I expect you and Gertrude will begin sessions on matrimony with me starting this Monday evening. I'll pencil you into my calendar. We're so pleased to have you as a member of our Christian family. You *are* Presbyterian?" he said.

"Yes, sir." Another strike in the book against my righteousness. I wondered about the matrimonial classes. I would have my pencil and paper handy those nights.

We emerged from the church victorious. Everyone asked how things went, and we told them we were to be wed in the church the second Saturday in July. His mother almost fainted.

We gathered in the rig and headed home. Cuyler was singing the melody part of the song he had whistled the first morning we were together. I asked him what the song was because, though the tune was familiar, I couldn't place it.

"Oh, it's just an old Irish tune I learned when I was a child."

"I thought you were Scottish."

"I am, but I can appreciate the Irish way with a ballad, Gertrude."

We arrived home around one o'clock. Johanna was waiting with a picnic lunch for Cuyler and me.

"You two run upstairs and change your clothes. I have prepared a nice lunch for you. Thought you might want to take a buggy ride. Have some solitude while you eat your lunch," Johanna said.

This wasn't 1897—this was paradise. I scurried upstairs to change into my shirt waist and skirt. Honestly, it was so hot, I wished that I had my good, old shorts and a T-shirt to wear. I'd slip into those and my running shoes, and we could hike through the mountains. I wondered where we might go for our ride, and what Johanna had made for lunch. I was starving.

It took Cuyler no time to change clothes. We fixed the smaller rig, took a blanket, the hamper, and bid goodbye to Mrs. Carr. Then headed for—the cabin.

"Is it far from here?" I said.

"No, we'll be there soon."

And we were. Back in our cabin with our mountains, trees, birds, and squirrels. I mentioned swimming with no idea of how we could.

"No problem."

He and I both laughed at the phrase. Inside the second cabin was a woman's swimsuit. Cuyler had his own in his family's cabin. So, I went modestly into cabin 2 and changed. You should have seen this suit. It looked more like a dress. Bonnet and all. And I was supposed to swim in this? When I came outside, he was fixing our picnic lunch.

"Is it safe to eat first? We might get cramps and drown," I said.

"Who told you that?" he said.

"My mother."

"All right, we'll swim first." There was this lengthy, astonishingly heavy rope that fell from the top branch of a big old tree. Cuyler took hold of it and swung his body out over the lake. He let go, screamed, and sank into the lake water. He emerged laughing and wet.

"Come on, Gertrude. The water's wonderful."

The rope returned for me, and I snatched it. Pulling backwards on it to check its strength, I ran for the lake holding on to it for dear life. "Look out, Cuyler." I screamed. I was not as perfected in this art form as he. I did my best and splashed into the lake. It was cold and refreshing on my hot skin.

We played a while in the water showing off each other's

swimming abilities. His were superior. I sort of doggy paddled around. The water was deep. He came over to me and held me close. "What was that about throwing yourself into the lake and drowning yourself to save me from embarrassment?" He grabbed me tightly around the waist.

"I didn't really mean it," I said. I tried to pull away from him.

"How do you know I might not have *lured* you here to finish you off?" He nuzzled my neck with his lips. "I'm good at making up stories." He said and dunked me and then pulled me back up quickly.

"What was that for?" I said.

"Water baptism," he said.

"You don't have that in your religion."

"You *do* know something about religion, don't you?"

"I'm a Methodist," I said.

"No problem," Cuyler said.

I kissed him and held him close to me.

"You remember this morning?" he said. His hand braced my head, and he pressed his lips to mine.

"I thought you wanted to wait," I said.

"We've set the date. Three weeks. I've no intention of changing my mind. How about you?"

"Not in the least. Despite the wonders of marriage the good preacher mentioned to us," I said.

Cuyler laughed and said, "I thought to myself, why does he say things to persuade you against marrying the woman you love?" He waded away from me and looked over.

"He just wants us to be sure. To know that the glow of new found love will wear thin after a few months," I said.

"I can't imagine you ever becoming dull, Gertrude." He floated on his back and splashed water with his feet. His wet black hair and sparkling eyes, flecked with merriment, made him more handsome—more desirable.

"After that little story you told today about the red house, I can't imagine *you* ever becoming dull either."

He paddled close to me and embraced my body. "Did I *scare* you?"

"Not in the least." I shivered sensing how close his legs were to mine.

"You lie. You were scared to death." He pulled my hips towards his. "You'll *never* go past that house without thinking about that story I told."

"All right, I guess it did frighten me a bit, but I knew it was all made up."

"Who said it was made-up?" he said.

"It isn't true, Cuyler. You never heard those sounds."

He kissed me. "Gertrude, as I stated once before, I never lie."

"No, but I've noticed you have no trouble bending the truth a bit."

The warmth of his touch mixed with the coolness of the water made my senses quiver. My temperature was rising to match the heat of the day.

"I've even more frightening tales, my dear. Why don't we go up to the cabin? I could tell them to you while we cuddle in bed. I was embarrassed at home. I've had all morning to think about what you told me." He kissed my wet neck while his arms caressed me. My body responded to his closeness, but I placed my lips next to his ear.

"Be patient," I said.

"What?"

"I went to church today, Cuyler. Do you have any idea how long it's been since I've been to church? I feel guilty about what I did to you this morning. Teasing you like that. My time period doesn't have the same attitude about extramarital sex as yours does. It was mean of me to seduce you like that. During the service this morning, I thought how nice it might be to wait until our honeymoon."

He let me slip into the water and threw up his hands in dismay. "And one of my rules *had* to be for her to go to church with the family." He laughed and splashed water in frustration. "Very well. We shall have our lunch and linger in the hammock together rather than the cabin."

"I have just one important question for you, Cuyler?" I surveyed the bank.

"What is that?"

"How do you get out of the lake?"

He laughed, and we struggled onto the bank.

We had a delicious lunch of cheese and fruit. There was a jar of lemonade, with two tumblers, and we drank it although it was warm. When we were finished with our lunch, we slept side by side in the large hammock.

I've never known such peace, such love, and so much happiness in my whole life. No deadlines, no plots to twist, no characters whose problems needed resolved. One blissful afternoon in Richfield Springs, in a hammock, with the man I loved snoring rhythmically in his sleep at my side. I was overwhelmed with the moment.

"Thank you, God," I said, "for whatever you've planned. Thank you for this one moment—one suspension of time moment—one memory that I'll never forget and cry about later when I remember it."

I'd try not to hurt when it was over. I understood what real love was now. Some people never find it, and I had. If I were correct, for three months I would experience the sort of love I'd reserved for my heroines but never for myself.

He moved on the hammock, and we both tumbled to the ground. It jarred him awake. I scrambled over to him to see whether he was hurt.

"Hello, sleepy head," I said.

"What happened?" Cuyler said.

"Moved too much in that hammock, that's all. Come on. We need to go home. It's getting late. I'll change clothes, and we can be home before dinner."

We went to our cabins and changed. I tidied the picnic area and tossed some of the homemade bread to the birds.

Our buggy ride home was quiet.

His mother was tending to her garden, and a delicious aroma of pot roast filled the kitchen. I asked to help with the cooking, but all the chores were complete. I mentioned to his mother that I would help her weed, but she laughed and told me it wasn't necessary. I went to the barn and asked Cuyler if he needed assistance feeding the animals, and he said not to worry he had it under control. There was only one thing I could do. Write!

I fetched my pad and pencil from the buggy and headed to the sun porch. I made myself comfortable in one of the rockers. I started to write the stories Cuyler had told me when my pencil's tip broke. Great! Where was I going to find a pencil sharpener? I knew I had purchased others from the store and went inside to find them. I changed directions on my way to my room and decided to peruse the second floor. I noticed an opened door to one of the other guest rooms. I peeked inside. I recalled Cuyler's tour but had only peeked at this room. It was no guest room; it was a *study.* I looked at the small writing desk in the corner of the room. There, sitting lofty and proud, was a *typewriter.* I'd only seen them in antique stores back home. And this one had typing paper next to it.

I sat near the relic—now shiny and new—with fresh ribbon securely wedged inside the gears. I took a sheet of paper and wound it around the cylinder. I set the margins. I wrote the title of my new book on the top of the first page in all caps. My fingers flew across the keys. Life was complete now. I had the one last piece of heaven I needed to be happy on earth.

I wrote six pages in one hour. I placed the script in one of the drawers of the office desk. How could I keep my writing a secret? I noticed the door held the key to it inside the keyhole. I would lock the door, only write when everyone was busy, jot notes during the day to make the typing go faster, and keep the key to the room with me always.

I sang the melody of Cuyler's tune as I skipped down the stairs to dinner.

Chapter Nine

Monday was a busy day. Cuyler woke me early with a hopeful knock on the door and a pitcher of warm water. Cute! I opened the door sleepily, and he was inside my room in a heartbeat. The door closed quickly behind us. He placed the pitcher beside the basin on top of my bureau. Without a word, he gently wrapped me in his arms. I smiled. "Good morning to you too," I said.

"You'd better dress with haste, Gertrude. We have much to do today. We go to the bank this morning to buy the store and deposit the money. After that, we need to purchase stationery in Cooperstown for wedding invitations and don't forget our first meeting with the reverend tonight. Tomorrow we'll drive to Oneonta to see what sort of office equipment I can purchase for the store. Then we need to buy furniture on Wednesday and begin setting up our household. I shall have them deliver all furniture and equipment on Friday, so we'll have to be in Milford all that day to establish our new home. My uncles gave me an advance so that I can start the store immediately. If all that weren't enough, each evening this week, we need to address the invitations mother is formally writing by hand during the day. Countless women will be bustling to the homestead to prepare for the reception and to ask you what we want for gifts."

I groaned. "I'm going back to bed. This all sounds to exhausting."

"No, Gertrude, it's positively exhilarating. Oh, and did I mention the Fourth of July picnic we are having here after the Cooperstown parade. I thought we might go to the cabin to watch the balloon races and the fireworks."

I eyed him between the slits of my slumbering baby blues. "I gather you're a morning person," I said.

"What does that mean?"

"You work better in the morning than the evening." I placed my arms lovingly around his neck and kissed him. "I'm a morning person too. After I've had my coffee that is."

His lips gently kissed my neck and shoulders. Who was teasing whom now? I was helpless within seconds. I didn't invite the activity, but I was responsible for it, so there wasn't much I could do. Poor Cuyler. First, she says yes-then she says no.

"In the book of manners, they say that an unmarried couple

should not hug and kiss too much. What fools," Cuyler said, stammering between kisses. "I know women don't enjoy this sort of behavior. My friends and I found a health book once. I understand, Gertrude."

I stopped him in the midst of his passion. "Wait a minute," I said. "What do you mean women don't enjoy this sort of behavior? What did this health book say?"

He looked at me with those innocent brown eyes his mother knew so well. "I *know*, Gertrude." He seemed embarrassed. "The health book said that husbands should understand that women don't like—you know—*sex*."

"We don't?"

"No, only men find pleasure in the union. Women just sort of endure it so they can be mothers. That's why men should never force their attentions on their wives." He embraced me. "On the other hand, wives should meet their husband's demands upon occasion because men enjoy it so much. It's expected a wife will want to please her husband even if she finds the act distasteful."

So that was the reasoning behind the no sex rule he set for our marriage. Oh, was this man in for the ride of his life. No wonder this era was repressed.

"I want you to listen to me *very* carefully. Women and men, under proper circumstances, enjoy the union equally. I can't wait until we're married, but I'm choosing to out of respect for our wedding ceremony. I want us to remember our wonderful honeymoon all the days of our lives. I can't speak for the women of your time, but I can tell you that the women of my time find sex quite pleasurable. Especially with the man they love. Some of them even take precautions to *prevent* pregnancy."

"Can you do such a thing?" He must have missed that chapter in the medical book.

"Sure. We've invented many different methods." I kissed him and held him close to my body. His skin was hot and smelled of the delicious spicy cologne he wore.

We held each other for a few more minutes and then stood apart. I said, "As you said, we have a lot to do today. I'd better get dressed."

I could tell he was thinking about what I had said and had no foundation with which to understand it.

We had breakfast and then rode in the tea cart to Milford. The friends in the bank were happy to see Cuyler and perplexed to see me.

I met James Von Dyke, and we both went to his office to sign papers. We now owned a business. Cuyler's uncles had provided the down payment. We opened an account, but *I* was not asked to sign anything.

"Excuse me," I said.

James said, "Yes, Miss Johnson?"

"Isn't this a joint account? Don't we both own the business? We'll be husband and wife in a few weeks."

James said, "Why would you sign the papers? Generally the husband's name is all that's necessary."

"Gertrude is correct," said Cuyler. "Put an extra line here at the bottom and add to the contract that the business and the bank account are joint ventures. Anything I own is hers and vice versa."

James said, "Well, that's most irregular, but I'll do it if you insist." He left the office and returned with an additional sentence added to the papers. I signed them. He handed Cuyler the keys to our new business and our new home.

Cooperstown was as usual when we journeyed through it that afternoon. We made our stationery purchases. Putt was washing the windows of his studio and spoke to me. He had my proofs ready. That was fast, I thought.

Cuyler and I examined the proofs, and I let him choose the one he liked. I thought they looked odd because of the hair being so short, but he thought they were beautiful. He asked Putt if he'd take our marriage photos, and Putt agreed. Cuyler paid for three photos to be made: one for me, one for his mother, and one for himself. Then Putt checked his journal, made a date for our wedding photos, inscribed the name of our church, as well as the place of our reception, and told us how happy he was for us.

Cuyler made a stop at Mrs. Sloat's. I looked at everything in the shop while he was sized for his wedding suit. He gave her an advance to hurry the work and winked.

As we were making our way back to the rig, we saw Daniel.

"Good morning, you two. When's the happy day?"

"The second week in July, Daniel. Consider yourself invited."

"Wouldn't miss it for the world. I'm working on a gift for you two. I hope I can have it done by then."

I smiled. "That's kind of you, Daniel," I said.

"It's the least I can do for two special people. Hey, Cuyler, you *are* bringing Trudy to the dance Saturday night at the hotel?" Daniel said.

"What dance?" I glanced Cuyler's way, but he seemed to be ignoring Daniel. "Cuyler, what dance?" I repeated.

"It's the summer sociable." He inspected Samuel's harness. "I don't usually attend. Sometimes the bachelors go and watch, smoke cigars outside, and talk. If you don't have a girl, it's rather boring."

"Well, you *have* a girl. May we go?" I said.

"I suppose if you want to. I don't dance much," Cuyler said.

"Don't worry. It'll be fun. What time is it, Daniel?" I asked.

"Eight o'clock. See you there." He tipped his hat and was gone.

"Why does he call you *Trudy*?" I detected a touch of jealousy in his manner.

"My friends and family call me Trudy back home. I told you that you could call me Trudy when we first met. I like the way you call me Gertrude, though, so I've never mentioned it again. Daniel, on the other hand, likes the name Trudy, so he calls me by that name."

"It seems a bit informal." I said nothing and smiled at the sound of irritation in his voice.

There *was* one sour note that day—Ellis. I saw him walking down the street and shuddered. When he saw me, he made a hasty change in direction. He crossed the street and sprinted into a tobacco store.

Cuyler noticed and laughed. "He's scared of you, Gertrude."

We purchased a newspaper before we left, and he asked me to read it to him on the way home. It was called *The Freeman's Journal.* I read many human interest stories, but my eyes fell upon the advertisements.

"Are we going to advertise our new business?" I asked.

"Of course, if you want to. Why?"

I started to giggle and then burst into uncontrollable laughter.

"What are you carrying on about?"

"Who are T. M. Hickey and Kenyon and Whitney?" I said.

"Oh, they're pharmaceutical sales persons in Milford. Why?"

"They have purchased a dozen ads in these three, small columns. Some of them are on top of the other and about the same item." I read a few aloud to him.

"The Cuban question and political issues sink into insignificance with the man who suffers from piles. What he most desires is relief. De Witt's Witch Hazel Salve cures piles," I said.

Cuyler tried not to laugh and said, "Piles are not something to snicker about, Gertrude."

I continued, "Late to bed and early to rise, prepares a man for his home in the skies; early to bed and a Little Riser, the pill that makes life longer, and better, and wiser."

"Well, I don't know what that one's all about," he said.

"This one is for women. It states here that women who drink sasparillo medicine will be better tempered and have a sweeter disposition."

"Well, you won't need that, dear. I couldn't ask for a more even-tempered woman to marry."

I folded the paper and placed it on the cushion next to us. "Do you see that farm over there, Gertrude?"

I told him that I did as it was not particularly hard to spot, it being the only one for miles. I knew this was a lead into a story, so I played along.

"That farm used to be owned by Dr. Nathan Winsor. The doctor studied medicine and practiced as a pediatrician for only a few years. He gave up the profession to become a teacher. Used to wear carpet slippers in class, and some say he smoked his pipe there as well. He was a small, spare man slightly stooped. He had been in the army and returned from the conflict with a large supply of army blankets."

I reminded myself that Cuyler was referring to the Civil War.

"He managed to get into a tussle with his neighbor over corn stocks," he said.

"Corn stocks?"

"His neighbor, a man named Steeres, owned some land which joined the Doc's by only a small fence. Apparently, Steere's corn stocks managed to skip the fence and sneak over into the Doc's property. Steere was madder than a wet hen about it, saying that the Doc was stealing his corn. I guess a royal argument started over it which was never successfully settled."

Cuyler continued, "The old Doc was a nice fellow though. He talked to me as a father would. Told me all about the Republican

Party, mentioning its policies. That's when I decided to become a Republican."

"Is your family Republican, then?"

"No, we're Democrats, or I should say; my *father* was a Democrat. However, in his later years, he claimed to be a strict Prohibitionist."

I remembered how Putt had said something about Cuyler not wanting to do as his father requested. I hedged into the topic. "Did you and your father get along?"

"Well, we got along all right, I suppose. When I was a child, he was busy on the farm. He hired workers since he had only one son to help him. I worked on the farm, but I didn't like it much. I did well in school so my mother suggested to my father that I might be allowed to go to the Hartwick Seminary for more education. My father allowed it because he had always been at the top of his class and believed that a person should have a good education. My head was turned towards the policies of the Republican Party, and I decided that I would be a business man instead of a farmer. Of course, this hurt my father very much, but I didn't see it at the time. I can see, now that he's gone, how much my stubborn pride must have hurt him. After all, I was the last son to inherit the Carr's homestead farm. If I didn't want to work it, who would? I asked if I could go to business school in Newark, and he said no at first. Then the farms all around us started to go under, and my father changed his mind with my mother's urgings. He kept the hired men to work the dairy farm, and I took off to business college My uncles had always told me that they would set me up in business if I wanted to own a store. As my father's health dwindled with age, I worked the farm for him. Though we disagreed on nearly everything, I couldn't break his heart. That Tuesday, last September 22, he went into Cooperstown to buy some supplies, visit his friends, and came home fine in the afternoon. At six o'clock that evening, he died unexpectedly. He was sixty-eight years of age. They said it was heart disease. It was quite a shock for me. I never thought my father would leave me so suddenly. I've been working the farm and dreaming of my own business all winter long. Then you showed up in my cabin, and my way was cleared."

"Who will work the farm when we leave?"

"That'll be up to my mother and my uncles. We have money to

hire farm hands, and I have a feeling she'll do that. Of course, I'm not going far, just Milford. I'll still drive over on occasion and see how things are going."

"So, actually we will have two businesses?" I said.

"I suppose my money from the store could aid the farm. I'd also thought about selling coal. My father left me a solid wagon and a good team of horses. We're directly across from the train station in Milford, and I could haul the coal from the train to the store or deliver it directly. People need coal to warm their houses. It gets very cold here, and wood is sometimes hard to fetch in twelve-inch snow drifts."

I shivered at the thought of so much snow.

"Of course, there's always the truss fund to help us should I need the money," Cuyler said.

"Your father left you a trust fund?" I said.

Cuyler laughed until tears filled his eyes. "*Truss* fund, Gertrude. Not trust-*truss*. My father owned a truss manufacturing business across the street from our house. He invented the ultimate, doctor approved, truss in the early seventies. He advertised too. Made some money from it and placed that in a bank in Toddsville."

Did I feel like a fool, or what? What's a truss anyway? I'd ask him, but I was already feeling mighty stupid.

"You go ahead with the coal business. I'll take care of the store. You show me the difference in the stock—teach me one nail from the other. I can help. Don't let a little male chauvinism get in the way of your true happiness."

"What was that?" he said.

I chuckled. "It means that just because I'm a woman, and you've a mind that women are meant for domestic chores alone; I can do the job of a man. Especially one as easy as this one. I can run a store if you show me how. You can tally the accounts in the evening. I want to help."

He took my hand and kissed it, and held it near his chest as we drove down the road.

I thought it odd that Cuyler never asked what political party I favored. But then why would he? I wouldn't be allowed equal voting rights in the state of New York until 1917.

We had a knack for making it home just as dinner was placed on the table.

Mrs. Carr had made some wedding arrangements of her own that day. After looking at the stack of invitations we had brought her, she said she knew what she would be doing while we were having our chat with the reverend that evening.

I asked Cuyler if I could drive the rig to Cooperstown, and he agreed to let me have my hand at the reins. It wasn't that difficult. The quarter horse obeyed me completely.

I put on my role playing attitude again, took a deep breath, and forged into the reverend's office anticipating more on the joys of married life.

"Cuyler has been a member of this church for some time," he said. "Well, as long as I've been here, anyway. I'd like to think I know him pretty well." Cuyler smiled his sweet, altar boy grin. "Cuyler, you understand that your role as husband holds many new demands for you."

"Yes, sir, I do," Cuyler said.

"You must be the head of the household now. You must be a good provider for Gertrude. I understand you two are going to own a business, is that right?"

"Yes, sir," said Cuyler.

"Well, that will be splendid," Reverend McBride said. "You must be the head of your house as Jesus is the head of His church. You have God alone to answer to, young man. Every day remember God's commandments and teach them to your wife and someday to your children."

Children? How does that fit into the scheme of our lives, I wondered?

"There must be time for prayer each evening. And if you have any questions, ask the Lord or your pastor."

"Yes, sir," Cuyler said.

"Now, Gertrude, I must admit I don't know you as well as I do Cuyler. I can only hope that you've been raised in a good Christian home."

Well, Mom went to church on Easter and when someone got married. Dad usually accompanied her unless it was fine golfing weather. I went to Sunday school as a child and sang in the choir. Does that count? I decided to lay it on thick. If Cuyler could do it, so could I.

"My *blind* mother took my sister and me to church every Sunday," I said shyly. "On Thursday, we went to our prayer group and prayed for my father. You see our father was much into drink when he was with us, before he left, and used to beat us blue if we refused to take his pail and a nickel to the saloon for his gin. That's how Mother lost her eyesight, you see. One night, when we came home from our prayer meeting, father was in a drunken fit. He swore he would kill us all and threw my mother across the room where she hit her head and lost her eyesight. My sister and I ran to the nearest church for fear he'd harm us too. I think it was a Catholic Church, and the nice priest protected us. My father ran off that night when the constables came around to help my mother to the hospital and take him to jail. We never saw him again. Mother, sister, and I continued to pray for him though. It was the evil drink, that horrible devil, that ruled him. He was nice when he was working and not drinking. The reason our house caught on fire was because my mother knocked over an oil lamp because of her blindness. It was lit so that sister and I could read the Bible to her. I must have fallen asleep and forgotten about it. My sister neglected to extinguish it when she went upstairs to bed as she's frightened of the dark. Mother must have tried to go outside to the Necessary, and before we knew it, the house was in flames. I ran upstairs to save my sister, and we made our way to the window of our bedroom. We were saved by the fireman's blanket when we jumped. Mother was lost, though. I thought she had made it outside to safety. Apparently, she went back into the house to save the family Bible." A tear escaped my eyes, my lip trembled, and I looked to Cuyler for comfort. He placed his arms around my shoulders and kissed my cheek.

"I wanted Gertrude to tell you herself," he said, playing along.

I peeked at the reverend whose hanky was wiping the tears that streamed down his cheeks. "I'd no idea. My dear, what trouble you have known. Cuyler must appear the hero to you to have taken you under his wings as he has."

"You've no idea. I could not manage one day without him," I said.

"That is how it should be, Gertrude. You must obey Cuyler in all things."

Did I miss something, or had he just reversed the discussion?

"Cuyler is the head of the household, and you must look up to him in reverent awe. Whatever he tells you to do, you must do without hesitation, no questions asked, in a humble and submissive manner, as befits a dear wife," he said.

I'd see if I could save this one. "But, sir, my father told me to get him *gin.* The gin made him evil, and he hurt us. How could obeying him be the right thing to do? Are you saying my mother was wrong to refuse to buy him drink and take us to church thereby refusing to obey her husband? Are you saying she should obey this evil man who wished to kill her babies?" Surely, he would see his error in logic.

"I can't speak on a situation I know nothing about," he said. "I would need to counsel them both. It appears that your father was led by the Devil not God. In any case, your mother should have obeyed your father. It was her duty. God would have intervened."

My anger rose. "Are you saying that if Cuyler goes berserk and asks me to kill someone, I must, because he tells me to?" I said.

He laughed. "Goodness, Cuyler would never ask you to do such a thing. He's a Christian man."

"I mean any woman—any man? Are you telling me a woman should be prepared to break the commandments because her husband says so?" I looked him straight in the eye.

"Of course not. If the husband asks his wife to break a commandment, then she should follow God's law always. Then she should pray for her husband's soul until it is reclaimed —loving him through this trying time."

I looked to Cuyler who was red in the face—unable to breathe lest he explode with snickers. "That will never happen to us, dear," I said. "You will always be my hero and my husband."

"Excellent. Well, I can see this session has proved worthwhile. I'll look forward to seeing you two next Monday then," Reverend McBride said.

"I shall look forward to it," I said truthfully.

"We shall discuss the physical intimacies of married life. How a man and woman can share their love through intercourse, so that they may have children in abundance. I hope that will not be too embarrassing a topic for you, Gertrude. I'm afraid it's a very necessary sermon, nevertheless. Until Sunday."

We walked silently to the rig. "Are you angry with me?" I said to Cuyler. "You asked me not to go on about my life. I broke my promise. I couldn't help it."

He turned to see whether the reverend was watching and then hugged me. "I said life wouldn't be dull with you around. I can't wait until you cross swords with him on the intimacies of domestic life next week. By the way, I was planning on murdering someone next week—say two in the morning—and I was wondering if you would pencil me into your busy schedule. I only need you to bring a meat cleaver. I'll take care of the rest. What do you say?" Cuyler said.

"That depends on whom you plan to do in, dear. Oops-I forgot." My eyes went wide with an automaton stare. "Yes, Cuyler," I said rote-like. "Who ever you want to do in; it will be fine with me, dear."

We giggled all the way home. He slowed as we passed the "red house." "Speaking of murder, dear Gertrude. Want to go inside the house?" he said.

I froze next to him. He slowed the rig and stopped.

"Why are we stopping? Cuyler? I don't like this place."

He leaned close to my ear and breathed seductively on my neck. "I want you to hear the sounds." We were quiet and listened. I did hear something. "Hear that?" he said.

"Yes, what is it?" I said.

"The sound a man makes when he kisses his lover until she cannot breathe anymore." With that said, he did as he had proclaimed.

"All right, you win. I hear the sounds, now can we go home. I'm sure your mother needs help with our invitations."

When we walked into the house, we saw his mother slumbering in the chair next to her desk. Her pen was lying on the stack of invitations. I pressed my index finger to my lips for him to be quiet and carefully pulled the pile of stationary away from her. She had a list, and Cuyler and I finished her work for her at the kitchen table.

While we were addressing the envelopes, Cuyler started to snicker and turn red again.

"What is it? What have I done now?" I said.

"Nothing, it was when you went on and on with that heart wrenching story about your father. He's not really like that, is he?"

"Only on weekends. No, seriously, he's a wonderful man, and

the two of you would get along nicely."

"As I told you before, my father was a Prohibitionist, so I've heard many sermons on the evils of drink. I do, however, remember someone else who preached to Toddsville on the subject. His name was Sam Wright, and he was a very strong temperance man and did some public speaking for the cause. To make his utterance more effective he had a 'speaking jacket' made of red material. At one of his meetings in the schoolhouse, he called for a collection on behalf of the cause." He looked at me and grinned.

"Did he make much money?" I said, sealing another envelope.

"He found in the hat: nails, buttons, tobacco quids, and three cents in money. He also devoted much time to music, as well as to the temperance movement." The wry smile had returned. "His instrument was a Jews harp. The only piece he tried to play was of his own composition called the 'Drunkard's Whale.' I've never observed the music for this melody on sale, and presume the piece, like others, are among the lost classics."

I suppressed my laughter for as long as I could. I didn't want to wake his mother. I looked at his face and saw the humor in his eyes and burst into uncontrolled giggling.

"It's true," he said. "I swear it. Well, we're finished. We should probably turn in. It's late and we've a long journey to Oneonta tomorrow."

I agreed, and the two of us closed the house and extinguished the lights. We didn't want his mother to knock over an oil lamp on the way to the Necessary and set the house on fire.

When we said good night, my lips yearned for his longer than I dared. It was a hot night. Too hot and still to breathe. We said little at first. He held me in his arms. I was so vulnerable. I was comfortable, happy, intellectually stimulated, up to page seventy on my writing, and in love. I had a roof over my head and meals prepared for me whenever I wanted them. All I had to do in this existence was be happy. Now that the stress and anxiety of so many hours of work were lifted; my body yearned for the one thing I had denied it for five years. It sent a message to my libido that I needed this man. I had never felt the warm caresses of a man who loved me and wanted my personality, heart, mind, and soul, as well as my body.

The look in my lover's eyes was helpless, pleading for us to combine our souls and our bodies selflessly and for all eternity.

"I *want* you, Gertrude. I can't wait any longer," he said. Tears rimmed his eyes. "We have *so* little time. I know I'm always lighthearted with you, but there's a great deal of sadness and loneliness that I've experienced in the past and will experience again when you leave me. How will I exist without you? Having you here—the joys we've experienced together each passing day—is so precious to me. And I'll have to remember them for, perhaps, an entire lifetime. I'll lose my soul mate—the woman I was meant to marry. I know I promised to live each day wholly and without thinking about what was to come, but the thoughts *do* come. I want to make each moment burn in my memory so that, in the evening, I can close my eyes and remember you. Remember how the wind went flying through this silly short hair of yours; how my favorite hillside flowers remind me of the soft blue in your eyes; the coolness of the lake water on my body when I swim reminds me of how we played and laughed on one hot summer Sunday afternoon; how the taste of the sweet strawberry jam my mother preserves for me every spring tastes just like your lips when you kiss me. And when I pass the red house, I'm reminded of how trusting and helpless you were when we first met in the cabin; how vulnerable you feel next to my strength; how I can tell your body is submitting to mine; and how you need me to protect you. All those thoughts remind me of how much you make me feel strong and powerful. And what will happen if you leave me? The fire will be gone, and I'll have no idea when, or if, I'll get it back. I'll ask myself—is she safe, is she ill, does she need me, is she thinking of me where she is right now, has she forgotten me and taken another lover, or is she burning in this fire with me. And will I ever know such happiness again? Let's not wait another moment. Satisfy my need for you. For each moment unsatisfied while you are with me, is the prologue to the journal by which I shall live all the rest of my lonely days."

Tears spilled from my eyes, and I cried against his chest, touching his face with my fingers like a blind person would, hoping to remember each detail–each feature.

"The Fourth of July. Not here where your mother is so near to us." I gasped for air and shivered from my emotions. "You said we'd go to the cabin to watch the fireworks. There. It's not a long wait until the Fourth—only a few days," I said.

I tasted his lips with my tongue. "I promise. No standing on ceremony any more, Cuyler," I continued, "our lives cannot continue to play by other's rules. We'll make our own rules. We're, after all, the only ones who really know the truth about this absurd situation, and even some of that has been denied us."

He took my hands in his. "Until the Fourth of July." He kissed my fingers and smiled. "I love you."

I kissed his fingers in imitation. "I love you, too." I went into my room and closed the door between us. I couldn't wait either. There was torture in pretending we could remain lively and cool in the midst of our passions. We were meant to be together. We knew it—so did our bodies.

I spent a restless night tormented by sweet intimate dreams.

Chapter Ten

I awoke the next morning happier than I'd ever felt in my whole life. The sun was shining; Johanna was singing as she made breakfast; Cuyler was on time with the pitcher and the affection. Cuyler had warned me that the trip would take all day. The trip was necessary because some particular equipment he needed for the store could be found only there.

As soon as we ate a hearty breakfast, we hustled into the carriage and took a new route. I had my pad and pencil ready to take notes and was relieved that, so far, my little secret was still undisclosed.

"I've been remiss in your education, Gertrude," he said. "I've not taken you on this route yet, and, therefore, much of your history lesson has been overlooked."

"I'm appalled, Cuyler. You promised to help me understand my surroundings. It's your duty as head of our soon-to-be household to inform me of everything."

He turned his head, regarded my expression, and pressed his lips together in a tight smile. His hand brushed his mustache and then stroked his chin in anticipation of a captive audience. "Yes, well, then we'll start. Must you write all of this down *again*, Gertrude," he said.

"Yes, dear. I might forget something. I'm rather slow."

He snickered. "Very well. Do you see the farm with the unusual hillock by the tall tree?"

"Yes, dear."

"That's the farm of Dr. Walter Almy Jr. M.D. deceased now, of course, who came to Toddsville at an early date. They called him, Old Doc Almy, and during his professional career, he had a large practice in the area. He traveled by horseback, as physicians did back in those days and on one occasion, while coming from Oaksville, on the back road by the Stone Mill, he was attacked by a panther."

I placed my tablet on the seat between us, folded my arms across my chest, and said sternly, "That's it."

"What?"

"You can't believe that I'm going to swallow this one. A panther? Really, Cuyler. When have there ever been panthers in this neck of the woods?"

"Forgive me for saying so, dear, but I'm afraid your historical information is lacking in this area, as well. Large cats did roam this area and frequently attacked when hungry. We called them panthers." He paused to let the information sink in. "May I continue my lecture for the day? It's clear I have much work ahead of me."

I shook my head in quiet submission. I *did* want to hear the story even if I wasn't sure about the panther part.

"As I was saying," he said, clearing his throat, "he was attacked by a *large fierce cat*. Putting spurs to his horse, he out distanced the animal at the woods near the Adam's burial ground, where the beast left the highway and went into the timber."

He continued, "The small building by the ruins of the old paper mill used to stand on the other side of the stream near the roadway and was used as the doctor's office. He was a gruff old fellow, and polish was not his middle name. On one occasion, he was called to a home in Toddsville to prescribe for one of the young ladies of the household. After taking certain medicines, they were to be followed by a dose of castor oil, but the patient refused to take the oil. Calling later and being informed that it had not been taken, he said, 'I'll give it to her.' Taking the girl by the nose he turned it down her and Miss Florence Todd said she always hated Old Doctor Almy after that. Doctor Ed Almy, his son, practiced his profession in Toddsville after the death of his father, and married Augusta Todd, daughter of Lemuel Todd. They have been dead many years."

I thought that was the end of the story and began to close the pad, but it was just a lead into the *real* story.

"Old Doctor Almy is in the vault which he built for himself, in the hillside on his farm, at the foot of the hill. He's sleeping there now; but Mrs. Almy, who died first and was buried in the vault first, is now buried in Sharon Springs. She made her son promise that he would remove her body, after the death of the Old Doctor, to her old home where she sleeps among her people the Millers. I have been told that Old Doctor Almy used to sit evenings in the vault door smoking his pipe. He was either getting used to the vault, or his wife would not let him smoke in the house," Cuyler said.

The carriage slowed so that I might see the vault from the road. It appeared to be run down, weathered, and frightening.

They dared me to prove the truth of it. So, one night, the four of us we "One time, I told this story about the wife being removed to another burial ground and some of my companions didn't believe my story. I've no idea why they didn't. nt to the very vault which you see before you. There was only one way to prove my point—go inside."

"Oh, Cuyler, no, you didn't," I said.

"I did nothing wrong. The outer door of iron was already slightly opened, while from the inner door of wood several lights of glass had fallen from the sash. By lighting a newspaper, I could see very plainly the interior of the vault. At the back side there's a stone platform, upon which rested the one internment. From my observation, it seemed to be in as perfect a state of preservation as at the time of death. The outer box didn't show any signs of decay, save for the discoloration from age. In those days coffins were made in Toddsville by the Carr brothers. A pine coffin then cost $5, while a cherry coffin was the talk of the community. I'm proud to say that Old Doc's cherry coffin, which my ancestors made for him, was in perfect condition, all things considered. As you can see, Gertrude, I convinced the doubting Thomases who came with me that night. They never doubted my stories again. Of course, that was a few years ago, and the doctor's daughter lays in the vault with him now. I've not visited it in years," he said.

"You didn't open the coffin, did you?" I asked.

He was shocked and looked at me in dismay. "Gertrude! How could you think that I'd disturb the Old Doc's repose? How gruesome an idea. Actually, Samuel Street Todd did, in fact, open Mrs. Almy's coffin when she still slept in the crypt. His exact words were: 'One night, when I was young, I took a screw driver, got into the vault, and opened Mrs. Almy's coffin. She had been lying there for some time, and her cheeks were covered with blue mold!'"

"*Cuyler* !"

"Sorry. You'll meet old Samuel soon enough. He's the oldest living Todd in the family. In his eighties. I think he'll make it to a hundred. The Doc's body would not have been the first dead body I'd seen anyway."

I was feeling ill. It was a good thing he'd told the story in broad daylight. I shivered to think that we might be coming home this way, in the dark.

He continued, "The first dead body I ever saw was Aunt Lemuel Todd, widow of Lemuel Todd, the paper manufacturer and mother of the same Samuel S. Todd. In company with my father, Samuel took us into the parlor and in the northwest corner lie Aunt Lemuel. How plain that white covering. And when Mr. Todd removed the sheet to explore the features—I was only six-years-old—that first vision of death made such an impression on my young mind that it seems only yesterday."

He paused and then said, "I'm not afraid of death, Gertrude. I know that there's a heaven we'll go to when we die. I know that my ancestors are there and that, when the time is right, I shall be reunited with them."

He spoke in a hushed tone. "Grandmother Carr died when I was young; I don't remember her passing. One day at play, I tore or destroyed some article she had made and mother said to me, 'Grandmother will not make you another' and I said 'Grandma is coming back?' As the years passed and she never returned, I understood she'd not come to me...but I could go to her. See, Gertrude. There's a place where we will all meet together some day. I believe that."

I closed my pad and returned it and my pencil to my purse. I took his hand in mine and bent low so that I could kiss his fingers. "Then that is what I believe, also. Time cannot keep us apart," I said.

He put his arm around me and smiled. "What did I ever do to deserve a woman like you?"

"Oh, I think I know, but you have a whole lifetime to think about it, *dear.*"

We entered Oneonta—you remember, the antique dealer's sexual fantasy—that I'd cruised in my Beretta. We found many large stores, and I was in a rush to see them all. The buildings seemed new and fresh in contrast to the way they looked when I went through the city. I noticed one bank thats cornerstone was dated 1770. I also noticed a house being built today that would someday be the Huntington Memorial Library.

First on the agenda, was the new weighing machine that Cuyler had had his eye on for so many months. It was very expensive and, for the first time, I saw Cuyler hesitate. He needed the machine, but it'd mean saying farewell to another dream. He purchased it and told the man that we'd pick it up before we went home. He turned to me and smiled. "There's a treat waiting for you."

Before I could ask him what it was, we were across the street. We walked into a store that sold jewelry, the Carr and Bull store to be exact. According to the sign outside, they sold almost everything. We were going to purchase our wedding bands. Plain smooth and gold was all I needed. The man, I think he was the Carr owner and related, sized us for the rings and said to come back later for them. Due to the urgency of the matter, and the fact that it was Cuyler wanting them, he promised to have them done before we left for home.

I became depressed over one matter again. I had so much money at home. I mean millions lie untouched in my bank account. How I wanted to help Cuyler financially. How I wanted to buy him something nice. He was paying for his own ring and that was my responsibility. He couldn't afford everything we needed.

This city was large and no one knew us like they did in Cooperstown, Hartwick, and Toddsville. We had lunch at a nice, inexpensive cafe. We talked about wedding details, and then an idea hit me like a boulder.

"I have no bridesmaids and no one to give me away. How are we going to explain to everyone that the sister, whose life I saved, *couldn't make the trip for my wedding?"*

He contemplated and pulled at his mustache. "Hmmm, you have a problem. Can you think of anyone who you know well enough to be a bridesmaid?"

I thought then said, "Sally and Mrs. Sloat."

"We have to go to Cooperstown tomorrow, anyway. Why don't you ask them? They can make the dresses in no time."

"I wonder if Putt would give me away. Except for young Daniel, I can't think of anyone else."

"Daniel has been my friend for some time. It would not upset me if you asked him. He did make your first evening in Cooperstown memorable, and he seemed very excited about our wedding. Putt will be busy with the photos. You have no idea how long it takes to set up for one of those shots," he said.

"All right. Now how do I explain my sister?"

Silence. We drank more coffee.

His eye blazed like flashlights. "We'll say that she is detained on personal family business. They're settling the will," he said.

"What could possibly be left to inherit?"

"She has moved into an apartment and cannot get away right now, but is planning on having us come to Brooklyn for a special dinner where we shall meet all of your relatives. The business of settling the estate, and planning a family reunion, is too much work for her, and she'll not be able to come all the way on the train to make the ceremony."

"Slim, Cuyler," I said.

He sipped his coffee. "I know, but it's the best I can do."

When we were finished with our afternoon meal, we window shopped the whole town. It had been a beautiful, sunny day, but the clouds were coming from the west and looked ominous. There was a gentle breeze blowing through the trees indicating the threat of rain. Cuyler retrieved the rings, and I put them in my purse. We reclaimed the new equipment and headed home.

"I suppose it would be a good idea to go back a different way and drop this off at the store," Cuyler said. "No point in taking it all the way home and then have to cart it to Milford tomorrow when you need to speak with the ladies and Daniel. We also have to purchase furniture and linens tomorrow. Of course, we may only be able to buy a bed right now. We're running low on finances."

I cuddled close to him. "Seems to me that a bed is really all we need, anyway. To be perfectly honest, I don't want to see Doc's vault again today anyway. I don't mind going to Milford. Besides, we'll be closer to shelter if it decides to rain."

Cuyler headed our little horse in the direction of our future home.

We managed to place the weighing machine inside the store just as the first burst of lightening hit.

"Why don't we go upstairs to the apartment?" he said. "We can ride the storm out and watch the rain from our front windows."

I shook my head in agreement.

We rushed upstairs as the deluge of rain brought pieces of hail to beat at the wood frame of our home.

Cuyler opened the door, and we dashed inside. It was dark

outside, and we had no lights. He and I focused our attentions on the citizens of Milford as they ran here and there trying to find shelter.

We were soaking wet, but the heat of the room dried us. Cuyler and I watched the lightening from our apartment window and dreamed our own private dreams.

"Well, Mrs. Carr, how do you like your new home?"

"It's cozy and dry, oh master of the household, god omnipotent, he who must be obeyed," I said.

"I do like the sound of your submission." He kissed the top of my head. "It makes my heart glad to see how obedient you are. Come here and kiss me."

I smiled with my eyes and was about to say something smart when it hit me. I doubled over as dizziness and disorientation twisted my perception. I felt the nausea and held my hand to my mouth for fear of vomiting. My head pounded and every wave of thunder made it worse. The blindness came also, and suddenly I was seeing nothing—not even my hand before my face. I was frightened just as I'd been at the Fenimore Hotel. "Cuyler!" I said.

He was holding me and trying to help. I heard him say, "Gertrude, what is it? What's the matter? Are you all right?"

"Hold me. Where are you? *I can't see you.* I'm so dizzy." I fell to the floor. I was shivering and could feel myself losing touch with reality. I started to cry. What was it about these storms that made me so ill?

"Should I summon a doctor? Oh, please tell me what's wrong." I detected the sound of fear in his voice.

He held me tighter as every wave of suffering swept me further from him. That was how it felt. Like I was dying, and my soul was leaving my body.

I blacked out. I've no idea how long I was unconscious, but Cuyler would not leave me nor release his desperate grasp on my helpless body.

The storm passed. I could hear the thunder in another county far from this one. I moaned and began to focus. A fuzzy haze still kept me from visualizing his face. The further the storm went to the east, the easier it was for me to see, and the calmer my stomach felt. Terror from the most logical answer overwhelmed us. *I was, for the moment, going back.* It seemed the only reason for my blindness. I held onto his comforting arms for my very life.

"What happened, Gertrude? What *was* that? Did you eat something unpleasant for lunch?"

I couldn't help giggling at his last statement. "No, Cuyler, I think I was being tossed back home; but I didn't go, and that's all the more intriguing. I guess the storm unsettles the atmosphere, and a traveler starts to feel the dark void. I saw no light, Cuyler. I saw no tunnel. I didn't experience those things when I first came to the cabin."

I knew he was scared, but he tried not to show it. "Well, you're still with me. That's all that matters, isn't it? We best go home before mother worries." He helped me up. I did my best but held onto him for support.

"We'll just have to be wary of storms, Gertrude. You can't go back yet. I won't let you. I have you until the end of September, at least. I won't let you leave before then."

I tried to balance on both feet, but it was no use. He picked me up in his arms, carried me down the outside steps, and put me into our carriage. Then he ran back upstairs to lock the doors and make sure the one to the store was locked, as well. I could sense the anxiety in him—the energy charged with stress that had changed his easy-going manner. There were no stories on the way home. I lay with my head in his lap and slept.

When we were close to Toddsville, an odd thing happened. I suddenly felt more refreshed than I had in days. I sat straight up as if someone had injected me with sugar. "Are we home?" I said.

"Yes, almost," he said.

"Good. I hope Johanna has something delicious for us to eat for dinner. I'm starving."

He examined my face. "You all right?"

"I've never felt better." It was just like my refreshed awakening the morning after the first bout with this silliness. I was experiencing a complete renewal. Whatever it was that hit me, had an interesting afterglow.

We spent most of the evening sitting on the sun porch talking with his mother about the wedding and the Fourth of July.

I asked some questions about the dance Saturday evening—*the sociable*—and saw Cuyler flinch, and his eyes inspect the tip of his cigar with abject fascination. What was it about the dance that had him so worried? Maybe he really couldn't dance.

His mother retired early, and we sat watching the new moon brighten the dusk. The day had taken its toll on both of us. He walked me to my room, hugged me, and pressed his lips to my forehead. Though no words were spoken about the Milford incident, I knew it had bothered Cuyler more than he would say.

I slept without dreaming.

Chapter Eleven

We rose early the next morning and ate a quick breakfast. Cuyler went to the barn to check on his cattle and horses, while I chatted with Johanna and had an extra cup of coffee.

"I've never seen him so determined," she said, spooning sugar into her cup of coffee.

"What do you mean?"

"I've watched him mature through almost every conceivable whim a young man can have, but I've never seen him act this way before. He seems to have a reason to live for the first time in six years. I think something flew out of his heart when he saw the farm become his responsibility, and his business dreams fall to the wayside. He's worked hard to keep the farm as his father wanted it. You know how a father and son can sometimes be at odds. That sure was the case with Chester and Cuyler, but when his father needed him; I saw Cuyler grow from a boy to a man right before my eyes. I also saw all his hopes abandon him. Life was once again ruled by circumstances Cuyler had no way of changing. It wasn't easy for him to put aside his dreams. Then you showed up out of nowhere, and suddenly the cloud that was hanging over him had a silver lining," she said.

She paused and watched my reactions. "I hope you mean it when you say you love him, Miss Johnson," she continued. "He trusts you. A confirmed bachelor doesn't need his heart broken right when he begins to open to a woman."

"I haven't always had it easy either, Johanna," I said. "I can't tell you everything, but I will tell you that I'll never knowingly hurt Cuyler. I love him too much. People laugh to think that two people could fall in love so quickly, and I surely don't understand it all myself. But, I do love him— his stories, his humor, his intelligence, his humanity, his kindness, his warm-hearted generosity. I've never known anyone like him, not in my lifetime." I smiled at that last phrase. I continued, "Not only that but he's a good kisser."

Johanna laughed and jiggled until I thought she'd burst. "Well, then I suppose that's all you need. I hope all goes well for you and Cuyler. I hope his little store is prosperous. I have to admit, I'll shed a motherly tear to see him leave the homestead.

I've grown quite fond of the lad. I tell you what. I'll give you some of my recipes—the ones for his favorite foods. I'll write them in a book so that you can keep them with you forever. It will be my gift to the both of you."

I thanked her, and she gave me a hug that would have killed a lesser woman.

When Cuyler came back into the kitchen, he examined both of us with curiosity. Innocent grins were all we were about to tell him of our conversation.

I drove the rig to Cooperstown. We parked by the Fenimore Hotel and began our search for curtains, linens, a bed, a small desk, a kitchen table and chairs, and the necessary pots and pans. We found the cutest miniature apartment-style gas stove. It had four burners and two oven doors with two side shelves and cost $18.00. I wondered what cooking would be like on one. I guess I would find out.

Daniel zipped by in a big hurry, and I stopped him to ask if he'd give me away at the wedding. He laughed as though he thought I wasn't serious. When he saw our facial expressions, he accepted wholeheartedly.

"I'd no idea you had no kin! Of course, I'll be happy to give the bride away." I think I made the guy's day.

I waltzed into Mrs. Sloat's dress shop as if I owned it. I asked them to be my bridesmaids, and at first they were reticent. I told them whatever they already owned to wear was all right for the ceremony. They agreed.

"Are you bringing Gertrude to the dance Saturday?" Sally asked Cuyler. "Because she hasn't a thing to wear."

Cuyler grimaced. I interjected. "We're going to the dance, and I'll wear the new blouse I've been saving for a special occasion and the black skirt."

"Oh, that won't do, dearie," Mrs. Sloat said, and swirled her petticoats out of the room and into the back of the shop. She returned through the archway with the most beautiful, summer-yellow, satin dress with an overskirt of white dotted-Swiss chiffon. The sleeves were a short mutton chop style which tapered to an abundance of frill and ribbon just above the elbow. It was seductively low in the bodice and would need just the right jewelry to make it outstanding.

"This is beautiful," I said, but didn't want to make a big deal about it in front of Cuyler.

"Wear it for me, dearie," Mrs. Sloat said. "It came in too late from my distributor. I was saving it for someone special, but Sally made her own, clever girl. You wear it Saturday and return it whenever you can. When everyone sees you in it, and asks where you purchased it, tell them Mrs. Sloat's shop. It'll be great advertisement for my store."

I thought that since she had the only dress shop in Cooperstown she needed no advertisement, but I wasn't going to mention it in lieu of her generosity. I asked Cuyler if I could wear it. Wouldn't Reverend McBride be proud of my humility? He looked at me and then smiled.

"Certainly, Gertrude," he said. "It'll look breathtaking on you. I thank you, Mrs. Sloat, for your generosity."

"Think nothing of it, Cuyler, my boy. You know I'd do anything for you."

She wrapped the dress in a box, and Sally added a ring of yellow roses for my hair.

Sally said, "I do believe your hair is growing, Gertrude. Don't you think so, Mrs. Sloat?"

"Why, yes, indeed, Sally. Growing so long you'll be able to wear it up for your wedding day. The wedding gown is almost ready. The big day isn't far off, y'know," Mrs. Sloat said. "And don't you start getting cold feet about it either, Cuyler Carr."

"I've resigned my bachelorhood, I assure you, Mrs. Sloat. I can't imagine one day without my dear wife."

We gave each other a quick and private look.

Chapter Twelve

Everything was ready for the Friday delivery of all our shop and home supplies. To save some money, Cuyler told me that he would use barrels from home to hold much of the smaller merchandise. I promised to use my imagination to create some money saving furniture ideas.

We had lunch at my first home, the Fenimore Hotel. I smiled and waved at everyone as I walked through the lobby and into the restaurant. Their faces illuminated with warm acknowledgment. I felt the same affection towards them. It was just like being back in the old neighborhood. Home? How *were* things at home, I wondered?

Don't get me wrong, it wasn't as if I'd forgotten Jennifer, Wainwright, Mom and Dad, and the Cooper boys. I remembered how Wainwright said he'd call every evening, and rush to the cabin if I did not respond. If he *had* come to the cabin, what would Jim have told him? "She's in the mountains sucking on wild berries and eating roots."

No that wouldn't do. Wainwright knows me better than that. How about, "She and my brother have gone on a search for authentic historical data." Much better, but that would only kindle Wainwright's jealousy.

Well, Jim could use those lines with Jennifer or my parents. I had visions of him frantically trying to answer Wainwright's Internet questions without my new screen name. *It was not my fault!* I hadn't planned this little trip.

After lunch, we headed home weary from our day's activities. We discussed how frantic our schedule would be until July 10. It occurred to us that Thursday would be our first free day. We decided to stay close to home and help his mother and Johanna with the picnic and wedding plans. Maybe we could sleep in and have a big breakfast. We could have another picnic. We could investigate Toddsville some more. I could WRITE!

When Cuyler knocked on my door early Thursday morning, I knew sleeping in would not be on the agenda at the Carr house. I opened the door, and we did our usual routine with the pitcher. I hugged him for a long moment because I knew he needed reassurance. He'd withheld his fears about the Milford incident from me. I could sense he'd closed a door to some secret chamber of his subconscious. A Victorian man must not show anxiety to his woman lest she lose confidence.

"Are you frightened I'll leave sooner than expected?" I said.

He tried to act nonchalant on the subject. "I...I just never *really* believed it could happen. It was logically feasible, I guess, but never real until the other day," he said.

"We don't know that it was a glitch in the time travel mechanism."

"It does seem to fit the puzzle we have before us."

"Maybe it was a sinus headache or a migraine." But, I knew the way it came and went so quickly it couldn't be a simple headache. I held him close. I didn't want him see the tears in my eyes or hear the grief in my voice. I wouldn't talk until I was free from the emotion.

I remembered the voice I heard that day in church. "Cuyler," I said, "maybe it'll all work out somehow. We need to give ourselves some time to learn more about our circumstances. Some people go through life never knowing a true love or any love at all for that matter. We're lucky to have found each other. Holding you in my arms like this gives me such sweet serenity. Something I've never known."

I touched my palms to his cheeks and cupped his face in my hands. I smiled into his eyes. "Come on, Cuyler. We'll make it through all this...somehow." I kissed his lips pressing all my love into them.

"You really want me?" He kissed my eyelids. "You won't change your mind when you go back home?" he said.

"Will you change your mind when I leave?" I said. Will you find someone else, tell everyone I died like you said you would if I never came back, bury me in the family plot?"

He laughed. "Did I really say that to you?"

"Yes. I thought it was sort of sweet." At least he was laughing again. "Maybe Johanna can fix us a snack, and we can go back to the cabin today. A sunny afternoon is a wonderful time to make love. I give up on the Fourth of July. It's too far away."

"Do you mean it? Today is a perfect day. My work is done. We could spend the morning with mother then slip away for the afternoon."

"Will there be anyone up there to disturb us?"

He frowned. "Well, Isaac might be there. There could be some other guests by now."

"In *our* cabin?"

"You mean our *Carr* cabin—privately owned? No." His hands surveyed my backside.

"You are becoming quite a '90s kinda guy, Cuyler Carr. 1990s I mean."

He tapped my nose with his finger.

I could see his mood had lifted as he hurried from the room to make plans. I whistled as I dressed.

We finished Johanna's big breakfast, and when Cuyler and his mother went their separate ways; I hurried to my secret place, unlocked the door of my private writing chamber, and lovingly inspected my manuscript. I had to "bond" with this antique typewriter. I was used to changing my spelling in a flash with my computer's spell checker, and discovering a variety of words with the thesaurus installed with my program. I had to painstakingly rewrite my pages now, after proofreading them by hand. I wanted this to be perfect—even if I had to rewrite it over and over again. I would need a lot more paper. I wondered how to get it without making the need obvious thereby disclosing my secret. After all, I had no money with which to purchase it. Perhaps I could enlist Johanna's help.

Three hours flew by. I was unaware of the time. I had to leave the room before my prolonged absence became suspicious and someone came looking for me.

When I went downstairs, I heard talking. There were three of the Carr aunts there, and they were chattering like hens.

"Oh, there she is now, the dear girl," one said. "Come sit with us a spell. We need to have some idea of what you and Cuyler need to start housekeeping."

I was anxious to be with my fiancé, but I explained to her our situation.

"We'll be pleased to help you in any way. I think there's some furniture in the attic you two could use for your apartment," said aunt number two.

"She needs a quilt. I have one stored away, and it'll be perfect. I made it myself," said another.

I thanked her and looked out of the window for Cuyler. I didn't see him anywhere.

"I have some dishes and silverware you can have. My first husband and I bought the set, but I used the ones we received for wedding gifts instead. It was a lovely, sentimental thing to save all these years, but Cuyler and you can have it. I've no use for it now." The tears in her eyes touched my heart.

I spotted my lover in the midst of the Carr brothers. It looked like quite a conversation. The aunts wanted to talk with me only to divert my attention from what was going on in the backyard. I caught brief glimpses between the curtains while remaining transfixed on the women's chatter.

I saw Cuyler shake his head no. The one uncle—the stern one who seemed to be the chief of the clan—took Cuyler's arm and patted his shoulder. The others looked at him and smiled. I hoped it was something good whatever it was. One thing was obvious. We were going nowhere this afternoon.

The day settled into dusk; the dusk into moonlight. We held each other as we rocked on the big swing on his porch and stared in silence at the moon.

"I know I'm supposed to wait until you tell me, but what was going on out there today?" I said.

"My uncles. They insisted upon helping us more than they already have. Our furniture and other supplies must come from their homes, and when I told them about our purchases, they were disappointed. Then they handed me cash. They said that if I had to break with tradition, they would at least help pay for it," Cuyler said.

My mouth opened wide. "You mean to tell me they bought our furniture for us?"

"Welcome to the Carr family, Gertrude."

The whole situation with the uncles and aunts that day had relieved his mind so much that he never mentioned the forgotten tryst in the cabin. I already felt married as we walked hand and hand up the stairway and kissed good night. My soft, cool bed waited for me.

Chapter Thirteen

Friday was the second best day of my life. We ate early and wore comfortable work clothes. Right! As if these clothes could be as casual as my jeans and sweatshirt. We hurried breakfast and put all the supples in an old buckboard type rig for we were carting more than the little tea cart could handle.

"Do you see the church? The Baptist Church there on the corner, Gertrude?"

A story was coming. "Of course."

"Well, one day Bill Witherall and his drunken friend Bill Wheeler conducted a funeral there. The point is that neither was the reverend, and the party—being from out of town—wasn't clever enough to tell the difference. This is a classic tale, Gertrude. Do you have your pad and pencil?"

Need he ask.

"Toddsville, like all other small communities, has had its famous and peculiar characters. One of the most notorious of these was old Bill Witherall. Clever, keen, witty, he was an awful liar who never worked unless the cider barrel played an important part in the day's activity. He traveled generally by one and sometimes two horses of that variety so common in the day's of the horsemen's convention at the *country tavern*. Witherall took for his bosom companion Bill Wheeler, tarred by the same stick. On one occasion, it is said, these pals were traveling together along the Mohawk Valley when it began to rain. They arrived at this church, and, the door being open, they went for the duration of the storm."

We were not far from Milford. My excitement to see our store was growing, but I wanted to hear the end of the story, so I didn't interrupt.

"While they were in the church," he continued, "a funeral procession also arrived. The folks were out-of-towners who had come home with their deceased baby daughter and wanted her to be buried in the old family plot—the plot associated with the *husband's* family. Of course, the area seemed strange to the man and woman who had been away for many years. A new pastor had taken the Baptist Church's leadership. The family of mourners came into the church and waited. So did the two drunks. After waiting about for some time, in an apparent uneasy mind, Witherall ventured to ask one of the mourners what might be the matter. They made reply that they were waiting for a minister. Witherall told them that he and his companion were traveling 'evangelists,' and that they would be glad to do anything they could to assist them. Their services were accepted, the coffin brought in and placed before the pulpit, the mourners took their seats, and the 'evangelists' took their places behind the desk."

I don't know shorthand, and I got a stiff cramp in my hand from writing so fast.

"Witherall opened the service with a prayer for a liberal collection: a hat was passed, the proceeds secured, and then 'Bub' Witherall arose to preach the funeral sermon from the words, 'Suffer the Little Children to Come Unto Me.' To soothe the sorrowing parents he told them that at that very moment their little one was playing a harp of ten thousand strings. The service was over; the funeral party went its way; while the 'evangelists' stopped at the first tavern and spent the proceeds they'd received for conducting the child's funeral."

"That is horrible," I said.

"You don't like this one?" he said.

"No, I mean, that the two men could do such an evil, low-down, skunky thing to grieving parents."

"Well, it's true. Every word of it. As a matter of fact, Charles B. Garrett, proprietor of the hotel in Toddsville, got into a dispute with 'Bub,' and, thinking he could tantalize his adversary, asked him when he would preach another fake funeral sermon, whereto Witherall replied,'As soon as you die.'" He smiled that boyish grin he had when he knew he had caught your interest.

"No one is that low," I said.

"*They* were. As a matter of fact, Gertrude, a Civil War veteran living in Toddsville, wishing to obtain a pension, employed Mr. B. to prosecute his case before the Pension Department in Washington. In all such matters, sworn statements are required, and Mr. C.—a man empowered to take acknowledgements—performed that part of the proceedings. The matter drifted along for months, as such cases usually do, until the veteran passed away."

He had me hooked for I could tell by the glint in his eyes

something devilish was coming. "It so happened, the next day, after the veteran's death; the pension check arrived. Not to be outdone by death, or the delay of the Pension Department, Messrs. B. and C., repaired to the home of the veteran and going into the room raised up the corpse, and, putting a pen in the dead man's hand—with their assistance—obtained his signature to the draft."

He said no more except, "Ah, Gertrude, home at last."

We arrived soon after nine o'clock in the morning. I had curtain rods, lace panels, kitchen paraphanalia, cleaning items, rags, and all the linen we had purchased in Cooperstown. Cuyler unlocked the doors, and I started to clean. Everything needed to be ready for the new furniture.

He took the barrels and tools from the back of the buckboard. The Carr family had insured us that their items would arrive by wagon sometime in the afternoon. All the specialty gifts and furniture had been brought to one brother's house. He and one other uncle would bring them to the store and help Cuyler set it all in place.

My hands would be full the whole day, but I went downstairs when I saw Cuyler having trouble unloading a large item.

"You *can't* help. This is *very* heavy," he said.

"Well, I can't stand around and watch you get smashed by it either." One by one the various men who worked either in the pharmacy or the bank came to help. Once they saw a woman lifting heavy equipment, their egos revolted. They made short work of it too. I chuckled as I watched the procedure from the upstair's window while I worked. The men unloaded an item, smoked a cigar, moved said item into the store, and stood on the corner chatting before they went to the next item. Male bonding at its finest. They were having such a good time.

Cuyler had ordered some supplies that were supposed to be on today's train. He would drive the wagon down to the depot when the train came to Milford. The furniture store men would deliver today too, so he really had little to do but wait.

I hummed as I cleaned and envisioned how I wished to decorate the apartment. Those moving men would not want me deciding where to arrange the furniture after they brought it up those stairs. It was rather obvious where the stove would go. The gas line that ran to the heater would hook into the new stove. I wondered if the gas were on. Did you have to tell someone like you did back in my time?

I opened the window and called to Cuyler. The men laughed and made comments that we weren't even married, and already I was running the show and slapped Cuyler on the back.

He smiled at them good-humoredly and told me that I would find the gas was on when I turned the little knob. Is this where I grin and blush and shake my head in wonderment at the grand knowledge installed in my clever husband's head?

There was a knock at the door. A tiny, silver head seated upon a frail body came through the door. The person smelled of strawberries.

"Hello. Are you here?" said the pixie.

"Can I help you?"

The old woman, who must have been in her late sixties, came into the room with a limping walk and a curved body which was held together with, what appeared to be, transparent silk rather than skin. She proffered a freshly-baked strawberry pie. I dashed to help her with it, and then wondered where I'd put it. I placed it on a box and then turned to her.

"I'm Mrs. Bates your neighbor," she said. "I live in the apartment over the bank. I just wanted to come by and welcome you to Milford and your new home."

"Pleased to meet you, Mrs. Bates." No, I told myself, don't make the *Psycho* connection she'll wonder why you're smiling. "I'm Miss Gertrude Johnson soon-to-be Mrs. Cuyler Carr."

"Oh, is that so. Well, marriage is a fine institution, to be sure. I've been married five times so I should know."

I looked around for a box for her to sit on. She waved her hand as if it were nothing, that she could stand, but she did sit on the sturdy box when I found one.

"You've been married five times?"

"Yes, siree, young lady. I can give you all the advise you need about being a good wife to your man. You just ask me, and I'll be pleased to help you with anything." She winked and giggled. *"Anything at all."*

There was no question that this woman would be a never ending well of information, and I had the feeling I would hear all of it whether I wanted to or not.

"So, you and Mr. Carr are opening a hardware store?" she

asked.

"Yes, and a coal dealership."

"Oh, a coal dealership? Isn't that nice."

"This is wonderful looking pie, Mrs. Bates. I'd offer you some, and we could share stories over coffee and pie; unfortunately, I have no dinner ware or stove. I have some pans." I laughed at the futility of having pans and pots with nothing to put them on.

"Oh, I just whipped it up this morning. Strawberries are almost out of season now, and I wanted to use all that I had and surprise you."

"Cuyler and I thank you. I'm sure he'll enjoy it. As a matter of fact, we're getting our supplies today. Maybe you can stop by later when the family brings our silverware and china. Then we can all take a break and talk."

Come to think of it, this is the only food I have in the whole house. We had purchased a small ice box, but of course, once it arrived, we would still have to take the wagon to the ice house for an ice block. I wondered how far away that was.

"Is there a market of any sort around here, Mrs. Bates?"

She smiled her quasi-toothless grin. "Yes, there is a general store a few blocks from here. You can't see it from your window, but if you go north a few blocks you'll find it. If I were you, I'd buy my produce from one of the farms—and your eggs too. I have mine delivered. Once you marry and settle in, I'll introduce you to the people I buy from, and you can order what you want. So, your husband's name is Cuyler Carr, is it? Well, I've heard of him. His father was Chester Carr, wasn't he? He died about a year ago last September, didn't he? That Cuyler downstairs?" She had moved from the box and hobbled to the window.

She and I looked down upon my husband-to-be. He had just unbuttoned his suit vest. The first three buttons on his shirt were wide open, and he had undone his tie. He was happy, indeed, smiling and smoking his cigar, storytelling, and laughing with his new neighbors.

"Yes," I said. "The one with the open and running mouth, mustache, and cigar." I pointed to him, and she raised her eyebrows in admiration.

"Well, he's a handsome one, for sure. He'll sure keep you warm on those cold, winter nights."

I was beginning to understand why she had gone through five husbands.

"I don't want to keep you from your work, Gertie," she said, "so I'll go home now. But, if you need anything just knock on my door."

Gertie?

I shook my head in bewilderment and finished placing the curtain rods over the windows. Each one had to be aligned exactly and bolted to the wall.

When I was done cleaning and adjusting the curtain rods, I affixed an attachment to the walls that would hold a small pole meant to support a large, heavy curtain as a room divider. Our bedroom would at least have *some* privacy.

Then I carefully placed our delicate lace curtains on the window rods, and the heavy panels of the room divider were placed on the pole. The apartment already had a homey feel to it. All it needed was some furniture.

I looked out of the window again, but Cuyler and his friends were gone. Fearing he had left me to visit more with his banking friends, I flew down the stairs to the porch. The door to the store was wide open. Cuyler was placing the barrels by the window.

"What do you think?" he said. He and the men had arranged the whole store, cash register, nail barrels, counter, and all.

"Amazing."

"All we need is a sign. Tom Banister, who works down the street, paints them, and said he could have one ready for us in a week."

"Utterly amazing. I just met our neighbor, Mrs. Bates, who left us a strawberry pie and thinks you look like number six.

"What?" Cuyler said.

"Never mind. She thinks you're cute."

A smile crossed his face, "Oh, really? How old *is* she?"

"About eighty," I said.

"Oh, well. I do like strawberry pie. Too bad we have no plates. I could go for a piece right now. I tell you what. While I finish this, why don't you take some money and run over to that small restaurant across the street and buy us some lunch. I'll stay here in case the furniture arrives. Here," he handed me his wallet, "take what you need."

"Okay. If you promise to eat upstairs with me and see what

I've done to our apartment."

I whistled the Irish ballad Cuyler loved all the way across the street. I ordered food and chatted with the waitress while waiting for it to be cooked. It was free of charge as a gesture of goodwill to the new neighbors. I thanked them and hurried home with the hot dishes.

We both washed from our sink's pump and dove into the food.

Cuyler liked the curtains. He inspected the "bedroom," and said it would do for privacy. I can't say that I've ever seen this man so exhilarated.

We had no sooner finished our lunch when the train whistled into the station. We both jumped to our feet and ran to the wagon. I would be free until the furniture arrived, and I couldn't wait to see the train unload all of our store goods.

It didn't take long to account for everything and sign the papers stating that we'd received the order.

We spent most of the afternoon placing the items around the store. I kept walking behind the counter pretending to wait on customers. One actually did come through the door. He thought we were open for business and asked whether we had feed for his horses. In one of the barrels, we had a mixture of molasses, oats, and corn—a dish any horse would die for. He asked our price. Cuyler became the ever-efficient businessman. He took one of the new sacks and, with a large scoop, placed the feed into the sack. The man counted his money, gave it to me, winked, and was gone.

We had made our first sale. We were in business. I placed the coins in the register. Its bell dinged satisfaction.

We had just decided that, plates or none, the pie would be devoured, when the Carr brothers arrived. They moved all the gifts upstairs, but let Cuyler and me place everything into the cupboards. It was hot, sweaty work.

With Cuyler's help we served the pie to our first guests. The two brothers had also brought home cooked and prepared provisions to place in the new ice box.

When we had everything the way we wanted it, we took them downstairs and showed them the store. They were impressed and told Cuyler he'd be a natural businessman.

As they turned their rig around to go home, the furniture from Cooperstown arrived. Excitement has a way of covering fatigue. The moving men from the Cooperstown store cheerfully moved it up the stairs and into our new apartment. Funny how my condo in Brooklyn paled in comparison with this modest flat. I'd chosen the furniture for my own home with intemperate boldness. I had more than enough money to do it, but the small items we had purchased together meant more to me somehow.

We locked the front door of the store and decided to put all our energies into organizing the apartment. We hooked up the stove and placed all the food in the ice box. Then we rode a few blocks to the general store to purchase a block of ice.

Cuyler told me that ice is harvested in the winter months by cutting blocks of it from the lake. Then it's carried to the ice house where they place sawdust over it to keep it from melting. It's purchased mostly in the summer months because most people have cold cellars to keep their food stuffs fresh during winter, or they place the meat on their icy rooftops.

We put the ice in our ice box. This was no small task and needed both of our hands to lug it up those stairs. I wondered how Mrs. Bates managed.

We thought about going home but collapsed on the bed as soon as I made it. The hand sewn quilt looked too cozy and teased us into napping. Our last precious ounce of energy was gone. We napped, cuddled in each other's arms, in the tepid room, on top of the quilt, for almost an hour. Summer's afternoon breeze played with my new curtains.

I awoke to find him staring at me. "I think I will like being married. It's quite pleasant to rouse from sleep and find you beside me." He flopped his head onto his pillow, and I rested my chest on the top of his, and let my fingers dally with his mustache.

"I'll make you breakfast every morning," I said. "Just name it, and it will be hot on the table after you shave."

"That'll be nice," he said.

"Then I'll dress, and we can open the shop at nine, close at twelve, come upstairs and make love for lunch. Then back to work until five," he said.

"That sounds perfect," I said.

I leaned further over his torso and kissed his lips. He rolled my body until I lay flat on my back. He placed his left leg over my right. This was a strategically seductive move if ever I saw one. Then he shifted his frame's weight until his body was on top of mine, trapping me under his long legs.

"Isn't it lunchtime?" he said.

I laughed. "We had lunch hours ago. We'll have to appease Johanna by staying hungry for her dinner, won't we?"

An evil laugh escaped his lips. "I have my meal here beside me. I should think devouring such a succulent dish as you would be supremely satisfying."

"It does seem to be the right time," I said.

"And it does seem to be the right place," Cuyler said.

"We'll tell everyone the train was late," I said.

"Perfect! Trains are notoriously late."

He tossed his vest to the floor, and then helped me unbutton the back of my blouse, kissing every piece of exposed flesh the very moment it escaped. I opened his shirt, and he tore it off and threw it to the floor next to the vest. I undid my skirt, scooted it and my petticoats from my hips first, then cast them on top of his clothes.

His eyesight rested on my bulging cleavage the corset pushed to its limit. My breasts pleaded with him to rescue them from bondage. Before I expired from lack of oxygen, my lover began to unhook the tortuous device until they were free from the lingerie. "You are beautiful," he said.

I rose from the quilt to fondle him and cupped his face between my hands, kissing him fervently.

I lay on my back inviting him to do whatever he pleased. I saw his brown eyes brighten as I surrendered my last resource of energy to his strength. I smiled into his eyes.

The cool breeze bathed my body. The lace curtains fluttered around me in the breeze, giving the illusion of gentle fingers soothing my skin. The wind tickled and tantalized my flesh, floating over my breasts—embracing me tenderly.

The heat of the apartment intensified the aromatic smell of his spicy cologne, sweeping its sweet fragrance around our tangled bodies. It mingled with my vanilla perfume.

My fiancé's eroticism swept us both into another dimension, and my eyes closed allowing my body to enjoy the sweet sensations brought forth from my lover's careful examination of every facet of my anatomy. I opened my eyes. His expression was amorous; there was fire in his glance.

I tenderly finger-combed his unkempt hair from his forehead, then let my fingers slide softly down his cheek tickling his lips.

I suffocated his mouth with my burning lips. He wanted no more movement from my vulnerable body. I was to remain powerless. No hint of speed lay in his temptations. My suitor's sensuous snare of his captive was slow, measured, and calculated for mutual pleasure.

One by one he undid my stockings from their garters, rolled them down my thighs, then tossed them to the floor. I could hear my heart pounding and feel my temperature skyrocketing.

I had always been a partner in the sexual endeavors with my first lover, but Cuyler had other ideas. I'd never received such attention and fulfillment.

Tears of remorse and love flowed from my eyes as I held his head against my heart and softly stroked his hair while kissing him. The thought that such ecstasy could be shared for such a short time made me melancholy even in my joy. This was our marital bed, and we could partake of it for only a few months—days—and then no more.

"I've waited so long for this moment," I said. "You've no idea how desperately I want you—have always wanted you. In some corner of my private thoughts, it was always *you* waiting for me. That's how I knew that I loved you the first time I saw you. I knew you were the man who would make me complete, fulfill my deepest yearnings, and extinguish the fires which have been burning out-of-control for years."

He tasted the tender flesh on my neck, where the vanilla rested, pulled boyishly with his teeth on my unprotected ear lobe, and then took my hand, turned it over, exposing the palm, and bit the soft mound under my thumb. I was beginning to think I *was* dinner.

"That was good, Gertrude" he said into my ear. "Did you write that speech for one of your books?"

As he tossed his trousers to the floor I said, "*Love's Tender Kiss!* It was my first million-copy seller."

"You know this reminds me of a story," he said, as I kissed him and thought 'go ahead and tell a story now if you dare.'

I said breathlessly, "I swear if you tell another story right now... "

He chuckled. "I was just teasing." And so were those lean fingers.

"I love you, Cuyler."

His eyes radiated desire; his kisses burned. "I love you too." And with those words he shifted position.

We both stopped what we were doing and froze.

"Hello!" said Mrs. Bates at the half-opened door to our apartment. "I have some dinner for you two young lovers. You must be starving for want of nourishment. Yoohoo." She was not inside yet. Proper etiquette forbade her to enter until asked. Unfortunately, proper etiquette had not prevented her unasked for visit.

With lightening speed, Cuyler pulled everything back on, buttoned it all in place, and ran his fingers through his tousled hair. No actress ever made a costume change any faster than I did as I hurled the corset back in place, hooked it, and buttoned the blouse—almost all the buttons—and my skirt back to its original place. To hell with the stockings, I could get them later.

Yes, indeed, Mrs. Bates had made dinner for us, the dear old thing. That wasn't all. As we pretended interest in the food, Mrs. Bates went through all the kitchen closets and rearranged our organization, justifying it all as the neighborly thing for a mature woman to do to aid the inexperienced young bride.

When she left—two hours later—it was almost dark. We needed to head home while there was still light. We had to wash the dishes, dry them, and put them back on the shelves Mrs. Bates had decided they should inhabit.

Cuyler looked at me; I looked at Cuyler. Then we both burst into the grandest fit of laughter any couple has ever had. He grabbed me and whirled me around until my feet were flying in the air. "I love you, Gertrude Johnson, even if it takes me forever to make love to you."

Just before dusk, we pulled the wagon into the yard of the homestead. Mrs. Carr came running to greet us. "I was wondering what happened to you two. I was about ready to send the posse."

"No need to worry, Mother," Cuyler said. "Gertrude and I had a long and exhausting day. A most satisfying one though."

It did look as if a greater power were helping us with the patience part. Cuyler took the horse and the wagon to the barn. I walked into the parlor, and Johanna asked me if we were hungry. I told her that we had met a new neighbor who had brought us food at five o'clock. Then Johanna winked and nodded her head telling me to go up to my room; she had something to tell me.

We hurried into the room and to my surprise, the yellow dress was pressed and ready for the sociable Saturday night.

"Now, my dear, you have a lovely dress, but have you tried it on yet? I can alter it for you if you test it tonight."

My clothes were dirty, and I'd been covered with sweat the whole day, so I ran to the kitchen sink and filled a pitcher full of water. Then I ran back to the room and washed. Johanna helped me into the dress.

"There you see. If you wear it that way, the shoulders will droop, and you will fuss with them all night and have no fun at all. You mean to dance, don't you?" I smiled my reply. She would have it fixed by tomorrow night.

"And, you can't wear black hose and those colorful petticoats of yours. I have some white stockings and white petticoats. I never wear them so just keep them. We'll fit them to your size."

"By the way, Johanna, have you any idea why Cuyler would not want to go to the dance?"

"Not really. He used to go just to smoke cigars and talk all night with his friends. Just looked into the dance and watched. You know, not just *young* people attend. Many older persons will be there too—like myself. Maybe he's worried about his dancing ability and what his friends will think of him now that he's entertaining his lady love instead of talking politics and baseball with them."

"I won't force him to stay with me if he wants to talk with his friends. I can amuse myself."

"If he leaves you for even a second, the young men will be buzzing around you like bees to honey," Johanna said.

"Why? They know I'm engaged."

"But you aren't *married* yet. And at a dance anyone can dance with whomever they please."

"I won't dance with them unless Cuyler says it is all right."

Johanna smiled a knowledgeable grin. "With *this* dress on, Gertrude, you'll be the most beautiful woman there."

"That can't be. There must be loads of prettier, younger girls in Cooperstown-with hair–for the men to flirt with. I'll be a wall flower while Cuyler smokes and talks about being a Republican and the presidential campaign." I wondered who was the president right now?

Johanna started to leave. "We'll see."

I shook my head in bewilderment as she left. Cuyler was my best friend and my love, nothing he could say or do would hurt me. I was beginning to trust him that much.

I went to my secret room and typed more pages of my manuscript. An all encompassing drowsiness came over me, and I blew out the light and locked the door as I left.

I went downstairs in time to see Cuyler returning from the barn. He still had chores to do even after his full day at Milford.

"Mother, Gertrude, I'm afraid I shall have to bid you a fond good night. I'm exhausted."

"I'll go up with you, dear. I'm more than ready for bed." He glanced at the expression on my face while I was saying the remark. As we climbed the stairs I said, "You *are* bad."

He smiled that wonderfully wicked grin. "Don't say you didn't like my dominant approach today. I'm very aware of every move you made, every impulsive reaction, and shall be replaying it in my dreams all night."

"Your dominant approach, hm? Well, just remember that only a liberated woman of the new '90s would have allowed you to go as far as you did this afternoon."

He lassoed my waist with his right arm and pulled me to his body. "Admit it. You liked the feel of someone taking charge this afternoon. I felt you surrender in my arms."

"Yes, you did. Just imagine how lovely it will be when you allow me to give you pleasure in return. As I said the first day we met, a partnership is much more fun. All things equal in work and play. You don't have to break your back to support us all by yourself, Cuyler. I'll share the load of work, and you'll help me at home. Men of your time period bled for twelve dollars a week while their wives stayed at home and picked new frocks from catalogues. For as long as I can help you, I will, because I know you'll do the best you can to help me, too. That is loving; that is marriage."

"I wish Reverend McBride could hear you tonight."

"It won't be long until we'll make love in our own cozy bed for as long as we can." I stood on tiptoes to kiss him good night.

I rose earlier than Cuyler and ran downstairs to heat our bath water. With private glee, I hurried to his door and knocked. A sleepy moan was the only reply, and then he answered the door.

"Here's your pitcher of water, dear." His hair was a mess, and he needed a shave. His large, brown eyes were half closed. He was wearing the robe I'd used that first day in the cabin.

"I'll meet you for breakfast, and then I want you to show me how to milk a cow."

He took the pitcher. "What?" he said to my back.

I went into my room, bathed, and changed into clean clothes.

A knock came to my door just as I was leaving. Cuyler was fresh smelling and clean shaven—ready to start his day on the farm.

We had breakfast, and I spent the day following him everywhere. We checked on the horses—feeding and watering them—then grooming them. Then we milked the cows while his mother fed her chickens and watered her flowers.

I was excited about the dance. Johanna promised to fill the only tub and boil water so that I could take a long, leisurely bath and wash my hair. She had a stove version of a curling iron and promised to curl my hair away from my face so that it would give the illusion that it was pulled into a bun.

Cuyler was decidedly detached from the event. The time to leave came none the less. He looked elegant in his three-piece black suit, and Johanna had helped me to look stylish in the yellow gown. When I came down the stairs, Cuyler averted his eyes and told me that I looked very nice. *Very nice?*

The rig had been hitched before we changed into our clothes and was ready for our ride into Cooperstown. Mrs. Carr told us to have a nice time, but Johanna was too busy preparing to attend the function herself to say goodbye.

The ride to Cooperstown was QUIET. If I had been unsure of his feelings before, this would have been the final tip off.

We arrived on time. The dance wasn't at the Fenimore Hotel, it was at the Carr Hotel which is in close proximity to the Mohican Club. "The old Carr Hotel was in Toddsville, which we've passed often on our journeys. It had a famous 'spring floor.' Dancing was more comfortable there because of it I've been told," said Cuyler. He couldn't resist a history lesson even tonight, but his manner was stoic.

Everyone was drinking punch and listening to the four-man orchestra. The Carr Hotel's ballroom was on the second floor and seemed to be over the kitchen area. You could see the lake from the north windows, and I could just make out the shimmering silver of the moon on the water.

The decor had been designed to celebrate the Fourth of July. Red, white, and blue half-moon banners fell over all the cornices of the draped windows like fans. There were small American flags everywhere, and I was thinking it all looked a little like the election hall of a presidential campaign.

When we walked through the door, Cuyler's friends and associates greeted him immediately. I was introduced to everyone. I noticed that I was the only one wearing a bright dress. As a matter of fact, it was the most beautiful dress in the hotel's ballroom.

Cuyler seemed awkward with his bachelor buddies. They walked by us and spoke politely, but they were headed outside to smoke and were not going to mention it to Cuyler for they knew he had company tonight—and for the rest of his life. You could almost hear what they were thinking as they traipsed past their old chum: "So, this is what happens to you when you decide to marry is it, Cuyler? Your free days are numbered, poor fellow. She's already pulling you by the ring in your nose. Soon, you won't even want to know the baseball scores. All she'll discuss with you are curtains and new frocks. No doubt your mind will give way, and you'll stop smoking cigars altogether."

I saw a perfunctory flinch of an eyebrow on Cuyler's visage, then he asked my hand for the first dance.

"I thought you couldn't dance?" I said.

"I can waltz," he said.

We went to the center of the dance floor and stepped slowly to the music. His friends stopped at the door and watched us. We were being watched; we were, after all, the gossip of the town. Most of the people there had not met me. I was being paraded, like royalty, before their eyes.

"Are you upset that I brought you here? Would you have rather gone with your friends?" I said.

"I've spent some twenty-six years with them. I *want* them to look at you. I want them to see how beautiful you are in your dress."

"But, you didn't even mention the dress at home and seemed put-out about coming here."

"I wasn't sure how it would feel to be on the inside doing what I'd always thought was a damn fool way to spend an evening. I watched as my chums strolled passed us just now, and I knew what they were thinking: 'Poor Cuyler's got himself caught. She's snagged him for good.' Then I looked at you and saw how the dress made you look like something out of a portrait. I realized that I had a new friend—one who would be mine for a lifetime."

I stared at him throughout the waltz.

When the melody ceased, we walked around the room and greeted everyone. There wasn't a soul there who didn't know and love Cuyler Carr.

We danced a few more tunes and drank some punch, but I could see his eyes stray to the front of the hotel where his friends were smoking and chatting.

I said, "I can handle myself if you wish to speak with your friends and smoke for a while. I think I can find the refreshments. I see Sally over there, and I must comment on her lovely gown. I can tell you're anxious to speak with them."

I had said the right thing. "If you're quite sure you'll be entertained. It won't be for long, Gertrude, I assure you."

"Whatever pleases you, dear. Remember, I love you, every aspect of who you are, and part of who you are is out there on that porch telling tales."

He kissed my hand and said, "I'll only be fifteen minutes."

I waved to Sally, but she was busy dancing in the arms of her boyfriend. I admit that I did feel very alone. I walked to the refreshment table and sampled the punch. No rum. I tried to act casual and hummed along with the music.

I was being watched. Two blue eyes were inspecting my every move. I heard a small masculine voice. "Excuse me, Miss. Might I introduce myself? My name is Clarence Peaslee. If I'm not being too presumptuous, are you not Miss Gertrude Johnson, Cuyler Carr's fiancé?"

I turned to look for the body that matched the voice but didn't find him until I glanced below my waist. The voice came from a small nine-year-old boy dressed like all the other men only in miniature. I reserved my smirk and played along.

"Yes, indeed, I am, sir, though we've not been properly introduced. How very nice to meet you. My fiancé has been detained outside," I said.

"So I've discerned. I hope you'll not think me too bold if I offer you a glass of refreshment," Clarence said. The tiny gentleman was playing a grown-up game, and I wouldn't hurt his feelings for the world.

"My throat is quite parched, thank you." He could barely reach the bowl, but I couldn't help him because I knew he wanted to show me how adept he was. I took the glass which was half-full of pink liquid.

"I understand you are from Brooklyn," he said.

"Why, yes, I am."

"Lovely music, don't you think?" he said.

"Yes, quite lovely."

"Would I risk your fiancé's ire if I asked you to dance?"

I blushed. "Well, Cuyler might become jealous, but I think I can risk it. Can you?"

He looked quickly to the front of the hall and saw Cuyler deep into a political conversation. He sighed. "I think I shall." He offered me his arm, and I thanked God my Dad had taught me to waltz.

Clarence stopped in the center of the floor, just like Cuyler had, and offered his arm to me as he tried to place the other one around my waist. His arms encircled my hips instead.

The music started, and I let the boy lead the way. He moved with small steps, and I followed him. He remarked, "I think you look lovely tonight, Miss Johnson. That color becomes you." I was wondering if this were a Cuyler clone. He had Cuyler's moves down pat.

When the dance was finished, and we applauded the musicians, Clarence asked, "Would you care for some fresh air? There are some benches set up on the banks of the lake. We would have a very nice view of the moon on the lake." He coughed and adjusted his too tight tie. Maybe I was wrong and old Clarence was a midget.

"Well, I don't know..." I looked out of the front door of the hall and saw Cuyler still in conversation. "Very well."

We exited from a side door, sauntered passed Cuyler and his friends without being noticed, and finally walked onto the green grass by the lake. He was correct. It was a picturesque scene with the moon shimmering on the ripples of the water. We sat on the benches. The cool summer breeze felt delicious wafting across my arms

"Tell me, Gertrude, what first attracted you to Mr. Carr; if you don't mind my asking?"

"Oh, I don't know. He's smart, well-versed, quite a communicator, and he has a wonderful sense of humor. He has a dry sort of wit and wonderful stories to tell."

The boy smiled roguishly. "Really? I've read extensively." I would have guessed that. I suspected his reading level was collegiate, and that he had an IQ of about 145.

"I can tell. You seem quite intelligent. What is your planned profession, Mr. Peaslee?"

"I plan to be a writer like James Fenimore Cooper." My heart flinched with a current of emotion, and a secret smile graced my lips. "Do you really? I write myself."

"I find that intriguing. What do you write, Gertrude, if you don't mind my calling you Gertrude?"

He moved fast for nine. "I write historic novels." I left out the romance part.

"Might I read them some day? Or am I being to presumptuous?"

"You may read them some day, I suppose. I'm far more interested in what you write."

He smiled, and his blue eyes twinkled. "I write poetry." He was actually wiggling with delight. "I would like to share some of my poems with you sometime, if it's quite convenient."

"I should love to read your poetry anytime, Clarence," I said.

His mouth twisted as if he had a lemon drop stuck to a molar. "Actually, I have one with me right now. I just wrote it this afternoon. It isn't finished yet. Would you like to read it?" he said.

He took from his pocket a folded piece of paper with large, ink letters on it, and handed it to me. I would break into a fit of laughter if it were a love poem. It wasn't. The poem read as follows:

The grasses nowhere grow so green,
As in Otsego;
The hills are nowhere so serene,
As in Otsego;

The skies are nowhere half so blue,
The lake nowhere cast such a hue,
And nowhere hearts beat quite so true,
As in Otsego.

"That's very good, Clarence," I said. It was a hell of a lot better than mine.

"Oh, it's just the beginning of the poem. I have more work to do on it. When I'm done with it, may I call upon you for your intellectual criticism of my work? Then, maybe you would let me read some of your prose?"

This kid had better moves than any man I'd ever met. "Well, I'd have to ask Cuyler first."

"Assuredly. When he comes back, might you impart my question to him?"

"I most certainly will."

He offered me his hand, and we went across the street, past Cuyler, again unnoticed, and inside the hotel. The ballroom appeared to be floating with dancers, and an eight-year-old girl on the other side of the room was eying my escort with a bruised expression.

He saw her. "Excuse me for a moment, Gertrude. Will you be all right here by yourself?"

"I'll manage somehow," I said, trying to look slightly disappointed. The little girl's eyes radiated joy when Clarence walked over to her. His evening card would be full all night. Perhaps she wrote poetry too.

I went to the refreshment table to try Johanna's cookies—which were her addition to the fare that night. No sooner had I munched one down when a more familiar voice caught my attention. It was low and secretive and came from the far hallway. I heard a young female sobbing. I decided to eavesdrop just a little. I eased my way to the wall next to the abandoned hallway.

"There, there, my dear. It isn't such a terrible idea. I'll be ever so gentle with you. My house is not that far away, or if you prefer, we could take a small buggy ride to an abandoned part of the county. No one will see us, I assure you, especially your fiancé."

"Take your hand from my arm. I can't. Don't you understand? Nathan would never forgive me."

"Nathan will never know, my dear."

"Don't touch my hair," said the girl.

"But it's such beautiful hair, and it flatters your face so. I long to kiss your lips and make you feel like...a *woman.*"

"Don't come any closer. I told you I was inexperienced."

"All the more reason for me to show you the way, my dear. You'll be a better wife for it. Besides, you're not married *yet.* You're the most beautiful woman I've ever met."

"I told you before; I can't. Please leave me alone. Don't ever ask me again."

"Then, my dear, I'm afraid I shall leave your fiancé alone as well. Nathan's parents have mortgaged their farm to the limit, and I'll tell him that. How it will break their hearts when he learns the truth, and how disturbed Nathan will be to know that I can't extend him a loan under these conditions. The family is already so far in debt that they would be buried in paupers' graves had they not purchased a family plot ten years ago. Isn't it true that Nathan's father has a heart condition? Doesn't his mother take in sewing and laundry just to pay the doctor bills which keep him alive? His mother didn't come through the last winter well, did she? Pneumonia, wasn't it? Pity," he said.

"You wouldn't be so horrid as to tell Nathan the truth?" she said.

"I will *have* to. I only told you because I thought we could come to a reasonable agreement. It appears we can't. I was only asking a small, trivial gift for lending, what I consider to be, a quite sizable sum."

"It's not a trivial gift to me. I don't want you to kiss me."

The voice became angry. "Then Nathan will have a virgin for his honeymoon but no home *or job* to return to. For I shall have to fire him, won't I?"

"Fire him? He loves his job at the bank," she said.

Good Lord, that slimy bastard, Ellis, was threatening one of his own employee's fiancés.

"Then come with me *now* for a short buggy ride. Such a little thing to give for so much joy."

I turned the corner and made my presence known, leaned against the wall, and folded my arms over my chest. I smirked. "Such a little thing is right. That's why it'll be a very *short* buggy ride. Provided he even makes it that far. Hello, Ellis. Still up to your slimy tricks?"

The girl was blushing. "Don't be embarrassed," I said. "You just go back in there and tell your fiancé what Ellis just tried to do, and he'll trot out of that bank job fast and find a decent one. I hear that they're hiring at the Milford National Bank. Come on. Do you really want the man you love working for this sleeze ball?" I looked at her, and she shook her head no. Then she hurried back to the man who had her future in the palm of his hands.

"You're being a bad boy again, Ellis," I said, moving in for the kill.

He tried to appear powerful and in control of the situation, but his knees buckled like jelly, and when he straightened them, he ran from me as fast as he could.

I returned to the refreshment table, snatched another sugar cookie, and looked for the girl. She and her beau were heavy into an expected conversation. I sighed with the pleasure one can attain from doing a good deed.

Cuyler's fifteen minutes were up. I noticed he was still puffing away on that thick cigar. So, this is what married life will be like for us—attending church and social functions and anxiously greeting friends because this was the only form of news correspondence besides the newspaper.

I heard a lively voice beckon in my ear. It was Daniel's.

He seemed to be having a good time, but I didn't see that he had a date. "How is it that you're alone tonight?" I said.

"I don't have a girlfriend, yet. I'm not as lucky as Cuyler, but standing around and discussing the joys of opposing political parties isn't my idea of having fun. I *love* to dance. I *love* the music. Will you do me the honor?" he said.

I gave my hand to the man who would, in two weeks, escort me down the aisle of the Presbyterian Church.

Lively on his feet, with a sparkle in his eyes that outshone the lights of the ballroom, and a smile that's only rival was the sun, Daniel whirled me around the floor to the melody of a brisk tune. At this point, it didn't matter if I knew the steps. He was a superb dancer, and any girl in the room would have counted herself fortunate, to have him as a partner. His form was like his sailing boat, free and spontaneous, as we breezed along to the music. There was something in this young man's personality that seemed so adventurous. He was quite different from the others, even

Cuyler. He laughed; he smiled; he joked; and he was authentic. He was not the stiff Victorian man at all. Nothing but goodwill and happiness issued from his lips. Life for Daniel was meant to be lived to the fullest—to be enraptured.

My dotted-Swiss chiffon shell flew with the satin skirt beneath it, daringly tossing my petticoats into view. He was, by far, the most energetic partner I'd had all night.

I giggled out loud despite my desire to appear the proper and cultured miss this evening. Daniel made comments engineered to make me laugh louder. He had me laughing so hard that my tears soon obstructed my vision. This only made him torture me with humor more fervently until the sniggers, combined with the speed of his turns, sent my head twirling, and I collapsed into his arms.

He guided me to the side of the room so that we wouldn't intrude upon the other's fancy footwork.

"Trudy, whatever is wrong with you?" he said, with a suspicious grin.

I couldn't catch my breath and continued with my fit of laughter. I waved my hands and arms as if that would help me speak, but it was no use.

He put his arm around me and said jokingly, "Shall I fetch you some water or punch?"

Again, I tried to suppress my giggles and sputtered incomprehensibly. Someone impinged our view, and there was instantaneous silence from both of us.

"Are you quite all right, Gertrude?" said the somber voice. It was Cuyler. He must have finished that cigar damn fast. Daniel tried to appear guilty but couldn't and grinned boyishly.

"She's fine, Cuyler. We were dancing, and Trudy got one of those funny fits women sometimes get. No harm done. I was going to get her something to drink, but since you're here, I'll give you the honor." He leaned over to my cheek and gave me a brotherly kiss good night. "Thanks for the dance, Trudy. See you soon about the wedding." Then he regarded Cuyler and said into my ear, "I hope."

"Well," I said glibly, "all finished with your discussion?" I tried to wipe the mirthful tears from my cheeks with the back of my hands and arrange my dress.

"I *told* you I'd return in fifteen minutes. I never lie about promises and things, you know that. What was young Watson saying to you that sent you into such a fit of laughter?"

I tried to tell him but kept interrupting myself with my own giggles. "He was commenting on the costumes some of the guests were wearing tonight. Oh, what a time I've had while you were visiting with your friends."

The music settled into a slow romantic waltz. "Yes, I can see that. Perhaps I shouldn't leave you alone at such affairs." His arms slipped into their accustomed position around my waist, and my laughter stopped immediately. The master's touch, with its soothing effect, brought me into his intimate sphere, pulled me into the warm solace of his love, allowed my soul to be close to its companion on earth. I slipped into his masculine aura and rested my head on his shoulder in helpless dependence. The dramatic change in my attitude reaffirmed our magnetic attraction to each other. I let him hold me a little closer than one should allow one's waltz partner. I didn't care. They were watching us, smiling at our closeness, but it didn't stop my wanting to be near him. The laughing tantrum had weakened me, and he was robbing me of all the strength I had in reserve. I wondered if he absorbed my energy into his own because I lost all of my willpower when I was near him.

I said, "Did you have a nice chat?"

He said into my ear, "It was somewhat educational. What did you mean by the comment that you'd had an interesting evening? With young Watson?"

"No, with Clarence, Ellis, *and* Daniel." If he were going to be jealous, he might as well get it full force.

"Clarence who? Ellis?" He almost stopped dancing for a second but continued with the melody.

"Don't get loud, Cuyler. Clarence is a nine-year-old boy going on forty who wanted to dance with me and learn my thoughts on his poetry."

"Really."

"Ellis was pestering the fiancé of one of his own employees before I intervened."

I didn't finish the whole story for just at that moment there was a shriek. The young lady's boyfriend had found Ellis skulking in a corner and hit him squarely on the jaw. Everyone tried not to smile and applaud. The girl was embarrassed but proud.

The boy said, "Consider this my week's notice. Don't you ever come near us again." Then he took his lady's hand and exited the ballroom. Ellis looked guilty and humiliated and scurried like the rat that he was to the side exit door. When all the cast members were gone, everyone gossiped about what had just transpired. I guess this sort of thing didn't happen at sociables very often.

Cuyler eyed me suspiciously. "Was this your doing?" he said, placing his hands on his hips.

"I just told her to be truthful with her fiancé. Wouldn't you want to know if someone were threatening your job through your fiancé's virtue?"

"I suppose, however, the situation had a rather dramatic and clearly public finale?"

I snuggled into his arms and said, "I know. Wasn't it wonderful."

"Gertrude! Really. What am I to do with you?" I could tell by the tone in his voice he wasn't angry.

"I'm certain you've had several thoughts on that subject tonight. Daniel was just having a good time. He has no date, and he's my escort down the aisle on our wedding day. You shouldn't be jealous, dear."

"Don't be ridiculous, Gertrude. *I'm not jealous.* I've already told you that Daniel is a friend of mine. I was simply concerned that you'd become ill, that's all."

"I see. Well, now I've filled you in on all the particulars of my evening with the young and the old men of Cooperstown. Now can I have some time with the man I love."

He gazed with affection into my eyes. "I shouldn't have left you alone. There's no end to the devilment you can get yourself into when I'm not around."

"I gravitate towards sin, dear." My words were a tickling whisper in his ear.

He smirked and tried not to show that I'd lightened his mood. He kissed me on the nose quickly. "It's a decidedly good thing that a sane, rational, sensible, traditional, Christian man is to be your husband," he said.

"Decidedly." My eyes closed, and I rested my head on his shoulder as we waltzed every dance until midnight. Then they informed us that we had to leave the hotel because they were closing the ballroom.

Serenity and intoxication come easy to a woman near Otsego Lake. I suggested a boat ride, but Cuyler thought I was being silly. "But, look at the way the moon shines on it." I waved my hands towards the water. "The surface looks like crystal. So smooth."

"Glimmerglass Lake, Gertrude. That's what Cooper called it in his *Leatherstocking Tales.*"

We spent a few moments meditating on the moon's reflection upon the waves of Glimmerglass Lake and then took an unhurried buggy ride home.

Chapter Fourteen

When I awoke Sunday morning, it hit me that I'd only been in Toddsville a week. I dressed quickly and was prompt for breakfast. I couldn't wait for my next Sunday sermon.

As we sat patiently in the pews chatting with the relatives, I noticed the same woman knitting again. "Exactly how did Mrs. Perry find so many husbands, Cuyler?"

"I don't know about the other two, but I do know the story about Reverend Perry. The reverend blew into town at the time of a series of meetings in the village. At one of the services, when those present were given an opportunity to speak, Mr. Perry arose and said he could say as his Savior did, 'The foxes have holes and the birds of the air have nests; but the Son of man hath no where to lay his head.' After he had finished, Johanna jumped up and said she had a place to lay her head and sat down. That evening Perry escorted her home, and they were soon married."

"It seems there's no end to the unusual reasons people in this time period marry."

A large woman, who almost took up the whole aisle when she strolled down it, went to the altar and bent to kneel in prayer.

Cuyler said, "Oh, no, not this again."

"What? What is it?"

"Mrs. Abner Dean. Her latitude, as you can see, isn't in proportion to her longitude. She sometimes gets down to kneel before the Lord and stays there during the whole sermon. One time, she fell asleep and started to snore loudly during the reverend's sermon. This would have been ignored except she lost her balance and toppled over. This awakened her but only to new peril. She could not get back up. The whole congregation was lost to the performance. Finally, several ladies went to her assistance, and when she had been adjusted, the sermon continued."

"Do you think she'll do that today?" I said.

"It *is* warm in here. It's entirely possible."

Reverend McBride began with a prayer. I peeked to see whether the lady was still at the altar. She was. Then the reverend asked for help for the poor and the destitute. I knew we had spent so much money that we couldn't help anyone now, but I was touched by the pitiful stories.

"As you know, one of our parishioners is in desperate need of help for her husband has left her with all the bills and the children to feed and clothe. This deserted wife with five children is making a brave attempt to be both mother and father to her family. Two of the children have been ill this past year; one required hospital care. Neighbors and kind Christian parishioners have helped with clothing for the children, but more is needed. Twenty dollars would help her pay her bills before she loses the roof over their heads. Naturally, all donations will remain anonymous. Just mark an envelope: To Mrs. K., and we'll see that she gets the money. May the Lord guide your hearts."

He continued, "Mrs. R's husband died three years ago, as you know, and she has been left with six fine children and a farm to run by herself. Her oldest son, Roland, has been much help to his mother by working the farm all by himself. They have done a grand job of keeping the family together. School starts soon, and the children walk a far distance to get there. This makes the need for warm clothing all the more necessary. But, the hard working mother cannot supply them with the clothing they need. You may wish to contribute money to the family with an envelope marked: To: Mrs. R., or the sisters among us may wish to prepare the clothes themselves."

Mrs. Perry spoke, "I'll make the mittens for them."

Soon, other ladies were offering until all six children were covered for the harsh winter walks to school. I was impressed by the charity I saw in the small church. This is what was meant by a community of believers helping each other. I shook my head to stop my tears.

"I wish we could help."

"Do you want mother to look for my old mittens?" he said.

I smiled at him and said, "No, I think we'll help some other way. I don't know how, but If God can show me the way, I'll do it."

The reverend told of those in the congregation who were sick; those who had been born; those who had died; and those who were about to be married. That was *our* introduction. He made us stand to be recognized. Everyone grinned and looked at us as if we were on stage.

The sermon was on love of all things. As if I needed to learn what that was, but he spoke of loving without conditions attached to the love. He said one should love others despite whom they were, or what they might have done to please us or distress us. This was true Christian love. We were to be good to those who had hurt us and forgive them. Did he mean I should forgive Ellis? Even if I did, I was still going to stay away from him. If there ever was a devil to be found on earth, it was that man.

After the service, many of the congregation welcomed me to their town. They chatted about Cuyler and asked about our plans. They offered to help us anyway they could. I could see that Mother Carr was becoming weary from all the wedding excitement. The week's activities had taken their toll. I mentioned this to her son, and we went directly home.

Johanna made us a nice lunch, and afterwards we napped all day on the side porch swing. Cuyler rested his head on the back rim of the swing and slept, and I snoozed with my head in his lap. It'd been the most exhausting week of my life. It had also been the happiest time I could ever remember.

Chapter Fifteen

The next two weeks were going to be equally demanding. We spent much of our time on the road. We would rise early and eat a large breakfast, then hitch Samuel to the tea cart and go to Cooperstown first. We picked up ordered items, purchased things we had suddenly realized we needed, and contacted Mrs. Sloat, Sally, Daniel, Putt, Reverend McBride, and the church's housekeeper, Mrs. Murphy. We sent thank you notes for presents that were delivered daily to the Carr homestead.

Then we took the snakelike, curvy roads to Milford and worked on our new home and business. We had customers already, and I was learning where to shop for supplies in the small town. I had asked Johanna to purchase typing paper for me when she went to town for groceries, and she had done so without questioning me. However, there was a pharmacy, with the unimaginative title of City Drugstore, that sold writing supplies. I wondered how I could convince Cuyler to bring the typewriter from the homestead to Milford without his catching on to my plans. I could always say that I needed it close by in case an inspirational muse attacked me.

I watched my wonderful fiancé as he chatted amicably with his customers. More often than naught, men came into the shop just to discuss politics or history with Cuyler. Before they left, they purchased something so they could tell their wives that the trip had been necessary.

Looking from the open window in my new apartment, I noticed the young man who used to work for Ellis stepping from a surrey with his girl. They walked into the Milford National Bank. I decided to help in the store so that I could speak with her when she came back outside. When she decided to allow her fiancé the freedom he needed in his business chat, I walked to the front porch pretending to sweep in front of the shop.

"I see you took my advice," I said.

"Oh, hello, is this your store?" she said.

"It's my fiancé's and mine. We are to be married July 10. By the way, my name is Gertrude Johnson, but you can call me Trudy. Your boyfriend has left Ellis, has he?"

"Yes. I told him what you said about the job here. I hope he gets one." Just then Cuyler came outside to see what I was up to.

"I'm sorry; I don't know your name. This is my fiancé, Cuyler Carr," I said.

"Nice to meet you, Mr. Carr. My name is Sophie Kent, and my fiancé is Nathan Justice. I suppose Trudy has told you about what happened with Ellis." She blushed. "I'm so embarrassed about the whole thing."

"No need," said Cuyler. "Gertrude had a run-in with the cur herself. She gave him a lesson he shan't forget soon. Forgive me for saying so, but your young friend managed a nice upper cut to Ellis the other night. How are things going?" The fresh cigar in his mouth was lit with the reappearing match from nowhere. This man could not converse without a strong cigar in his mouth. I actually don't know whether he smoked it or just used it for a prop. I mean, he lit the thing, but I never really saw smoke coming from his lips.

"Well, he left the bank, as you heard," she said. "There's one problem though. His parents are mortgaged to the teeth with the old bank. Ellis still has that to hold over us."

A stern look from Cuyler reminded me that I'd been told not to interfere with these Victorian people's lives. Too late now.

"Make sure your young man takes on the obligations of his parents," he said. "So it would be Nathan Justice Sr.'s farm of which we're speaking? If there is anyway to change the mortgage to this bank, try to do it. I'm sure the Milford Bank would be happy to give him a new loan. Then you'll have a safe roof over your heads to start your matrimonial career."

"Nate will be furious that I brought this up," she said.

"That's a nice bit of farmland," said Cuyler. "I can understand Nathan not wanting to farm anymore, though. It's hard work for one man."

"Nate's asking for a job right now. No bank will give a man a loan when he has no job. He can't ask for a job and a loan at the same time, can he? We don't even know if he'll be hired. That's why I stepped outside while he spoke with the manager," Sophie said.

"Is that all that's troubling you?" With the words still dangling from his lips Cuyler entered the bank. A few minutes passed, and I nervously chattered like an idiot about my forthcoming wedding while asking her about hers. I swept the porch so accurately one poor ladybug, who had tried to crawl onto it four times, decided to give up and find another place to nap.

Cuyler emerged, still puffing away at the cigar only this time he was grinning with victory. "Nathan has a new job," he said. "He's signing the papers right now."

The young girl said, "Oh, thank you, Mr. Carr. Did you say something on Nate's behalf? Oh, I just know you did. Trudy, I can never repay you for handling Ellis for me and helping us get started here in Milford. We would still be under the thumb of that horrid man, and who knows what trials there'd have been for us if you hadn't interfered, Mr. Carr." She shook Cuyler's hand vigorously. "You are a saint." She dabbed the tears from her eyes with her lace handkerchief. "And your fiancé is an angel from heaven."

The boy exited the bank door and hugged his girl. Then he walked over to us.

"Thanks, Mr. Carr, Mrs. Carr. Sophie and I will always be grateful to you for getting us started and away from that ba--, oh, forgive me, Ellis." He was a forthright young man in speech as well as action.

Cuyler tapped the ash from the tip of his cigar, and said, "No problem. If you need any help at all, such as asking for that loan for your parents' mortgage, you just let me know. Of course, if you decide to move closer to Milford, you know where to buy your coal and hardware supplies."

"You needn't worry on that score. We'll make this town a big success. When are you two speaking your vows?"

I spoke. "In two weeks. We can hardly wait." The look I gave Cuyler was triumphant. I had interfered where I shouldn't have; he'd interfered where he dare not. We had combined our charitable natures to bring joy to this couple's life.

The two climbed into their surrey, hugged each other again, and waved as they departed.

As he waved to them he said under his breath but loud enough for me to hear, "I told you about being too independent."

"I know, but I couldn't sit by and let Ellis win this girl's virtue and rob her and her man of a terrific honeymoon, depriving both of them of a perfect, once-in-a-lifetime-memory, now could I?"

His arm went around my waist, and he tugged me to his side

affectionately. "Of course you couldn't. That's why I intervened on the boy's behalf. Not only did I get him a job, but he won't have any trouble obtaining that loan since I've been asked officially to sit on the board of directors of this bank. I accepted five minutes ago. I think there are many good things a man can do for others in such a position."

"What an honor, Cuyler. You must be very proud. Your reputation for honesty and good business sense must have done the trick."

"I suppose, it was something like that. And I'm especially proud of the new member of the Carr family for going against my wishes and doing the Christian deed which was placed before you by Providence. Obviously, I was to help in this, as well."

I kissed him on the cheek. "Then you aren't angry with me?"

"I was until the girl called you an angel. I remembered that I had dubbed you the title when I first saw you in the cabin. I also once told you that whatever new adventure you tossed my way would add the needed excitement to an otherwise boring existence. I can't be angry with you, Gertrude. I love you too much."

"I never consciously meant to disturb you," I said. "I just saw something bad happening, and, without thinking, plunged into the middle of it."

He kissed my forehead. "Let's call it a day. I'm hungry for dinner and tired from all the traveling. We have to meet with the good reverend tonight, or had you forgotten?" he said.

"No, I hadn't forgotten. As a matter of fact, I'm looking forward to it."

He gave me a curious look.

The ride home was a quick one, and Johanna had dinner hot on the stove for us. She was spending much time preparing for the Fourth of July banquet á la Carr this Sunday.

Mother Carr motioned to gifts in the parlor. She'd had company all day. She told me about a party Sally and Mrs. Sloat were preparing for me on the Thursday before the wedding. I would have Cuyler show me Mrs. Sloat's house because this time Mother Carr, Johanna, and I were on our own with the buggy. It was an all girl party.

The Carr men, who would be ushering and standing in as best man at Cuyler's side, had their own plans for his bachelor's party. He knew all about it but hadn't mentioned it to me. I couldn't imagine what they would do since they were against drinking. Well, this is one historic tidbit about which I was never going to learn. Cuyler was as closed-mouth on the subject as a tomb. I surmised they would smoke cigars and talk politics at the Carr Hotel or the mysterious Mohican Club.

Chapter Sixteen

Once more we traveled passed the "red house" and into Cooperstown for our lesson on marital joys. The sun had not fallen over the ridge of Glimmerglass Lake, and it stayed light until 8:30 or sometimes 9:30 these days. This made the trip to the reverend's office much easier.

He was happy to see that we had remembered our appointment and asked many questions about our plans. He jotted the things we said down in his reference book. We were to come to the church the night before the wedding for a rehearsal. Everyone in the wedding party, as well as the reverend, was to have dinner at the Fenimore Hotel that night. The Carr family had helped with this too. Then he came around to the discussion at hand—SEX.

"I know that you are inexperienced in these matters, Gertrude, but I want you to understand that I must mention how much this means to Cuyler."

Okay, let me get this straight—despite my obvious repulsion towards sex—I was supposed to do Cuyler the big favor. I thought I would lose every ounce of Victorian prudishness and burst into a fit of laughter right in this poor man's face. If he had only seen the two of us last Friday. I had my role, and I hoped I was a good enough actress to perform it.

"We find in the Song of Solomon that a husband greatly delights in the pleasures his wife offers him. Because it is in the Bible that such delight does not displease the Almighty, and, in fact, God even tells us to be fruitful and multiply; we can see that it is right and proper for a man and woman to well...have...once in a while...joys of the flesh, so that they can conceive children. You love Cuyler, don't you?" he said.

"Yes, of course," I said.

"Good. It's important to remember how much he loves you when the time comes for the consummation of your marriage. For the two shall become one. The woman shall leave her family and join with her husband's."

He looked at Cuyler for a moment. "You're a kind man, Cuyler. You must understand that Gertrude will need some tenderness and patience before she can submit to you in all things. No matter how strong you desire the stimulation of the flesh, you must realize how repulsive it is to your wife."

I saw the sheepish smirk skim across Cuyler's face, and I knew he was remembering last Friday's interrupted interlude.

"Women are not as physically capable of enjoying the act as men are. Something not right anatomically speaking, of course. They hesitate." A cough from my fiancé? Or was that a stifled chuckle? Bite the bullet, Cuyler. You're losing the battle.

"Be patient with her, and she may finally be able to relax, so that your home may abound with the joy of your own little children. Children, although they are a handful at times, and strain an honest man's patience to the limit, are wonderful additions to a couple's domestic bliss. Only then will Gertrude be able to fully comprehend that the act of intercourse has a reward for her, too." The man was beaming with a grin that would rival Santa Claus.

Some reward—10 hours of labor. However, he *had* brought up something which should have, but had not entered my mind earlier. Pregnancy. I had discovered that the ever-recurring monthly curse had followed me through time. I was shocked to realize the fact this Monday morning with no clue how to handle the situation in the 1890s. History books, as a rule, never mention this sort of thing. I had managed a line to Johanna which I'd hoped would initiate her help in the matter without making me sound completely stupid. After all, a young woman of 26 would know what to do. I couldn't ask her, "Hey, what do you do for Tampons around here?"

So, I resorted to the fire and thunderstorm story again, and due to the delicate nature of the circumstances and my clear panic, she waved her hands and cut off my question while running to the laundry for the needed supplies. How embarrassing! The point is—if one can do *this* in a time travel situation, it stands to reason that the other is conceivably possible, also. Forgive the pun.

Cuyler glanced my way to see whether I was playing the innocent Victorian virgin with emotion, and smiled at the odd, helpless look on my face. Method acting at its finest. I simply was frightened by the possibility of becoming a time traveling mom, and the look was there on my face. I had a feeling the Cooper men might not know much about this topic. Hadn't Jim told me that he wouldn't answer any more of my questions, so that I might figure the whole thing out on my own?

I had a flashing mental picture of me having a baby in Brooklyn circa 1998, in a hospital full of hygienic niceties, while my husband paced in Milford circa 1898. What if I never was able to come back through time, and my child would grow up never knowing what a great dad he had. What would I do? Would I have the NYSHA black and white picture of Putt's photo in a frame on one of my condo walls, and point to the handsome man in the Victorian clothing and say, "Daddy-say-Daddy?" He or she would never know how hard Cuyler had worked to make a family and a home he never enjoyed.

What if I miscarried when I went through the tunnel of time? How would I tell Jennifer and Bruce that I was married in Cooperstown during my summer vacation, conceived, but gave birth in Brooklyn without the presence of the man who I've said is the love of my life? Then tell Wainwright when he questions—and you know he will—that my loving husband can't manage to get away from his work to watch the birth of his own child, or even come to the hospital to see his kid, in a time when travel from Toddsville to Brooklyn would only be a few hours driving time. How could I lie to a research analyst who wants my body before and after delivery that my soul-mate husband never telephones, e-mails, or sends the kid a birthday card?

"Sure, Trudy," Bruce would say after the second year of no Mr. Carr. "You just had a fling with one of those mountain men and didn't want to tell us you were having a baby out of wedlock. That's okay," Wainwright would say with clear sexual and domestic intent. "I'll be happy to play husband and father."

And what about the responsibility of being a single, married mom who has no help at those four o'clock feedings I've heard about?

What if I could travel back in time next summer? That would be wonderful, for then I could at least see Cuyler secretly in the three months I'm supposed to be in the cabins for my vacation. However, you can't be secretive with a child who has to be breast fed one season and watches cartoons with his bottle in another. Would Cuyler be supremely surprised when I showed up in cabin 1 with baby Carr? Would he also be hurt that he couldn't watch his own child mature?

Could I leave the kid with my parents while I played for three months in another era? Could I lie to the last son in the Carr line, telling him he could have no heir?

Will my child need therapy at three months because he's wearing Pampers in Brooklyn and linen didies in Milford? How does a kid explain to his first grade teacher that he knows more about American history than she does? How do you explain to the grandparents when the six-year-old mentions playtime with his Macintosh to Mother Carr; or how he loves to help his father deliver coal to the farmhouses because he gets to ride in the 'awesome' wagon with his dad's 'cool' team of horses, to Grandpa Johnson? Staggers the mind, doesn't it?

When Cuyler, or Trudy, Carr II is ready to accept the Einstein business, and wises up to the gimmick, what new headaches will unfold? Will he want to stay with his Dad because Otsego is where that cute, little red-haired girl lives? Will daughter Carr want to travel to Europe one summer with her junior class, breaking her father's heart when she doesn't come home to see the man who has waited half a year to see her? If it's tough for Cuyler and me to handle the separation, imagine a kid trying to cope with it. Well, if some people tell their kids about Santa Claus, maybe I'll just have to tell him that we have to keep quiet about our secret Never-Never Land, or that the Looking Glass world is our *private* place.

"I'm sure you two will figure it all out on your own," said Reverend McBride. "When two people are as much in love as you and Gertrude are, nothing can keep them from happiness. All you need, Cuyler, is a little patience. Patience and understanding will keep a marriage joyful and everlasting. May your love keep you together throughout eternity, and may you have a wonderful life here in New York until then."

Patience? PATIENCE! Huh? What? I must have missed the whole sermon. Cuyler was shaking hands with the reverend, and I must have had a tranced-out expression on my face.

"Next Monday will be our final session," he said. "I'm not going to preach to you that night. I know how tired, and nervous you both will be then. You certainly don't need my words to add to the many ideas floating through your heads. So, I ask you two to think of anything you want to discuss with me at that time. I'll not say nay to any problem you may wish to discuss."

The famous hormone-driven emotions came to my soul, and I

started to cry. "Oh, Reverend McBride, pray for me."

"Why, Gertrude, don't cry. Physical pleasure isn't all that bad. You'll get used to it."

"Please pray for the two of us. I feel lost right now."

Cuyler caught on fast that I was worrying about something altogether different from what our preacher thought. "I think she's upset that her mother, father, and sister can't be here for the wedding," Cuyler said. "You know—the fire and all. She has no mother with whom to discuss feminine things—things a girl might want to ask her mother before her wedding night." Good boy, Cuyler. Ever creative with the non-lies.

"Oh, yes, I see." The middle-aged man blushed, and an empathetic look came to his visage. "In such circumstances, a girl would not want to discuss this matter with a mother-in-law, no doubt. Well, Mrs. McBride, my dear wife, would be happy to chat about anything you might want to discuss, dear Gertrude. I can well imagine how alone you must feel right now. I shall certainly pray for you and Cuyler."

We said goodbye, and I could tell Cuyler was anxious to hear what was troubling me. "Whatever is wrong, Gertrude? I can see you're genuinely upset."

I wasn't sure how to approach this one. "Cuyler." I eased into the discussion. "When he mentioned children, I realized that I don't know whether I can have babies while I'm a time traveler. And if I can, what sort of life would it be for all of us?"

"I see." He stared at the leather reins of his buggy. "You're correct. There doesn't seem to be a pamphlet on this business, does there?"

"It just occurred to me, that's all. It made me realize how scary going home will be." I hugged him, and he stopped the tea cart. "I want to stay here, Cuyler." I understood fully what that statement meant. "I want to be your wife, forever, remaining in the Toddsville of 1897, working in our Milford shop, living in our tiny apartment. I want to see your mother on Christmas, and celebrate Easter morning in our church with the Fat Lady and the Knitting Queen. I want to find out what happens to Sally and her beau, Sophie and Nathan, and whether Daniel finds a girlfriend before next July's dance. I want to wake up EVERY morning and make your breakfast. I want to have our child and have the two of us raise him."

Yes, indeed, folks. I SAID IT! And I meant every word too. How far down the emotional highway had I traveled? Only three weeks ago I was trying to avoid an emotional commitment to Wainwright. I didn't want marriage or children. I didn't even want *people* in my life and had buried myself away from everyone. I was attached not only to Cuyler but to my new friends. I cared what happened to them. I wanted to share the good and bad days with these unusual but pleasant folk who had taken me into their hearts on a lie. I wanted to help them when they needed someone as they had aided me in my distress. They had accepted me with only a minuscule amount of hastily relayed information. Their keen sense of character had decided that I was a kind and charitable person. They were willing to give me the benefit of the doubt. They were a part of my life now, attaching themselves to a secret chamber in my heart—a chamber whose door had been locked for years.

As much as I loved my own friends and family back in Brooklyn, I'd always had to prove myself. My mother expected me to be perfect, and my father had wanted a boy. Jennifer cared about me enough to rent the cabin for me, but I always produced for her, didn't I? I wonder how she and Sydney would feel about me if I went belly up and couldn't write anymore. Hopefully, we had been friends long enough for her to call once in a while.

Then there was Wainwright. No question the man was as loyal as Lassie. If I kept telling him no, would he leave me? Would he stay no matter what happened? Would he call if I forgot to answer his message on my machine?

Was I running from Wainwright because he accepted me for who I was? Is this really what had been driving me to isolation and detachment? My heart had been destroyed by that college boyfriend turned lawyer. Was I still reeling from that pain? Had I dropped from sight because of my own feelings of unworthiness? Low self-esteem? Was I unlovable? That young man had hurt me both physically and emotionally. What had I ever done to deserve that?

Then there was Cuyler. This whole crazy situation had been a blessing for him. His life had been altered, and he had planned a new course based on our marriage. What would happen when I left, and he had to make up that story that I'd gone back to Brooklyn to visit my sister? For nine months? What would happen to their trust when I never returned, and my husband had to make his own way without the companion who had promised to love, honor, and obey until death? Would Mrs. Bates make him dinner every night? When he came home from a hard day's work, would he light the stove, make some tea, read a book for a while, and curl up beside my pillow on our bed, falling asleep without his wife snuggled tightly in his arms? Would Johanna send him home with baked goods every Sunday he drove his mother to church? Sooner or later they would wonder why a wife stayed away from her husband for so long. A distraught and lonely shadow of a once jovial Cuyler Carr would shed its darkness on the memory of a woman who had been their friend but had left them. Even Daniel's famous smile would fade to think that the woman he had walked down the aisle of the Cooperstown Presbyterian Church preferred her one sister in Brooklyn to the man she said was her eternal love.

I turned to see his reaction to my melancholy mood. What could he say? He held me in his arms and kissed me. He'd had the same thoughts last week. I'll never forget the kiss he gave me then. A kiss which held such emotional intensity. It said, "I'll love you forever and beyond, no matter what's in store for the two of us."

"No one—not fate—not God, not even something evil, would try to keep us apart. You told me once to have some patience, and the reverend mentioned it again tonight. We'll get through this, and we'll *stay* together somehow. There's no one else I want to live with, and I think you feel the same."

I glimpsed his expression in the dimming light of sunset and knew that *nothing* would keep me from living with this man from this day forth and throughout eternity.

We sat in silence all the way home. We walked into the house and spoke little to his mother or Johanna. Instead, we went straight upstairs and said good night to each other with a simple hug.

I changed into my nightgown and went to sit by my window. I stared long and hard at the moonlight on the pasture where the cows grazed by day. The sky, its own Glimmerglass, reflected every star. Sparkling diamonds on a black velvet night. Was there anyone who could make sense of all this? Two intelligent people were doing their best to comprehend.

I bowed my head in the direction of my dresser and observed my reflection in the half-lit mirror. What a difference! Sally had been correct. My hair had grown long enough to pull it up into a sort of chignon. My face glowed with an illumination of the love that burned inside my heart. A new twinkle, like the stars in the heavens, glazed my eyes. I had put on some much-needed weight. Johanna's cooking, and a renewed appetite, brought about by a stronger will to live. How clearly I could see everything now that I had returned to the land of the living.

Reality is really nothing more than a perceived observation of the human soul. The tenderness I felt in my heart was not fiction. I needed no fancy words to describe what I'd always known existed in true love stories. I had found what I was searching for and hadn't realized it. Passion was nothing more than pure, honest love from a wonderful man like Cuyler. The photo had drawn me to him. I'd known before that fateful day in June that I loved him. I'd found his persona and fallen in love with him before I'd ever met him in real life. The healthy pink in my cheeks was the blossom of the new-found knowledge that I'd saved my heart for this man. So you see, Jim Cooper had been correct. The discovery that my dream had come true had made my life complete. I'd placed that poem on my bedside and willed Cuyler into my life. Perhaps Cuyler had had a similar vision of the woman he'd marry before I dropped into his. In any event, the moon and the mirror reflected an altered life for two people who deserved to have this joy. Sometimes, in the darkness, you seek the light, and, if you're very lucky, you find it.

Chapter Seventeen

The rest of our busy week went quickly. I was adjusting to the laborious days and early nights. Exhaustion took us to bed by nine. Chores woke us at dawn for another active day. It was becoming increasingly more difficult to secure time to write my manuscript. I escaped to my secret room right after dinner; when Cuyler went to the barn to take care of the animals. I had close to four hundred pages finished. I found myself completely involved with its plot and its characters. Why shouldn't I? I was the heroine, and Cuyler was the hero. I sympathized with her troubles. It was also good therapy for me to write down my thoughts. I could grapple emotionally with my own feelings, and, through my character, try to solve them.

I helped Cuyler in our store during the morning hours. I talked with Mrs. Bates during the afternoon. We were becoming great neighbors. The other citizens in the town stopped by and chatted with both Cuyler and me. We belonged to this tight knit community. I cared about them, and I knew they would be there for me if I ever needed them.

We stopped by Cooperstown to converse with Sally, Mrs. Sloat, and Daniel when we had a chance. They were excited about the party and their wedding clothes. Daniel told us that our present would be finished by the Fourth of July. We informed everyone for the tenth time about the dinner at the Fenimore Hotel and all the other times and dates. In this manner, we hoped to have the celebration run smoothly.

In the early evenings, I sat by Cuyler's mother on the porch steps by her garden. The two of us plucked the enemy weeds and watered the beautiful petals. She lectured me on the flowers' names, and how you cared for each. She promised to help me start my own window box in our apartment next spring. I could see that she was upset about us leaving.

I learned as much as I could about the Carr-Todd lineage from her. I knew she was aching for an heir to the Carr line. One poignant aspect of this whole time traveling scene was that I might be leaving during the autumn equinox—near the twenty-second—which was close enough to the anniversary of Chester's death to matter.

For the moment, Cuyler remained communicative on daily life and our plans, and so I no longer heard the histories of Toddsville. Once the marriage had begun, I was sure we'd return to my lessons.

Sunday morning, July fourth, was a blur of activity. We had a hasty breakfast and went to a quick service at church. Even Reverend McBride wanted to see the parades. We hurried home and changed into more comfortable clothing.

The Carr and Todd relatives arrived thereafter. By ten in the morning, everyone was laughing and active. The men smoked and talked. The women helped Johanna in the kitchen. Mother Carr greeted everyone and showed the small boys and girls how to use the ice cream maker. Then we hurried to the main street of Toddsville for the annual parade.

The place was decorated to the limit with ribbons and banners of red, white, and blue. Flags were flying from every house. The parade was quite different from Macy's or your local town's. There were fire trucks on display, and teams of horses clomped down main street. Clubs, organizations, and secret societies—with men in odd hats—marched by us. A local band, smaller than a high school one, played through the streets.

When the procession finished, we climbed back into the carriages and traveled, en masse, to Cooperstown to watch its promenade. It was grander by far than Toddsville's.

I saw Sally and her boyfriend on the other side of the street. They were with her little brother and her aunt. I finally met Mr. Sloat who was as jolly as his wife. Many of our church members were there and stopped to greet us, but I did not see Daniel. I was curious about this secretive gift of his.

When we returned to the homestead, the food was on the makeshift picnic tables. Cuyler had strung a huge, silk flag over the picnic area which would act as our shield from the sun.

I saw Putt driving home from the Cooperstown parade and asked him to stop and have some lemonade with us. He did and took a picture of everyone eating dinner. The vision struck me as cold as freezing rain. I'd seen that picture in my photo book. The big family reunion. The corn on the cob. I now knew with certainty which family and which house was displayed in that photo.

I was forced to entertain the young ladies, my new cousins,

who were my age or younger. They talked about my wedding ad nauseum. They hoped there'd be sunshine for the outdoor reception on Mother Carr's lawn. They begged me to tell them about my wedding gown and for me to recite the sad tale of the fire. When that story was through, they asked about the day I fell in love with Cuyler and promised I'd marry him. I could see how important conversation and storytelling were to the people of this time period. Except for the newspaper, face to face dialogue was the only way to learn anything. I could remain true to my Victorian persona by remembering Penelope, her voice, and my book.

Cuyler was having almost the same discussion, with small changes, of course, with the young male cousins who seemed to have a never ending love for teasing the outspoken bachelor about tying the noose around his neck by marrying me. I overheard Cuyler telling them about his love for his bride, and how life had new meaning because I was in it.

Around six o'clock, he and I bid farewell to the family and headed for the cabin. We were still planning to watch the fireworks from the ridge of Canadarago Lake. Above the trees, he promised, we would see the bolts of color as they gleamed against the twilight.

We had eaten pie and ice cream, feasted upon deviled eggs and salad, and swallowed all the fried chicken and corn on the cob we could manage. Johanna insisted we take a snack for later. She had lemonade in a huge jar for us, and white cake with chocolate icing carved into slices and wrapped with linen inside a picnic hamper.

His mother warned us to be home as soon as the fireworks were finished because of the darkness and the threatening thunderclouds. The weather had teased us, prophesying a wash-out for a picnic during the afternoon hours.

We stopped in Richfield Springs before climbing the hill to the faraway cabins. There was a large field there that could hold a whole circus, and it was crowded with people watching the balloon races. I assumed the race would be finished shortly as the fireworks would begin in several hours.

It's rather difficult to tell how far along a manually driven balloon race has progressed. I think the spectators were anxious as well because of the menacing rain clouds. We watched the colorful balloons fill the air with their peaceful grace and chose our own particular favorites. Then we encouraged Samuel to pull us up the long hill to the cabin. I could swear Samuel's ears were flicking, and his head turned left and right as if he knew there was a bad storm coming.

If there were any guests in the other cabins, I surely didn't see them. I was wondering if I'd finally meet Isaac Cooper tonight. I felt sure that he had to be kin to Sam and Jim. He was nowhere in sight though. I asked about this and Cuyler hadn't a clue why the caretaker would not be near his cabins on July Fourth. Cuyler said the Cooper property was the best spot in all Otsego County to view the fireworks display. He wrapped his arms around me and hugged me.

"Who cares where he is tonight? We'll curl up on our blanket, eat, drink and watch the fireworks together and alone. *Finally alone* ."

"I thought you had decided to give up the pursuit of premarital sexual gratification because of the constant interruptions. After all, next Saturday we'll be legally man and wife," I said.

"Well, if you feel like it now, and no one is near enough to interfere; we could always make fireworks of our own."

I kissed him playfully on the nose. "Are you sure you are as good a boy as you claim to be Cuyler E.? I could swear there's a bit of the devil in you."

"It's because I'm near you that my moral fortitude weakens. You've this way of turning my thoughts to lust and sin," he said.

"Do I? So, you're going to blame it all on me?"

"You distract me from the straight and narrow."

I giggled. "That's funny. I thought I'd be distracted *by* your straight and narrow."

He hurled me playfully to the blanket and began the sweet seduction his lips had learned from our last assignation.

"There, you see what a bad influence you are on me. Such a wicked derivation of a righteous statement," he said.

I submitted to the wonderful sensations his lips created on my skin. Then we heard the voice.

"Cuyler! Trudy!" Only one person in *this* world called me Trudy.

It had to be Daniel's voice. We looked at each other and said in unison, *"Daniel!"*

We inspected the bank of the lake nearest our blanket. There was Daniel waving to us. "I thought the two of you would come here to watch the fireworks. Come down to the bank. I have a surprise for you."

We examined one another's peeved expressions and then smiled. Daniel had made us something that could not be wrapped in a box and given to us at our wedding reception. He'd been waiting for us by the lake all day to show us his gift. We rose from the wool blanket and walked down to the bank of the lake. There, freshly painted and bearing the name TRUDY, was our fishing boat. *The same boat which was still harbored in the lake outside cabin 1 in 1997.* This was that same boat only on the day of its birth. How it sparkled on the water. Our wedding present had cost Daniel hours of labor, and it was a beaut.

Cuyler grinned. "Did you make her all by yourself?" he said.

"Of course. I could see the love of the sea in Trudy's eyes the night I took her on my sailboat. She never asked what I did for a living, so I decided to surprise her with her own boat on her wedding day. Knowing how much you like to fish, Cuyler, I just knew you'd love her too."

FISH?

"Boy, you have that right, my friend. I've always wanted my own boat." Cuyler looked like a boy who had just obtained his first baseball mit.

FISH?

"Cuyler," I said coyly, "you never told me you fished."

"Well, sure I did, Gertrude. When you first met me, I told you I came to the cabin to relax and fish. Why? What's the matter?"

I decided to bring the objectionable subject up later. I didn't want to diminish Daniel's ecstatic mood. Cuyler was obviously thrilled with the gift which meant any jealousy about Daniel and myself being friends was finished. That was a miracle I did not wish to destroy by mistakenly mentioning that I hated the very sight of fish and would only want to row around the lake in the boat bearing my name. For that same boat was the little one whose name I had tried to decipher, that had survived wear and tear, to sit on the bank one hundred years later waiting for its owner to return. This was an important moment for me, and I let the two men chat boat talk as I reflected.

The boat was here in 1897 and there in 1997. This meant, unless there was a really strange coincidence, I had been here and there too. If I could have only made out that name. Then there could be no denying that the TRUDY's existence linked me to the past, the present, and the future. If I needed any significant clue to the reality of my time travel experience, it was now sitting docked in the water before my eyes.

I had stumbled onto some sort of compelling truth. I had existed in 1897 or a reincarnation had taken place. A reincarnation so exact to my 1997 life, so much a replica to my present birth, that I had actually been baptized my predecessor's name. I doubted that happened much in the tomes of reincarnation literature. I had stumbled upon my fate. I was meant to be Cuyler's wife. Even if that meant I would have only been his wife during the summer months of our lives together. It meant that time travel was real and interjected people into a slot they were meant to fill for whatever reason heaven only knew. I found comfort in these thoughts.

"Well, Gertrude?" asked Cuyler.

I must have been zoned out for I hadn't heard any of their excited patter.

"What?" I said in a trance.

"I said, do you want to ride around the lake?"

Daniel and Cuyler were smiling up at me like little boys from the bank of the lake.

"Of course I want a ride. After all, we have to christen it the TRUDY, don't we?" I ran to the picnic basket and found the jar of lemonade. When I returned to the bank, I held it dangerously close to the helm, or starboard, or whatever the front part of the boat is called, and said, "I hereby christen thee TRUDY, the first and only boat of Cuyler and Trudy Carr."

The men applauded as I smashed Johanna's jar against the boat breaking the glass jug in half. One part remained in my hand. I placed it on the bank and lifted my skirts to navigate myself into my boat. Daniel helped me and Cuyler rowed. Soon, we were in the middle of the lake. The sunset was every bit as lovely from my boat on Canadarago Lake as it had been from Daniel's sailboat on the Glimmerglass.

"Why don't we watch the fireworks from here?" Cuyler said.

"Oh, I can't stay," Daniel said. "I have to return to Cooperstown. I promised to help with the fireworks. So, if I'm not there, there won't be any."

A sleek smile curled Cuyler's lips. "Oh, then I guess I'll row you back to the bank. You'll not make the first display if I don't."

"Right you are, Cuyler. Do you like the boat?" Daniel said.

I said, "We love the boat. Thank you so much." I leaned over and kissed his cheek, and we almost capsized.

"*Gertrude!* Until you get your sea legs, I suggest you sit still while I row us to safe ground."

I just loved it when he got that stern little sound of leadership in his voice. I guess I was learning to appreciate the Victorian male's magnetic spirit and power. Well, this Victorian male's anyway. He was so sensitive beneath that cute, dominant attitude that I came unglued whenever I heard the sound of it in his speech.

"Yes, Cuyler. Sorry, Cuyler," I said.

We thanked Daniel and watched him ride his horse down the hill and disappear.

"So what's this about fish?" he said.

I rolled my eyes heavenward. "Oh, Cuyler, I *hate* them. I can't stand the sight of them."

"Well, that *is* a problem. Almost everyone I know fishes in these parts."

"You aren't going to insist I clean them or anything, are you? I can't even eat one," I said.

"Hm. A good Otsego wife should be willing to fry a skillet full of her husband's catch of the day, especially when we come to this cabin for vacations."

"Does that mean the wedding is off?" I said, looking at him with wide-eyed sadness.

"Well, I must say, I have some serious reservations now that you've told me how you feel." He did not indicate that he was kidding. I was frightened.

"You can't mean that you wouldn't marry me just because I don't like to fish?"

"A man in this area spends a great deal of time fishing, Gertrude. I think you should have at least mentioned it before now," Cuyler said.

"If it means so much to you...I suppose...I could *try* to like them."

He turned to face me, and his boyish grin proved that, once again, he had frightened me for the fun of it. "I guess that's the best a man can ask from his obliging wife."

"You had me going. I thought you meant to leave me at the altar over a simple, bug-eyed carp."

"Good heavens, woman. How shallow do you think I am? Race you back to the blanket," he said and was gone.

I chased him as best I could with the boots and the skirts, but I tripped on a root or something and fell onto the blanket.

BOOM!

It was the first of the fireworks, meant to signal the beginning of the display.

Cuddled in each other's arms, we watched the reds, blues, violets, sparkling silvers burst onto the panorama of a velvet, blue skyline. I could see the skyrockets' flare mirrored on the lake and in Cuyler's observant brown eyes. He was hypnotized by the spectacle, but I only had eyes for his wonderful face. I watched him during the whole cavalcade of spangles and sparkles.

I took the back of my fingers and stroked his cheek. "I love you," I said tenderly.

He stared at me and read my hidden meaning. He took my hand in his and kissed my palm never altering his gaze from my eyes. Our lips embraced, and the finale of bursting noisemakers echoed the explosion of passion in our hearts.

When two persons are as united in spirit as we were, they need no words. We left the supplies and strolled to cabin 1 hand in hand.

Nothing had changed there. It looked exactly the same as it had the day I left for Cooperstown with moccasins on my feet. The tulip quilt would be my love bed. The cotton sheet toga would wrap around Cuyler's body when we lay in each other's arms afterwards.

It began to rain. I could hear the thunder and see the lightening flash across the skies. There couldn't be a better excuse for staying here in the cabin until it blew over. I didn't feel uneasy either. No headache-no dizziness.

He started a small fire in the stove, and I began to undress before him. My lips parted in anticipation of his lips' caress as, one by one, I pulled the lace sleeves from my arms. The blouse fell to the floor as I walked towards him. My hands reached around his neck, and I kissed him. He lifted me in his arms and carried me to our bed.

The storm grew in intensity. So did my ardor. He looked at me warily. "Are you sure you feel all right, Gertrude?"

I gave him a long slow kiss in reply.

"I can see what you mean," he said.

He stood and removed his coat, tie, and vest. I watched as he unbuttoned each one of those cute Victorian buttons on his shirt. His chest was bronzed from the summer sun. His broad shoulders and arms were strong; their muscles taut.

I discarded my skirt and slips but stayed in my corset and stockings. I wanted him to take them from me as he had before.

I sat up on the bed and shifted my weight to my thighs, so that I could reach my arms up to his shoulders. He stood towering, so tall, above me. I ran my hands over his chest and shifted the shirt from his back. I looked lovingly into his eyes. "I want you. I love you. There'll never be anyone but you in my life. Whether it is now that I say these words or next Saturday, I mean them. I never knew love until I knew you. I want to give you pleasure and make you happy. I'll do whatever you ask of me to bring you joy and delight."

He scooped me into his arms and kissed me. "Does that mean you'll go fishing, after all?"

We laughed. It relaxed the sexual tension. His skin, against my cheek when he hugged me, was as hot as the fire in the cabin's stove, and I could smell the aroma of his wonderful cologne.

"Gertrude, I..."

"Please. Let me love you." I gazed into his eyes. They burned with a sensual light yet seemed wary. A bolt of lightening flashed its brightness into the room, and a clap of thunder shook the small cabin. It frightened me, and I hesitated.

"Are you afraid of storms?" he said, playing with my hair.

"I never used to be. I suppose the last few storms have made me apprehensive."

He sat next to me and cradled me in his safe warm arms. "Then we'll wait until the storm is over, or until it at least stops exploding in our heads. I don't want you nervous tonight. Not tonight. I'll hold you and ease your fears until it stops."

I closed my eyes and rested my head against his arm. I *did* feel secure. The next sensation I had was not of my lover's warm embrace. When I opened my eyes, I saw the glare of my computer screen, and Jim Cooper typing furiously.

Chapter Eighteen

"No," I screamed. "No!"

Jim Cooper heard my voice and came into the bedroom. He quickly shielded his eyes and groped for the robe that I'd left on the bed. "Goodness, Trudy. You look like something out of a Frederick's of Hollywood catalogue. Here, put this on."

He threw the floral robe to me. I was in too much shock to do anything but hold it in front of me.

"No! No! I want to go back! You *can't* do this to me. I insist you place me back in time this instant!" The Victorian lady was here. Gertrude—not Trudy—had returned.

"Ooh, I love the Victorian sound in your speech. How far did you go back? Let me guess. A century ago by the look of the corset. Now take it easy. I'll explain everything." He tried to come near to comfort me, but I recoiled.

I began sobbing and screaming. "*How dare you do this to me.* I was to be married in a week."

"Married? That's wonderful. Do I know him?" said Jim. There was no way to shock this man.

"How should I know? When was the last time you were in 1897?" I said.

"Well, I was never in 1897, but I was once in 1890. Met a great guy who fished up here and used this very cabin."

"I think he's my fiancé."

"Cuyler? Well that *is* something. He told me he was born to be a bachelor. I told you you were beautiful. Guess Cuyler thinks so too, huh?"

I flung the robe into his face. "What are you doing here? Why am I here? How do I get back? What are you doing to my computer?"

"Look, just calm down and control yourself. I know it's hard to adjust. You'll return to 1897 as soon as the storm has passed. As you can see, we're having the same storm. I should shut off the computer." He sat in front of it. I tried to breathe in and out slowly and remain calm.

"By the way, what secret screen name do you use with Wainwright? I've been trying everything under the sun, and I think he's getting suspicious."

"Wainwright?"

"He's been after you day and night. You haven't answered him. I've been trying to think of something to say besides: 'Trudy went on a hike;' or 'Trudy went for a swim'.' I don't think he believes me. He's *really* hot for you."

"Why are you here?" I said.

"I thought I might make things easier for you when you returned by keeping your loved ones at ease about where you've been for several weeks. Your friend, Jennifer, called twice, and she believed me. Your mother thinks I've kidnapped you, so I'd call her storm or no storm. Once your father threatened to drive up here and hunt for you. But, good old Wainwright has sent you tons of e-mail and tried to IM you every night. I guess you're 'Trudy112,' but you must have said something to him about changing it."

I started to cry. "What's going on?"

"Trudy...you've gone back to the time you dreamed about, and, apparently, found the man you were in love with before you left. I read the little poem you wrote to Cuyler, the one by your bed, so I figured that's where you were. Sam and I travel too. This cabin is a portal to the past," Jim said.

"May I have a drink?" I said. I sat on the couch, and he made me a rum and Diet Coke. I reached for the drink and halted. I placed it on the table. "Could I have some tea? I'd feel better with a nice cup of hot tea. I don't drink anymore."

"Sure." He whistled as he boiled the hot water and readied the cup and tea bag. He handed the soothing beverage to me and sat across from me.

"This cabin has been in the Cooper family for years. As far as we know, our ancestors have always traveled through time. Until two weeks ago, we never knew anyone else could do it. Our fathers have traveled everywhere and recorded their travels in several surviving journals that we still write in to this day. Sam goes in the summer months; I go in the winter months. He's been traveling to the 1700s for years. He has a sweet woman there named Abigail and has been married to her for fourteen years. Every summer he returns to her. The two of them have three children. They live in a log cabin on this very spot."

I remembered Cuyler's shock when I arrived in his bed. "How does he explain his disappearances? Doesn't she wonder where he goes, and why he leaves her with no protection?"

"She can shoot pretty straight for a woman. He tells her he's trapping. Then, so that he doesn't actually have to bring them home, he tells her that he has sold them and brings the money home."

"He lies. And you? Where do you go in the winter?"

"I don't have a woman like Sam does. I'm still looking. I go whenever I want to find antiques for my business, or sometimes I just do research. I can usually travel back with some light pieces. When I travel in the winter, I try to go somewhere warm," Jim said.

"You can bring things back and forth?" I said.

"Whatever you have on your person will travel with your body."

I sipped the soothing tea. "You can go *anywhere?* Like where?" I said.

"Anywhere. If your heart wants to be there, you'll go at the change of seasons: any time period—any location. Sam and I stay close to home so that the transfer is rapid. We have a business to run, you know."

"Then where's Sam? Why isn't he here if I am?"

"During a bad storm your molecular structure gets all scrambled," he said. "If you are near the portal, you'll come back so that you're not interfering with the atmosphere. If you're not near the gateway, you'll experience sickness."

"So that's why I was so sick during the bad storms, yet fine when they ended. If I stay away from the portal during storms, I won't travel back."

"Correct. Sam deliberately stays away from his bed when a storm comes up. It's worth the sickness to be with his beloved Abby as much as he can. He tells her that he's going to the barn to settle the livestock who might be frightened by the storm."

The Internet clicked and needed a reply. I walked over to it. It was 'Prince Charming' all right.

"My new screen name is 'Snow White.' " I sat at the computer and typed.

Jim said, "And of *course,* Wainwright is 'Prince Charming!' " He smacked his head for stupidly forgetting the children's story.

I typed, "Hello, Prince Charming. How are things at the castle?" and e-mailed it to him.

I received an immediate IM. "Snow White? Where the hell have you been? I was close to buying airplane tickets to find out what had happened to you."

I smiled at his concern then switched our conversation into a private chat room. I typed, "I went hiking. I've been having a wonderful time. Sorry if I frightened you. How are things in merry old London?"

"Not as much fun as they would have been if you were here. I did spend some time researching the medieval time period for you. How about a good sword and sex romance? I've got a great hero for you—a heroine, too."

I started to cry again. I was home, and the transition had been too quick for me. I thought about my true hero holding air and half-naked on our tulip quilt. What he must be going through. At least he would believe my story now. I wondered if he would place it in his "Tales of Toddsville" some day: "There I sat, holding the woman I loved, when she just disappeared into thin air. Wondering what had occurred, I lit the end of a rolled up newspaper with the tip of my cigar and cautiously inspected the cabin." I hoped Cuyler would wait before going home tonight. He'd have too, wouldn't he? He couldn't go home without me.

I typed my response to Wainwright, "That sounds wonderful. I haven't used that time period since my first book. Go ahead and investigate if you want to, friend. I will be out of touch for a while. I met some other campers here, and we're going camping. Real camping. Don't worry about me. I'll take my survival kit and band-aids. Be careful, Bruce. I'll see you around. Yours, Snow White."

"Well, just remember to stay away from those black snakes," he said. "And dwarves. And don't bite any red delicious, if you know what I mean. Yours, Prince Charming."

That was the end of our correspondence. I glared at Jim. "All right, what's the gimmick? How long have I got in Toddsville? Can I stay if I want to?" I said.

He dragged his hand across his mouth and squeezed his lips while raising his eyebrows. It seemed he was saying, "Well, here goes."

"The portal opens during the summer and winter solstices and the fall and spring equinoxes," he said. "Now, if you choose one for travel, you must return the following season. There's no getting around that as far as we can tell by our journals. Whether you are near the portal or not—whoosh—you're gone. Actually, this came in handy once for one of my relatives. He was about to be hanged by a judge for stealing the man's wife's affections and trying to run away with her, when suddenly he was gone. Swoosh. Anyway, this means you can travel twice a year and return twice. The winter months are horrible traveling time, and I wouldn't advise trying it. One journal entry talks about frostbite and catching pneumonia. Which brings up another bit of info. Yes, you can get sick, and yes—if it is your time to die in this life—you'll die there instead of here. So, just like real life, you'll never have any idea when your time is up. Of course, you might have found your slot," Jim said.

"My slot?" I went to the still warm tea kettle and refreshed my hot beverage.

"If you're really lucky, you'll find the spot you were meant to fill. You see, unlike those time travel movies, you *can* affect the past. If you move things away from their real juncture with fate, all records after the move will convert," he said.

"So, if I had my picture taken in 1897, it'll be housed in the NYSHA archives?"

"If you have filled your slot, yes. This means that you actually were born to travel back in time and meet your destiny while fulfilling others. Not a reincarnation of another person, you understand. You were born in 1970 to be the woman he would marry in 1897. Do you see what I mean?"

"You mean to tell me that all through time—from the beginning—people were meant to fill spots before they were born?" I said.

"We think Sam was. Sam told me that until he showed, Abby had been the twenty-year-old unmarried maid of the town. Now she is happily married and the mother of three lovely children."

"How do you know whether you're filling the time slot or just cruising through?" I sat comfortably on the couch and shook every time the lightening flashed outside the cabin.

"Lots of ways. Primarily by doing research. You have a wedding date planned, right? All right, when you return in the fall, do some research. If you go down to the NYSHA records and find out that Cuyler married a Gertrude Johnson in 1897—it's you. Before your visit, Cuyler would be listed as a bachelor;

however, if you find a wedding date for him, and it has your name on that record, you've found your slot."

I thought about the boat. I stood up, and, unafraid of the storm, ran out of the front door. Jim ran after me as if I were crazy. I didn't care. If Daniel had given us that same boat, the name might now be visible, and I would have my proof. I slipped in the mud and almost tore open the flesh on my feet, but I *had* to know.

I watched as the wind rippled the waters around the boat. It howled through the trees, like an angry ogre, at my audacity. I moved closer to the edge of the lake. Jim screamed for me to be careful and mind the lightening, but I waited, and slowly the boat's backside hobbled into view. There it was. Much clearer than before—TRUDY—but still not as bright and beautiful as it was when it was given to us as a wedding gift.

I shouted to Jim. "What if you've left a mark or a sign? The boat docked at the ridge of this lake was a gift from Daniel Watson to Cuyler and me for our wedding. It was just given to us today. He's the only one who calls me Trudy in 1897. The boat was painted with my name on the side. When I saw it before, I could not make out the painted name. Now look. The boat rotting in the water tonight is the *same boat*."

He told me to hurry back to the cabin before I chilled, and I obeyed him. Oh, how excited I was! I had the proof.

"Well, it's a very clear and identifiable clue," he said, as he poured me another cup of tea. "Congratulations. It doesn't happen to all of us. I told you I knew him. We spent a whole summer solstice fishing and chasing babes who came up for the resort's activities," Jim said.

"Chasing babes?"

"Sorry, Cuyler. We chased and flirted, but none ever caught his eye. I was not so choosy," he smiled. "That's why he told me, just before I left in the fall, that he had given up all possible hope of finding his kind of woman."

"Did he ever tell you what he was looking for?" I said.

"Sure. You." Jim had this habit of smiling with his eyes first, then his lips. "I was hoping you'd transport and meet him. You see, you've filled the heart of a lonely man. Isn't that worth traveling and searching?" he said.

"Well, the marriage idea was just a way to solve the problem of my showing up in his cabin's bed half-clad." I chuckled at the memory. "You should have seen that one. I'll never forget it as long as I live. Which reminds me."

He interrupted, "If you've filled a slot, can you research your time there? You see, I don't know much about this. If anyone did find their slot, we have no permanent record of it. You *can* find out what happened to the people you've met-though I've got to warn you-it would not be a happy task to find the truth about the death of your loved ones and friends. It's ironically prophetic. Sam is a different matter. No permanent records. He travels once a year, so I suppose that limits you, as well. It might not be the perfect setup, but you can at least travel to your slot twice a year. Of course, you don't have to."

"You mean you have a choice?" I said.

"Sam does. He chooses to go in the summer. If you don't want to fulfill your own destiny, and stay unhappy and unfulfilled, that's up to you. I'm beginning to think I have no slot. I'm going to have to live my life on present soil," Jim said.

"If you can choose to change things, can't you choose your own destiny?"

"You can change things like, for instance, the books may say that Cuyler ran a farm, but, you talk him into buying a store. The record book, after your interference, will change like a domino game for not only the man you marry, but your influence will alter others' lives, as well. The shove of one detail will cavalcade the rest into focus. Like the name on the boat. It *can be* rather spiritual. Let's say that you save a boy from drowning, and he becomes a famous scientist who invents—ah—a part for computers, or something like that; or, you nurse someone back to health, and through your kindness they save someone else's life. You could encourage and support people towards their true calling in life. As a matter of fact, if it weren't for time travelers, nothing would ever have been invented, and we'd still be living in caves."

"That far back?" I was in awe.

"Uh-huh. What I've been trying to do with your computer is to find the other holes," he said.

"Holes?"

"The atmosphere around the earth is like Swiss cheese. It has small and large holes, like black holes, spaced around the globe."

"You mean like those people who disappeared in the Bermuda Triangle might have time traveled instead?" I said.

"Check when they dropped out of this world, and I'll bet it was during the change of seasons. When the earth and the seasons make their change, the hole opens and out you drop. Well, not everyone. I've been Internetting the known travelers, the ancient families who've traveled, and I've been finding some great information. I've taken a toy globe and marked the holes that exist in Europe. Before the summer is over, I'll have every continent. When one traveling family member finds that he has a 'brother' in America, the communication explodes. I tell him about my cabin; he tells me about his castle, and then informs me of a hole in Scotland he knows. There are more in America I'm sure, but I haven't recorded them all."

"But you only travel close to your portal?" I said.

"We try to stay close most of the time. The portals and the traveling time will differ if you do long distance transports. You can get a mean jet lag from it. Generally—from what I'm hearing—it's best to travel in your own time and then go through the portal. So, if I want to travel to Camelot, I would go to England, find the portal, and then travel to the past from there. Actually, I was thinking it might make a nice winter trip. I'd love to come back with a suit of armor. Who knows, maybe I'm Lancelot? I'm jealous to have the knowledge that you have, Trudy. You and Sam know where you belong."

"So, if I'm hearing you correctly, my life in 1997 mirrors my longevity in 1897."

"By, Jove, she's got it. The river of time keeps flowing, and you can hop into it wherever you want."

"And you say your forefathers have been doing this for some time?"

He snickered. "Yes, in fact, one of my forefathers had several women in several time periods. He was married in his own life and transported twice a year. Once to 1600 to meet his Indian woman, and once to a school marm in the 1700s. He says in his journal writings, that he even traveled by ship to Europe every other year to go to an Italian contessa he had in the 1400s, and his 1600s Irish temptress whom he wooed and won. In those days, husbands could be gone for long periods of time, and no one ever questioned it."

"Where was his slot?" I said.

"I'm not sure he ever found it," he said.

"What would that mean then?"

"Probably that his own time was his true life and wife. Or that his days will be invaded by and changed by a future time traveler. Oh, and that's another myth I should clear up right away. Forget *The Time Machine.* You can't travel uncharted waters on the river. In other words, you can't go into the future because it doesn't exist in time yet. It hasn't been written so you can't become part of it. Nix the idea of finding that weird looking Cooperstown of 2080. Can't happen. Einstein's theory you know. You can't hear a voice in space that hasn't spoken a word."

"Well, that makes sense, I guess. Still, I have another question," I said.

"Shoot, Mrs. Carr."

"How do you handle finances? I mean, I have all this money in 1997 that would be so useful to those in 1897. I want to help."

"I understand. You're a kind person, Trudy. Unselfish. Most travelers want to take money so that they can buy castles and property. We handle it a couple of different ways. We buy a lot of antique money and store it away. Come home with coins from one time period to help someone on another trip. I've been saving all sorts of coins and so have my ancestors. We keep it in a safety deposit box. Becomes a hobby like other antique collecting. If we can, we open bank accounts with whatever coinage, gold, or silver seems to be needed. Man, you should see the interest. Sam opened an account in the 1700s with some fur-trapping money he had, and when I went to Cooperstown in 1890, the account was in the millions. Like I said, you're the first non-family member that has traveled. If you want, I'll write you a special letter, and you can dip into the Cooper funds all you want. I'm sure you're good for it."

My heart leaped. "Do you really mean it? Where's my mail?"

He motioned to the box by the door. I ran to it and tugged at the tape. I found, amid the catalogues from Chadwick's of Boston, my check from Jennifer.

I opened the envelope and asked him for a pen. The check was for ten thousand dollars. "Write the letter. I'll sign this check over to you. It's for ten thousand dollars."

"That'll do it. And don't be thrifty, either. Take as much as you want. Sam was planning on entering more money this summer. So, the balance by now should be way into the millions. It was three million in 1890."

We did the writing and handed each other the notes. I placed the letter in my bodice. Oh, I could just see Cuyler's face when he saw a letter with another man's mark on it in his favorite bosom. A letter from a man handing me all of his money.

"You say that I'm the first woman whom you know of to travel through the portal?" I said.

He smiled. "If any of my fore-mothers did, they didn't mention it to anyone. And they never told father. I suspicion that a spinster aunt in 1886 traveled because she always was gone in the summer. Most people in Cooperstown leave in the winter not the summer. I wish she had told us. She was a religious woman and probably didn't want anyone to know what a wild time she was having with the Mohicans or something. I can see that something's bothering you. What is it?"

"If Sam can make children, can I give birth to them?" I said.

I had thrown him a tough question. He went and opened another beer-his third. Finally, he said, "There's no question that you can physically make one, I don't know if you can transport one."

"You said that I could take and bring back anything that was on my person. A baby is rather attached," I said.

"You'd have to travel back during the pregnancy at some point," he said. "Whether it would have an affect on the unborn fetus, I just don't know."

I was angry now. "But, *I* don't change when *I* come back. I mean, I gain a little weight from Johanna's cooking, and my hair grows a little longer and all. My attitude about love and living is altered, but my body isn't."

"You've discovered that your biological cycles are the same?" Jim said.

"As healthy as ever."

"I suppose there'd be no problem then. Of course, you're taking a risk. You would be the first, I suspect, and the consequences would be surreal."

"I know. I've thought about that."

"The best thing to do, in my opinion, would be to avoid it. If you can't, then I'd keep the child in one time or the other. It might be too hard for the kid, and besides, nothing says he'd be a traveler anyway. Keep him at Grandma's house for the three months you're away. If you deliver in *your* time, I wouldn't tell Cuyler at all. It might be too hard on him to know that he can never see his own kid."

"Then you're saying that Cuyler can't travel forward?" I asked.

"First, you must have a view of the time period. How can he fixate on something he's never envisioned? Secondly, the river has already swallowed him. He is reflected in the glimmer of the water. How could he come to the bank of the river? He has no understanding of time travel. He would have to imagine everything."

"Well, I was in the same boat on your river once. I had to view the past from my imagination. There were no pictures in 1600, so how can you bring that to your vision anymore than Cuyler could imagine 1990? If his heart were set on coming forward, why couldn't he?"

"You can't go to the future," he said. "It's never been done. Besides, do you think he could handle the changes? He can't fill a slot that hasn't been created. How can he go beyond his time?"

"You're telling me that I can. I was just a sparkle in my great-grandfather's eyes, so how could I exist beyond my time?"

"All right, Trudy." He threw his hands into the air in exasperation. "I suppose, I don't have all the answers. Sam and I research our brains out but can't explain everything even to ourselves. That's why I'm e-mailing all over the world. Maybe when you get back, I'll have the answers. No one has done it. That's all I know now," Jim said.

"Because no one ever tried. Cuyler isn't some Indian in a cave, or a Barbarian, or a Viking. He's an intelligent man who has managed to accept much of this considering his time frame. He *loves* me." I started to cry again. "If he could, might he not try?"

"I can see that this is too much for you, and the storm has reached its peek. Call your mother."

He returned to the computer to "play" with his portals in Spain, and I went to the phone. I dialed my mother's number.

"Hello, Mom. It's me, Trudy. How was the wedding?"

"Oh, my God, Trudy. Dad, it's Trudy," Mom said.

I heard his voice in the background. "Where the hell's she been?"

"I don't know. I'll ask her. Trudy, you've had your father and I worried sick. Where've you been that you can't call your mother?"

I restrained the giggle that was creeping into my voice. I wanted to say, "I've been in 1897, and I met a great guy. I'm getting married next Saturday. Sorry, my dear blind mother, but you can tell your drunken and abusive husband that. Say 'hi' to Sis for me. I'm going to church regularly with my fiancé and his mother. I'm eating terrific food, and I look much better than shit because I'm ecstatically happy for the first time in my life. Oh, yes, if Daddy asks tell him my man owns his own hardware store and coal dealership. No, I'm not pregnant."

I did not say any of those things. I said, "I went hiking with the man who owns these cabins."

"You went hiking? In the woods? With a strange man?" she said.

Dad said, "What strange man? I told you something was going on."

"Yes, but you don't need to worry. He's married and has three children."

"Well, that sounds better. He's married, Dad, with three kids. Did you spray yourself with insect repellent, dear?" Mom said.

I sprayed myself with vanilla scent, and Cuyler loved it. "I surely did, Mom. And I had a survival kit, too. With band-aids and everything. We cook on an open fire the fish we catch each day."

"FISH? Trudy. Since when do you eat fresh fish? I've been trying to get you to eat fish for a whole childhood."

Since Cuyler said that Otsego women helped clean their husband's catch of the day. "Well, I have to, Mom. There isn't much else but berries."

"So, she's eating weird stuff, huh? Probably smoking the weeds, too." Daddy in the background again.

"Don't eat any berries, dear, or toadstools," Mom said.

"Is she sick? What's the matter with her stools?" said Dad.

"*Toad* stools. Honestly, your father's hearing is going. Did you meet any nice, young men?" The lilt at the end of the question was flirtatious.

"As a matter of fact, I did. His name is Cuyler," I said.

"Cuyler? What a nice name. Is he your age?"

"One year older," I said.

"Well, older men are better anyway," Mom said.

"How would you know?" Dad said.

"Drink your beer and shut up. I'm trying to talk long distance here," Mother said loudly and then changed to a softer tone. "Well, this *Cuyler*, what does he do for a living?"

"He owns his own store in Milford, Mom." I knew she'd never take the time to check.

"A business man? Well, that's nice. Already established, is he? Are you being nice to him?"

I remembered gently stroking my lover's mustache. "I'm being *very* nice to him, Mom."

"You're not boring him with any of your silly romance novels? Remember, dear, men don't like women who talk continually."

I thought of the endless stories he told on our daily trips. "No, Mother, I'm letting him do all the talking."

"And remember, men don't like women who are smarter than they are? Does he like you?" she said.

I thought of Cuyler acknowledging my intelligence as a personality priority over the other women he'd met. I also remembered his accessment of my corset. "Yes, Mom, I think he likes me."

"Well, marry him. Don't wait a second longer. Drug him if you have to. Your biological clock is going to start sending you signals soon, you know!"

"She's marrying someone? The married guy with three kids?" Dad said.

"No, he owns a store in Milbrook," Mom said.

See, I told you.

"I didn't say I was marrying him, Mom. I said, I met him while I was hiking, and we got to talking. I think we'll join a campers' group and camp for the rest of the summer. So, this may be the last call you get for a while."

"She's going camping, dear. Don't drink any of the water. Take bottled."

Oh, right, I was going to lug bottled spring water around in a backpack.

"Okay, Mom." The storm was quieting its intensity. "Look, I've got to go. See you when I get back in September."

"All right. Have a nice time. Send postcards if you can. Dad and I love you."

I thought of the Smith and Telfer postcards I had seen for sale in Putt's studio. Oh, boy, would that be cute. A picture of Cooperstown in the 1890s and a message on the back:

Been to the balloon races July 4th. Saw fireworks. Going to the parades and an ice cream social next week. Married Cuyler last Saturday. Presbyterian Church-Cooperstown! Honeymooning in the Cooper cabins. Having a grand time in 1897. See you soon! Love,

Gertrude

"Okay, Mom. I love you, too. Tell Dad to layoff the beer, and I love him. Bye."

I perused the evening sky from the cabin window. "Why do we fall back when it storms? If the portals open to let us in and shut to lock us there, how can a storm bring us back?"

His features were lit by the bright light of the computer screen. "The atmosphere goes off kilter for a while, and the gateway opens a crack, until the alignment shuts it again. Whatever falls out, will go back when it closes. Remember, it only occurs when you're near the archway. Because you are not synchronized for the natural way of the earth in your new time period, the atmosphere spits you out until it's been cleansed, and then puts you back as you were. Actually, you'll fit more evenly with the natural world then. A sort of peaceful contentment comes over you." He was glued to the computer. "*Rome A.D!* Now that's one I'd like to visit." He had found another friend in Italy.

He was correct. I had never felt better than after the two storms. I had hummed Cuyler's tune in the hotel bath and eaten voraciously when we got back to the homestead.

I was quiet, and Jim noticed. He came over to me and gave me a brotherly hug. "I'm sorry. I've been quick with you, and it's your first time. Of course, you have many questions. Some I can't even answer. Sam will understand. He'll have lots of time to talk with you and answer the queries of your heart. He'll be more sensitive than I. I'm just looking for a little fun and some choice antiques. It's more to you, isn't it?"

I looked at him, the tears filling my eyes. "Much more."

He handed me his hanky. "You really love him, don't you?"

That did it. His shoulder would have to do. The tears were flowing. "Yes. When I came back tonight, I thought I'd never see him again."

"I'm glad you're so happy. You look great. I can tell 1897 becomes you. Your eyes are sparkling, and you have such a strong will to live, an energy force you didn't have before. You seem alive—not like some Xerox copy of Gertrude Johnson. Authentic. Real. Caring and compassionate. Shall I tell Jennifer the one about the camping trip?"

"Don't I have time to call her?" I hadn't realized the thunder was so distant.

He looked into my face with gentle compassion. "Got my letter?"

I looked down into my bodice. He did not. "Yes. Thanks."

When I looked back to say goodbye to him, I was once again in our cabin. I felt wonderful, but I did not see Cuyler. Frantically, I searched the room. Then I heard it. Soft coughing. A gasp. I turned the corner and peeked.

Cuyler was staring out of the doorway and onto the porch as though he were watching the storm subside. He was making those little sounds in his throat that men make when they're crying.

"Cuyler?" I said softly.

He turned with trepidation— afraid it was a dream. I waited for it to become reality.

He walked across the room, staring at what must have appeared to be an apparition, and then held me tightly to his chest. We kissed as if the very air we needed to breathe was in each other's lips.

"Where were you?" he said.

"I just took a hop back to my own time because of the storm. It only happens when you're in the station of transport—so to speak. When I got sick before, I didn't travel. When you aren't near the doorway, you won't go back, but you feel lousy. It's all because of the storm. I have *so* much to tell you, but not now. Let's go home. I want to go home now." I cuddled against his chest, feeling the security I always felt when I was close to him.

"I think I can find my way home in the dark, but the roads will be muddy. Perhaps, we'll try to make it as far as Cooperstown. If it looks dangerous, we'll stay at the Carr Hotel."

We found the soggy remains of our picnic and bid goodbye to the 'Trudy.' I smiled at the little boat. "Thank you," I said to her.

Samuel was having a fit in the small lean-to stable Isaac had erected near the cabins. Cuyler calmed the poor animal and then hitched him to the soaked tea cart. I went into the cabin and found a towel. Drying the water from the leather upholstery gave me time to decide what to say on the ride home.

Carefully, Cuyler trotted our horse down the hills, and we soon found the main road to Cooperstown. The air was warm and smelled fresh and invigorating. I'd never felt so alive in my life. Of course, that was the pay off for the chaos of the storm, wasn't it?

I began *my* lecture with a general science of time travel lesson, trying to explain it as simply as I could. He listened to every word I said, and—if he'd had any doubts before—he believed me now.

"You mean you can come through the holes twice in a year?" he said.

"Yes, once in the summer and fall, and once in the winter and spring. You go through one to the past and travel back in the next. So, I'll be leaving sometime at the end of September—just as I originally thought."

"But, you *could* come back in December?"

"I could, but it's considered risky if you're going to a particularly cold climate. There's the possibility of frostbite or pneumonia. You'd have to come to the cabin in the snow to get me. It'd be around Christmas. If you want me to, I'll do it."

He was quiet for a while. Pondering everything I had said.

I launched into the stories of Sam and the other Coopers. I told him about the possible risk in having children. I reminded him that I'd return every summer.

"At least we know the truth now," I said. "I was meant to love you and to marry you. I'll be with you for as long as you'll have me. Every summer."

"What about my traveling to your time?" he said.

"Well, I put it to Jim, and he argued against it. He said you'd become part of this time, and, therefore, could not travel in it; but he wasn't sure. He was looking into the possibilities of traveling around the world via different foreign locales."

"Jim Cooper? That name sounds familiar." I could not see his face in the dark, but I would have loved to see the evading-the truth-expression his mother knew so well.

I said, "You should. The two of you spent some time together in 1890 fishing and checking out the summer babes."

"Excuse me. Why would I be interested in newborns?" Nice try, Cuyler.

"Don't play innocent, pal. You remember Jim, don't you?"

"Vaguely." Even in the dark, I could tell his free hand was pulling on one side of his handle bar mustache.

"And *he* had some luck with some Gibson girl beach bunnies vacationing around Otsego Lake."

"Oh, yes, *that* Jim Cooper. Well, I just went along to watch how he handled himself with the young ladies. I can assure you, Gertrude, I was not in the slightest bit interested in any of the 'babes.' I told you that, until you came along, I found women boring. Wait a minute. How do you know all this? Are you telling me that he was from *your* time?"

"Installed my computer for me. Used the same cabin to fly the friendly skies. Are you changing the subject?" I said.

"What do you mean—computer?" Yes, he was.

I could see Cooperstown ahead, and he was traveling right through it. We went east and turned up one long hill heading through the pitch of night to our family's home. I didn't like this route. The road was like a roller coaster, and it would take us passed the infamous "red house."

We tried to make the trip less frightening by talking about my new-found information.

"He told me that you decided to become a bachelor because none of the girls were your type. Is that true?" I said.

"Precisely. I think I made that perfectly clear when I met you in my bedroom several weeks ago."

Then we switched the topic before the inevitable questions were asked. I discussed the wedding plans. We chatted about the gifts we'd received from all the families. Sally and Mrs. Sloat had been in and out of the homestead discussing their gowns with Johanna and helping her choose decorations. We still had one week to go until the final vows were spoken. There were parties to attend, the rehearsal dinner, the preparations for the reception at Cuyler's home, not to mention a household to establish and a business to run. When all that was done, we could plan the honeymoon in the cabin.

"I hope it doesn't storm next weekend or, for that matter, all next week," he said.

"Oh, yes, how *did* it feel to lose the woman you were making love to," I said.

"It was *not* amusing." He hesitated. "I...felt...as if someone had wrenched my heart from my chest."

"I screamed loudly and demanded to be returned immediately, if that makes you feel any better," I said.

"I suppose, we'd better check the Farmer's Almanac or the Freeman's Journal to see whether there's a possibility of another storm during our honeymoon," he said.

"If there is, we'll just move to another cabin. I wouldn't want disturbed again," I said.

He put a comforting arm around my waist. "That's my idea too. Let's have as much of a good time as we can. I love you; you love me. The family is sending us to a happy life even if it will be lived one season at a time."

I checked on my letter tucked snugly between my breasts. "I have some other wedding surprises for you. We'll have to make a trip to Cooperstown tomorrow, followed by a trip to the Milford bank later the same day. It's vitally important."

I would follow Jim's advice and dip wholeheartedly into that bank account. When I returned to 1997, I'd see that the Coopers were reimbursed. I would see that the Carrs were repaid for their charity, the homestead refurnished, and the church given a fresh coat of paint. The two women with the sad tale of loss would find a bountiful check delivered to the reverend the day of our wedding. Cuyler would be repaid with more than my love. I'd see to it that this man wanted for nothing for the rest of his life. Call it my dowry if you want.

I had nothing when I met him, and he gave to me without a shrug of worry. He'd changed his whole life for me. I'd see that Cuyler was taken care of forever. All of his dreams would come true. He could build that house in Milford if he wanted. He had never asked anything from me, but he would marry into money—big time.

Jim had said that we were sent back to fill a slot in an empty life and to make dreams come true. We should aid and support every one of our loved ones and even show kindness to the strangers that came before us. Who knows? The woman with the hard-working teenage son may be nurturing the next philanthropist or president. This young man could be a reverend, or an attorney, or save a man's life in World War I. Even be the grandfather of the doctor who saved my father's life in Viet Nam.

I had, at last, found my destiny and my love. I knew where I belonged—where I was happy—in Toddsville next to Cuyler. And if it took years, I would find a way to stay here for the rest of my days.

Jim and Sam didn't know everything. If I were destined to fill this slot, then I'll be damned if I'm going to fill it just once a year. Even if I get frostbite, I'd find a way to return in the winter. And, as soon as we started housekeeping in Milford, I would teach Cuyler all about 1997. Then, maybe he'll get the vision he needs to find his way to me. I want a son to give Cuyler. The heir he needs to keep his homestead going. I want that life to stand as living proof of our love. Someone who will go beyond us into the future—into the 2040 Cooperstown.

I'll continue to write too. I'll buy tons of paper and drag the typewriter to Milford. While I work on Cuyler's stories, I'll research the Sam and Abigail tale, if I can, in the local libraries here. That romance would make a great novel. People don't have to be rich and glamorous to have the best love stories, do they?

That's just the beginning. Jim Cooper has some great stories in that journal of his. I'm sure he won't mind my rewriting them into several great romance novels since we're from the same time traveling clan. I'll make Jennifer so happy she'll cry. The more the money flows, the bigger and better store for Cuyler. In fact, someday he can just quit altogether. We'll spend the time we've been allotted riding through Cooperstown, picnicking at our cabin retreat, going to church, helping the poor, and living for all our time in the homestead at Toddsville.

I've got to make it happen.

"My, my, Gertrude, you seem deep in thought," Cuyler said. "We're just turning westward and will be home soon. What's on your mind?"

I squeezed his arm. "Oh, I'm just thinking about our time together, our wedding, and our future—our wonderful, wonderful future. I can't wait until Saturday. I'm rather glad we kept getting interrupted all the time. I want next Saturday evening to make history. Our own history. One you won't divulge to *The Freeman's Journal*, Cuyler."

He laughed. "Why, Gertrude. I've only just begun. I have so many stories for you. I've been holding back so that I might entertain you for a longer period of time. Sort of keep you in suspense, so to speak."

Mental note: buy new ribbon for the typewriter, too.

Chapter Nineteen

I awoke Monday morning with the energy of a woman on a mission. I had decided to take care of all the banking business today so that I could give the money to Reverend McBride at our last Monday night session. I had wanted to give it to him next Saturday, because we would not be in church Sunday morning, and that would keep our gift anonymous. It had occurred to me to get rid of the money soon. To hold it one full week would make me too nervous.

I was downstairs with Johanna before the others. I boiled my own hot water and took it to my room to bathe.

I noticed that my hair was long enough to pull up and tried to do so failing miserably. I ran to the kitchen, and Johanna helped me fix my hair with some hair pins she had in her room. It was only an illusion of a Victorian style, but it would do. I helped her make breakfast in return. I wanted to surprise Cuyler with my Gibson girl look.

Mother Carr and Cuyler joined us and remarked about my appearance. The fire had not harmed the growth of my hair his mother exclaimed. I smiled at Cuyler, and he lowered his eyes and simpered. It seemed as if I would live with his story for the rest of my days.

I followed him to the barn and watched him milk the cows. The new hired hands would start tomorrow allowing Cuyler time to show them how he wanted the farm handled. I spoke with him about my plans for the day.

"I want to go into town and stop at the First National Bank this morning." I touched the paper hidden in the top of my corset.

"Why? I don't have an account there," he said.

"I have inherited some money from my mother's will." His gaze probed for the joke, and his right eyebrow lifted. He shook his head and said, "Am I supposed to understand this one?"

"No. You're supposed to agree with *me* today. Anything I say I wish to do; you must agree to. Then we have to ride to Milford and take care of another matter. You can open shop, and I'll see to the upstairs. We see Reverend McBride tonight, don't we?" I said.

He nodded his head as the cow sighed.

"Then maybe tomorrow we could talk with Daniel and Mrs. Sloat before we go to work. We're working this week, aren't we?"

"I was planning to start today. I'll need to break in those new men tomorrow, so I won't be going to Milford Tuesday. You can go into Cooperstown on your own, Gertrude. I'll prepare the rig, and you can talk and shop all you want."

I was frightened and excited about my plans, but would he appreciate my interference? He couldn't refuse a girl's dowry, could he?

When he had freshened his hands and clothes, we hitched Samuel to the tea cart and maneuvered the hilly road to Cooperstown.

"You're a mystery today, Gertrude. That grin and the bizarre twinkle in your eye," he said.

"You could use another rig and a team of men to help you with the coal business, couldn't you?" I asked.

He lost his carefree mood. "It will be difficult. I could bring in a variety of coal, heap it into large mountains down at the depot in Milford. Then, when the orders come in, I could let my men do the hard work and deliver it while I ran the store."

"Then you need to start looking for some men and a new rig. You did say you wanted to build a house in Milford for us, didn't you?"

"That will come eventually, Gertrude. One thing at a time."

"I noticed some nice property near the train station. Why don't we build there? I'm sure I could help you find a lovely design."

He stared at me, and Samuel made that noise horses make with their lips when they're hot and tired. The record-high heat was unbearable.

"Are you sure that when you 'flashed back,' or whatever it was you did, that it didn't do something to your mind?" He touched his right temple with his index finger.

I slapped him good naturedly on his arm.

We were at the bank by nine o'clock. I told him to wait outside for me. He saw his friends by the fence of the Mohican Club. They were discussing something in *The Freeman's Journal* and smoking cigars.

"Are you sure you don't need me?" His eyes were riveted to

the men's body language.

"I won't be long. Go over and talk. Maybe I'll check in with Sally and Mrs. Sloat if we have the time now."

He went his merry way. I took a deep breath and prayed for a woman teller. I walked into the bank. It was richly decorated, and an antique compared to the rest of the town. It had the same style and grandeur as did the Fenimore Hotel. There were awnings of forest green on all the windows. The brass on the door, and everywhere inside, had been polished to a sheen.

I saw a male clerk counting money and went to him. I unbuttoned my blouse, away from anyone's eyesight, and retrieved my note.

"Yes, Ma'm, may I help you?" He had beady eyes under the rim of his cap.

"If you'd be so kind. I'd like to withdraw thirty-thousand dollars from your bank."

He gulped. "Do you have an account with us?"

"No, but my benefactor does, and he's asked you to help me in this matter. Here's his note. You can check his signature with the one on his records."

He read the note. "I know Mr. Cooper quite well. As a matter of fact, his was the first account I opened when I took this job. He was here several summers ago, as I recall." The man smiled. "We had quite a time that summer." He had lost track and blushed. "Yes, well, I haven't seen him around lately."

"He travels extensively." I couldn't resist the inside joke.

"Well, everything is in order. Shall I write a note or do you want cash?"

He had me there. "Cash will be fine. I'm taking it to my bank in Milford. I'll be living there soon. I'm to be married Saturday."

"You're Cuyler's girl, then? I've heard so much about you from friends of mine."

"Ah, don't tell Cuyler about the money. I want to surprise him."

"Oh, yes, of course." He walked to the safe, and I could now tell that he was Jim and Cuyler's age. He came back with a small package, counted the money onto the desk, and I stuffed it into my bag. "Good luck to you, Mrs. Carr. Hope you and Cuyler have a wonderful life together. He's a nice fellow."

Yes, he is, I said to myself as I thanked the clerk and walked away from the bank. Cuyler was standing with his back to the Fenimore, his hands in his vest pockets, puffing on a cigar as fast as his friends were chatting. That's my guy. I thanked God for his disinterest in my actions.

I stopped by the lingerie shop and purchased some fresh under garments including several more nightgowns for my trousseau. Then I crossed the street to Mrs. Sloat's.

"We've been shopping, Gertrude? You *dear* girl," Mrs. Sloat said. She was in rare form today. I don't suppose she was asked to be matron-of-honor at too many weddings these days.

"Good morning to you too, Mrs. Sloat. I hope you're ready for Saturday."

Sally popped her head from the sewing room. "Gertrude! Good morning. We're so busy with our dresses. Will you have a look?"

I regarded the plain, pink frocks. "I think you need some satin here and some lace there. Some rosebuds here would be nice."

Mrs. Sloat and Sally laughed. "She's losing her mind under all the strain. Poor Cuyler. She'll have a nervous breakdown before she stands at the altar."

Nervous breakdown? Well, I hadn't heard that phrase for a while. I sauntered over to the dresses, suits, and jackets. "Give me one of each," I said, pointing to the ones I liked. "In my size, of course. I need a trousseau."

Sally giggled. "You're just going to the cabins."

Mrs. Sloat silenced her. "We're not supposed to know that, Sally." She regarded my crazed expression. "Why do you need all these clothes, dear?"

"Well, I'm moving to Milford, and I might not get into town for some time. I thought I might need them now that I'll be helping my husband in his business."

"Cuyler's going to let you work beside him?" Sally said.

"Of course. We're a *modern* couple." Sally giggled again, and Mrs. Sloat crowed.

"I don't think my boyfriend will ever let me work when we get married," Sally said.

"Why not? If you like working here with Mrs. Sloat, why shouldn't you make a little extra money for your family until one comes along."

"Oh, Gertrude, such nonsense!" Sally said. "She must be delirious. So in love with Cuyler, huh?"

Mrs. Sloat winked. "I'd say Cuyler's the one delirious. She's got him wrapped around her wedding ring finger." We all chuckled at Cuyler's expense.

"Well, do I get my dresses?" I was showing no signs of giving up this purchase.

Mrs. Sloat and Sally dropped their jovial expressions. What they had assumed was strain was real illness. "You *mean* it, Gertrude? Why that would cost more than a hundred dollars."

I took out two one hundred dollar bills and placed them on her counter. "This should pay for my dresses and your wedding gowns. Add the trim. I want you two to look gorgeous on my wedding day." They looked at me as if I were a ghost. "Not enough? Very well." I took out another one hundred dollar bill. "Will that do?"

"Did you rob a bank?" Sally's mouth dropped when she saw the money. Mrs. Sloat examined the greenbacks.

"My sister just sent me my half of our inheritance for my wedding present since she cannot attend being otherwise occupied with our family's estate. It appears that there was an account set up by our grandmother. It was to be ours in 1895. My mother forgot about it. My mother also had some accounts that she hadn't touched for some time for fear that my drunken father might squander it. I happen to have quite a bit of financial assistance from my losses."

Mrs. Sloat clasped her hands together, ran to me, and hugged me. "Glory to God, I asked him to help you. Poor pitiful lamb. The Lord has come to his true servant. Glory to God."

Sally cried. "I'm so happy for you and Cuyler. Does he know yet?"

"No and don't tell him. I want it to be a surprise. Where's his wedding suit?"

They brought out the white shirt, tie, and formal jacket and a nifty hat—but no trousers.

"Are you still fixing the pants?" I said.

They snickered until they broke down into tears.

"She doesn't know. We best not tell her," Sally said.

"I think we should," said Mrs. Sloat.

"Let Cuyler tell her when he wants to," Sally said.

"What? Tell me what?" Now what was the man up to?

Mrs. Sloat went about getting my packages prepared. She secreted the money into the cash register. Sally ran back to the sewing room and began to sew like mad on the wedding dresses. She would add the expensive trim. Neither was talking.

"Now run along, Gertrude," said Mrs. Sloat. "If you can keep secrets from Cuyler, I guess he can keep some from you." She propelled me out of the store.

The packages almost fell from my arms. "What? Tell me what? What secret?"

Sally said, "We'll see you Thursday night at six at Mrs. Sloat's. Cuyler will give you directions. She lives here in Cooperstown. We have a wild time prepared for you."

Probably some left over cider gone toxic and party games. I doubted they would have ordered any naked male model to pop out of a cake. Mrs. Sloat made sure the packages were level and then patted me on the arm and said, "I'm so happy for you; I think I'll cry."

"What? Tell me what?" I said, as I tried to find my way to the carriage. The rest of my money was safely in my bag.

I managed to get to the cart without mishap. I saw Cuyler and his friends and decided to walk right up to that stuffy old men's club and say good day to the chaps. I'd not spoken to them since that first day in Cooperstown. Perhaps their communication skills had improved.

Jim Wheeler said, changing some subject quickly, "Well, here's your girl now, Cuyler. Look out now. She's been shopping. There goes all of your money, Carr."

Cuyler turned and displayed a look of fear on his face. I smiled and took his arm reassuringly. "Why, I'm just picking up our orders. Isn't that right, dear?"

"Yes, of course. Orders," he said, playing along.

Cliff's eyesight had not improved for he was still looking just below my chin. "Fine weather we're having, wouldn't you say? Hope it will be nice Saturday for your wedding."

"*The Freeman's Journal* says that it's unusually hot this summer as compared to summer's of the past," I said, presenting my best Penelope imitation.

Robert looked like a man in love as he stared with adoration into my eyes. He did have cute, blue eyes. "It will be such nice weather for swimming sports up at the cabin in Richfield Springs."

Joe coughed; Jim whistled.

"Er...I mean the temperature will be quite conducive to the water of Canadarago Lake."

Another low whistle of warning from Joe.

"What? I just meant to explain that it should be *hot* at the cabin," he said.

My cheeks held a maiden's blush; my eyelashes fluttered. Cuyler smiled at poor Robert's predicament.

Jim said, "No one's supposed to know where they'll be next week."

"Oh!" Bob had lost the battle and was embarrassed. "Dreadfully sorry, Miss Johnson."

"That's quite all right, Mr. Stiffler. I do hope you'll attend our wedding."

Joseph said, "We'll all be there, Miss Johnson. We wouldn't want to miss Cuyler's day of imprisonment." You had to love this quy's candor.

Clif silenced him. "That isn't nice to say, Joe. Cuyler and Gertrude will be very happy. Especially after the send-off we've planned for Cuyler at the..." Joe stopped him with his palm on the guy's mouth.

"Well, my dear," Cuyler said, "we have work to do, and you did say you needed to be in Milford early."

Let's see if I have this act down cold. "Oh, yes, dear." A shy smile escaped my lips. A breathless voice rich with submission. My eyes gazed adoringly into my master's face. Cuyler wrinkled his eyebrows and pressed his lips together trying to refrain from laughing at my performance. "I wanted to check on some things at the apartment," I said. "But, only if you're finished with your conversation, dear. I do hope I didn't interrupt anything important."

He gave a wry smile as he rolled his eyes heavenward, "Nothing earth-shaking, dear."

The men bid good day to us both. I heard one of his friends say, "Lucky Cuyler." And another one said, "If I'd met a girl like her, I'd be headed to Richfield Springs myself."

Soon, I was seated in our rig, had the newspaper on my lap,

my packages in the back, and Cuyler's mind twirling.

"Not that I mind, my dear, but where did you come up with money for new clothes?"

"I'll tell you when we get to Milford. Meanwhile, you drive, and I'll read to you." I opened the paper to the social page, which was my particular favorite.

"Did you know that the number of Club men wearing white cloth shoes is increasing, and that R.H.W. is no longer classified as a 'dude?'"

"Well, I guess that's reassuring," he said.

"Also, only once in the past ten years has the temperature reached 87 as it did last Monday. On June 28, 1892, it was 88, and on September 23, 1895, it was 86."

"Well," he said, "that explains a lot, doesn't it?"

Where was his mind?

"There weren't as many firecrackers set off this Fourth of July because the little boys hadn't the money for their usual purchases of explosives."

"That's too bad."

Earth to Carr. Hello?

"There's an article here that says that it's to our advantage—as a nation—to purchase Hawaii, because the United States will then own the two greatest *volcanoes* in the world."

"Really."

And we're going to bring the volcanoes to Milford and sacrifice a virgin in one of them to bless the harvest. Why wasn't he *listening* to me?

"Yes, and it goes on to say that scientists deduce that the heat from the volcanoes may be harnessed to generate power," I said.

Maybe he didn't like volcanoes.

"Oh," I continued reading, "we missed the Third Separate Co. which came by on a separate train last Monday morning on their way to Richfield Springs. They went up the lake on the 'Natty.' I guess when they got to Richfield, they had a parade or something. It says here, that everyone wished that they had known they were coming in advance."

"Read the baseball scores to me, Gertrude."

I should have known.

It wasn't hard to find them. "The C.A.A. team and the Richfields met here for their third game. The Athletics won 11 to 9, and they didn't play the ninth inning. The Richfields started off well, scoring five runs in three innings, to two for the Athletics; then the latter ran away from the Richfields, scoring 8 runs in the next four innings, to 0 for the visitors; in the eighth inning the later scored 4 to 1 for the Athletics. I guess it was a close game. They play again this Saturday."

I went on with the news. "Friday morning the post office in Fly Creek was robbed of stamps and cash, but no one is sure how much has been lost. A boy at West Winfield was injured while playing baseball when a broken bat hit his face. Edwin Betts and his wife were killed by lightning in last night's downpour. They stopped their carriage under a tree because of the severe storm, and the tree was struck by lightening, and they were killed. They left behind two children. He was a farmer and 43 years old." The storm had certainly taken its toll in more than one way. I folded the paper onto my lap. I didn't want to read anymore. I wanted him to talk.

"Two little children." He shook his head. "That's sad."

I started to read his thoughts. I could tell he was waiting for the moment of truth about the money, but I wasn't ready to divulge anything yet.

"Are you excited about our wedding? I am. I think it will be perfect." Chatter away, Trudy. He's a man on a mission.

"I wonder what I'll ask the reverend tonight at our last meeting? What are you going to ask, Cuyler?"

Probably how soon he can divorce me after the wedding.

"Oh, I don't know?" He looked at me. "Gertrude, how did you pay for the clothes?"

I shielded the guilt from my eyes with my lashes. "I paid with cash," I said. "It ran over one hundred dollars. I hope you don't mind." I was being truthful, but I had a feeling the answer set the fuse.

"Well, actually, Gertrude, I thought we had discussed our financial problems thoroughly last week, and that you understood that all our cash must go into our home and business."

"Yes, I did understand that, Cuyler. Look," I pointed, "the river is high after the rains last night. I think the horse looks tired. Maybe we should give him something to drink." I wondered if he could read my anxiety.

"I believe you're ignoring my questions. I'm in earnest." I

could see he was doing his best to control his temper. Once I settled our accounts at the Milford Bank, I would show him his new savings account book.

"Are you looking forward to being married? I am," I said.

He slapped the poor horse with the reins for no apparent reason and grumbled under his breath. "I had been until today."

I stifled a merry chuckle at his expense as we pulled into Milford.

"You open the store, dear. I have to go to the bank and do some business," I said.

"Well, I should come along," he said, as he tied the horse to the post.

"No, I need to do this by myself."

His voice rose. "*Gertrude Johnson Carr*, if you plan on withdrawing money from our account, I think I should know about it this very moment," he said.

He was cute when he was angry. Hands planted on his hips. Mustache twitching.

I stood on tiptoes to give him a kiss on his lips. "Don't you worry. Have a little faith in your fiancé."

He suffused his swollen cheeks with exasperation and opened the door to our store. He gave me a warning glance. Big, brown, beautiful eyes with inner dialogue that said, "This had better be good, Gertrude." I was walking on thin ice with him.

A woman clerk grinned when she saw me, and waved that I should come to her window. "Hello, Gertrude. How can I help you?"

"I need to open a savings account under Cuyler's and my name. Can I do that without his signature? He's really busy right now."

"Sure. I'll have you sign the paperwork, and then you can place his name as co-owner of the account. I guess I know the two of you well enough. I mean he is one of the Board of Directors."

I watched her hurry to the office to get the necessary papers. Then I noticed Nathan Justice who smiled and waved.

"How are you today, Gertrude?" he said, stuffing bills into a beige bag.

"I couldn't be better, thank you."

"Excited about Saturday?" he said.

"Thrilled."

The clerk returned.

"And with what amount would you like to open the account?"

"Twenty-five thousand dollars."

A hush fell on the room. Nathan stood still with his mouth gaping. The young woman thought she hadn't heard correctly. "Did you say twe...twenty-five *thousand* dollars?"

I opened my dainty bag and withdrew the bills. "Yes, I've come into an inheritance from my mother's death. You know, the fire and all. I didn't tell Cuyler yet, so mum's the word. My sister sent me the notice Saturday, and I've just now had the time to see to the business of opening an account with the Fourth of July being on a Sunday and all."

"Oh, yes, well, certainly." She counted the money twice. I was glad I'd asked for large bills. I still had some money in my bag. I had other plans for that.

Nathan walked over to supervise the procedure. He was trying to learn. She had me sign the papers. I hesitated one moment before signing 'Cuyler E. Carr' on the line where it asked for the co-owner of the account. "This means that if I'm unavailable to withdraw funds, he can without my signature?"

She beamed. "Yes, he can withdraw it anytime. His signature is good. As a Board member, he'll never be questioned."

Warm tears filled my eyes, and I choked back my emotion. My heart felt heavy inside my chest. Now, my love, no matter what happens to me, you'll always be taken care of. This is just the beginning. You'll never want for anything. It's my way of saying I love you.

The procedure was finished quickly. She penned in our account book: $25,000 under the column entitled deposits. "It's been wonderful doing business with you, Mrs. Carr."

"Well, I'm not Mrs. Carr yet. Next Saturday." I sashayed my little bustle to the door and opened it to leave.

Nathan said, "You've been Mrs. Carr since the day you walked into town."

I turned to regard his expression and smiled in response to the remark. Yes, I had indeed. I placed the little account book into my bag. Now to face an angry Cuyler.

He was speaking with a man about ordering coal for the winter months, and how much he would charge.

"Well, I plan on selling chestnut, stove, and egg coal at the coal yard for $5.40 per ton of 2,000 lb., and $5.70 if you want it delivered in the village. I'm planning on having the coal from my corporation delivered by my team. My terms are strictly cash, sir."

The man agreed to the conditions and placed an order. Cuyler looked at me and glared while he wrote. I was in big trouble.

The man continued to ask Cuyler about the different feed and flour we were planning on selling. He told the man, but I could tell he wanted the guy to leave so that he could have it out with me.

Eventually, the man left. Cuyler waved as the man walked down the street. Then he turned to me, took my hand, and nodded to the outside staircase.

"Upstairs, Gertrude!"

He locked the front door behind us and flipped the sign on the door to read: CLOSED. We climbed the stairway. He unlocked our back door and hustled me into the apartment. I stepped out for a quick moment to respond to Mrs. Bates's salutations.

He said, "*Are you mad?* We haven't the money for trifles right now? I suppose you're over-excited about the wedding and feel you need extra items; but, I must tell you, that I'm perfectly happy with the details we've planned thus far. If you're going to insist on falling back onto your 1997 ways, our agreement is in serious jeopardy."

"Don't you love me anymore?" I used my wide-eyed, innocent, blue-eyed look.

"Love has *nothing* to do with it. We had a bargain. You were to obey me and to never make a single move without my knowledge. I'm taking care of you remember."

"Oh, yes, indeed, you are. Taking *very* good care of me too," I said, cooing as I swayed dangerously close to his body and ire.

He quivered for a fraction of a second at my nearness. There was a clear, seductive intent in my mannerisms.

"Now, don't start that. I'm in earnest. We had a deal." He moved away from me, paced, and pulled at his mustache with his long fingers. "I was to marry you and take care of you, and you were to follow the path of a woman of my time period. Talking only when I was around and about things I knew. I asked very little of you that I would consider to be difficult to live with except to speak submissively in front of my friends."

"Yes, I remember. I remember that you said we could do whatever we wanted when we were alone." I tried to place my arms around his chest. I knew this was too much feminine independence for a Victorian man to handle.

I reached up and smoothed his mustache delicately with my fingers. It twitched involuntarily, and I giggled.

"Stop that!" he said. "I'm trying to have a legitimate conversation with you about this...this...financial secret of yours. Spending money we don't have on frivolities. Sneaking in and out of banks without a word to me." His arms jabbed the air at intervals to accentuate his points.

I kissed his cool lips.

"*Stop that!* Answer me." He stood much like he did that first night he told me to leave his cabin.

"I do love you." The emotion was right in front of him inside a pair of blue eyes.

He weakened. His lips quivered slightly, but I saw them. "Well, Gertrude, I would like an explanation." His arms were crossed over his chest. This really was our first husband-wife argument. Domesticity at its best, and we hadn't even said, "I do."

I reached into my bag and retrieved the small black book. I handed it to him.

"We don't have a savings account at this bank," he said. I watched as he inspected it closely. His mouth softened, and he said quietly, "Gertrude, where did you get all this money?"

"It's my dowry. I told everyone that I inherited it from an account my grandmother set up for my sister and me. I said it was part of my mother's will. Of course, it isn't. And there is more if you need it."

He was astonished.

"Cuyler, you extended kindness to me, asking nothing in return. I told you that I was a well-known author in my time period. I make thousands of dollars. Jim Cooper and I conceived of a way to transfer my 1997 money to your 1897 currency. It has aggravated me to watch us pinch pennies when I knew I could help with my own money if I only had access to it. Now I do. On my first day here, Daniel and I had a long talk about the way things were in Cooperstown during your time's depression. I decided right then that I would help where I could, and that I would repay you for your Christian charity: for helping me stay out of an asylum. I know you would never ask for a reimbursement, Cuyler, but I have some pride, too. Gertrude Johnson repays people. I plan to repay your relatives and help your mother fix her homestead. I plan on assisting the church, and donating money to those women who are down on their luck: the ones the reverend mentioned in church a few weeks ago. See. You have had a great influence on me. I've become the spiritual woman you wanted me to be, and the modern woman you dreamed of loving. Please accept the money. I was afraid that if I told you ahead of time, you'd stop me. I want to be reassured that, no matter what happens to me, you'll always be taken care of. I want a home to come back to next summer. I want it built and furnished by next June."

I tried to read his thoughts. How much help could you offer a proud Victorian chauvinist when you were a well-off Brooklyn feminist?

An idea came to me. "It's God's way of helping you because of your good Samaritan behavior. I was naked, and you clothed me." I tried to remember the verse. "I was sick, and you comforted me. I was hungry, and you fed me. I was without shelter, and you gave me a home. Isn't that right?"

I had never seen his eyes light up the way they did right then. His face glowed with pride and love.

"My word, Gertrude. There's twenty-five thousand dollars in this account," he mumbled.

"The account is in both our names. From now on, every donation and financial gift will be offered in the names of Mr. and Mrs. Cuyler E. Carr," I said.

I waited patiently.

"Why there's enough for two homes, two teams of workers, two rigs, and many more horses. I could expand the whole business."

"Yes, dear. And as I said, it's just the beginning. This is my way of telling you that I love you. I want you to be happy all your days—with or without me."

He grabbed me around the waist and held me. His eyes looked right into my soul. "I could have managed. You didn't need to do this."

"I know, but, since I can, please accept it in the manner in which I give it. My love is represented in this gift. I love you, Cuyler," I said, cupping his face with my hands and kissing him tenderly. "Forever and throughout eternity." I gazed into those deep, all-knowing eyes, hoping to read his thoughts.

"I want you to always be the happy and wonderful man you are throughout whatever hard times lie ahead. There'll be no bad times for you. Remember, I'm from the future. I know what's coming in American history. No matter what's in store for Cooperstown, New York; whatever you want you shall have. You didn't believe me that first night when I told you that I was a famous writer. You thought I was a vagrant." I laughed. "I hope you aren't still angry with me. If I should ever make you unhappy in any way..."

"You really do love me, don't you?" he said.

I stood away from him so that he could see the emotion in my eyes. "With all my heart," I said. "Finding you has made my lonely life complete. You don't know how much meeting you has meant to me. I was in such a state only a month ago. Everyone told me how sick I looked. I can't believe, for one moment, that all this wasn't meant to be. No matter how far away from you I am—my heart will be right here." I touched his chest with my finger. "Inside this big heart of yours."

Our lips touched, and we stayed inside this embrace for some time.

"Are you sorry you met me? Have I disturbed your life too much?" I asked.

"I've told you before, you've given me what I never realized I needed, what was lacking in my life. I spend each day trying to forget the reality last night's storm showed me. I think that's what's been bothering me all day. I was trying to pretend you were just a woman—just *one* woman—not more or less than I had a right to."

He held onto me with a desperate need to be told I'd stay forever. I couldn't say the words. I couldn't tell the lie he wanted me to say. I wasn't going to stay. The best I could do was come in the winter or the summer, and even that was not a certainty.

We walked to our little bed, sat down on the quilt, and rested for a few moments. We said nothing to each other, just held on, as if touching alone could keep me beside him.

"Come on. We need to make our little home ready. You need to make friends and future customers. We have to be at the homestead in time to eat dinner, meet with the reverend, and make final arrangements. I do hope the week flies by quickly. I want to be yours, in all ways," I said. I slid from his side and offered my arms.

"I'm sorry, Gertrude. For my anger. I should have trusted you. I was unkind."

"No problem." I smiled, and he laughed.

"No problem," he said.

The rest of the day was made full with trivial things. Cuyler sold feed and flour while making future orders for coal deliveries. We would eventually have to travel out of Milford by train and make some business arrangements with the coal company, as well as hire men and purchase horses to make up his team.

I tidied the apartment. Around four, he hurried upstairs to fetch me for our ride home. He was excited and had something in his hand. It was some sort of pamphlet.

"While we're riding home, take a look at these house plans. I just picked them up down the street. If you want a home, I'll have to start the plans and construction now. I won't have to look far for a builder. The Todd side of my family built almost all Toddsville. If the weather holds, I could start building on that bit of land up the road from the store as soon as we return from our honeymoon."

Everything was back to normal. His mind was alive with ideas, schemes, and dreams.

It was a hot day, and the ride home was as uncomfortable as it could be. I wanted to run to Otsego Lake and jump in. These 1890s clothes could be stifling in this heat. The horse was exhausted after a few miles up that long hill to Toddsville.

We were having fried ham, corn on the cob, and what smelled like sweet potatoes, for dinner. I inhaled the wonderful aroma before I even entered the house. I reveled in these moments when someone *else* did the cooking. I hugged Johanna in appreciation, and then I went to find my mother-in-law.

She was in her own room sitting in her rocking chair by the cool, open window of the master bedroom. She was sleeping upright in the chair. I hated to awaken her.

"Mother Carr," I said gently.

She heard me and opened her eyes. "Why, Gertrude, I must

have fallen asleep. Did you get everything accomplished in town?"

"Yes, and more." I sat on the floor in front of her curling my skirts around my knees. "My sister has sent me my inheritance. We are all quite surprised that there is any at all."

"That's wonderful news. Cuyler will be happy. Just at the right time, too. Of course, under the circumstances, it must make you sad that you had to receive it in this manner, dear."

"Yes, but some good should come from adversity, don't you think?"

"Yes, I do, dear."

I opened my bag. "I want you to have this." I gave her one thousand dollars in cash. She stared long and hard at the money.

"Why, my dear, this is a lot of money," she said, her hands shaking.

"I want you to fix up the homestead anyway you want. Whatever your heart desires. Don't worry. This is just the beginning. My sister only sent me a portion of the net."

"I don't know what to say." Her eyes were warm with affection.

"Don't say anything—just take it and have some fun with it. I just gave Cuyler my dowry. I opened a savings account in our Milford bank, under both our names, for twenty-five thousand dollars. He can have the business he's always wanted. He can build us a house. I want him taken care of no matter what happens to me."

"Why, my dear, nothing will happen to you," she said. She touched my hand with hers.

"Well, I just want to be sure. I never thought there would be a house fire, either. I suppose I'm just a bit frightened by such things now. Do you understand?" It never ceased to amaze me how his 'stories' helped me through every adventure.

"Yes, I guess I do, but Gertrude, you are young and healthy. Nothing will happen to you or Cuyler. You must not live in fear." She looked at the money. "Oh, my, whatever shall I do with so much money?" She was smiling.

"Whatever you want." I threw my hands into the air.

Then she turned somber and confidential. "I must admit that the speed of this romance between you and my son had me worried for some time. Not anymore. I can see how much you love my son, and I know that you will be the best wife any man ever had, except for Chester's, of course."

We laughed and discussed the approaching celebration, but the irony of the time travel situation was always in my foremost thoughts. How would Cuyler explain my disappearance to this woman, and what would she think of me then?

Chapter Twenty

Our last trip to the church for another lecture from our reverend would start the wedding week off with the proper absurd touch.

The reverend and the organist were waiting for us. We talked mostly about the ceremony and the dinner Friday night. We were not asking for anything different or special. We wanted a nice church wedding. The men of the Carr clan would be the ushers, and that famous uncle, who had given him the Poe book, would be Cuyler's best man. Daniel would be by my side all morning as he would when he walked me down the aisle. Decorations were being handled by the aunts and cousins on both the Carr and the Ingalls side of the family, and I had been told, politely, not to intrude.

I had two envelopes, with five hundred dollars in each, inside my bag. One bore the name of Mrs. K. and the other Mrs. R.

"This is a contribution from Mr. and Mrs. Cuyler E. Carr for those ladies who need assistance." I handed him the envelopes. He looked inside and gasped. He wiped his eyes with his hanky to keep us from seeing his emotion.

"My word, this is most generous. God has answered our prayers. I'm sure the women will be very grateful."

"Cuyler and I are happy, and we wanted others to share in our happiness. I want you to realize that it's given because of my husband's generosity. Some of my inheritance came to me this past week. We decided that the Lord wanted us to use it to help others. Cuyler listened to the Spirit, and I listened to him."

The preacher was overjoyed. "Please keep this anonymous," I said. "I'm sure you understand."

Cuyler was amazed, as well. He looked at me with such pride. I don't ever want to forget that moment.

We left after the good reverend read our vows to us, acknowledged the Scripture, and prayed for our life together. Amen, indeed, I said under my breath.

It was getting dark and Cuyler, once again, chose the road that crossed the "red house" path. I'm quite sure he did this on purpose. I think that he enjoyed the fear it sent through my body.

"We shall take the second road over the hill which I call my 'short cut,' but others call the 'Haunted Road'."

Those last two words were said slowly and dramatically.

"Oh, Cuyler, no."

"Why? You aren't afraid of ghosts, are you? I shouldn't think a bonny girl like you would be afraid of anything."

"This wouldn't be some perverse male idea of getting even with me for keeping you in suspense today. It's too dark an evening for this, isn't it?"

His voice lowered. "Yes, my dear. Very dark, indeed. But, I'm here to protect you from the ghosts of the murdered and insane."

Shit! "*Don't* do this again," I said.

"I thought you appreciated my stories," he said.

"I do," I said.

"You can take notes on your *little pad.* Local color tales are always the best, aren't they, Gertrude?"

"Yes, of course." I cuddled close to him. The trees had a way of bending their limbs over the road, and if it were daylight, I'd say it was chapel-like, but in the evening, it was macabre.

"This road has been known as the 'haunted road' for years," he said. "Persons using this road at night have observed a figure, clad in white, darting from tree to tree and crossing the path while making weird noises and striking terror into the hearts of the good people of Toddsville." He stopped the carriage.

"I can sometimes hear those screams still. Many persons felt that the 'ghost' was a crazy woman who lived in the 'catch all.' You can never tell. It could be the one from the grave who searches eternally for peace. One night, when several men were passing over this road, they heard a noise that did not sound like a crazy woman. It was the squeaking and creaking of something altogether supernatural. Something which the men swore to the day they died they'd seen." His voice had a low and eerie sound to it. Full of proper pauses and hushed words, slow phrases and whispered sentences, he had me on the edge of my seat.

"The men decided to stop their rig and inspect the premises. It was much darker than it is now, Gertrude. They lit matches to find their way to the gasping and creaking noises. The wind blew fiercely, just as it's doing tonight. They separated and searched until they had no more matches. They were about to return to their rig when one of them felt something cold on his cheek. Like something unnatural, dead, clammy, and chilling. You probably think it was the moist limb of a nearby tree, or the wind as it sometimes blows on the back of your neck, but it was none of these. The object happened to be a dead man hanging from a tree."

I shuddered and said, "Can we go ahead now? I'm getting chilled."

"Chilled? On a summer's eve? Perhaps the haunting happens once more for our courageous curiosity. Upon closer inspection, they found that the corpse was a resident of Toddsville. It was Thomas Lester, who committed suicide March 18, 1864," he said.

"Oh, God," I said.

He tried to stifle a satisfied grin.

"There he was swinging from the tree, with his face distended and purple. His mouth was opened wide in death. His eyes were rolled back into his head, and his tongue-dangled from his cold lips, as if it reached for the last breathe it never received. The men cut him down and lifted him into their rig as best they could. They took him to his house, but he lived a solitary life, and there was no one there to prepare him for his grave. He had been dead for hours. The men knew nothing else to do but to bury him in a shallow grave. Shallow because of the lateness of the night. No coffin for the dead. No service to see that his spirit found heaven. To take one's life is a sin against God, Gertrude. With no sermon to ease the spirit's rest, they say it walks in the full moonlight on this road to this day. They say that on a windy night, you can still hear the tree limbs creaking where the rope was stretched around that poor man's broken neck. Whatever bothered the man in life, they say, follows him still to his grave. He cannot rest. He cannot sleep. A faithless woman? Loss of his business? Drink? One theory is that he killed a man and could not live with the dreadful secret. If that is so, then he will walk through hell and find no peace."

"Cuyler?"

"Yes?"

"You are making this up."

"I don't need to. It's the truth. I never lie, Gertrude. I told you that when I first met you." Then he kissed me quickly and resumed driving the rig.

"Today, when I was in Mrs. Sloat's shop, she said that your

suit was ready for you to take home, but they were very evasive on one issue."

"What is that?"

"They had no trousers prepared. Then they started to giggle at my expense and said that it was up to you to tell me."

"That's true enough." I could hear the grin in his voice.

"Well, aren't you going to tell me?" I said.

"If you can keep secrets, my dear, so can I."

We were home in minutes. The house was quiet. We went upstairs and kissed good night. Soon, we would not have to go to separate rooms.

Chapter Twenty-One

The next few days held as much excitement as the first of the week. We had visitors from all the families, presents to unwrap, hired men to train, dishes to sample, horses and cows to feed, relative's names to mispronounce.

We did get a chance to travel to Milford by way of Cooperstown. We decided to slow the pace by strolling along Main Street.

I pointed to various shops and told Cuyler what they looked like in 1997. He was intrigued yet melancholy on the subject. Cooperstown was as he saw it. There could be no other. He loved his county and wanted me to forget my old home. It did not exist for him. I sighed remembering Jim Cooper's words. If he could not conceive of my home, then he could not dream it; and if he could not dream it, he could not be with me.

We went to the lake's dock and spoke with Daniel. He was bringing his beautiful sailing boat into port. "Well, how are the two love birds today?" he said. "Want a ride?"

"Yes, of course," said Cuyler faster than I could answer.

There was a breeze combing its fingers through the branches of the tall, majestic pines. I listened as Cuyler and Daniel spoke about Saturday.

"I surely do remember your saying that you would stay a bachelor, Carr. How things have changed."

Cuyler shook his head in mock irritation. "Well, I *had* to. She begged me. How was I to handle a sobbing woman? I'm not cruel, Daniel."

Daniel picked up on the cue to tease me. "Well, I suppose some good will come of it. She can cook, can't she?"

I turned to Daniel and glared.

"Moderately. Johanna's far superior. Did I ever tell you the story of Samuel Spinner and Miss Carrie Cotton, Daniel?" Cuyler said.

"I don't believe you have," Daniel said. "I'll take her out a bit, and we'll rest there and enjoy the coolness from the lake water. Feels good on such a hot day. Then you can tell me the whole tale."

I groaned—no note pad.

When we were out in the lake a ways, I rolled onto my back, snatched a large pillow he kept there, and listened.

"During my boyhood days there lived in Toddsville a Samuel Spinner and a Miss Carrie Cotton, two young people employed in the Union Cotton Factory. After admiring each other through rose-colored glasses over the 'mules,' they decided that life for them was one long honeymoon, and the only way to reach their hearts' desires was a voyage on the sea of matrimony. With love as their pilot, the couple went to Rev. John Perry for sailing orders."

"Cuyler, is that Mrs. Perry's husband?" I said.

Slightly annoyed by my interruption he said, "Yes, Gertrude, it is. As I was saying, the marriage day was pleasant enough, the benediction solemn enough, and the congratulations of friends profuse enough, and the old factory bell pealed forth tones of joy, while Aunt Johanna Perry, over her knitting, shed tears of sympathetic gladness, supposing the craft containing those new-found joys had started on a placid lake—but it proved to be a schooner stranded on a bar," said Cuyler.

Daniel laughed so hard I thought we almost lost him in the "placid lake."

"In consideration of the services rendered," Cuyler said, as he found a hidden cigar, lit it with that magical match from nowhere, and threw the match into the water where it fizzled, "by the Reverend gentleman, the groom was to deliver, or cause to be delivered, a sack of flour—to help replenish the larder of the divine—which was never bought, never paid for, and never delivered."

Daniel grinned. "Did the reverend annul the marriage then?" he said.

Cuyler puffed on the tip of the tobacco and said, "No. At the conclusion of the services the groom went to Burke's hotel for a 'stabilizer' and found the liquid 'Trace' was dispensing contained more than one-half of one percent of alcoholic content by volume. The bride sat patiently in the salon waiting for the return of her husband while the groom sat in the saloon taking on supplies. Love, the pilot of the undertaking, jumped through a porthole and was lost in the drink," he said.

Symbolism was rampant in this one, I thought.

"After several days," he said, and I coughed.

"Days?"

"Yes, Gertrude, *days*, the groom came to the realization that his tankage capacity was unusually large, and the success of the undertaking became a failure before the start. Several days after the 'happy event,' the reverend gentleman met the bride, and, being asked how she enjoyed married life replied, 'I tell you, elder, it is a little better than hell.' "

Once again Daniel lost the rudder, or whatever it is you steer a sailboat with, and we almost had the sail collapse on us, while Daniel laughed until I thought he would expire. No doubt the boys on bachelor night would like this little wedding story. There was more.

"If you like that one, I have another. Soon after the Spinner-Cotton wedding, another couple employed by the cotton company decided to take a whirl at the marriage business, but on account of parental objections on the part of the bride's people, postponed their venture from time to time. In fact, their courtship was conducted under difficulties, and their spooning after the old people had hit the hay. At last the day came, and the daughter, sneaking out of the back door, met her lover and made haste to the Rev. John Perry, who performed the ceremony. The marriage had hardly been completed when the irate father appeared on the scene to find his daughter married to the man of her choice. The father, after expressing his opinion in language I will not quote, and deciding they could all go to that unspeakable place, went home and left the bride and her husband to 'Paddle their own canoe.' "

At the end of the second story, Cuyler grinned and shot his cigar ash into the water. Daniel had enjoyed the "nautical tales." I just watched Cuyler's face as he told them. He was used to telling the salty men's tales as well as the history lessons. I turned my face to the sun and let the warm rays kiss my skin. This was heaven—this was peace—this was happiness. If only the people who lived in the time of my days could understand what life in the "slow lane" was really all about.

It wasn't the safest time nor was it the easiest. It was hard, back-breaking, physical labor that made you sleep like a baby at night—no Sominex. It was pinching pennies and no frills entertainment. It was endless chats with friends who meant it when they said they wanted to hear what you had to say and stayed to listen. It was knowing that others cared what happened to you, and that you meant it when you asked how they were doing. It was looking forward to small affairs and social get-togethers where people, not items and costs, made happen.

I'll admit to missing many comforts of my old-new world, but not the hurried, stressed-out people who passed my condo's front window. Our modern medicines would have cured the people who would die in Cooperstown this winter. Strong people-survivors-who would bow their heads and pass into the next world, but who might have been healthier than those I saw coughing and wheezing on the subway in New York City. Jennifer had six different pills she took a day for various allergies and anxiety attacks that plagued her. I lived an easier life. I was a writer. I lived in the twilight. One step in reality and one step in my imagination. I liked it there!

Lying in Daniel's boat, watching Cuyler sleep on the opposite pillow while Daniel faced the wind in his sails with reverent joy, inspiration struck me. The words to a poem tiptoed into my thoughts. I was excited. I hadn't written a poem since the one I wrote for Cuyler back in my cabin. I promised myself not to forget it and to write it down as soon as we docked. I needed the pencil and the paper from the carriage. My heart and mind were pulsing with creativity. Cuyler had that effect on me.

He wondered at my speed in racing upstairs to my writing room without a comment to anyone and shutting the door behind me. I hadn't written for some time. I was hungry for it. The typewriter would be taken to Milford next, and I would have to tell Cuyler something about why I wanted it. I wrote:

I Live in the Twilight

by Gertrude Johnson

I live in the twilight;
Between crimson and gray.
Bid good night to the morning;
Tell the sunset good day!

Shadows of sun beams;
Shield me from the moon.
Bright, bursting star dust;
Weaves dawn's threads on her loom.

The Past tells its stories;
A whisper in my ear.
The Present speaks of sadness;
Creating nothing from its tears.

I live in the twilight;
Between crimson and gray.
The River of Time is my home now;
And what was-is my today!

There. It was finished. I looked at my words and hurriedly wrote the little verse that I had written to Cuyler before I was transferred to 1897. What a difference. The change in my writing was because of the man and my undying love for him. Poetry had found its way into my heart and my art.

When I came downstairs, I was surprised to see the Carr men waiting for me. Mother Carr was nowhere, and Johanna was somewhere in the garden, I suspected. Cuyler was staring at the floor, and I had the faint feeling that I was about to be told something serious and solemn.

The one I called Poe spoke. "We belong to a proud Scottish family named Carr. The name was once spelled K-E-R-R or K-E-R, and it may be British or Norse; we don't really know. We know that it originally meant the 'Hunter of Swinhope.' It was first used as far back as King William the Lion, and it stands for your husband's clan. It's now your family clan, too."

I shut my mouth and stood stone-like next to a small, tapestry chair. Cuyler would not look at me. Had I finally insulted the brethren? Was I to be taken outside and stoned? What had I done? All the females in the household had forsaken me. Why was Cuyler so intense? He had told them the truth—that I came from 1997—because of some ancient blood brother and full moon thing about saying no false word before your wedding day.

"Gertrude Johnson, you have been chosen by our cousin, and nephew, Cuyler, to be his bride. Where his heart goes, so goes ours."

Had I missed something?

"And it is right for you to hear the words that the family wish to speak to you before the wedding day. You should know that you will be a part of our clan, and you will wear our tartan, but you shall learn the truth about the family whose colors you will wear even to the day you die. And you shall hear of the oath we spoke years past. Sit," Poe said.

I sat as fast as I could on Mother Carr's favorite chair. The men angled themselves and lit various cigars and pipes. Cuyler noticed my chagrin, and when I caught his eye, showed sweet simpering lips.

"Many years ago, in Scotland, the Carrs fought one another. In the fourteenth century, two brothers, Ralph and John Kerr resided near Jedburgh, and they did not share similar political views."

Ralph?

"The Kerrs of Ferniehurst descended from Ralph—the eldest brother— and the Kerrs of Cessford descended from John."

Ralph?

"Such a bitter feud it was, they even spelled their names differently: one choosing to leave off the second 'R'."

Now showing: Mel Gibson in *Ralph: Terror of Scotland.*

Their homes were only a few miles apart, and the two families shared the title of warden of the Middle March. Sir Andrew of Ferniehurst was appointed in 1502; and Sir Andrew of Cessford held it after Flodden."

"They were both named Andrew?" I said.

"Does your woman often break into a speech, Cuyler?" said one of the eldest men in the room.

I glanced at Cuyler. I had promised to keep my mouth shut. The wedding would be canceled due to *attitude*.

"Frequently," Cyler said.

"Shows spirit."

Cuyler winked at me.

'Poe uncle's' countenance appeared peeved. "Although the two families combined their forces at times against the British, their frequent brawling among themselves brought much violence and destruction to Teviotdale. This rivalry became a political problem in the sixteenth century because the Kerrs of Cessford supported the Pro-English policy of the Douglases being led, at the time, by the Earl of Angus and his wife Margaret. She was the widow of James IV, Gertrude, in case you don't remember. The Kerrs of Ferniehurst stuck with the party of King James V."

I was wondering if we were Kerr one or two. It didn't seem to matter.

"At the siege of the Castle of Ferniehurst by the English," 'Poe uncle' said, "the attackers claimed that its defense was assisted by 'spirits' and even the devil himself. Horrible atrocities were committed there when the castle fell. The women, who had tried to defend the castle alone, were raped; some were also murdered. The Kerr men vowed bloody and heartless revenge."

He had my full attention now.

"Upon its recapture from the English in 1549, great efforts were made by Sir John Kerr's men to take their prisoners alive so that they could be slowly tortured to death in revenge for the rape of the Kerr womenfolk by the English. One account of the bloody executions, described by a Frenchman, tells how the Scotsmen purchased one of the violators from this same Frenchman for a small horse. They laid the villain upon the ground, galloped over him with their lances at rest, and wounded him as they passed. After he was slain, the victors cut his body into smaller pieces and bore the mangled gobbets in triumph on the points of their spears."

I heard myself say, "Good!"

Cuyler pressed his lips together and subdued me with a private gesture.

"An eye for an eye," said the older man. "That's what it says in the Good Book.

Another cousin, about Cuyler's age, said, "We all know that the British tyrannized our borders and were barbarous to our people...especially our women."

I listened to all 'Poe uncle' had to say.

"This rivalry between the two houses continued. It's a long

and very political tale of hatred. I'll not go into the details today. Their houses were, however, united by marriage. In 1631, Anne Kerr of Cessford married William Kerr of Ferniehurst. Many prestigious titles have been wreathed around our ancestors' heads since that time. Eventually, Robert Carr's father brought his wife to America, and I'm sure Cuyler has filled you in on what happened after that."

"We are a proud family, as we have already said," said the old man. "Civil and yet temperamental, we bear the fairness and the fight in us from our ancestors."

This explained why Cuyler did not duke it out with Ellis that day and simply took his money to another bank to punish the banker's impertinence.

"We protect our women, Gertrude. If Ellis or anyone else hurts you, as your former beau did, we shall not sit idly by," said the uncle who had spoken of the past.

So that was the reason for my love's solemn visage when I came down those stairs. He had told them that I had been abused by my first "beau" and was wondering if I would be angry.

The cousin said, "Cuyler will tell you more when you get married, I'm sure. We want you to know that we'll not allow anyone to harm any Carr. Especially our women. We speak this oath to you in secret. It is not meant for others' ears. You have gained more than a family in this marriage, Gertrude. You have obtained a group of men who will kill any man who touches you."

Kill?

The old man said, "He gets a tad dramatic sometimes." But, a glint was in his eyes when he stared at the young man.

"Chester's sister, Cuyler's aged aunt, made this for you. The head of the clan, the 'Poe uncle,' took from behind the couch a woolen scarf. Its pattern was beautiful and, at first glance, seemed like a standard plaid, but, upon closer inspection, I saw a complex design.

There were four different squares: two were solid with colored lines passing through them, and two were shadow squares blending the two bold colors together. One was bright red and was divided like a cross with one solid, bold line of deep blue. The square to the left was red shadowed by this dark blue.

Underneath this red line was a completely different plaid. Beneath the shadow red box was a beautiful teal green square.

This square had no center line running through it. It had a margin of red and green blended together, and the combination made the margin stand out. I had no clue what each color and each box represented.

I placed the tartan scarf around my neck and cuddled it close to my throat. I saw the men were touched by my action.

"This is the Carr clan's Tartan, and you are giving it to me because I'm going to be one with you on Saturday, isn't that right?"

"Yes, Gertrude. You're one with our family. We wanted you to have your own woolen replica of your man's Tartan, but first we wanted you to know what the Tartan of borders means when you wear that scarf on a cold Sunday in January when you bundle yourself off to church. When Cuyler told us how bold you were in striking a man bent on doing mischief to you, we all knew. We wanted to accept you into our clan with our love, and with our strength, we'll protect you for as long as you live."

He made his way across the room, held out his hands to me, and when I rose to meet him, hugged me. I was shocked. All the uncles and cousins did likewise. Cuyler just watched, and when they were finished, he stood and took my hand in his.

"Welcome, Gertrude Carr," he said.

Then they all laughed.

"You told it better than you did the last time," the younger man said, acknowledging the head of the clan. "But, I was hoping for more blood with the violence. She can take it."

The spokesman said, "Cuyler tells us that you wish to pay us back the money for your furniture from your dowry. We told you that it was our tradition to install Cuyler into his new home. We expect nothing in return. You keep the money and use it for something new for your business or apartment. And don't be angry with Cuyler for telling us. He didn't want you to insult the clan before you even entered it."

He motioned to the men. "We have to leave you now. We shall see you tomorrow night, eh, Cuyler?"

They all departed, and we waved to them from the front porch of the Carr homestead. Cold winters-warm scarf. Would I be there to wear it? One thing I did know for sure. This Tartan wool would be around my neck the day I went back to my own time. It was my Carr connection. We returned to the front parlor and shut the door behind us.

"Well," Cuyler said waiting.

"Well, what?" I said.

"How do you feel about the oath and the clan?" he said.

"I feel proud." I stuck him in his side with my straightened finger, and he yipped.

"But, you *could have* warned me. I thought I was the next blood sacrifice when I came down those stairs."

"I came to fetch you when I saw them line up their rigs by the house. I couldn't find you. Where were you hiding?"

"Ah, I've been sneaking into that little guest bedroom by your room and doing a bit of writing. I really love to write, as you know. Could we please take the typewriter with us tomorrow when we go the apartment?"

"Writing what?" His brows knit together.

"Poetry." Half lie albeit it, but: *I never lie I only stretch the truth.* "Oh, well, if that's what you want, of course. Mother certainly doesn't want it."

A small knock came from the front door. Cuyler answered.

It was Clarence on his bicycle: a lovely, old-fashioned two wheelers with a small bell on the bars that rang as he peddled.

Cuyler knew the boy was the one who had danced with me and read poetry to me at the sociable, so he role-played with him.

"How may I help you, sir?" Cuyler's manner was stern as if the boy were twenty-six as he earnestly perceived himself to be.

Clarence removed his hat, out of respect, and rested it upon his chest. "Perhaps this is not a convenient time?" he said.

"That all depends, sir. What is it you wish?" Cuyler said, and leaned against the door frame blocking Clarence's view of the interior and me. Then he folded his arms across his chest and glared at the boy.

Master Peaslee never faltered, but his voice didn't sound as courageous as before.

"I've come to sit with Gertrude for a while and chat."

"Chat?" 'Is-that-all?' query from Cuyler.

"Yes, Mr. Carr. Chat. I have a selection of poetry to recite to her."

"Really? And what sort of poetry might I ask?" 'Love poems?' was the subtext here.

"I read the first stanza to her at the dance, and she encouraged me to finish it. It's about Otsego County." The boy squeezed his lips tightly together making them crinkle, and his nose dip humorously.

"I see. Gertrude did not inform me that you wished a visit. I have not given her my permission to have a gentleman caller share such an intimate moment with her. She's to be married Saturday. You're aware of that fact?"

"Oh, yes, sir, and she couldn't have chosen a fairer or kinder man to marry in all Otsego County."

Cuyler smiled. He turned and looked at me. "Well, Gertrude, what do you say? Do you wish to sit on the porch and hear young Master Peaslee's poetry?"

"If it's all right with you, dearest," I said.

"I suppose he's a modest man, and it'll do no harm. I shall see whether Johanna has some lemonade and cookies close at hand should Master Peaslee perish whilst reading his verses." Cuyler winked and privately patted my posterior as he disappeared into the kitchen.

I left the front porch and motioned that we should go to the side porch.

"Sorry about the interrogation, Clarence."

"Quite understandable, Miss Johnson." He tugged at the small bow tie he had tightened like a noose around his neck. "I can well imagine his concern. I mean, I did walk you away from the party and dance a waltz or two with you several Saturday's past." He became secretive. "Competition from a younger man," Clarence said.

"I should think. You have your verse completed then."

"Yes. And I have come by for your criticism of it." He reached into his pocket and removed the same dogeared paper he'd had the last time. It was now covered with words.

"Now don't feel you need to be kind in your critique lest you break my heart, Miss Johnson. I'm fully aware that it's not perfect, but I shall deem it a great honor for you to tell me how I might improve it."

I unfolded the paper, noticed Cuyler smiling from the kitchen window, and read:

In Otsego
by Clarence L. Peaslee

The grasses nowhere grow so green,
  As in Otsego;
The hills are nowhere so serene,
  As in Otsego;
The skies are nowhere half so blue,
The lake nowhere casts such a hue,
And nowhere hearts beat quite so true,
  As in Otsego.

There is nowhere a land so sweet,
  As in Otsego;
Where storied past and present meet,
  As in Otsego;
The corn shocks in the autumn haze,
Are wigwams of old Indian days,
When Natty trod the forest ways,
  In old Otsego.

I've wandered far in distant lands,
  Far from Otsego;
I've joined my strength with stranger hands,
  Far from Otsego;
Yet, when my time has come to die,
Just take me back and let me lie,
Close to the pine-capped hilltops high,
  In old Otsego.

I was moved to tears. I reached for my lace handkerchief. The poem touched me in a way I was certain Clarence couldn't have ascertained.

"It's beautiful, Clarence."

He was in shock and very excited. "Do you really *mean* it? You like it?" I viewed the nine-year-old just then.

"I think it's perfect. You shouldn't change a word of it. However, I do have one question. How does a man so young learn to speak of foreign places?"

He took back his poem and carefully folded it and placed it into his pocket. "My father died when I was just a baby. My mother and I moved from one relative to another. We went everywhere, Italy, England, France. We have family in nearly every port. I hated it. I wanted to come back here and live on my father's farm. I begged her, and she finally listened. Three years ago we returned, and our farm was so run down she almost left. A nice man helped her fix and paint our house, then the barn, then groom the land, and finally, he married her. I like him. Since I never really knew my father, I've accepted him as my own. They shall have a baby soon. I'll have a brother or sister. Then I shall be the eldest, and it's a grand responsibility."

"Yes, I can see that it would be." All came into focus. The courtly manners, the worldly outlook on life, the poetry.

"I shall not leave again—ever. Do you understand how I feel?" he said.

I thought of my own poem. "Oh, yes, Clarence. I do understand, indeed."

Cuyler flew through the kitchen's back door with a plate of sugar cookies and two tumblers. "I'll just be a second with the lemonade."

About a second and a half by my recollection. The master of the house poured the yellow liquid into the tumblers, stood awkwardly to see whether we liked it, and then disappeared.

"He's frightfully cautious with you, isn't he?" said Clarence.

"He loves me."

Clarence blushed. I offered him a cookie, and he took two. Then we both sipped the sweet summer juice.

"Oh, well, I know something about that," Clarence said.

"You do?"

"I have a girlfriend. Her name is Jennifer. She's younger.

Just a baby. Seven."

"And you love her?" I said.

"I'm *wild* for her." He rolled his eyes with enthusiasm, and a few crumbs trailed down his vest. "She has the prettiest hair and the sweetest smile. Of course, I haven't approached her on the subject of matrimony yet. She can't even read my letters and poems. Someday, I shall approach her father on the subject. Meanwhile, I plan to sow a few wild oats before I settle down permanently with only one woman."

Then he became confidential. "You see, there's an older woman. I passionately love her, but I'm afraid her heart belongs to another. I shall worship her from afar."

"I see. Well, would you like to read one of *my* poems, Clarence?" I asked.

He said that he would, and I rushed passed Cuyler, flew up the stairs, and grabbed my new poem hot from the typewriter.

"What's going on?" Cuyler said.

"Clarence wants to read my poem."

I sipped my tumbler of lemonade and waited. I knew he would have no clue what I meant by living in the twilight—the past and the present—but I wanted him to sample it anyway.

"It's beautiful, Gertrude." He was in love. I had no intention of heating this crush, but I'd just done so.

"Do you understand what it means?" I said.

"Of course. You're saying that you live in two worlds. One full of fantasy and fiction and the other reality."

That wasn't what I meant in the time traveling poem, but it was a fantastic summation of my personality in general and could clearly be the unconscious symbolism represented by my work. This kid was a genius.

He choked on a swig of his beverage and handed the poem back to me. "It's *typed*. I shall have to buy a typing machine someday. Maybe Mother could get me one for my tenth birthday. Well, I realize you have many things to do to get ready for your wedding. I came by today because I've heard that you won't be living here after your honeymoon."

"My husband and I will be maintaining a small apartment above our own business in Milford."

"That's quite a way from Toddsville on a bike, but I might see you when you visit the homestead. Our farm is not far from here. Closer to town though. You've passed it often, I'm sure. Who knows, I might just ride my bike to Milford after all. Is it a hardware store then?"

"You've heard correctly."

He stood and bowed to me then kissed my hand. "Good day, Miss Johnson. Congratulations on your forthcoming wedding. I hope you and Mr. Carr will be very happy."

"Thank you, Mr. Peaslee. I'm positive we shall be. Please feel free to visit our store in Milford anytime. Thank you so much for allowing me to read your poem and for your critique of mine."

He placed his little hat on his head, and I accompanied him to the road. He sat upon his bike, tipped his hat, waved to Cuyler—who came to the porch to say farewell to him—and jingled down the road. I watched as he turned the corner at the end of the road and headed back to downtown Toddsville.

Cuyler stood beside me and wrapped his arms around my waist. "It's a good thing we're getting married soon. I shall have to beat them away with sticks. You have this *magnetism*."

I turned inside the circle of his arms and kissed him right on the lips. "Did you ever get a chance to tell Isaac Cooper about our private honeymoon?"

"Come to think of it, no," Cuyler said.

"Well, I think a quick trip to the cabin might be in order. I'll assemble some of the items I want in a bag and leave them there."

"You don't need anything much, Gertrude. I'm not planning on taking you anywhere for at least two weeks."

"Do you mean it—*two weeks*? Two?"

"We can start the business anytime we want to. It's ours. We don't seem to have any financial burdens presently. I plan to keep you all to myself and ravish you daily. Occasionally, I'll go into town for supplies so that we can eat." His sharp teeth nibbled on my neck.

We took our small provisions to the cabin, and I got to meet Isaac. You guessed it. Just a little over five feet eight inches-blue eyes-long brown hair pulled back into a ponytail-only he had a beard and mustache. I suppose I expected him to smile some sort of recognition since I had met the whole family in 1997, but, of course, he didn't know me. He was just as charming and mysterious as the rest of the family. I wondered if he time traveled, and if so where he went in the winter months.

Chapter Twenty-Two

Thursday began the final hours before our marriage. No more trips to Milford, and no discussion that didn't begin with a question about what still needed to be done. Johanna had a million last minute details to handle about the reception, so I handled most of the house and garden decorations. Luckily, there were many stores in Toddsville for last minute items.

As we traveled into Cooperstown to bring home our wedding outfits, check with the Fenimore Hotel about the reception, talk with the organist and the housekeeper of the church, speak with the florist, and say hello to Daniel and my two bridesmaids; it suddenly occurred to me that I had not purchased a wedding gift for Cuyler. Who had time or opportunity? He was with me hourly.

I saw a pleasant jewelry store across the street from the Fenimore Hotel. I had plenty of money with me. Cuyler would try on his wedding tux—or what was supposed to be his tux. I whispered to Mrs. Sloat to keep him occupied until I could purchase a gift for him. She winked and said that she could keep him forever if need be.

I hurried across the street and entered the store. Now the problem. What could I buy Cuyler? I wanted it to be special, but men are not so easy to surprise. He had a pocket watch—the one his father had given him. He had mentioned to me that it had "ceased to tell the correct time just after my arrival," and he no longer wore it. I saw one that would be perfect.

"May I help you, Miss?" said the young man.

"Could I see this watch? The one with the scroll and the smooth, plain, gold face." It was exactly what I wanted to purchase for him, and I wanted it engraved.

The man was pleased to make such a quick sale, but hesitated when I said I wanted it engraved by tomorrow. I'd make up some stupid excuse to come to Cooperstown to pick it up.

"I don't know, Miss. Why the rush?" he said.

"It's a wedding gift. I'm getting married on Saturday. Today's the first day I've had an opportunity to come and find a gift," I said.

The man's face brightened. "You don't mean the Carr wedding? You're not Gertrude, are you?"

"I am. I want this watch for Cuyler. Please."

"If it's for Cuyler Carr, I'll have it done for you today. Can you get rid of him for an hour or so? I'll engrave it and wrap it for you now. Just pay for it, and I'll slip it to you just as you're leaving town. That's his rig by the hotel, isn't it? I was supposed to go to lunch but for a rush job like this, I'll go without."

"Oh, thank you. It means so much to me."

"Just tell me what you want on the inside of the face. Don't be shy."

"On the outside, where it's smooth, could you put his initials-C.E.C. in that pretty, Old English script? It'll match the edging around the watch."

"Sure, Miss Johnson," he said.

Now the hard part. "On the inside could you put: To Cuyler from Gertrude. I shall love you beyond mortal time."

"That's an interesting twist to the usual." He chuckled. "I'll have it done for you in an hour."

He rang up the sale for the watch and the engraving. He told me that the watch was the best and most expensive in his whole shop. It hummed with precision. I didn't care about the cost; it was for Cuyler. I knew that exchanging rings was all the gift he would expect from me, but I wanted him to have a gift from me; one which would last forever—tick-tocking my heartbeat for him alone to hear.

"If I have trouble shaking him, leave it with Mrs. Sloat. I will be at her house this evening for an all girls' party. I'll tell her what I've done. Oh, and here's a little extra for your patience and understanding," I said.

"Thank you, Miss Johnson. By the way, you picked the right gift. He's brought his father's watch in for the last three months to have me fix it. I gave up. He was real disappointed. The timepiece was something special to him. This'll be a nice replacement. A man shouldn't go into business without a good, gold watch in his vest pocket," he said.

"You're correct, sir. Thank you." I was gone, almost running down the street to Mrs. Sloat.

I could tell Cuyler was losing patience when I heard a "Blast!" from the dressing room.

"I don't *mind* the button. If *I* don't mind it, why bother?"

Cuyler said.

Mrs. Sloat hurried up to me. "Oh, he's fit to be tied. Did you find something nice?"

I told her the entire story, and she smiled with satisfaction. She would be my accomplice in this and all things. Then I tried on my wedding dress while Cuyler went down the street to his favorite spot to smoke a well-deserved cigar. I must admit he was quite surprised when Mrs. Sloat no longer seemed concerned about the worrisome button.

The gown was the most beautiful satin explosion of feminine Victorian rose and lace. She had added reams of satin onto the train and bragged that when I stood at the altar the train would hug the last pew. I believed her. Sally came out of the sewing room with the rose wreath and veil for my hair. Since, all was paid for, there was only the matter of carefully boxing it and preparing it for its ride home.

The women showed me their gowns. The dresses were quite different from the skimpy ones I'd seen before. We had the same lace and rosettes on our gowns and for our hair.

"How can I repay you for helping us prepare so quickly? I haven't had much time, and I have no gifts for you," I said.

"Just be happy, that's all we ask," said Sally. "You've made us beautiful for a historic wedding. It isn't every day that a bachelor is snared." They both laughed.

I was given directions to Mrs. Sloat's house for tonight's party, then hurried down the street to witness Cuyler saying farewell to his friends.

"Lovely timing, Gertrude. We can go home now," Cuyler said.

"Home?"

"I'm exhausted. All this wedding business. And the hired men. Into the cart."

"Ah, I'm famished. Why don't we have lunch?" I said.

"Fine. Johanna can make a plate from all the food she's cooking."

"Ah...no...that isn't fair. She's working so hard. Why don't we eat here in town? Just the two of us. Why not try Tunnicliff's restaurant? I've never been there, and it looks charming. If you didn't bring any money, I have some."

"Tunnicliff's restaurant? Now?" he said.

"Please? Couldn't we just slow the pace a bit? Have some

peace and quiet before the mind boggling events crescendo?"

"Well, if that's what you wish, Gertrude."

We walked two blocks to the cozy inn on the corner. I couldn't help notice the Federalist-style home next to the inn that had been built with almost the same stone facade as our homestead.

I ordered dishes that would take forever to cook.

"Did you get your suit?" I said.

"Yes, though Mrs. Sloat *would* go on and on about the tiniest details. And your gown? Is it as beautiful as the bride?"

"Much prettier by far," I said.

He took my hand. "I'm glad we decided to eat here. I like this place much better than the hotel's restaurant." He touched the back of my hand with his lips. "I like the crystal chandeliers, the brass decor, the fireplace, and the warm atmosphere. We shall have all our special dinners here. You know, when we want to celebrate cherished days or special holidays—like our anniversary or Valentine's Day. Whatever we find substantial." He kissed the palm of my hand.

"Cuyler. Tunnicliff's restaurant is still standing. I ate lunch there a few days before I came to your time."

"Really? How extraordinary," he said. "Well, that *is* significant, isn't it? This restaurant can be our private rendezvous. Whenever you are lonely and thinking of me, go to Tunnicliff's. And whenever I'm melancholy, longing for your presence, I shall come here too. Who knows, we may end up here on the same night, different year. I think I'd know if you were with me somehow."

"All right. It's a deal. I'll come here, order a nice meal, and pretend I'm with..." I couldn't go on. The tears flashed too quickly into my eyes for me to stop them.

"Gertrude, don't cry. This is our first true connection with the future and the past excluding the cabin. Tunnicliff's will be our place because it's stood the test of time. Like our love."

"How did I ever deserve anyone as wonderful as you?"

"Sinful living," he said. I chuckled despite myself. "Those *books* of yours. God must have felt that you needed me to keep you from your dishonorable way of life."

We laughed and ate, paid the bill, and left. As I was strolling down the street to our carriage, I took a departing look at Tunnicliff's restaurant so that I would remember.

Miracle upon miracle, one of his friends stopped to discuss an item he had read in the newspaper, and Cuyler asked me to go to the carriage and wait for him.

I entered the jewelry store like someone in a James Bond movie, picked up the beautifully wrapped gift, placed it gingerly into my bag, and smiled my gratitude as I rushed from the store. I leaped into the carriage and waited patiently.

"Sorry I kept you waiting," he said, jumping into the cart and pulling at the reins then clicking his tongue against his teeth to snap Samuel into action.

"No problem," I said, as I patted the treasure in my bag.

Chapter Twenty-Three

The day wore on, and we indulged ourselves in an early dinner, not that I was particularly hungry after that great lunch at Tunnicliff's.

Cuyler's young cousin came to retrieve him for his party at six.

"Now, bring him home early," I said, pretending to be his mother.

"And you too, Gertrude. Don't become over-excited at your ladies' party."

Mother Carr and Johanna were ready with small, wrapped gifts they giggled over. I drove us to Mrs. Sloat's. I wondered who could possibly belong to all these rigs. I didn't know this many people.

We walked inside the lovely, if rather small, two story house. The place was packed with women. There were wedding-white satin ribbons, bows, and flowers on everything. There were refreshments and a large table full of gifts. When I walked in, everyone cheered. They must have been Mrs. Sloat's friends. Upon closer inspection, I saw many Todd, Ingalls, and Carr relatives.

"Come in, dear," said Mrs. Sloat. I waved to Sally who grinned with the excitement of their surprise for me.

After refreshments, I opened the gifts. They had been chosen with care: kitchen utensils, linen towels, pots and pans, tea cups, tea kettles, and other household lace and linen products, a Bible, and some stationery, a scrapbook to put favorite items in, small, throw pillows, and a honeymoon peignoir from Sally and Mrs. Sloat. They had all been wrapped in plain white paper and purchased for Cuyler and me. Johanna gave me Cuyler's favorite recipes in a nice book she had made herself.

The best gift of the evening came from my mother-in-law. Inside a small box, was a lovely, gold necklace with one large ruby dangling from its center and smaller rubies on either side. Matching ruby earrings came with it.

"Mother Carr, these are lovely," I said.

"They are antiques, dear," she said.

I had to remind myself that, for her, antique meant further

back than 1800.

"These came from Scotland and were given to Robert for his wife. They have been handed down, through the years, to the next daughter on her wedding day. I have no daughter save you, Gertrude. I want you to have it with all of my love."

I stood up, walked over to her, then leaned over and kissed her cheek. "Thank you so much." Some of the Carr women wiped their eyes with their lace hankies.

"It's the least I can do for the poor child who will marry Cuyler," she said. This comment lightened the mood in the room.

We didn't play any party games, but there was one game for the unmarried women. They tried to read their future husband's name in the wax of burning candles.

We sat around in animated conversation and drank strong black coffee from tiny china cups. I was given much advice and learned their ideas on married life.

"Well, I'm glad Cuyler has had the good sense to marry. So many young people these days choose celibacy," one woman said.

One of the Todd women said, "That's because so many are restless— always on the move. Don't want to settle down like Gertrude here."

Right! Hardly the traveler me.

Sally said, "Well, it costs more to live these days—to provide for a family."

"Poppycock," said another, with little care about her rough language, "they just want to buy more for *themselves.* Don't want to share with a spouse and children."

Sally said, "You have to go to school so many more years these days—college time—like my beau. When you've graduated and set up your business, you've lost interest in starting a family. At least that's what most of the bachelors in Cooperstown say."

"Rubbish," the older woman said, continuing her string of interesting profanities. "It's because of these men's clubs. That's the problem with men these days. If you can go chat with your friends at these private men's clubs who needs a wife. Who wants children to disturb your completely selfish lifestyle?"

Mrs. Sloat added her two cents. "The men's clubs can be a refuge for them, and, I dare say, single and married men alike seem to harbor there; but, Lillian, young men and women are more independent these days. Girls can get *jobs* and sometimes make more money than their husbands. They want to be independent and don't want the responsibility of a family and cleaning up after a husband."

An ugly girl who would never marry said, "I think the problem started when those *summer girls* showed up around here. Summer girls spring up all over the place in Cooperstown in June."

I was wondering if she were placing me in the category of a "summer girl" since I had shown in June for a supposed vacation.

"They see the young men and flirt and carry on like hussies. Then when the boy is in love with them and wants a commitment —poof—they're gone. Our moral and mannerly boys soon learn to flirt and fawn all over them-realizing that they can get what they want without a wedding ring. If you read my meaning."

"Lucy, such shameful talk," Mrs. Sloat said.

"Well, it's true, isn't it?" Lucy said.

Many young ladies in the room agreed with her.

"It's education's fault. More and more education. Our men would rather trade culture for the love of a good woman. Have a substantial library and intellectual discussions with their male friends instead of a woman's companionship."

I was realizing what a gem I had in Cuyler. I also felt proud that I had managed to turn his 1897 ideas around.

"Education? Oh, Ethel, how can you say that?"

Ethel said, "They learn so much about economics, business, hygiene, and mental growth until they value *it* above living with a family."

"She's right. A man grows fearful as he gets educated. Knowledge is less expensive than a wife and her charms. Education refines away the natural inclination to be married, I think," said another.

A few older women agreed to this last statement.

"Doesn't have any 'gross' instincts after a while, if you know what I mean," said one, as she raised her eyebrow and signaled that she was speaking of lust.

Gross instincts? Does she mean that the more knowledgeable a man becomes; the less he needs sex?

"And a woman is such a comfort too. She can decorate his house, teach his children, make him good, healthy, nutritious food, plan a nice dinner table, and care for the whole family when they're sick."

That's it? I was beginning to see the problem. No wonder this era was repressed. I knew something they didn't, however. Despite his mannerly devotion to his mother, church, family, and friends, and in every way the most Victorian of all men I have ever known: Cuyler was *not* repressed. He might have been, but he wasn't now. That was what they all needed to learn. Men and women weren't cold to sex. They never had been. They never would be. The mores of society might have changed the outwardly appearance, but the inner man and woman craved exactly what they had craved since day one. To pretend differently would only cause more problems for society: adultery, abandonment, broken marriages, broken hearts, and villains like Ellis. They were lying to themselves if they thought differently.

The sad point was that the young ladies in this room believed that they should not enjoy sex, and that they should stay home and let their husband's work for them. The reverend's lecture was not a novel notion for Christians exclusively. Cuyler mentioned the hygiene book he and his friends had secretly read. Not a helpmate, not a friend, a Victorian wife was just a noose around a poor guy's neck.

It was time for Trudy to set the record straight. As Victorian as I may have to act, I had to help the young women see their way into the new century. I took a deep breath and forged ahead.

"Excuse me." Everyone became silent. "If men and women are both being educated, and both finding jobs, why can't they both work, or at least work side by side in the same business? Maybe men would marry sooner if they saw they had a helpmate, as the Good Book tells women to be," I said. Did you notice I got the Good Book in there in case I would be lynched?

Gasps

"Oh, Trudy, you can't mean that you would stop cooking, cleaning, and raising your children to take a job."

"Well, Cuyler and I have a small apartment that doesn't require much maintenance. I plan on helping Cuyler by working in the hardware store while he runs our coal business. He approves too."

The young girls swarmed to my side grinning.

"I'd love to do that too, Gertrude. How did you convince such an educated man like Cuyler to agree to it?"

"It's precisely because he is educated that he agreed. We can make a great deal of money this way, keep the farm, and build our dream house for our future family. And when the day arrives to have children, I'll still help him in the store while suckling my child."

"You can't mean that," said Ethel.

"I do! After all, we're in this together. Why should Cuyler do everything by himself while I choose drapes? We need the money. We have no fortune." Little did they know.

Lillian said, "She's been reading *The Ladies' Home Journal*, hasn't she, Olive?"

"These notions you have about the woman's place being in the home are erroneous. Our pioneer women worked alongside their husbands, and in the Middle Ages many women owned land and fought battles to save their homes while their husband's were off with the king on some crusade. This is not modern life I speak of; it is as old as Adam and Eve."

"A suffragette, oh, Olive, I'm so sorry," said Ethel.

"A woman should not be placed on some ancient Greek pedestal. She's not some tyrant on a throne for a man to toil for. She should share his sorrows and his successes and should be entitled to equal consideration when she is sick etcetera."

Sally's little friend said, "My friend, Grace Bowen, gave a lecture on that very subject at the Methodist Episcopal Church just this June."

Ah, those lively Methodists.

"There was a full congregation there when she spoke on 'Women's Work in the World.' Many people thought her speech was very wise. And not just women were there to hear her. She said the same thing Gertrude just did. The new woman of the new century."

I was winning the war with the young women, but the old women in the room would hand me a new battle.

"What about your own artistic pursuits, Gertrude?" said one.

"I write, and I can do that after my chores are done. This lightening of the strain of man's labors will aid not destroy the family and our society. Your husbands will have more time for leisure and start to enjoy their children and the time they spend in their warm, comfortable homes. This revised standard of educated men and women building homes, rather than simply worrying about money, will keep your men out of the men's clubs and in their favorite easy chair."

"What about the home? Who will clean and cook?"

"I should hope that a man would help there too," I said. "I mean, if the woman is pulling in her share of the money, I think he might not mind washing a dish or two."

The ugly one said, "Cuyler? Washing dishes? That'll be the day!"

My face turned beet red. "He does and happily too. If the most solid bachelor you have ever had in Cooperstown can wash a breakfast plate, just think what will happen to the more domestically inclined."

Ethel smiled. "Well, don't expect us to tea soon, dear. Without a woman's touch, I suspect your apartment will be chaos."

"What's more important, a doily laden chair, a finely draped window, a carefully organized cupboard, or a happy and satisfied husband?" I said.

"They'll starve for want of nutritious food. Gertrude won't have *time* to cook."

"There is a pleasant restaurant across the street in need of a few solid customers. You needn't worry, though, I like to cook. The one thing Cuyler will never starve for is my love. That I shall give him in tremendous portions." I looked over to see Mother Carr's reactions. She was grinning from ear to ear and her eyes were twinkling.

"Many husbands are probably going to the men's clubs to have a conversation that doesn't require them to make a judgment on disciplining the children or choosing the color of the drapes," I said. "I'm sure they dare not smoke or discuss politics at home."

One lady, who probably had only been married a few years, said, "I wish he *would* talk politics with me. I'd like to find out what his thoughts are on matters I've read about in *The Freeman's Journal*."

"The next time he goes to fetch his hat to leave for The Mohican Club, ask him to sit down and talk with you about some subject...any subject. Ask him whether he wants a second cup of coffee and light his cigar. Show him how knowledgeable you are on the news since you're obviously well read."

"Did you say you're a writer, Gertrude?" Lillian said.

"Yes, I write novels." I added quickly, "But, I haven't published any yet. Fiction," I grinned, "not political."

Mrs. Sloat said, "What are they about?"

"They're love stories," I said.

Sally's eyes glimmered. "Love stories," she gushed. "Oh, tell us about one. I should think a love story would be just the thing for a wedding party to hear."

"Well," someone filled my cup with coffee, "I just wrote one about Charles Hemingway and Penelope Chauncer. Do you want to hear that one?"

They did. We did not get home until eleven o'clock, and I was forced to make my own way home with the horse and buggy on those dark, hilly roads of Toddsville. I didn't mind at all. I was able, for the first time in my life, to see the eyes and facial expressions of my audience as I told the romantic tale of the heir of Hemingway estates and the proud and courageous beauty who stood by his side and helped him all the way from chapter one to chapter twenty-four. I had been in writer's heaven.

Cuyler was waiting for us. He looked none the worse for wares and smelled only of tobacco.

"I was worried sick about you three," he said. "Where have you been all night?" I wanted to tell him that we had been watching male strippers and drinking champagne, but, of course, that was too 1990 for Mrs. Sloat. We had stuffed the gifts into the rig as best we could, and Cuyler helped me bring them into the house so that his mother and Johanna could go to bed.

After we had settled the horse I said, "How was your bachelor party? Naked women jump out of huge cakes? Lots of jokes about married life?"

He grabbed the usual spot and hugged me tight enough to stop my breathing. He passionately kissed me causing an immediate physical reaction from my weary anatomy.

"What's wrong?" I said.

"Nothing's wrong. I just sat there all night and listened to them. Those who were married—those who were single. On and on they spoke of their horrible lives and their boring wives, and how there would always be a spot saved for me at the Carr Hotel's social room if I wanted to chat or have a smoke. It was *expected* that I was heading for a *horrid* experience. I began to have 'cold feet' as they call it. Then I thought of you, and what it would be like to *not* be married to you, and...well...I just had to hold you in my arms and tell you that's all. Tell you that I can't wait to start my life with you."

"I know exactly what you mean. I had the same experience only in reverse. We really aren't like all the others, are we?"

"Out of the loop with the rest of time, to be sure," he said.

"We have a busy two days coming. We should go to bed. It's late." I touched his cheek lovingly and started to walk across the street to the front door. He pulled me back. His lips were fire. He wanted me. I felt likewise. His body was lit with a new flame; and my body wanted to burn forever in his; but we closed the door between us after we said goodnight.

Chapter Twenty-Four

We moved Friday. While everyone else in the household was bustling into each other—some aunts had shown up to help Mother Carr—Cuyler and I made matters worse by driving all the gifts and our own personal items to Milford...including the typewriter. Cuyler even volunteered to purchase some new paper for my art.

"Your uncles mentioned that you might have more to tell me about the Carr tradition. Is now a good time?" I said.

"I suppose the family skeletons might just as well come out of their secret chambers all at once." He slapped Samuel's rear with the leather reins, and we headed to Milford with our buckboard full of treasures. It would be the last time we would be in Milford for two weeks, so there was extra significance added to the trip today.

The sky was overcast—what else is new—but the breeze was warm and the air comfortable. I found my tablet and took notes as he talked.

"According to the records of the First Presbyterian Church in Cooperstown, Lucy Carr, a sister of my grandfather, Ephraim Carr, married Levi Kelley May 22, 1817. Kelley was a millwright. Many mills, now demolished, along Oaks Creek, contributing to the business life of this section, were the result of his labor. He was a wonderful mechanic, and his sense of adjustment was so keen that he could 'true' a corner or set a post without the aid of a plumb."

"I'm not sure I understand why this is a big secret?"

"Be patient. He possessed an uncontrollable temper, and, during his fits of anger, would throw a fellow workman any tool he might have in his hand or was within his reach." He checked my spelling by glancing over my shoulder.

"Kelley purchased a farm in Pierstown, and Aunt Lucy furnished one-half of the money to pay for the property with the understanding that the deed should be a joint one. When the transfer was made, he had the papers drawn in his name, ignoring the agreement with his wife. She requested him to transfer one-half of the place, but he shook his fist in her face exclaiming 'That is your deed.'"

I put my pencil down in my lap. "The bastard."

"Precisely."

"He used to sleep with a loaded shot gun at the head of his bed, and his treatment of his wife became so abusive that she left him and returned to the home of her bachelor brother, Robert Carr, where she lived until her death in 1855."

"So, that's why you agreed to joint deeds and accounts. I thought it a rather open-minded attitude for a man from this time period. This, plus what happened in Scotland, is why the Carr's hate any man who hurts a woman," I said.

"Yes, of course, but there's more to the story. In April 1827, Kelley leased the farm to Abram Spaford. From almost the beginning, he began to find fault with his tenant, and on several occasions stated to neighbors, 'I'll put a ball through him before summer is over.'"

He leaned over to me and checked my notes again. "No, that's spelled wrong, Gertrude. It's Abram not Abraham."

"Thank you. Go on with the story."

"The dreadful day occurred September 3, 1827. Spaford was drawing oats, and the place where he was unloading them displeased the landlord. Spaford went to the house while Kelley repaired to his part of the dwelling. He went into his bedroom, got the gun, and, passing around to the Spaford side, entered the kitchen and shot his tenant. The unfortunate man received the charge beneath his right breast exclaiming, 'Oh Lord! I am dead,' and sank into the arms of his distracted wife, who was left a widow with seven small children." As he put more animation into his storytelling, he almost lost Samuel's reins.

"Am I talking too quickly, Gertrude?"

"Go on. I'll catch up."

"Kelley was arrested and removed to the jail at Cooperstown. While there, one of his neighbors called to see him and upon leaving said, 'I hope you will receive justice.' The murderer replied, 'That is what I am afraid of.' While in prison, he sent for his wife, but the Carr brothers said to their sister, 'No, you cannot visit that murderer!' And she never went to see him."

This was even better than the "red house" story. I wrote furiously.

"On November 20, Kelley's case was moved to trial. The Honorable Samuel Nelson presided at the term. Stakweather,

Campbell, and Collier defended the murderer while E.B. Morehouse conducted the prosecution. The jury rendered a verdict of guilty, and the prisoner was sentenced to die, the Honorable Justice speaking as follows: 'The sentence of the laws is: that you, Levi Kelley, on Friday, December 28, between the hours of 12 at noon and 3 thereafter be taken from the prison to the place of execution, and there hung by the neck until you are dead; and God have mercy on your immortal soul.'"

I shivered when he said the words.

"Your aunt never regretted seeing him one last time," I said. "I mean, even if he were a rat; he was her husband. They might have shared some nice times together."

"When the Carr men take over a situation, and a decision has been made; no one in the family shall overrule it. That isn't to say that the heart of the woman may not have, at least, wanted to make her peace with the man. Of that, I cannot be sure. Anyway, Kelley was executed at a public hanging in the village, and people came from far and near to view the gruesome spectacle. Seats were constructed about the gallows, and at one place the weight of the people became so great the timbers gave way, and several persons were injured. The murderer hearing the noise inquired of the sheriff the cause, and when told of the accident said, 'I'm sorry.' The black cap was adjusted, rope tightened, trap sprung, and Kelley went to meet his Creator."

"After his death," Cuyler continued, "several relatives requested permission to inter his body in the Carr burying ground near Toddsville, but the five brothers said that: no murderer would ever be buried in their cemetery, and the resolution of one hundred years has never been broken. Several years ago, in conversation with Mr. Benjamin F. Fish, he stated that his father told him that Kelley was buried back of the Presbyterian Church in Cooperstown, in an unmarked grave dug nine feet deep and filled in with alternate layers of brick and earth. Ah, we're home!"

Even writing as fast as I could, I was not finished writing the story, nor ready to start unloading our cargo. "That's the end of the story?"

"Death, Gertrude, has a way of finishing a tale, yes. However, my father used to quote verses about the murder of Spaford and Kelley's execution. I can't remember all of them, but I do remember this one:

In eighteen-hundred twenty-seven,
Old Kelley broke the laws of heaven.
He murdered his poor tenant there,
Who took his farm to work for share."

"Could you repeat that? A little slower this time?" I said. He did so as he tied Samuel to the hitching post then opened the door to the apartment.

Mrs. Bates peered from her door. "Well, how's the happy couple today?"

"Just fine, Mrs. Bates," I said. "We have to unload some gifts. We won't be around for some time. Can you keep an eye on the place for us? We're going on our wedding trip," I added.

"Well, of course, Gertie, I know what that's all about." She winked.

How do you tell your sweet, old, neighbor lady that if she keeps calling you 'Gertie' you might have to pull a Kelley number yourself.

I have to admit; we made short work of moving in. We dropped everything in the middle of the floor, except clothing, which we placed in our closets and new bureau.

We made our way back home discussing all the excitement that would start tonight at our rehearsal dinner. Cuyler asked about the rings which I still had in my drawer.

We managed to fly through the front door at three o'clock. I hurried to my room to get the smaller, gold band, which would be placed on my finger. He was waiting at my bedroom door. I handed him the precious gold ring. He held it between his thumb and index finger as if it were a diamond.

"Who would have guessed that only a few week's ago a bizarre incident would turn into such joy?" he said.

We changed clothes quickly and hastened downstairs. The house looked beautiful, and Johanna looked tired. I wore one of my fancier dresses, the one with the lace on the collar and sleeves, and my newly inherited necklace and earrings. Cuyler wore his best suit, the one that reminded me of the photo he had taken. Mother Carr was sporting her Sunday best. We had to wait for Johanna to change clothes, but soon we were on our way to the Fenimore Hotel.

We were ushered to a private room resplendent with flowers,

lace tablecloth, and linen napkins fanned and clasped with a brass ring at each seat. Beautiful cream china, adorned with pink roses, twinkled with the reflections from the lit candles and crystal chandeliers. A burgundy tapestry rug lay on the planked wooden floors. A delicious aroma of onions, beef, and hot coffee permeated the room.

One by one everyone arrived, and we said grace and sat down to the feast. Savory roast, steaming hot red potatoes, and beans filled our plates. We drank wine with the meal and some champagne with our raspberry truffle dessert.

The head of the Carr clan made a toast wishing happiness, love, and a life-fulfilled for both of us. Daniel made a toast for the bride and groom to have a happy life and to remember the rings.

Then Cuyler stood.

"Tomorrow is my wedding day." He hesitated while everyone giggled and made surprised-he-remembered comments. "And I want all those whom I love, gathered in this room tonight, to know how happy I am. I have found the woman who has already made my dreams come true, an eternal friend, and a lifetime lover. Not only is she beautiful on the surface, but she is lovely, beyond words, on the inside, as well. She is an angel, whom I've been lucky enough to find on earth. I want you to show Gertrude the friendship, love, and laughter you have all shared with me in the past, and bestow your blessings on this union from this day forward." Everyone sipped their champagne again as if he had proclaimed a toast.

"Furthermore..."

Someone said, "Shut him up quick, or we'll never make it to the rehearsal."

Even I had to snicker at that one.

He glared at his cousin. "*Furthermore*, tomorrow is my beloved Gertrude's birthday."

How could I have forgotten that Saturday was my birthday?

"And, as it is bad luck to see the bride before the ceremony, and we will be far too busy afterwards at the reception; I have this gift which I would like to present to her on the eve of our first birthday together and the first day of our lives as a couple." Everyone clapped.

He produced a lovely, wrapped package which reminded me of

the one I had for him. I was stunned. I unwrapped the gift and opened the box. Inside was a strand of pearls and at the center was a cameo. The white face had been etched by a local artist, and it was me. Of course, it was far prettier than me, but it had the Bertha collar of lace—which I had on all of my dresses and blouses—my profile—with a smile upon the lips— and it had fine, curled, *short* hair.

"Do you like it, Gertrude?" he said.

I was speechless. "Oh, Cuyler, it's lovely. Is it me?"

"Of course. Do you know any other Gibson Girl with short hair?"

I stood, hugged him, and then kissed him in front of the whole party.

"Wear it tomorrow for me with your wedding dress. Happy birthday, Gertrude."

"Wait a minute. Don't sit down. I have a wedding gift for you too. And for like reasons, I suggest you open yours tonight.

I would etch the expression on his face into my memory book forever. He was thrilled with the watch. When he opened it, and read the personal inscription inside, he wrapped his arms around me and everyone cheered.

"My father's watch is irreparably broken. How could you have known? I'm overwhelmed."

This started the whole evening on a most pleasant and joyous note. We decided to walk to the church. It was a few blocks away, and the evening was warm. Daniel skipped and jogged. The older ladies were driven in a rig.

I felt as if I were living a dream. The music of the organ—whatever hymns the organist had chosen—the soft light of the church; Daniel grinning as I placed my arm in his; the processional; Sally and Mrs. Sloat taking their places at the altar; Cuyler's face glistening; the words the reverend spoke; his mother's tears; Mrs. Sloat's tears; the Carr's smiling then teasing their brethren if he so much as hesitated on a word.

"Come on, Cuyler. Spit it out. It's too late to back out now," said 'Poe uncle.'

When we had completed the fake ceremony, everyone went outside while Cuyler and I had a few last minute words with the preacher.

"I'm so happy for both of you. Don't worry about all the particulars of the wedding. They shall take care of themselves. You only get married once, praise God. Enjoy every minute of it." And then, he prayed for us and hurried down the aisle of the church and out into the yard.

"Are you as excited as I am?" he said.

"Of course. I'm a little sad that my family is not here to see me marry you. It's difficult to believe that all this started as a sham because I dropped into your bed. Remember how you said that you would just go to the next cabin, and I would fade out of the picture?" I said.

"Yes, and do you remember going on and on about floral negligees and city hall?" Cuyler said.

"I also remember how you believed my story on faith alone."

"Whatever supernatural power has brought us together, I'm supremely grateful It has. Someone, somewhere, was certainly making it very clear we were to marry."

"Probably your father," I said.

He chuckled. "Well, I wouldn't put it past him to drop a gorgeous woman into my bed so that I would take the hint."

We exchanged a soft and reverent kiss before the altar. As far as we were concerned, we were man and wife.

Chapter Twenty-Five

I must have overslept because when I came down for breakfast Cuyler was gone, and a tub of lukewarm water was waiting for me. A bath? Glorious! I ate rapidly and plunged my naked body into the soapy water. I scrubbed every inch of me until my skin was crimson.

Then Johanna did my hair, making it look as if it had been wrapped into a bun, with small curls framing my face. Some powder dabbed here, and some perfume there, then into my wedding-white satin and lace lingerie.

I complimented Johanna on the spread of food she had prepared. Barrels of ice and jars of punch were ready for the guests. Cake and cookies, trays filled with cheese and meat for making sandwiches, salads, deviled eggs and so forth were waiting in the pantry.

She showed me our wedding cake. Four round layers decorated artistically with my pink and white color scheme. Tiny rosettes and ribbons of pink icing caressed its sides.

Mother Carr tiptoed into my room and hugged me. She was dressed and ready for the twelve-thirty wedding.

I stayed in my room and remained quiet while they finished their last minute chores.

The full extent of this wonderful dream struck me. I would marry the man of my dreams in two hours. Sally would come by to help me into my dress, and then I would arrive at the church in time to be escorted down the aisle by my new friend Daniel. How lucky could I be? I took the necklace Cuyler had given me from its box and smiled at the perky, pretty face he had fashioned for me. This is who I am—this woman changed by love. He sees me as this happy, beautiful woman; therefore, I have become the reflection of his love—his ideal—in the image on this cameo.

If Jennifer could see me now. I looked quite different from the author who needed a vacation from my work. There was a special shimmer, a glow, and I could see it in my reflection in the mirror. A little twinkle came into my eyes when I thought of Cuyler.

My life had new meaning. It was more than a deadline or a

story line. I had a lifeline. I suppose I had been kidding myself all along. I was rich and famous, but, I wasn't living. Only love can resurrect the lost life that exists within a person's broken heart. Only love can bring your soul back from the dead. It had blown its sweet breath into my living corpse. You will see who you really are when you find your reflection in the eyes of the one who loves you. It's up to you to return that gift of life. *And I had given life to Cuyler.*

You can read all my romance novels, but you won't find what you're searching for there. My stories can never replace this special reality. When you find it; you'll doubt it's real. You'll see it twinkling in some special person's eyes like a heavenly star. If you see it—run to it. Little stars have a way of fading when they can't find their partner's glow.

Today was a beautiful, bright, and breezy day July 10, 1897. My birthday—my wedding day.

Sally rushed upstairs and threw open the door of my bedroom. My first thought was to tell her how pretty she looked in her gown.

"Hurry, Gertrude!" she exclaimed.

We placed the gorgeous ivory satin gown on my small frame. The rosettes made me blush and smile as soon as they were in my hair, and the veil was not so long as to be cumbersome.

"Cuyler asked me to give you this," she said grinning.

It was a full bouquet of pink roses tied with ivory satin ribbons. They smelled of summer, fresh mountain water, and cotton candy. I slipped into my satin boots, and Sally laced them for me. We flew out of the bedroom. Then I hurried back to get the satin bag that held my wedding ring for Cuyler.

Daniel was waiting to drive us to the church in his rig. He gave a low whistle when he saw me.

"Like I said before, Cuyler is one lucky man. Do you have everything?" I shook my head yes after I checked the bag to make sure the ring was there.

We made good time.

Sally adjusted my veil and train and watched the gown as it followed me up the steps and onto the sidewalk that led to the green door. Mrs. Sloat was waiting there.

She started to cry. "Oh, my, Gertrude, it's as if you were my own daughter. You're so gorgeous." She played with the gown and the veil so that it would be perfect for my entrance. I adjusted the cameo on my collar so that it fell correctly at the base of my throat. I wanted Cuyler to see that I was wearing it.

The chapel was decorated with pink roses and white satin ribbons cascading to the floor. The end of each pew had a white satin ribbon, and three fresh roses attached to the center of it. The altar had baskets of overflowing roses and ribbons which covered the altar. Candles were lit upon the altar, and large candle sticks with white candles stood by the first pews. The empty first pew on the bride's side of the church threw me unexpectedly.

The stained glass windows gleamed as the sun sifted through their colors. The white runner was placed on the ailse to protect my gown, and its chapel length train. The perfume of a floral garden filled the chapel. This scent blended with the aroma of the burned wax from the candles. The sanctuary whispered reverent peace.

Sally and Mrs. Sloat looked like princesses in their lovely handmade gowns and both held smaller bouquets of roses and ribbons.

The audience was chattering, but when the music grew louder all discussion ceased.

My heart was pounding so hard it hurt my chest. My mouth lost all moisture. I started to breathe deeply. Daniel patted my hand to reassure me. My gloved hands were wet with nervous perspiration. My head felt dizzy. I was wondering if Cuyler was sensing this exhilaration too. If they didn't start the wedding soon the bride would faint.

The wedding march began. First, Sally waltzed down the aisle, then Mrs. Sloat. The guests rose and the music crescendoed. Daniel took my arm. This was our cue. I looked to him for support, and he smiled.

"You wouldn't want to live without him, would you?" he said.

I trembled. "Not a second." I took my first step onto the white runner with my "father." Everyone stared at us.

It was at that precise moment that I had my initial glimpse of Cuyler in his starched white shirt, bow tie, pink rose boutonniere, black tuxedo jacket and tails, and tartan KILT!

So *that* was the big secret. We were having a traditional Scottish wedding. All the Carr men, who were ushers—and the

'Poe uncle,' who was the best man—were wearing formal kilts. And it's a real good thing they had that little chat with me, because with my sense of humor, I might have had a giggling fit just as I sailed down the aisle.

I'd never seen a Scottish wedding in my life, and, therefore, would never have guessed what he had in mind. I'd heard about them from Jennifer and my mother, but I'd never encountered a solemn man wearing a kilt who wasn't playing a bagpipe in a parade. If I didn't know that these men had a history of warfare and mayhem, I would never have understood the proud wearing of the Carr family tartan.

Daniel murmured after noticing my shocked expression, "Didn't tell you about the kilt, did he?"

"No, he didn't. But, it is *my* Tartan now. I'll be a Carr in ten minutes."

"Well, you know Cuyler. He likes you to be just a *wee bit* surprised. It's his personality. We wouldn't love him any other way." He winked at me, and I smiled.

After the music's introduction, we proceeded down the center ailse. Daniel grinned and greeted everyone with a wink, wave, or a nod of his head. I was looking in only one direction, at my future husband who was grinning with pride as his beloved, in her beautiful satin and lace gown, swished past each line of pews. He grinned a personal tribute to me. I returned a radiant smile. I wasn't nervous anymore.

When the music ceased, the reverend asked who would give me to Cuyler. Daniel acknowledged his role, kissed me on the cheek, and offered my hand to Cuyler. Cuyler's hands were warm as my gloved palm touched his strong fingers.

"Gertrude, you look unbelievably beautiful today," he said in a hushed voice.

"You look sort of Scottish," I said.

"I suppose I should have warned you," he acknowledged.

The reverend was giving a sermon on married life as we eyed each other and ignored him completely. I'm sure you can just guess what his lecture was about. I didn't hear a word he said until he wanted us to repeat our vows.

"Do you, Cuyler Carr, take this woman, Gertrude Johnson, to be your lawfully wedded wife?"

"I do," Cuyler said.

"Do you, Gertrude Johnson, take this man, Cuyler Carr, to be your lawfully wedded husband?"

"I do," I said.

We held hands and repeated the reverend's phrasing of our vows: "I, Gertrude, take thee, Cuyler, to love and to cherish-to have and to hold-for better or for worse-

-from this century to that century -

-for richer or poorer, in sickness and in health, and forsaking all others for as long as we both shall live. With these words, I pledge my love."

We exchanged our rings and smiled into our newly married spouse's face.

"You may kiss the bride, Cuyler," the reverend said.

My husband embraced me before the congregation. Cuyler whispered into my ear, "Happy Birthday, darling."

"It is my esteemed honor to present to you—Mr. and Mrs. Cuyler E. Carr."

The organist played; everyone applauded. Daniel whistled; Mrs. Sloat cried some more; Mother Carr was crying buckets now; and Sally was jumping up and down as she clapped her hands. The best man hugged Cuyler, and I think I saw him brush away a tear. We stepped into our own new world.

As we would forever and ever, passed this life, and well into the next.

Putt snapped a family portrait in the front yard of the church. We had the church's door and the bright white walls of the church as a backdrop. We froze waiting for the picture to take. The brass hands of the clock above us touched the one. The bells chimed. We had been married one half hour.

Rice cascaded like tiny apple blossom petals over our heads as we ran to Cuyler's uncle's formal carriage. Everyone else raced to their rigs. And didn't all Cooperstown come out onto the streets to wave and proclaim their good wishes to us. I felt as though I were the queen of the Rose Parade. We heard even more cheering as we rode through Toddsville and out into the country.

Johanna had somehow beaten her own path before us in Cuyler's tea cart. She greeted us and offered refreshments. Cuyler and I met all of our guests and noticed a fresh array of new gifts to open in the parlor. I guess we had more friends than I knew.

I didn't feel much like eating and enjoyed the discussions with the family, as my husband and I opened the gifts and shared stories with the eldest member present, Samuel Street Todd.

Soon, it was time to cut the wedding cake. With our hands clasping the silver knife, we sliced a piece of white cake. I fed him a small piece. He did likewise. We kissed. There was just no sense at all in not embracing each other repeatedly. We were married now. Mother Carr hugged us both and begged another photo for the album. So Cuyler and I posed under the archway of the front porch and waited patiently for Putt to take our picture.

A three piece orchestra, I think it was the same one at the dance, played various tunes and everyone danced on the green grass. We twirled in each others arms, but I suddenly froze when one particular tune began to play.

"Cuyler, that's *your tune*. The Irish one," I said.

"Yes, the one I like to whistle. Why?"

"Because I can't place the name of it."

"Oh, it's an old one. It's *I'll Take You Home Again, Kathleen.* It was popular when I was a lad. They still play it quite a bit, especially at weddings. I think my cameo looks splendid on your wedding dress."

"I see you've slipped my watch into your vest pocket." I whispered into his ear, "I only have one question."

"What is that?" he said.

"What do Scotsmen wear under their kilts?"

He grinned. "Come upstairs and find out." With that said, he grabbed my hand, and we raced into the house, up the stairs, into my room, and closed the door behind us.

"Time to leave, Gertrude. Change from your pretty dress to your traveling suit. We have a cabin waiting for us."

"Just let me throw the bouquet from the window." I called to all the eligible bachlorettes to hurry to the window. Their excited pleas to have me throw my beautiful bouquet to them made me sad to part with Cuyler's gift.

"Take the center out," he said. When I did, four small roses tied with ribbons eased from the bouquet. "Just for you."

I hurled the church bouquet from the window, and Sally caught it. I said, "You're next, Sally." All the girls squealed with delight and hugged her generously.

He removed my veil but let the tiny rosette band stay like a halo around my curled hair. "You're beautiful."

He removed the necklace. "I love you," he said. Then the long satin gloves were gone. He eased the train from the back of the gown.

I undid the bow tie from his throat. "You look as if this is choking you."

Then I slipped the jacket from his shoulders and undid the vest button by button. I slipped the starchy, white shirt from his tanned and muscular arms.

"Gertrude, my clothes are in my room. I can't run naked from room to room." He slipped the shirt back onto his shoulders but did not bother to button it.

"Very well," he said, "two can play at this game."

He undid the clasps on the back of the dress and carefully liberated me from the classic gown. He found the satin covered hanger and placed the dress there buttoning it to make it stay. I wore an elegant satin camisole with tiny pink roses and ivory ribbons which I had special ordered from the lingerie store's catalogue. New ivory stockings were fastened securely at mid-thigh. Two garters lay beneath the lacy tops of the stockings and one tiny, pink rosette lay upon each. The rest of my honeymoon attire lay folded inside the tapestry bag that I was taking with me. I wore thin, satin panties with lace at the rim. I knew the sunshine, that was glowing behind me from the window, gave a perfect profile of my femininity.

An innocent yet seductive smile played upon my lips. "I'm all yours." Sauntering, with a sway to my hips, I slipped my arms around his chest and gazed intently into his eyes. He curled his lip devilishly which made a dimple in his cheek. There was a wicked twinkle in his eye. I closed my eyes and waited for his kiss.

"You want me to kiss you?" he said.

"Yes."

"No!" he said.

"No?" I asked.

"No! And you will never get the answer to your question either. Not until you change your clothes and meet me, with your packed bag, precisely five minutes from now, in my rig. We need to find our cabin as fast as possible. It's five already. I'm going to my room to change," he said in a deep voice ringing with true Victorian authority. "Tarry not lest I find displeasure so soon with my new wife. *Five minutes.*" He was gone.

I made rapid work of the suit, placed vanilla scent behind each ear, grabbed my bag, rushed down the stairs, and leaped into the tea cart that had been transformed like magic with flowers from Mother Carr's garden and ribbons.

Cuyler came from the house with one bag. He called to the people in the back who we were leaving. So much for formality. He jumped into the rig, snapped up Samuel's reins, and watched as every guest hurried from the left side of the house to say farewell. I'm sure they had many wonderful things to say, but I heard none of them.

I did see Daniel who said, "You can do some fishing in your new boat, Cuyler, when you get bored with other things." The men laughed; the women blushed. Cuyler's pals just shook their heads as if they were watching the executioner fasten that black covering over his head and tighten the noose.

The Carr men looked proud. Mother Carr blew us a kiss. I could tell she was about to cry again. Johanna winked at me.

The other women wore painful expressions on their faces. Their brows knit together in a grimace; they waved and tried to smile for me. "Be brave, Gertrude," it seemed they were saying, "maybe it won't be so bad." Oh, Lord, what a time period to live in.

We took the road into Flycreek and tried to soothe our tangled nerves. I laid my head on his arm as he whistled his Irish ballad to Samuel and me. He was taking me to our first home.

There was gray between the cream colored clouds when we arrived. The sun was scribbling its saphire and magenta signature across the sky as it bade farewell to the earth.

I was hungry. I peeked under the seat, and, sure enough, there was a picnic lunch filled with samples of all Johanna's wonderful goodies we had turned down when we were too exhilarated to eat.

We took our bags into the bedroom and placed our clothes into the bureau. I put any perishable food into the icebox and was surprised to see that someone had left a bottle of champagne and two crystal goblets for us. I wondered who.

Cuyler suggested that it might be a gift from Isaac Cooper. That was cute, I thought. From Sam, Jim, and Isaac. Congrats. We did not open the bottle. Right now we needed to relax and eat.

It'd been a tiring week and a dynamic day.

We had our wedding repast on the porch and observed the sunset together. Hugging each other as married couples do, we watched until the streaks of orange and violet diminished. We kissed. "I don't see any signs of a storm, do you?" he said.

I thought that was clever. "And Mrs. Bates would have a horrid time bringing us stew all the way up here," I said.

"Unless Daniel has a sail for the boat, I can't imagine why he would need to 'drop in.'"

"There's so much food at the homestead, I can't imagine the Carrs riding over to share anything with us."

"I think we've finally made it. Alone at last," he said.

One of the squirrels, climbing down the tall tree in front of us, wiggled his nose asking if we might share some crumbs from our dinner. "Well, almost alone. Pay him off-quick," I said.

Cuyler threw some bread crumbs to the 'critter,' while I hastened to our room and put on the seductively beautiful satin and lace peignoir that I had purchased in 'Victorian's Secret.'

I placed it over the corset and stockings. If he were going to indulge in this sweet teasing, so was I. There are precisely 14 hooks on a corset, and I would make him undo every last one of them.

I gazed at my feminine reflection in the small bureau mirror. We were going to have some honeymoon. Two weeks. Pure heaven in his arms, but this time we were going to play by *my rules*. I'd been devising a plot for days.

I opened the door of our bedroom and posed, leaning my shoulder on the door frame, and looking as inticing as a woman can look. I toyed with the satin ribbon ties on the robe and smiled coyly. He was just bringing the last of our dinner into the kitchen and placing it in the icebox.

"Gertrude!" he said.

"You know something, dearest, I've heard many wonderful stories since I became your intimate companion," I growled provocatively. "But, you have *never* heard one of mine," I said.

He was not certain what I had in mind, but he was willing to do anything the lady in the satin nightgown wanted.

"Oh, well," he said. His throat must have felt like the Sahara desert, because his voice sounded hoarse and parched. "Of course, Gertrude, anytime you want to tell me one of your novel's plots, I'd be happy to hear it."

"*Tonight!* "

He grinned, like a child whose best friend has just invented a game he knows nothing about. He was a good sport. It was one of his finer qualities. He sat on the wooden arm chair at the front of the cabin nearest the couch and placed a pillow on its seat for comfort then crossed his arms to listen.

"Once upon a time," I said, "there lived a strong-willed, handsome, intelligent, baron who lived in England in ancient times. He owned much land, great wealth, and managed it all in a firm and businesslike manner. He was the last of his family's line—the final Baron of Toddsville. His father was anxious that his son should take a wife for there were rumors that the Norman's would invade soon, and there would be terrible blood shed and loss of property. Baron Cuyler was not afraid. He welcomed the fight. His father was concerned because their lands were easily accessible to the Normans; plus, they had few knights and fewer weapons. The Baron Cuyler vowed to kill all Normans with his family's infamous sword: The Legend of Carr. His forefathers had sliced many an enemies' throat with this weapon."

"Oh, Gertrude, I *like* this story."

I smiled and continued, "The Baron's father was concerned that his son had not taken a wife, had accepted no woman's dowry, and sired no heir. What if anything should happen to either of them? So, against Baron Cuyler's wishes, his father prepared a marriage for his son. He found an anxious father with a daughter who was Cuyler's age. The woman was the last daughter of a proud Anglo-Saxon family. Her father had much wealth and property and was renowned as a fearless fighter. Why they owned half of the county of Brooklyn by the city of York on the ocean side of the continent!"

"May I take notes?" my husband said.

Very cute, Cuyler! "Certainly," I said.

In sublime imitation of me, he scurried to my tapestry bag, that I had left on the kitchen table, and found my pad and pencil. He returned to his seat and flipped to a clean page. With pencil in hand, he nodded that I should continue.

"Lady Gertrude of Johnson had no plans to wed, however. Fighting beside her father on the bloody field of battle, they had tried to erase the Norman warriors' path from their doorstep.

They had succeeded thus far. With the enemy leaping into the fray, Lady Gertrude had no intention of leaving the battlefield nor submitting to any man. She doubted that there lived a man who could win her respect. Her father feared that her virtues and property would be seized by the conquerors; her land used as a reward for victory on the battlefield; and her hand given to the strongest of the King's men. However, if she were already married to the valiant Baron of Toddsville, who was well known as a fearless fighter; he would not only have a husband for his daughter, a champion protector for his land, but a future for his family's homestead. Unbeknownst to Lady Gertrude and Baron Cuyler, their marriage was arranged for them."

"Go on. I'm trying to keep up," he said.

"I was rather hoping you were," I said, with a different interpretation of his line.

"The Lady was rushed to her castle's chapel to stand next to a fool who would be the proxy husband for Baron Cuyler. The Baron was thrust into *his* chapel to witness a greasy kitchen wench standing in for the Lady Gertrude. The wedding was quickly completed with miles between the real spouses. They were married in the eyes of the church, however."

" 'I shall never submit to this-this Baron Cuyler! You are wasting your time on futile hopes,' said Lady Gertrude. 'Father, you might just as well have married me to this fool!' " I portrayed her voice with dignity.

"And the Baron said to *his* Father, 'Am I to risk my life for not only *my* land but some simpering wench's also. This marriage is ill-conceived for I shall never bed her thus never consummating these forced nuptials.' "

" 'Well,' said the Baron's father, 'suit yourself, but now her lands are yours. The union of both houses forms a vast kingdom, indeed.' " I relayed their words by acting the characters' gestures and facial expressions.

" 'Only after her father's death, and I'm sure that won't be soon. I've heard he's quite a warrior,' mused the Baron." I had to get that one in for my Dad.

" 'Art thou mad?' screamed Lady Gertrude to her poor father. 'Do you think I will let this country fool slide between my sheets and conceive for you a grandson? He'll take my virtue to win your lands?' "

"Virtue...win...lands. Got it!" Cuyler said, scribbling on the pad.

"Not yet, but you will," I said sweetly.

"The Baron leaped onto his famous warrior steed, Samuel, and, with his army, departed to protect his newly united kingdom. When he arrived, he was amazed to see the land so much in peril. Fighting courageously at the head of the knights was the small frame of a soldier who most certainly would be killed soon. Cuyler could tell the lad was losing strength with every thrust of his heavy broad sword. Not wishing to see a fine and valiant warrior killed in perilous battle, he pledged his men to the fight."

I waltzed my frame closer to Cuyler. The satin and lace of my gown swayed in the night's summer breeze. My vanilla fragrance sweetened the air around his head. I positioned myself beside his pad and pencil. He really *was* taking notes.

"Go on, Gertrude. I've caught up with you."

"Baron Cuyler swung his infamous sword across many a Norman's throat. With the added strength of numbers, the battle favored the homeland now. His family sword wore the bloody scarlet of warriors who had met their Maker this day. They were no match for the strength and courage of this mighty hero. Baron Cuyler heard the groans of the wounded. All around him lay the mangled pieces of useless limbs and decaying lives."

"Oh, Gertrude, this *is* good. I'd no idea you could write like this."

I gave him a 'don't-interrupt-me-while-I'm-telling-a-story' look and smiled. "But, as his knights conquered countless cowardly *cads*," I continued, "Baron Cuyler beheld the young knight who had led the knights into battle so courageously. To his chagrin, the boy lay on the ground. A giant of a warrior, obviously the leader of the Normans, towered above his still form. The tip of this predecessor's sword rested on the young man's throat. Baron Cuyler knew that even if he raced to lend aid to the valiant warrior, he would be too late. Just then, he noticed some sort of conversation happening between the two. Baron Cuyler could not decipher the words. He moved closer," and so did I, "and saw the brave knight's blood-stained, helpless, left hand raise to fend off the enemy's fatal blow. He heard the ogre say, 'Aye, I see. Married! Ha-ha. I'll find him and slay him. This golden symbol will not alter my plans for you. I'll pluck the offensive joint and its band from thee.' "

"Baron Cuyler could not believe what the man was doing. The mammoth dragged the young knight to a rock, flattened the boy's left hand upon the smoothest part of it, cruelly positioned his knee on the young man's elbow, thus bracing his helpless arm for the harsh thrust of his blade, and cackled with glee as he swung his unyielding sword back and forth before the eyes of the wriggling form. The rapier would sever the third finger on the boy's trapped hand."

"Good Lord, it's the girl, isn't it, Gertrude?" he said.

I smiled to find him so immersed in *my* tale. "The monster emitted a cruel curse as he raised his sword high over the small warrior's head. " 'Tis not thy finger I desire. I'll slay thy father, take thy lands, and marry you this day. I like a woman with fire in her eyes, and I shall enjoy the challenge of watching you submit to me.' He laughed cruelly. 'And as for thy husband, what coward is he who does not protect what is rightfully his, allowing his wife to fight his battles for him.' He leaned low to speak into the squirming soldier's ear. 'I shall slice a piece of him, as well, and well you know which limb I mean. Then let him live to watch what I do with his woman and his land. So I shall end two houses—two estates—by marrying you and killing your husband's seed.' "

"Baron Cuyler knew the identity of the frail warrior instantly." My husband's face illuminated with self-gratifiction. "It was Lady Gertrude! He remembered hearing many tales of her courage. He raced to her side, and just as the villain's sword would forever carve the gold band from her ring finger, Baron Cuyler parried the blade with his own."

" 'Her husband is before you!' snarled Baron Cuyler. 'Stand and fight me, coward, or are women the only ones you fight? For I've heard your curse, and I'm here to protect this land and this woman who is my wife.' "

Cuyler loosened the tight black tie from his shirt collar. He unbuttoned his vest. Next, he slipped his feet from his shoes and coughed. He kept on taking notes though. I knew where his healthiest erogenous zone was.

"It was an evenly matched fight. A swing and a parry. Clearly Baron Cuyler was the superior warrior."

"Well, of course, that stands to reason," my Cuyler added.

"Sssh, must you always interrupt?" I said.

"Sorry," he said.

I leaned over his chair, allowed my robe to caress his cheek, and blew the battle scene into his ear.

"Baron Cuyler had the enemy on the ground and on his back. The Legend of Carr lay on the villain's throat. The loser begged for mercy."

" 'Please, I meant no harm,' begged the coward. 'I would not have hurt the lady.' "

" 'You lie! You would have killed her, then me,'" said Baron Cuyler.

" 'Nay, good knight, the field is yours this day.' "

"Baron Cuyler slackened his grip for a second and the coward pulled the hero's feet from under him so that now their positions were reversed."

" 'Now, Baron Cuyler, husband to this Anglo-Saxon slut, I shall cut off your legs, rape your woman before your eyes, then finish you for good.' "

"Gertrude!" he said, chastising my gore, but he sat less comfortably on that cushion, and I noticed.

I reclined on the couch across from him and toyed with the ribbons on my robe, smoothed the satin gown over my hips, and made sure my breasts did not crinkle the lace.

"The family sword had been thrown far from the hero's hands," I continued, "and Baron Cuyler could not reach it, try as he might. The Norman beast declared his triumph over the brave heir to the Toddsville and Brooklyn estates."

" 'Aye, and when I'm done with you,' he said to the hero, 'I shall slice your body into smaller sections, throw the bloody pieces to my valiant men, and let them place your guts on the tips of my warriors' spears. I shall behead your father-in-law and let the bloody stump sit upon the gate of his own castle. I'll take his land as my own, dividing it among my top three men. Then I'll make war on *your* father and his lands, conquer them, as well, and behead the last of the Barons of Toddsville—your father—allowing my dogs to feed upon his entrails.' "

I watched Cuyler write. "He looked to the helpless figure of the girl-knight," I continued. " 'When I've had my fill of the beautiful and spirited Lady Gertrude, I'll let my six, top captains enjoy her flesh, and then burn her at the stake for being an Anglo-Saxon witch.' "

"Good heavens, Gertrude, do you really write like this?" He shifted in his chair and straightened his trousers.

"Only when I'm feeling mellow." I stood before him. The warmed vanilla scent filtered into the air around us. I let my robe open provocatively and watched as the pencil slipped from his hand. His face burned brightly from the excitement and suspense of my story.

"Well, how does it end? Baron Cuyler? How does he win? He *does* win?" Cuyler said.

A demure smile covered my lips. "As the cad's sword glistened in the light of the burning torches..." I lowered my body to the floor below his chair and settled before him arching my back in a pin-up pose.

"Baron Cuyler made his peace with God."

"No!" said Cuyler.

"He could not move under the weight of the villain's foot pressed upon his chest. His sword was too far away for him to grasp, though he strained with all his might to touch it. His adversary witnessed the effort and thrust the sword even further away with his other foot. Baron Cuyler closed his eyes and prepared himself for the severing slash that would amputate his legs. He had fought courageously that day. He would enter Valhalla."

"Ah, excuse me, Gertrude. Valhalla? Isn't that historically inaccurate?" Cuyler said.

I skimmed the tip of my tongue slowly across my lips. "It's *my* story."

"Lady Gertrude could now reach the Baron's sword but not her own. Quietly, she raised her body from the side of the rock," I arched my body towards his, "clutched Cuyler's saber, and as the Norman's sword was about to trap her husband's movements forever, she plunged The Legendary Sword of Carr into the assailant's back and speared his lungs. The aggressor gagged and wretched but was not dead. He turned in fury towards the lady warrior."

" '*You bitch!* I'll kill you for that!' he said."

"But he spoke no further word," I continued. "Taking the lady's sword from the ground nearest his torso, Baron Cuyler punctured the scoundrel's heart. Blood spurted from his lips; no further breath did the man take. He fell forward to the ground and to his death."

"Yes! Good story, Gertrude. Fine ending. Of course, when I tell it, I may rearrange some of the Baron's actions and lengthen the fight scene between the two men."

"Who said I was done?" I said.

"Oh, sorry."

"The Baron, wet with sweat and blood looked towards the small frame of the woman warrior." I moved so that I was on my knees and only inches in front of him.

"He gave the lady his hand lifting her so that he might better behold his bride. He was grimy from the battle, but Lady Gertrude only saw how handsome he was. She examined the cut on his shoulder with her fingertips." I eased my own hero out of his vest.

"She smoothed his tousled hair." I ran my finger through the dark waves of my husband's hair.

"Her hands brushed away the dirt and mud from his wounds," one suspender down, "which he had sustained saving her father's estate and her honor," second suspender down. My eyes studied my husband's muscles. "She was *amazed* at his strong body." I unbuttoned Cuyler's shirt.

"He was tall. His face lean and rugged, and his fingers long and well shaped." I held his two hands in mine and gently kissed those fingers.

"His eyes were warm, topaz, jewels of the night." I fondled his brow and cheek with my fingers.

"His arms were strong...muscular." My hands massaged his chest.

"His chest swelled proudly and was full of dark curly hair." I leaned close to his face and kissed him tenderly on his lips, pulling at the shirt until it slid from his shoulders and out of his trousers.

" 'Are thee then my wife, warrior?' asked the gruff soldier."

" 'It appears that I am,' answered the woman mesmerized by his soulful eyes." I leaned across his lap and gave him a long and passionate kiss.

"Baron Cuyler eyed his bride curiously," I said. "For all that he could see before him was a soldier in armor, tiny loops of a chain mail tunic, her head covered with chain mail netting." I stood before my husband.

My Cuyler stood not being able to write another note. I privately claimed justice for the ghost stories. He stared at me full of yearning—full of desire.

My voice softened. " 'Then let me have a look at you, woman,' said Baron Cuyler."

"The armor breast plate dropped from her breasts," I said. I pulled the satin ribbons that tied my robe free; I let the garment fall to the floor. "And he could see the voluptuous curves of her feminine body."

" 'You are my wife?' he said. The hero was searching for words to speak, but his body was on fire. He longed to take her in his arms and claim his legal right to her."

I continued, "She pulled the chain mail netting away from her face, and he saw how lovely she was. He lost his heart to her the moment he saw the bright, sky blue of her eyes, the flashing light playing in her auburn curls, and the full red lips which begged for his embrace."

" 'I shall see to the killing of the prisoners, ascertain the needs of my men and your knights, feast at your father's table, and *then* come to thy room for our marital union,' the Baron said to her."

"Lady Gertrude stood stubbornly on her two legs, placed her hands on her hips, and stiffened her lower lip," I said.

" 'Oh, you think ye shall? Must I suffer to be treated as some reward, given to *you* the victor, when I, myself, fought this battle as well as you this day.' "

" 'Aye, you hot-tempered wench,' he said grinning. 'Well, do I like spirit in my women.' " My Cuyler watched my lips as they formed the words.

" 'Well, sir knight, I'm *not* so easily won. I may be your wife by proxy, and you might have saved my life this day—though I have returned the favor I think—but, it shall be a cold day in hell before I'll submit to you! I'd rather see you dead, than in my bed, husband.' "

My Cuyler's hands went around my waist and pulled me towards his body.

Cuyler interjected his own words into my story. " 'Aye, a wench like you must be won.' Then Baron Cuyler pulled her into his arms and kissed her passionately until she weakened with his ardor."

As Cuyler spoke the words, he role-played the Baron's actions with me playing the part of the lady. He had caught onto my plan. He must have determined that two could play this tickling-the-libido game. You know Cuyler, winning this game would be his goal.

I somehow found the words to say, " 'I'd sooner mate with a cur!' Lady Gertrude thrust her body away from the Baron of Toddsville." I struggled to free myself from his embrace so that I could tell the story *my* way.

"Wouldn't you rather have a Carr?" He pulled me back.

Cuyler had taken hold of the plot with ferocity and tightened his grasp on my satiny form. "With that said," he continued the storyline, "the Baron decided to hell with the men, the food, and the execution of prisoners. *The woman was all that he wanted.*"

His kiss held such fire, such passion, I could not free myself to speak. Which was what he wanted.

"Her submission would be his greatest victory, besides, rationalized the Baron of Toddsville, she *was* his wife," said Cuyler.

Cuyler swooped me up into his arms and headed for the doorway to our bedroom.

"Wait! I'm not finished with the story," I said, trying to kick my way out of his hold.

"Oh, yes you are." His voice held a merriment and a dedication to purpose with which I could not argue.

"Baron Cuyler broke down the door to the Lady's chamber," —my Cuyler pushed it with his foot—" kicked it shut behind him," —he did—" and tossed Lady Gertrude onto their nuptial bed."

It was a soft landing. I was not to be undone.

"Lady Gertrude screamed for her *father*," I said loudly.

He pulled on my legs causing my back to fall flat on the tulip quilt, clamped his hand over my mouth, and positioned his physique above mine so that I couldn't move.

Cuyler continued, "But no help came as her father was making merry in Brooklyn with the soldiers."

Even I had to giggle at that one, and I kissed his palm so that he would take his hand away from my mouth.

"Baron Cuyler slid the chain mail tunic from her sleek and beautiful body." His warm hands slid my satin nightgown passed my thighs, over my shoulders, and above my head, allowing it to fall onto the bedpost. "Before him was a *vision.* Part warrior—part Goddess—*his wife.*"

I let my back relax against the bed cover.

He stared in dismay at the corset. "He wasn't aware that he would have a chastity belt to contend with." He undid my garters and slid my hose down to my feet. Then he stood at the side of the bed.

" 'Tis most unseemly, wench, to keep your husband from his lawful pleasures.' " His eyebrows came together at the top of his nose, and he placed his hands on his hips. He wanted me to do something with the corset. He was having too much fun making up the story and had no idea how to put a corset into the tale.

"Lady Gertrude knew where she had hidden the chastity belt's key," I said wickedly, "but she would not tell him."

Pleased with myself, I continued, "'Fie, you braggart!' said Lady Gertrude. 'My father's final security that I should remain a virgin. Thinkst thou that ye shall take me at thy will?' "

Cuyler smiled and wagged his index finger at me as if to say that I was being naughty.

"Oh, all right," I said.

I continued my part of the storyline. "Lady Gertrude stood away from the bed," I said and stood up, "and found the key in the place where she hid her jewels."

"That's a nice turn of a phrase, Gertrude." He stroked his moustache with his thumb and index finger while he watched.

"Thank you."

"Then Lady Gertrude proceeded to unlock her charms." One by one the fourteen hooks slowly opened. He was thrilled with Lady Gertrude now.

"Baron Cuyler's passion rose," he continued the story, and pulled me onto the bed.

"He thrust the beauty to the tulip quilt—I mean—the *nuptial bed.*"

"Such sweet and tender thoughts of united joy came to his mind. He kissed her gently," Cuyler said and did, "then more forcefully," he said, as he pressed his lips tightly to mine, "and knew that she would yield to him." I did.

"The Baron had found the perfect woman in this prearranged marriage," he said. "A woman whose courage matched his own." He pulled away the last shred of covering I had. "A woman whose exquisite beauty was unparalled. Intelligent. Passionate." I moaned and let Baron Cuyler tell his side of the tale forgetting completely Lady Gertrude's interests in the plot. "And the sort of woman he would be proud to have at his side for the rest of his life."

I gazed lovingly into his eyes—into the face I loved to see. "Lady Gertrude's thoughts raced like the blood in her veins, hot, wild, uncontrollable," I said. "Reaching a fevered pitch, she held her warrior close to her breasts. She touched his hair, his cheek, his lips. Her eyes spoke of her insatiable hunger for her husband."

The actions matched the words, and the story's pace quickened. Ancient bride and groom became Victorian bride and groom. A perfect blend of story and storyteller bonded our bodies into one united soul. I had not planned for him to enter my story, or my prearranged seduction scene, but now I understood all to well how perfectly our souls matched.

"She could thrust the warrior from her side no longer. Her desire for him surmounted all reason."

"The Baron let drop the armor of war to don the amour of a more fiery confrontation," he said.

"Nice play on words," I said.

"Thank you," he said.

He released what was left of his clothing. Two eyes never left my focus. Two lips burned into mine.

"His hands touched her soft skin," I said, pleading for him to continue. "She knew that the Baron was the only man who could free her, fulfill her, and love her for whom she was."

He told the rest of the tale. "The woman, who lay beside him, would now yield her heart, her mind, her body, and her soul to him. He saw it, not as a victory of the flesh, for his love for her *grew* with every kiss."

He stopped the story abruptly and said, "Oh, God, Gertrude!" He caressed my cheek with the back of his fingers. "*I love you so much.*"

My hands grazed his taut skin. My gaze never left his, but as my own ardor rose, I closed them so that I could sense it all. My heart was pounding rapidly and belonged to him alone.

He pressed his lips to mine and then refused to remove them. I couldn't breathe. I think that was what he wanted. Suffocation, compliance, panic, thrill, and then release. I gasped, and felt such a desperate need, with so much ignited power and energy, submission was the only sane path to follow. Authority—his. In charge—him. Mindless defeat. Joyful surrender. Our hearts were pounding with combined joy. We had waited so long for this moment. Perhaps, not as patiently as we should have, but now we were rewarded with rapture.

I whispered into his ear while I held him and kissed his face, "I can't breathe, or live, or love, if you're not mine." I closed my eyes, and, together, we soared above the heavens.

One body-one mind-one spirit-one love-one life!

We wrote the poetry our bodies shared:

Pomegranate, azure,
Magenta,
Mauve, white,
Scarlet,
Lilac, plum!
FIRE!
Gasping for air,
Surrender!
Blindness-Death
Follow me!
Fear
Trust,
Twin-Panic,
Twin-Heat,
Twin-Thrill!
All
Is
Possible
Now!
Thirst!
Hunger!
Need!
Covet!
Climbing-Higher!
Soaring-Euphoria!

Bliss!

Ecstasy!

Joy!

Rapture!

Husband!

Lover!

Cuyler!

Never

Leave

My

Side!

And in this shared moment, when the world goes away, when there is nothing left but a new sphere, one man and his woman, one husband and his wife, hold each other against the darkness of the night, against the inevitability of time, and discover the wisdom of the ages.

I knew. Oh, how I knew the truth of our shared destiny now.

"Cuyler." My tears wet my cheeks as I held him close to my heart and kissed him. We listened to our hearts' pattern.

He studied my face for a moment and then smiled. "Why are you crying, Gertrude?" He kissed my lips. "Is something wrong? Didn't you like it?" he said. "Well, I suppose I'll just have to do it again?" A wicked grin creased his face.

He knew.

I snuggled into his side and held onto him.

Then his voice grew solemn. "It was more than I could ever have imagined."

"I know...I know," I said.

That was the beginning of the best two weeks of my life. Nothing would ever compare to the day to day, night to night, joy of making love, and being in love, with a man with whom you embrace every precious moment.

We woke when we felt like it, changed into our swimsuits, and ran down the hill to the lake. Whether it was cold or warm, we threw ourselves into the lake water and splashed and swam happily working up an appetite for a big breakfast.

While he shaved and dressed, I made breakfast. The small icebox only held so much food, so we had to travel into Richfield Springs for groceries every few days. We picked up *The Freeman's Journal* for the news, and the baseball scores, and, of course, the article that mentioned our wedding. We cut it out of the paper and placed it in our keepsake scrapbook—the one which I had received as a shower gift.

According to the paper, we had missed the Rev. Dr. T. L. Cuyler's—who had journeyed all the way from New York City—speech at our church the day after our wedding. Appealing last name, huh?

Apparently, the 'soda water fountain' was doing big business. The temperature on our wedding day had reached 88 degrees. A grand piano had been delivered to the Fenimore Hotel so that the 'musicale' on Saturday evening could continue as planned.

The Pierstown Epworth League was having a social at Fred Bates' home on July 23. Carr and Bull, the Oneonta family store we had visited, had a huge ad for their tremendous winter stock.

I learned about an opera house called the Bowne Opera House that prided itself on having a seating capacity of 500, a 'gas lit stage,' and *plenty* of scenery. I was sure the vocalists appreciated the management's sense of box office appeal.

There were the usual comments about alcoholics on the streets, and foreboding statements that vagrants were generally thieving and running amuck in Cooperstown as well as in all the smaller communities.

And in the shade of that wonderful tree, that held the long rope, cuddled in our comfortable hammock, that swayed lazily in the breeze, I read the baseball scores to my husband.

I cooked breakfast and dinner, and we made a small snack of sandwiches, meat, or cheese for lunch.

We had a disagreement about fishing and finally decided to take our boat into the middle of the lake and rest it there without hassling the poor fish. He had the fishing gear stowed in the front room's closet, from his first June vacation, just in case I changed my mind.

My own home was far from my thoughts. I never thought about Wainwright's trip to Europe or his e-mail problems getting in touch with me. My mother and father had probably taken their usual summer vacation by now. Jennifer and her husband would be enjoying their traditional July vacation. That world was not worrying about where I was or what I was doing.

We were in a tiny world of our own—in a cabin made for two. No one bothered us, and Isaac never came by.

It rained for a few days, making it mandatory for us to stay inside and in bed, *but it never stormed.* We had planned to run to cabin 2 if the weather looked threatening. I'd no intention of going back to 1997 for even an hour.

We made love whenever we felt like it which was as often as possible.

In the evening, we would sit on our porch, in the rockers, and watch the sunset together. We sipped lemonade on hot evenings and drank coffee on the cooler ones.

I wore Cuyler's undershirts around the house with my satin and lace panties because they looked like the runner's outfits I wore around my own home in the summer. Cuyler said I looked indecent, but I told him that no one was around but himself to notice. I'm quite positive he changed his mind about the attire.

We took walks down the various paths and hiked into the mountains.

Every night we slid our naked bodies between the cool cotton sheets of our wee bed, then made love like two people obsessed with each other.

We did not always tell stories to enhance our libidos, but when we did, we took turns. Sometimes he would begin a fictional story based on some historic tidbit he knew; sometimes I told him the plots of my books. He loved my romantic tales as much as I loved his historic ones. We had found a common ground of understanding, an intellectual fusion, and were more intimate than ever before.

Most of all we laughed. He could make me howl with glee at any given moment. He loved to see me break up right while I was doing something tricky, like cutting potatoes, or frying chicken for our evening meal. And when I begged him not to torment me while I cooked, he came behind me and kissed my neck with intense delight, knowing how it aroused me so, until I simply placed the food on the hot tile and gave up on preparing the meal. Obviously, *I* was to be devoured—not the chicken.

I found nothing about living with this man objectionable. He had no temper, and his passion was astounding. He talked, opened to me, like no other friend I'd ever had. He never let me work alone and always helped no matter the chore. I did likewise. He remained the dominant man in charge of our family, and I didn't mind it in the least because I loved that Victorian side of him.

The combination of prim, proper, and passionate was a heady aphrodisiac to my uninhibited nature. I simply let him row the boat of our lives as he did on Canadarago Lake. We treated each other with the best of care because our days were precious to us—and numbered. We had no time for arguments and did not really have the temperament for them anyway. We gave each other what we needed to be happy on this earth. We knew only to well that it could all be taken away in the blink of an eye.

We talked about the winter months one afternoon. Cuyler did not want me to attempt coming home and risk illness. I wanted to try. He held me close and said, "If you want to come home, and it seems safe in your time, then I suppose you could try it. I mean that. If there's bad weather in your time and a quantity of illness, don't come. I'll bring a sleigh up here and wait for you. I'll have Isaac place some logs in the cabin and keep warm while I wait. I'll examine the *Journal* for the exact solstice date. Our house should be finished by that time. I arranged everything so that we could start the project right away. Of course, if you don't like the design I chose, we'll build something else. I wanted to begin construction while the weather is agreeable in hopes of moving in around Thanksgiving." He looked lost for a moment. "I admit moving in without you will be a bittersweet prospect. I'll just remind myself that the house must be ready for you when you come home."

"I'm sure the design you chose will be fine. In fact, I'll see whether it's still standing in Milford when I return. Do you really think the house will be finished by December?" I said.

"Well, the outer shell and the rough interior work should be done before you leave. You can choose the furnishings now so that I can move from the apartment around Thanksgiving. By that time, our business will keep me hopping, and I'll not have time to bother with it further. I don't want to spoil your fun. I assume my wife will want to properly arrange our home."

I kissed him for saying that. I said, "I'll withdraw some more money and make sure you have enough. Will it be a lot of trouble to come to the cabin to pick me up?"

"If the weather is difficult, it might be. Just stay in the cabin until I can make it there. It's probably time to ask Isaac about his time traveling. He might not even be here in the winter months," Cuyler said.

"Jim said the whole family traveled whenever they wished," I said. "If we can get him to divulge the family business, he might prove helpful."

"I couldn't bear having you come all that way only to become ill, especially if the medicine in your time would save you. Our people die of pneumonia in the winter. I'd have no medicine to give you. I'd lose you for all time. That's why the summer is the best for you to travel." The Victorian logic was in evidence. "Though I shall miss you so." He hugged me and let the true emotion show.

"Look. We have flu shots and vitamins and pneumonia shots et. al., and I'll store up on all those before I come home. I'd love to spend the holidays at the homestead with your mother and Johanna. Spend the dreary winter months snuggled close to you in front of our own fiery hearth. Besides, you'll be so busy with the coal business, you'll need me to run the store," I said.

"I just don't want to lose any time we have together." He stroked my brown curls. "I want it to last forever. I never want to be lonely again."

"I don't want to be morbid, dear, but Jim said that my longevity directly parallels my lifeline in 1997. If I'm to die this winter, it won't matter whether I'm here or in Brooklyn."

I turned in his arms and looked into his beautiful eyes. "Nothing will separate us, Cuyler. No matter what happens to us, or how long we have, we'll always be together. *We're one.* From today and into eternity, we will always be one."

I laid my head on his broad chest, let my arms encircle his waist, listened to his heartbeat, and smiled. He kissed the top of my hair and placed his cheek against my head. I detected that sound he makes in his throat; the one he tries to disguise.

Chapter Twenty-Six

I saw Isaac the day before we had to leave. I thought it best to speak with him privately.

"Hello, Isaac," I said. "Not many tourists here right now? Nice of you to let us keep Cuyler's old family cabin; I mean considering what goes on there."

He stopped grinning. "What do you mean by that remark?" he said.

Boy, I hope I'm right. "Well, I mean, it has been in the family for over a hundred years, hasn't it? Many relatives have used it, haven't they?" I moved in like Sam Spade hot on the hunch that my instincts were correct.

"Who told you that?" He gave me that James Bond sideways smirk that Jim had inherited.

"Your son, well...I mean your great-grandson-Jim Cooper."

His eyes grew large, and I could tell he was wondering if he should tell the truth or retain the lie. "I'm not married. Hard to have a son, or even a great-grandson, if you're not even married. Are you sure you haven't lost your mind with all this...ah...stimulation?" he said.

"Oh, come on, Isaac. I'm sure you know what I mean. Do you leave in the winter? You're a young man; you've got plenty of time to have a wife and children. Besides," I went in for the kill, "you know who I'm talking about, don't you? He was here in 1890 and spent a great deal of time with those 'summer girls' he and Cuyler met in Cooperstown."

He dropped the facade. "How's he doing?" he asked

I smirked. "Just fine. Oh, and his brother Sam travels to 1797 and has a lovely wife, whom he adores, and a small family he has to leave behind in the fall."

His eyes grew wide, his brow furrowed, then he said, "I always wondered if they'd lend the cabin to someone who would slip through the window of time."

Window of Time? I liked that. "They weren't sure I'd fall through it. They suspected I would but didn't tell me about it until I went back a few weeks ago during that terrible storm. You were still in Morris, I guess."

"Uncle died. So, Cuyler married a time traveler. Oh," he

started to howl with laughter, "you must have come while he was in the cabin on his fishing trip. Oh, my, that must have been quite a scene. I'm sorry I missed that one. So *that's* why you two married."

"It was the initial answer to a compromising situation, but it soon became the reality of our hearts."

"I can see that. Well, I'm glad for you both—and sorry too. Does Cuyler believe all that you've told him?"

Cuyler came up the back of the hill behind Isaac overhearing the question. "He's gaining confidence in the story daily," my husband said. "Well, Isaac, it seems you've a great deal of information for us. What did you mean by saying 'you're sorry for us too?'"

Isaac was trapped. He dropped the axe he was using to cut logs for winter. "I just meant that it seems a shame to discover your wife has to return to her time and can only be with you in the summer."

"Jim told her that she could return in the winter if she wanted to."

"You can travel two times a year, but it isn't recommended that you travel to a climate known for its bad winter weather in December. She can travel winter to spring, but I'm sure the summer holds the best of your memories. The coal business will be less trouble then, affording you more time to spend together."

I said, "Suppose I wanted to try traveling in December?"

"Well, that's your decision," Isaac said. "I could help you out there, Cuyler. I have a sleigh, and I could watch for her and bring her to Milford for you. That way you wouldn't have to rent a sleigh and travel up the hills alone."

"Then it *is* possible. It *can* be done." Cuyler's voice was jubilant.

"I can keep the cabin warm for her if we get a nasty blizzard like the one we had last Christmas."

"During the summer months, I can travel back home when a bad storm hits. Right?" He nodded in agreement. "Is it the same with winter storms?"

"Yes, but you need not worry about that. I doubt that you would come back to the cabin in the deep snow *for anything.*"

They both laughed. They had a better understanding of the Cooperstown climate than I did.

"Oh, if you don't mind," Isaac said, "when you go back home in September, I'd like you to take something to my two great-grandsons. I'll get the package ready for you. It won't be heavy. I know you're probably planning on taking many personal items with you, so I won't bother you with much."

"No problem. Oh, and I should tell you that I have Jim's permission to take money from your account," I said. "You see, I have a great deal of money in my own bank and can reimburse Jim when I get back."

"Not a worry." He turned to Cuyler. "Are you aware of how wealthy your little Mrs. is?"

"She gave me some clue. Why?"

"She can hand over millions to you from our family account," he said. "We replenish the account by placing money in the bank years in advance so that the interest is abundant. If she's placing money from her 1997 account to our 1797 account through Sam and Jim, by next summer you could own all of Toddsville. You're an extremely fortunate man, Mr. Carr." He patted Cuyler on the back. "Course, I always liked you. Even told Jim when he was here that I felt you'd never find a wife in your own time. Wouldn't doubt they took one look at Gertrude, knew who would be in this cabin June 1897, and prayed."

"You mean *they* knew we would be right for each other?" I said.

"They knew that if you were the type to fall through the 'window,' and wake up next to Cuyler; you were meant for each other. If you didn't, no one's the wiser."

"Do you know of any women in your family who've traveled? I would love to ask them an important question," I said.

"None have admitted going anywhere; although, I suspect my sister is a summer-fall traveler when the spirit takes her. She disappears and turns up in the fall with this silly grin on her face. I've asked her about it, but she's a lady spinster, and you can't get that sort to talk. Rather fond she is of the Middle Ages, and I suspect she's having her own form of recreation A.D.—if you know what I mean," Isaac said.

"Does she go every year?" I asked.

"Not that I know of. She might be skipping a year or two because of the wars."

"Wars?" I said.

"English campaigns, Holy wars, you know. Traveling to the Dark Ages is very tricky. Pop up in the middle of some medieval feast, and you could be burned at the stake the next morning for witchcraft. Not open-minded as we are in the 1890s. However, she wears the most beautiful necklace with a gold cross at the end of it—not our sort of jewelry at all—and I suspect she has a warrior for a husband. They sometimes left home on campaigns and were gone for years. I'm thinking she'd rather stay with family than head the defense of her castle."

That wasn't going to help. How could she get pregnant if her husband was off in the Holy Lands? "Any other women in your family take the trip?"

"I don't think so, but I'll look through the attic in my grandmother's house and see what I can find."

Cuyler leaned against the oak tree and crossed his arms over his chest. "And you—have you ever traveled?" Cuyler said.

"Once a year I take my little trip to the Cooperstown of the 1600s. I'm the only white member of the Mohican tribe. There's a girl there, if you must know, but it seems I'd better get busy settling down in this time period if I'm to have such a fine family," he said grinning.

"Another question, if you don't mind?" Cuyler said. "Is it possible for someone from the past to travel forward? Say for instance if your Indian maiden wanted to come back with you, could she?"

"I know what you're thinking, Cuyler." His eyes lowered, and he kicked a wood chip he had spied on the ground with the toe of his boot. "Granted you're probably the first one to appreciate and understand the time traveling theory, but, I'm sorry, Cuyler; when you become a part of time, you can't leave it. I wish that I could see the Cooperstown Jim, Sam, and Gertrude know, but I can't. I'm sorry. I just don't have any information in the record book to support such a theory. I'll research it for you if you want me to."

"I'd appreciate it, Isaac," said Cuyler.

Isaacc tried to lighten our mood. "But, the cabin is always yours. I'll not lend it to anyone else. If Gertrude wants to come home to you in the winter, I'll stay and help out. Wasn't planning on traveling until spring anyway."

I gave him a quick hug. "Thank you. I'll take back anything

for you," I said.

"You two forget about September right now. Live each day to the fullest. Don't let anything prevent you from having the greatest marriage—if not the strangest—a couple could have. Probably why it's happier than most." His faraway look spoke of an Indian maid.

"Maybe he's right," I said, as we rowed to the middle of the lake and let the oars rest on the side of the fishing boat. "Maybe we are living a charmed life knowing that our days are numbered. Unlike those couples who bicker with no clue how many days they'll share."

"You may be right."

We spent the last day of our honeymoon wishing there were more weeks of relaxation before the rigors of daily domestic life resumed. We packed all that we had into our tea cart, said goodbye to our cabin of love, and urged Samuel down the familiar path to Toddsville. One quick trip to see how his mother and the homestead were doing and then home to Milford.

"I don't want to leave the cabin." I started to cry.

He reached over and pulled me to his side. "It's been the happiest time I've ever known, but we need to start our new business and the construction of our own home."

I smiled and wiped my tears with his handkerchief. I think what was really bothering me was the fact that the next time I would see the cabin would be on that fateful September evening when I would leave him for God knows how long.

Mother Carr and Johanna appeared oddly transformed when we greeted them at the homestead. They were quiet—subdued.

Apparently, all was well. The hired men were working as instructed, and the barn and pastures had never looked better. Mother Carr had hired some construction men to build a new section onto the back of the house; however, she didn't appear excited about the prospect, as I knew my mother would if I'd surprised her with a lot of money and told her to splurge on new items for her home.

They welcomed us with hugs. The filtering process known as "reality," or what some people call "post-wedding blues," was visible in their smiles and veiled their eyes. They had missed us and no left over wedding cake or satin ribbon would wipe away the fact that Cuyler and his perky fiancé were now a married couple and moving to Milford. Mother Carr had gone to church alone for the first time in her life.

Our sunny disposition changed their mood. Johanna had a feast waiting for us. We sat at the dinner table and talked until the sun became an apricot streak across the sky.

"Well, Gertrude, it's time for us to head home. We have a booty of wedding gifts resting in the middle of our apartment. How we shall ever manage to find our way around the place tomorrow is beyond me. Maybe we should wait one day to open the store."

"Nonsense," I said valiantly, "I can handle all that. You have to open the shop tomorrow." I turned to my mother-in-law. "We'll come for you next Sunday for church, Mother Carr, and save a hearty appetite for Johanna's lunch afterwards. We do take Sundays off, don't we?" I looked at Cuyler.

"And Saturday around noon," Cuyler said.

"Noon? Why noon?" I asked.

His eyes twinkled merrily. "Game time. Next Saturday we're attending *your* first baseball game, Gertrude."

Dad had taken the three of us to many baseball games while I was growing up. What a thrill it would be to see a real old-fashioned game, *Casey at the Bat* uniforms, and those marvelous handlebar mustaches. I wondered if we were going to cheer for the Richfields, the Athletics, or the Cubans.

"Once in a while, we might go to one of the local musicales or something at the opera house?" I asked.

"Whatever you wish. Perhaps mother would like to attend with us as well."

It turned out that Mother Carr had always wanted to see the musicales at the Fenimore Hotel and the local community theater's productions, but had never had anyone to accompany her.

Johanna mentioned that I might want to try my hand at preserving food for the winter. I was polite, but it sounded like too much work. She and Mother Carr entered their jams, jellies, and preserves in the September fair. I promised that I would ride over to the homestead, help them cook and set up their displays at the fair. I wasn't sure I'd be ready for an actual entry this year.

When Cuyler told them about his house plans, they encouraged him to build a huge house. They couldn't remain somber with such wonderful news, and our cheerful attitude soon reclaimed their smiles.

Johanna insisted we take a basketful of food home with us when it was time to depart. We kissed Mother Carr goodbye, then trotted Samuel to Milford on the old Indian Trail.

When we parked in our *own* backyard, stabled and fed our horse in our *own* barn next to the outhouse; my heart raced with anticipation of spending our first night as man and wife in our own little home.

As soon as I saw the mountain of gifts in the middle of the room, I groaned. We took a few quick stabs at the boxes of gifts, stacked one on top of the other, and surrendered.

Cuyler and I found our bed, opened the window beside it to allow the cool, summer breeze to come into the room, took off our clothes, and lay almost naked under the quilt on our own bed for a peaceful and happy rest.

The next day proved to set the agenda for all succeeding days—hard work after grueling hours of hard work.

We awoke to an empty icebox and had to make breakfast from the bread and rolls Johanna had given us. I told Cuyler to open the store, and that I would attempt to find storage for our new items.

I worked from sun up until sundown and only stopped for a one hour break.

Cuyler found me in the midst of my domestic war zone around noon, took us to lunch across the street, and afterwards we walked to the general store and purchased all that our arms could carry. Until we had ice, we could only store dry or tinned goods.

We snickered for no apparent reason as we filled our pantry with food. He'd had a wonderful day. In one day he had met more people, made more friends, and sold more horse feed, than any other businessman in all Otsego County. *He was happy!* He smiled, teased, sang, whistled, and laughed so loud that I could hear him all the way upstairs while I worked that afternoon. My back-breaking chore soon became delightful because of the lightsome sound of my husband's whistling.

I prepared a meager repast of thick-sliced bread and ham sandwiches, some leftover hardboiled eggs, cheese, and an apple pie Mrs. Bates had made for us. That first dinner in our new apartment was memorable; I felt a wonderful womanly pride as I watched my husband eat our first real home cooked meal.

I thought we would be too sleepy to make love but not so. After we crawled into our small, brass bed, I felt his hands sneak under my nightgown and find their way to my breasts. I knew what he had in mind. The best aphrodisiac a man can have is the joy of a satisfying day at work and the knowledge that he may return to his happy home, a hearty meal, and an affectionate wife who wants to make love to him. Simple? Right!

How could I be more pleased with my life?

Chapter Twenty-Seven

On the first Saturday of our new domestic life, we closed shop at twelve and headed for Cooperstown, to the C.A.A., to watch the baseball game. We purchased tickets at the gate and found seats. We bought peanuts and popcorn and munched away as the young athletes came to the field. I noticed few women and wondered why. Then I found out.

Clifton Clark spotted Cuyler, waved, and came to greet us. "Well, didn't expect to see you at a baseball game, Cuyler," Clif said, ignoring my existence.

"Thought Gertrude might want to see the chaps play ball," he said, ignoring Clif as the sports took to the game at hand.

"Gertrude? Why would Gertrude want to watch a baseball game? Surely, she has more *feminine* things to do with her time." I think this was one of those 'Okay, you're married, but you don't have to let that spoil your fun' comments.

In unison my husband and I turned our heads and examined his intent with curious looks.

Cuyler said, "Why wouldn't Gertrude enjoy the game, Clif?"

"Well..." he stammered, surprised that he had been put on the spot. "It isn't a *lady's* sport, is it? Not like croquet or golf. I've heard some modern women are taking up golf these days. But, baseball?"

I targeted his eyes with an icy glare. I had information researched from the Hall of Fame to support my data, and I was going to lay it on old Clif. "Women have actually played the game, Clif." I smiled just the same.

Even Cuyler was shocked.

"In 1891, there was a women's baseball team. They wore official uniforms and had their photo taken as well. Really, Clif, are you trying to be old-fashioned and narrow minded? Why shouldn't I enjoy this sport with my husband, *my friend*?"

"Friend? Oh, Cuyler, next she'll be wanting the vote! Make sure she never waltzes into the Mohican Club, or it'll set Cooperstown tongues a-wagging," Clif said.

Cuyler put his arm around me. "Gertrude doesn't want to attend any stuffy old men's club. Really, Clif, I think you need a girlfriend. Someone with whom you can share the joys of living.

I can tell you that my life has never been more fulfilled." Cuyler kissed my cheek.

Clif gasped while his fingers tore at the rim of the plain, braided, straw hat he clutched.

"May I offer you a peanut, Mr. Clark?" I held out the bag and smiled.

He sat down next to us, to ease the shock, took a few peanuts and smashed them between his palms, threw away the shell, and nibbled on the nuts. He regarded my face for a long time, and then stared at Cuyler, who was in some world of his own called "Who's on First."

Soon the other fellows surrounded us, offering snacks and lemonade until I thought my stomach would turn inside out. I'm not sure how I managed it, and maybe I didn't, maybe it was Cuyler; but I had just passed some sort of test and was now allowed to be one of the 'guys.'

Jim Wheeler said, "The Richfields and the Athletics have their work cut out for them this day."

"Take a look at that team, Cuyler," said Robert Stiffler.

"I can see. Our nine will have a tough match," said Cuyler.

"Their team is fully as strong as ours, Cuyler," said Joseph.

"It's going to be a close one, for sure. I've heard that they were a strong aggressor in their last three outings. It won't be an easy victory," said Clif.

The ball soared, was caught by the second baseman, he lunged at the man who had run from first to second, and soundly tapped the player on his foot as he slid to second base.

"Safe!" the base umpire screamed.

Oh, the crowd went wild with accusatory declamations. Cuyler lit a cigar. Calmly he said, "They'll have to contend with these umpires, too, it seems." The cigar's tip was guillotined between his white teeth. "They shouldn't allow blind men to perform such delicate work."

We watched as the scowling baseman glowered at the umpire, and the grinning opponent wiped the dust from his hands and uniform.

It wasn't long before the Richfields had all three bases covered in the first inning. The fourth man sent the ball over the rear fence and brought them all in scoring four. The Athletics scored one.

The men continued to complain about the condition of the diamond, easy outs which should have been caught, and smooth grounders which should have been smoother. The umpire was called every name a Victorian man can get away with calling him. By the end of the match, all five of my escorts were convinced that the umpire couldn't decipher the difference between an out and a strike, nor a home run from a fly ball.

It was a wonderful day. I think our team won after all. I was to learn that Cuyler and his friends, who had pleaded impartiality earlier, were rooting for the Richfields. I assumed this team was from Richfield Springs, so I cheered loudly when they made home runs. After all, I had a special reason to favor anything from Richfield Springs.

I told Cuyler that if he wanted to attend the Tuesday or Thursday evening games I would come along. He said that he liked the Saturday games because they didn't interfere with his work nights. So, every Saturday, we went to the C.A.A. and sat with the 'boys,' ate snacks, and cheered for the Richfields.

On Sunday morning, we awakened early, fussed in the small apartment to get both of us ready to leave for church, and still managed to eat breakfast.

Mother Carr was sitting on the porch and ready for us to take her for her Sunday ride.

The first service we attended was interrupted while a grinning Reverend McBride told the congregation how pleased he was that Cuyler and I had been so generous to the needy families of Otsego County. My face turned scarlet. Everyone turned and stared at us. The Carr brothers smiled with pride. So much for my *private* donation. Cuyler didn't seem to mind the comment as much as I did.

When we had chatted with everyone about our honeymoon and our new life, we went to the homestead for Sunday dinner.

The feast resembled Christmas. We had turkey with all the trimmings, homemade bread, cranberry and apple salad, fresh beans, and cherry pie. I wasn't sure if Johanna was just happy we were back, or if she felt this was the best way to feed a starving husband after a week with his new wife's cooking.

We did not tarry long. Cuyler was ready to give me my first *real* historic adventure he said. We rode on a back country road—as if any weren't—until we found a wide, golden pasture.

He tied Samuel's reins to a tree, grabbed my hand, and said, "Follow me."

"Ooh, are we making love on a hill this time?" I said.

"Well!" he said, smiling at the notion, "that's an exceptional idea and shows some merit; but, no, I'm going to introduce you to Natty Bumppo."

"Now I suppose you're going to tell me that there really was a Leatherstocking. Even *I* know he was made up."

He turned me around by my shoulders so that I could face him. "He was not made up, Gertrude. He really existed, and I'm going to show you where he lived."

"I don't mind running up this long hill after you, Cuyler, but James Fenimore Cooper made the lanky hunter up in his over imaginative mind. I'm a writer, remember. I know about stuff like that."

He eyed me, crossed his arms across his chest so that his one hand rested beneath the opposite arm socket, while the fingers on the other hand pulled at his mustache, and gave me a wry look. "Do I make up *my* characters?"

"Well," I said, "I don't suppose so."

"Then why should Cooper. Trust me, Gertrude, people who live in this area don't have to fictionalize anything. There's enough history and mystery for several novels."

"Oh, all right. Lead on MacDuff."

I climbed, walked, hiked, and collapsed. I wasn't used to all this long distance walking. "I can't go one step further," I said gasping.

I sat on a grassy place filled with old stones and pulled off my boots.

"You don't have to, Gertrude, we're here." He sat down beside me, took off his jacket and vest, undid his shirt and tie, and rolled up his sleeves. I attacked.

"Gertrude," he said laughing.

I kissed him, and we rolled over each other playfully in the tall grass. I embraced him further and began tugging at his shirt.

"*Woman*, what is it that you want?" he said.

"*You!* You just brought me out here to make love to me under the sun, didn't you?"

"No, I meant you to write some notes about the history of David Shipman."

I stared at him. "You mean there really was a Natty Bumppo, a Leatherstocking, a last of the Mohican?"

"Yes, pull that 'stuff' from your hair."

I pulled the long grass from my soft curls.

He stood up and pointed to the shell of what had once been the cellar of a hidden cabin. He moved towards it. I accompanied him and then remembered my pad and pencil. Frantically, I searched for the purse I had carried all the way up that hill, found it, and hurried after Cuyler.

"At the termination of the Indian Trail at Oaks Creek," he said, indicating the various directions by waving his hands in the air like some ancient Indian, "stands the remains of the cabin owned by David Shipman, the famous hunter. As a boy, I well remember this hole in the ground where the cellar was, and hearing it stated that this was where Leatherstocking lived."

I gazed upon fiction's greatest secret. I wrote.

"Shipman was a famous hunter, Gertrude, and with his dog and gun roamed over the hills in quest of game, and he whipped the stream for the abundance of fish which swam within its borders."

"Just north," he said, pointing as far as the eye could see, "of Toddsville on the farm of Mrs. Albert Quackenbush..."

I hurled the pencil down to the ground, twined my arms stubbornly across my chest, and started to laugh. "Oh, Cuyler, you made that name up."

His eyes became solemn. "I assure you, I didn't make the name up. It's a real and true family who still live in this area. They live right over there." He pointed. "Really, I would have thought by now the validity of my tales might have become solidified in your mind. May I continue?"

I coughed apologetically. "Yes, dear, sorry. Continue."

Then he smiled. "I never lie, Gertrude."

"As I was saying," he continued, "north of this farm and near the trolley, is a large mound that was thickly covered with timber. It was on this mound Shipman hid three days from the Indians, although his home was but a short distance from his hiding place. My Grandmother Carr used to say, so I've been told, that as a little girl she was afraid of Shipman because he looked so rough and wore leather breeches, his clothing being made of tanned deer hide."

A vision of Daniel Day Lewis as Hawkeye flashed into my mind. I could *never* be scared of someone like *him*.

"Shipman's cabin stood on old Doctor Almy's lot, known prior to this as Shipman's lot, for we learn that Shipman set apart a small parcel of land for burial purposes which became known as the Shipman burying ground."

"Most original he was in naming."

"Gertrude!"

"Sorry."

"He also selected this last resting place under a large tree that stood within the enclosure. This has led me to believe that he owned the lot bearing his name, probably having purchased it from the Adams family."

You know what I'm thinking...Gomez et. al. Knowing Cuyler's stories as well as I do, I wouldn't be surprised if that was where the family dwelled before their fame in the comic pages.

"How many internments," we're back in burial lots again, "were made in the Shipman plot, besides his wife, I don't know. But, this plot was abandoned on account of moisture and the present Adams cemetery—north of Fork Shop—came into being."

I couldn't see any statues from this vantage point, so maybe I'm wrong about the ghoulish family.

"When Mrs. Shipman died, the Reverend John Bostwick, pastor of the Baptist Church at Hartwick, conducted the funeral service. Upon the arrival of the funeral party at the grave, they found it partly filled with water, and the minister said to the hunter that it was a poor place for a burial. The hunter said, 'I know it, but I expect to be buried here myself if I live to die.'"

I giggled and stopped writing. The usual look from Cuyler. Silence.

"I've heard my father state that his father told him that at the burial of Mrs. Shipman, one of the men present steadied the box in the water with his cane while others shoveled in the earth."

I placed my arms around him and held him. "Your father told you many stories, didn't he?"

Cuyler looked at the ground and was silent. I saw the moisture rim his eyes. "We shared more than I ever realized. I...I...just now realized how much." I hugged him and then looked at him.

"Is that the end of the story?" I knew it wasn't, but I needed to get him out of this mood and onto the story he wanted so much to tell me.

"No...ah...David Shipman had one son, Samuel Shipman, who raised a large family of sons and daughters."

Cuyler said, "The old hunter passed away in his cabin, right here, and several neighbors came to prepare the house and make ready for the funeral." He smiled suddenly.

"The deceased was lying on the bed, when to their horror and astonishment the old hunter sat up, as if taking a parting shot at a bounding buck or flying fowl, and missing his mark, groaned, fell back on his pillow and gave up the chase. This unusual incident coming from a 'dead' person so frightened the women that one of them fainted."

I tapped him on the nose with my finger. "You're bad."

He grabbed me in his arms and swirled me around in the air and then deposited me on the earth that once was David Shipman's cabin. "He'd broken his last pigeon's wing. He'd whipped Oaks Creek for the last time; but the name of David Shipman, the famous hunter, 'Deerslayer,' or, 'Leatherstocking,' will remain long after the teller of this tale has been forgotten."

I don't know why that last line got to me, but an immediate reaction came upon my countenance.

"Oh, Cuyler!" I kissed him and looked longingly into his eyes. "No one will ever forget you, my love." He observed the emotion on my face and quickly comprehended the truth in my last statement. Time—life—love—mortality suddenly became as clear as the waves on Glimmerglass Lake.

"But, Gertrude, I'm no one. I'm just a simple businessman from Milford."

"No, don't say that," I said hugging him. "You're more than any man I've ever met in my life...so much more."

"But, I'm not Baron Cuyler of Toddsville, Gertrude, like in your story."

I held him close to my body and smiled behind his back; my face radiant with the love I had for him. "You don't *have* to be a Baron or a King. Just be *you*, because I love you just as you are and wouldn't have our life be anything but what it is."

He pulled me down onto the grass and rolled on top of me.

"Whatever would have become of me if you had never entered my life?"

Submitting a coy smile, I said, "I've no idea, but I'm just as lucky. My life was headed into a downward spiral. Fame—plenty of that. Fortune—lots of that. Happiness—none."

His fingers touched my lips, and then his hand moved down my side. "I think I shall partake of my wife at this very moment, right here by old Natty's home."

"Are you sure about this?" I said. "Suppose little Clarence and his girlfriend should happen by." He kissed my neck and bit my shoulder. "Proper Victorian men do not do such things, Cuyler."

"How would you know?" He kissed my lips and nibbled on my earlobe. "You're just a writer and from another time to boot."

With that said, we shared an interesting and very satisfying encounter high above the sleepy Toddsville hamlet.

Chapter Twenty-Eight

The August months drifted by in a sleepy haze. I was learning my way around my small kitchen. I ground my own coffee and soon was making my own breads and noodles supervised by Mrs. Bates's experienced tutelage. I tried to bake on my miniature stove, ruined several cakes, and burned dozens of cookies. I wasn't too terrible at fruit pies, however, and soon I accomplished a variety of home cooked goodies. It didn't hurt to own a general store. The restaurant was across the street, and the farms were close enough to reach quickly.

We eventually had the ice delivered. Soon, butter, milk, and eggs were brought to my door by a dairy wagon.

I started making tea and chilling it with chips from my own ice block. I squeezed the lemons and sweetened the juice with sugar to make my own lemonade.

Breakfast was fried toast, scrambled eggs, bacon, and steaming fresh coffee. Lunch was homemade soup, or a fresh, green salad with slices of homemade bread. For dinner, we had a pasta dish with my own homemade tomato sauce streaming over it, fried or baked chicken, or roast beef or stew on occasion.

It was hot work cooking in the summer with no air conditioning. Sometimes I would cook in the evenings, and we would have cold boiled eggs, or fried chicken, and potato salad made with my own dressing. One of my bachlorette presents had been a White House Cookbook, and, boy, did I use it.

When the faithful 'little curse' came around, I decided to do some investigating at the local Milford Pharmacy. You would not believe what I found! It was a Ladies' Faultless Serviette Supporter that looked just like the one I had worn as a girl—sort of. I was ecstatic because they came with napkins instead of the linen Johanna had given me that I felt ill-served my needs. Since disposal was a real chore, I went back to the washable linen. Talk about a recycler's dream.

Mrs. Bates had a clothesline hanging from two trees in our backyard, and told me that I could wash our clothes in her washing machine that was housed in our combined cellar. I rushed downstairs to find a mechanical contraption that in no way resembled a washing machine by any stretch of the imagination.

She had an Anthony Wayne Washer, two Gardner clothes bars to dry private items, two tubs and a double-faced wash board sitting on folding wash benches, and a folding ironing board, which she told me I could take upstairs to use with my iron—the one I sat on my stove to heat. I decided to use the two tubs and wash everything with the board as I was never going to figure out how to use the washer. I bought soap and started the work of washing our clothes *by hand.*

On sunny evenings, Cuyler and I made ice cream with our White Mountain Ice Cream Freezer that had also been a wedding gift. Mrs. Bates would join us to sample the sweet vanilla ice cream, and we placed any leftover cream in the ice box for Clarence.

Yes, Clarence had found a way to join us in Milford. He was turning into a strong little biker. He peddled all the way from Toddsville with his bicycle bell jingling all the way. I would serve him ice cream, or pie, lemonade, and when I finally learned how to make them—cookies. He wrote tons of poetry and carried his verses in his pocket to read to me.

Cuyler and the boy became good friends, and soon he accompanied us to the Saturday afternoon baseball games in Cooperstown. Cuyler would attach Clarence's bike to the carriage, and we would take him home after the game. The two sat side by side ingesting popcorn, peanuts, and drinking root beer. Invariably, Clarence became ill and had some gastronomical trouble on the way back to Toddsville.

His mother and father were pleased at our interest in the boy as his mother's delivery date was close at hand.

Mother Carr, Cuyler, and I attended the "musicales" at the Fenimore Hotel. We were able to hear Mr. Riesberg in concert. This vocalist was well known for his "free concerts" and was always afforded great reviews in *The Freeman's Journal.*

We heard Mr. Earl read selections from his own writings, which *I* found most amusing.

We were also able to enjoy the trilling melodies of Kathrine Hilke, a soprano who had come from Brooklyn to sing with Mr. Riesberg. This one was not a free concert, however, and we had to reserve our seats by purchasing tickets at the bookstore for fifty cents each.

We secured our seats for the opera house at Winegar's Drugstore. We were able to see Delly perform a very entertaining hypnotist act. The house was packed for the show because it had been advertised as good clean fun with no debauchery or violent acts. The entertainer would take people from the audience and hypnotize them to do all sorts of wild things. He wanted me to appear on the stage, but Cuyler and I both shook our heads no. Imagine what I might tell under hypnosis.

Then he suggested that Cuyler come on stage, but the whole audience exclaimed that my husband couldn't stop talking long enough to go "under." Mother Carr and I both chuckled at poor Cuyler's red face and good humored smile as he waved his hands for everyone to stop teasing him.

The entertainer put a young woman under his spell, and she slept for twenty-four hours. He moved her to the lobby of the Fenimore Hotel, and there she lay the whole time peacefully sleeping while all the citizens gawked at her.

One day, the Fenimore Hotel almost caught on fire. It was big news. Someone had turned on the gas in one of the upper rooms, and at first, it streamed up to a great height. Some boys, misjudging what they saw, cried, "Fire!" Just before that, a janitor in the club house had lit a fire in the parlor, and smoke was issuing from the chimney causing the situation of the "hotel fire" to appear more dramatic than it really was.

The fire department was called, and hoses were strung along the streets. The water was released. One lady in an apartment on the corner of the hotel, who had not closed her window, was deluged with water from the fire hose when she turned on the gas in her room. The curtains and carpets were soaked. The fire department was perturbed about the false alarm, the hotel managers were exasperated because of the damage, and several guests demanded calming.

The local ball clubs continued to entertain Cuyler, the chaps, Clarence, Daniel, Mrs. Sloat and her husband, Sally and her boyfriend, and eventually, Johanna and Mother Carr, at the Saturday afternoon baseball games. The Richfields beat the Cubans 13 to 4 on August 18. The Cubans made a grand show of "coaching" their team to *defeat*, and we enjoyed their antics. On August 22 our team beat the Gillams 17 to 9.

One Saturday, we watched the Athletics and the Wilkesbarres instead of the Richfields. The visitors did not have a very good team, and the game was rather one-sided. It was the loudest group we had ever witnessed at one of the games. Rowdy crowds became the norm as the summer ensued. The Athletics scored 11 in the eight innings they played, but the Wilkesbarre team scored only one in the fourth inning and two in the sixth.

Oh, how Cuyler loved the baseball games! Come to think of it, there really wasn't anything he didn't enjoy. He never scoffed at the musical even when Mr. Reisberg was over dramatizing and hitting wrong notes. He never said negative things about the elocutionary acting style of the local Milford theater group who preformed, upon occasion, in the Presbyterian Church in Milford—right next to our store. They did modern comedies whose titles were unknown to Cuyler or me. We pretended to laugh at the jokes and then started howling at our own pretenses. We had to leave at intermission and went home to our bed giggling all the way.

On some Sundays, Daniel took us out in his sailboat, and we lounged trailing our bare feet in the cool water of Glimmerglass Lake. We enjoyed the respite. We worked our fannies off all week to enjoy a Sunday picnic at the park, a sailboat ride with Daniel, a carriage ride into the country, and an afternoon of uninterrupted lovemaking in our own bed with the refreshing breezes fluttering our curtains. Then we would sleep as if we were dead until the sun began to lower behind the pine trees.

Cuyler promised to give me a train ride as I yearned for one every time it whistled into town. He said we might even go to Brooklyn, and I thought I'd die with excitement.

He worked all day in his hardware store and drew a large clientele. He did the labor alone not planning on hiring help until the coal business became more demanding.

He moved his team of horses and his large wagon into the livery stable in Milford. It was an astonishing sight to watch him handle the horses. Every muscle in his arms and upper torso strained and yet controlled the strong quarter horses. This is why he was so muscular; why his body was so strong and handsome. His long fingers were defined from the fierce grip he held on the reins. I watched him work them in the pasture across the street from the homestead for hours until they obeyed his every command.

No one would have thought to buy their hardware goods or feed from anyone else. He chatted with his clients about their families and their health. He remembered all their children's names and their ages. He inquired about their wives and added flour, sugar, and other dry goods into the store's stock. Soon the whole family shopped in our store. I had plenty of meal, flour, coffee, tea, sugar and other baking goods to create his evening desserts, which was really the reason I think he brought in the baking supplies in the first place.

His birthday was celebrated with a family picnic at the homestead. Johanna allowed me the honor of baking his birthday cake. It was lopsided but tasted delicious. He told me that I was his birthday present when I gave him a typed copy of that first poem I'd written about him for a gift.

You are probably wondering if I had time to write. It wasn't easy. Like I said, I tried to cook in the evening when it was cool so that I could write for four hours in the early mornings. I managed to do this five days a week, but Saturday and Sunday were our days together, and I cared little about that typewriter then.

On our trips around the county, I heard more tales and more history. I took my notes, then transferred them into the novel.

One Sunday, when we were traveling home from the homestead, Cuyler pointed to a building that used to be the Union Cotton mill owned by Graville Quackenbush. It was senseless for me to think that the name was made up for comic purposes because he referred to the people constantly and even showed me their home.

"You needn't feel that you have waited too long to marry, Gertrude," he once said to a comment that I'd made about being an old maid by his time period's expectations. "I know of a spinster by the name of Dora Darling who was quite mature when she married. She applied for a position as a weaver, in that very building that you see before you, and was assigned to a loom adjoining one operated by John Aaron."

"Rather advanced for those days, wasn't it?" I said.

"Precisely. The next day she called on the superintendent and requested to be transferred to another loom giving as her reason that she did not want to work so close to a man."

"Reverse chauvinism?" I said.

"Exactly." He continued his story. "The superintendent, after giving the request due consideration, refused to grant the change. As time passed, she began to learn that possibly men were not such terrible creatures as she had depicted and there arose an admiration for the weaver she had previously scorned. As time went on, Mr. Aaron found opportunity to pick up broken threads, replace shuttles, and do other cast that fall to the lot of a weaver, and the couple soon discovered beside weaving 'Union Mills A Sheeting,' they were also weaving a friendship that would be hard to break."

"Like ours," I said, snuggling close to him.

"Precisely," he said. "The old dam came into being as a lovers' lane, while the tall steps on the west end of the factory afforded a restful place for holding hands, and 'poverty row' extended its good offices to speed the lovers on their happy way."

"You mean they..."

"Well, it seems they did, Gertrude, but they planned on marrying."

"That's good." I continued writing my notes.

"The bride, clad in her new, robin's egg blue ensemble, that was very fashionable; and the groom clad in the finest weaves in Piccadilly, repaired to the residence of the officiating clergyman, Rev. John Perry, who, in well chosen and solemn words, pronounced them husband and wife."

"Rev. Perry certainly does a lot of marrying in these parts, doesn't he?"

"He's quite the romantic. At the conclusion of the ceremony, the couple went to their apartment, the 'Third floor back' on the 'Four family house,' where they began housekeeping immediately. During the evening, they were visited by the 'Coquine Band' of Toddsville, a musical organization noted for the varied instruments played and harmony produced. After the passing of cider and cigars by the groom, the organization disbanded and left the newly wedded couple to themselves."

"I like that one. I'm soft hearted when it comes to a good love story."

"Like ours?" Cuyler said.

"Precisely," I said giggling.

We did not find much call to travel to Cooperstown during the week. If something truly necessary came up, I was allowed to drive the horse and buggy by myself into town. I enjoyed the independence.

I didn't see my friends except on rare occassions or at Sunday services. When they began attending the baseball games, we were able to chat more.

One particular Saturday afternoon at the baseball game, Mrs. Sloat relayed a frightening experience she had had the previous week.

"It just isn't safe on the streets of our town these days—especially at night, Gertrude. They've hired extra security and deputized more men."

"Whatever for?" I said.

"We've had a rash of burglaries. My store was entered while I was out, and the small amount of money I had in my drawer was stolen."

"How?"

"There are so many vagrants in Otsego County these days. And the drunks are everywhere at night. The police do their best to haul them into jail, but decent people are now locking their doors and staying inside on these hot summer nights. We have even started locking our home too, Gertrude," Mrs. Sloat said.

"Have you been robbed, Mrs. Sloat?" Cuyler said, overhearing our conversation.

"I have been, Cuyler, dear boy. And if you're smart, you'll see that there's an extra lock placed upon your shop door and one on your apartment as well. Many people have been mentioning your good fortune and new business. Being as it's in a small town and your store is right on the main street, I suppose they'd have to be mighty bold to rob from you. Still, you never know. You two have a fairly obvious schedule."

"Thank you, Mrs. Sloat. I appreciate your advice and will heed it, I assure you. I only hope my mother is all right, considering she lives so far west—so out in the country."

"They seem to harbor near the cities. Mostly drunks looking for money to purchase liquor. The constabulary is ever watchful. Still, I won't let Sally walk home alone anymore. My husband, or her boyfriend, sees us to our doors every night."

"I'm glad to hear that. Will they retrieve your money?" I

asked. She was a decent, Christian woman with a good heart and didn't deserve to be harmed.

"They caught the villain, Gertrude, but I shan't see my money again," she said.

The woman was agitated, and I was anxious for our many friends who had entertained nightly walks, bike rides, and social gatherings without fear in the past. I suppose crime knows no specific time period, traversing all equally.

Cuyler spoke of the new concern during our night ride home.

"I think she's correct. We should place a barricade on our door, too," he said, concerned that the tools would be desirable to a thief.

"If you wish. Would you like me to travel to Toddsville to see to your mother? She wanted me to help her preserve her jams and such for the winter and the fair."

"If you like," Cuyler said, and I could tell I'd eased his mind.

Chapter Twenty-Nine

It had turned September in such a short time. My days were numbered, and we neared the equinox date with great trepidation. Every August storm reinforced this fact by my usual show of illness. Love making had become more earnest, passionate, and bittersweet. My writing became manic. Cuyler found more reasons to close the shop and spend time with me. His rationale was that he had plenty of time, after I was gone, to attend to business. I painted and decorated my home wholeheartedly. I tried to purge the thought of this heartbreak from my soul by plunging headlong into a project that would make our domestic life seem more permanent. We worked on the house plans more diligently.

Of course, Mother Carr and our friends did not understand any of this. The fair would be held within four days of my departure, and everyone's focus was on that event.

Cuyler gave me permission to help his mother and keep her under cautious eyes while he ran our booming business. There was only one hard and fast rule to which I had to promise. Under no circumstance was I ever to tarry after dark.

The temperature dropped. The welcome breeze made cooking the fruits over the hot stove with Johanna and Mother Carr easier. We spoke of family as we boiled and canned the fruit, and I kept to Cuyler's story when asked about my sister, mother, and father. I could tell Mother Carr wanted me pregnant soon.

Our new house plans were agreed upon, and they had started to build on our lot. The advance we gave them made them more agreeable about completing the project before winter.

As expected, the house was a classic Victorian structure and a mansion to my way of thinking.

It had a basement with three chambers: a laundry, coal cellar with outside chute through which Cuyler could deliver his own coal, and of course, a place for the furnace near the coal cellar. It had a 15' wide room in the cellar for storing fruits, preserves, and the canned items Mother Carr was hastily teaching me how to create. There were outside steps from my laundry to the backyard for me to use when I wanted to hang my clothes out back on the clothesline in the warm seasons.

The first floor opened from the street by an enormous wood

and glass door to a wide vestibule. To the left of this hallway was a parlor with a specially designed bay window and another window wall which would have bookcases on either side for nick nacks and other items. This room had a fireplace on the inside wall.

A large arched doorway would lead to the library. This room had a fireplace on the inside wall also.

Outside this room was a piazza and a doorway which led back into the house and connected the vestibule where there were stairs leading to the second floor or to the cellar. If you continued walking, you would find yourself in the kitchen which had some neat built-in shelves and another fireplace. It also had a small porch extending from the kitchen door. It had two pantries, one for storing cans and jars of food, and a butler's pantry that had many glass covered shelves for dishes and glasses etc. I loved the pantry concept even though we weren't going to have a butler.

The butler's pantry led to the spacious dining room. It had another fireplace on the pantry wall and a ten-foot wide window. There was another piazza outside this room too. If you walked out of the dining room, you would see the stairs to your right and there was a storage closet there. The stairs took you to the second floor.

The second floor had a master bedroom, two chamber rooms, a nursery, and a bathroom. We were going to have indoor plumbing. Next to the bathroom was a guest bedroom with a turret, castle-style tower window in it.

The master chamber, that we were going to use as the master bedroom, had a window and a roof porch, a dressing room for me and a closet as well as our own fireplace. I loved our bedroom having a romantic fireplace. You could get to the nursery or sewing room from here.

To the left of this hallway were two chambers; one had a roof porch with a closet and an interior fireplace; and the second had a closet and a fireplace too.

If you continued up the stairway, you would see a four chambered attic. It mimicked the second floor in many ways and was not as small as you might think. The roof line on this house did not taper. It had what was called a French, or mansard, roof which was shaped rather like a box. The chimneys were visible atop the attic which had many windows making it a cheerful and bright addition to the house instead of a dark storage area like most modern attics. I planned to use the attic exclusively as my own. It would be my office. I would store my research data here, my typewriter, a huge desk, and all my office supplies.

The house would be made of wood and painted white. It would have a large stairway to the front door, a stone walkway, and a carefully designed, wrought-iron fence—that would surround the entire yard—closing with an ornate gate. And best of all...it only cost $6,000 to build. We would decorate it in style with the money we had. I had already withdrawn more money from the Cooper's account and started ordering furniture and rugs for our home.

Naturally, I loved the look of the house design and could not wait to see it finished. I watched the progress daily, envisioning every aspect. The vision would have to sustain me for many months.

The county fair would begin its festivities on Monday, September 20, 1897. It was to be held on the grounds of the Agricultural Society and continue for three days. Opening day would be reserved for setting up all the entries. Johanna and Mother Carr told me what to expect at the "fair."

"They have spent much money on improving the fair this year, Gertrude. I expect it'll be grand," said Cuyler's mother.

"Doring's celebrated military band will play most of the time. Mr. Edwin Clark directs the Troy band," said Johanna.

"Yes, Johanna, we know why the band is your point of interest," she teased. "She has a thing for that Edwin Clark," Mrs. Carr said.

Johanna turned beet red. "Hush now, I do not."

Mother Carr winked.

"Cuyler will be sure to watch the horse races because they've improved the track, and it promises to be a grand show. Cuyler so *loves* horses."

"On the second and third day of the fair there will be balloon ascensions, with a parachute drop made by Professor Frisbee, the world renowned expert," said Johanna.

Frisbee? Nah, it couldn't be!

Johanna continued, "In front of the grand stand, every day, there'll be free air exhibitions, by those famous athletes and acrobats, the Rice Brothers and Etta Victoria. There'll be lots of things to catch your eye, Gertrude."

"Cuyler will want to inspect the thoroughbred stock; as you say, he's looking for another team to deliver coal this winter," said Mother Carr.

"She wants you there to see her win first prize in the canning exhibition," Johanna said.

"Oh, now, no one said I would win, Johanna."

"She wins every year and that's fifteen years in a row," Johanna said wryly.

"Well," I said, "it looks like fine weather for a fair."

"What's the matter, dear, you seem troubled by something?" Mother Carr said.

"Maybe Gertrude would like to enter an exhibition. Can you sew?" Johanna said.

I shook my head no.

"We know you can't can or make jam nice enough to win."

I shook my head in agreement.

"Well, Gertrude, what would you like to enter? What do you like to create?"

"I doubt that they have an exhibit for writing, do they?" I said.

"Well, of course, they do, Gertrude. Have you been writing on that typewriter of mine?"

My heartbeat faster with excitement. "I've been writing some poetry. Do they take poems?"

"They take anything and everything; and sometimes, if it's very good, they publish it in *The Freeman's Journal.* The award is given to the best poet and the best story writer. It's called the James Fenimore Cooper Award for Literature, and they say it's judged by the new publishers that are looking to set up shop in Cooperstown. Not many people enter this exhibit which would make it even easier for a newcomer, such as yourself, to win."

My mind turned heavenward, and I knew what I had to do.

"Well, where do I apply, sign up, submit?" I said.

"Johanna, look how excited she is. My dear, just go down to *The Freeman's Journal* office at the Fenimore Hotel and apply.

You can enter as often as you want, but the deadline for your final pages is September 17, so you'd better hurry up."

I would enter the writing exhibit with my small poem. Then I would enter the manuscript and submit it under the name Cuyler E. Carr's *Reflections of Toddsville.* Although he had never written a word of it, they were his stories. All I had done was compile them into a manuscript. I couldn't be sure of the judges, but I was sure everyone knew Cuyler's history stories by now. They would identify him as the author, and I would tell them that I'd merely typed them for him so there would be only "fibs" told.

I would leave out the personal things between us and save them for my own book, but I would give Cuyler what he deserved most in this world—recognition. I couldn't wait to see his face when they called his name as first prize winner. How thrilling it would be if they published the manuscript under his name. It would be the best gift I could give him next to a permanent 1897 address or a son. Then when the time came to say goodbye, whatever story he made up for my departure, might not be so difficult for my friends to understand.

As far as my poem was concerned, well, no one would understand it, anyway; so I would encourage Clarence to enter his little Otsego poem because I felt sure he could win. Wouldn't that little girlfriend of his sit up and take notice when he went to take the prize? I would help by typing it for him.

I raced home by way of the newspaper office. I took several applications and asked about the dates and the official manuscript style, word size, and sentence spacing they expected. They sort of looked bewildered and told me to type it on paper if I could. I laughed to myself. Yes, I thought I could handle that one.

I never drove that rig home faster in my life.

Chapter Thirty

The next few days were a blur of editing, writing, and revising. I have to admit that the apartment took second place to the manuscript. Cuyler pretended not to notice his cold dinner.

I filled out the application and took it back to the news' office. The problem was keeping it secret; so I told the man at the desk not to make a big deal out of the entries lest there be partiality by the judges.

Cuyler was amazed when I seemed detached and secretive about my "poetry" writing for he still thought that was what I was typing. I hastily wrote a love poem to him, so that he thought I was just writing verses.

I helped with the hardware store in the afternoons, and we both inspected the construction of the new home during our free moments.

In one week the manuscript was finished. I placed the pages in a large box that he had received merchandise in and put it in our rig. I had my poem as well. Clarence had visited the previous Saturday and allowed me to enter his poem. He brought it to the homestead Sunday.

On that fateful day, I kissed my husband farewell as he leaned against the front door of his store to chat with his customers. He smiled and waved goodbye as I headed to Cooperstown with my secret gift. That picture of my wonderful husband would sustain me over the horrendous days that followed.

I took our labors into the office of *The Freeman's Journal.* The clerk smiled, winked, and wished me good luck. We needed luck, for I desperately wanted Cuyler to win. After all, nothing but my heart said that we were going to. I sort of figured I had an edge because I was a published author, of course, you never know what budding Cooper was out there dying to get published.

On the return trip to Milford, I saw a man unconscious and bleeding, lying in the middle of the road. He seemed to have been thrown from his horse for the animal was standing to one side of the man quizzically looking at me. I stopped the rig and calmed my horse. I went to the man, kneeled to check for signs of life, and then smelled the worst chemical one could ever imagine wrapped around my nose and mouth. The darkness covered my eyes, and I felt myself falling into large, masculine arms.

I've no idea how long I was out. When I awoke, I determined that I was in a room, an old, musty bedroom, with ripped wall-paper on the walls. It smelled of dust and old rags. My hands and feet were tied with rope. I tried to call out but a dirty rag stifled my screams.

Where was I? What could anyone possibly want with me?

I heard voices. It sounded like two men talking. I couldn't make out the words, but once in a while I heard "Carr" and "woman." I must have been kidnapped for some reason, because I was still alive and relatively unharmed. I tried to decipher where I was.

An old house was my first guess. No sounds of trains so I thought I might be somewhere in the country because you could usually hear the train from almost anywhere in the county. The window was open; I could smell fresh air and hear the sound of a bubbling brook. The combination of sounds was familiar, but I still could not place my location.

Then I thought of Cuyler. What must he be thinking? Had Samuel and the rig returned without the mistress?

Just then the door opened. I admit I was frightened. A rather basal and dense looking man, with a large forehead, prominent eyes, brown bushy hair, cracked teeth, poorly-fitting farmer clothing, who smelled of sweat and dirt, regarded my demeanor.

"Yeah, she's awake. Come on in, Tweed," he said.

Tweed came into the room and smiled a toothy grin. This man was thinner and might have been older than the first man by a few years. He looked more muscular though than the fat and soft first man. Both men had lecherous looks on their faces.

"Oh, God, girlie, ain't you sweet?" Tweed said, and licked his lips.

I panicked. Struggling to remove myself from the bed, I managed only to confirm my own helplessness.

"Ain't no use squirmin'," said the first, and as yet, unidenti-fied man. "We got you good and hog tied. You cain't go nowheres lessen we want you to."

"Can't believe Carr's woman fell for that old stranded stranger act, eh, Clint? She was so easy to ketch. A little chlo-roform, and she went out like a light," said Tweed. "Take off the rag."

Both men smelled like a barn full of cow manure.

The horrible cloth was taken from my mouth. "Who are you? What do you want with me?" I said.

Clint said, "Hooo, don't you like them spirited gals, Tweed?" He came close to me and touched my hair. I wanted to tear him to pieces. My dread of the psychotic killer was finally coming true. All I could think of was Jim Cooper's words that a traveler could die anytime whether here or at home.

"What do you want with me?" I repeated.

Tweed laughed in a low-toned voice. "Why money, of course, sweetheart. Word's all over town that your dowry set Carr up sweet. Why shouldn't we get some of it, huh?"

I relaxed. Was that all they wanted? "You want money?"

"At first that was all we wanted," admitted Clint, stroking a broken tooth with his long tongue, "but now that I see what a woman Carr's got, well..." he said, as his eyes inspected the ripped blouse and the cleavage shown by the missing two buttons, "maybe we should plan a little party for the three of us." He came close to me, and I was nauseous at the thought of his filthy hands touching my body.

He reached up to my face. "Such a pretty gal. Got a sweet face, sugar." His eyes regarded my body. A low whistle. "I can see why Cuyler wanted you, baby face."

Tweed intervened. "Enough of that," he said. "You heard the man."

The "man?" Was there a third man involved? Some operation!

"How's he gonna know if I take some," said Clint. "She ain't gonna see him. He ain't gonna know."

"Well, let's not piss him off, okay? You don't know what he's got planned."

Then Tweed leaned over my body and brushed the other man away.

"We got you and Cuyler's got to pay to get you back. We left a note with your rig. If he wants you back in one piece, he'll have to come up with ten-thousand dollars. When he's got the money ready, he's got to give us a sign by closing the store at noon on a week day. That night, he'll bring the money to Oaks Creek and leave it in the middle of the bridge. There'll be instructions for him saying how he's to find you."

"You lie. You won't let me live," I said.

"Sure we will, honey pot, as long as he comes up with the dough," said Tweed. "We ain't murderers. By the time he finds you, we'll be long gone with the money. He's got to have the money ready in three days," he came close to my face, "cause if he don't," he placed his dirty finger on my throat and made a slicing gesture, "we'll *have* to leave him a bloody corpse."

Clint found the comment particularly amusing and laughed the most perverted laugh I've ever heard.

"That's when I get to have you," said Clint.

"Shut up!" said Tweed, and smacked him across his shoulders.

"Well, I do if we're gonna kill her."

Tweed hit the bumbling fool across his mouth this time to shut him up. I was beginning to have some respect for Tweed. "I just told her we was gentlemen. What you make me out a liar for?"

Clint smiled at me. "But, she's pretty, and she ain't gonna complain. Are you, sugar? I got something for you, baby face." Yeah, I thought, and you can just keep it, Bub!

God in Heaven get me out of this one! Please, Cuyler, get the note, the money, *and get me the hell out of here.* Call the Carr Clan. Call the F.B.I. Call Arnold Schwartzenegger.

"Go get her the food." Clint hurried out of the room. Obviously, Tweed was the smarter of the two. I would try innocence and helplessness. That wouldn't be a tough act.

"Please don't let that man touch me." My eyes were rimmed with tears, and my blue eyes glowed with angelic innocence. "My husband will give you the money. We just got married, and I'm pregnant." This was a lie but a good one because an instant look of empathy came over his face.

"Pregnant? Shit! I didn't know you was pregnant. 'Course your husband's gonna pay," he said, trying to reassure me. "Now don't you worry about old Clint. I won't let him near you, but I do have my orders. Two days is all your man's got."

"Who are you working for?"

"I cain't tell you that."

"Well, if you free me now, I'll see that you get double the money. You can divide it between yourselves."

"Cain't. Got my orders. The man gave us money up front for our work and our silence." He shook his head. "Cain't."

His eyes looked at my helpless form. "So you gonna have a little one. I sure hope your man comes up with the money quick." His eyes lowered to my abdomen, and he showed true compassion. "I'd hate for you to get into trouble or sick. I shore would hate to have to slit your throat." Well, as much compassion as a thug can muster, all right.

"I kilt a man once," he continued reassuring me. "I know how it feels to have a man's life in your hands and watch it slip away." The poetry of a murderer.

"It was in Albany," he said, as he rubbed his calloused hands together in a sort of Lady Macbeth style all his own. "But, I was drunk and got into a fight with him first. I never murdered anyone for money. I ain't never kilt a lady." His eyes glanced at my helpless figure.

Clint came into the room and put the tray of odd smelling food on the bed.

"I can't eat with my hands tied," I said.

"Tie her feet to the bedpost so she cain't run; then untie her hands so's she can eat. The man didn't tell us she was pregnant."

Clint's eyes opened wide. "Pregnant! Shit. I cain't hurt no pregnant woman." I thanked the Lord for forgiving my lie. "Her old man better come up with the dough."

My hands were untied, and my feet retied. My wrists hurt from the rope. It had cut into my skin, and they were red and bloody.

I kept remembering the Carr oath. These men needed to fear, not me. If they hurt me; they would pay. I had to find out where I was though. Trudy Johnson Carr could take care of herself. I'd figure a way out of this mess and save shelling out the "dough."

Clint stayed in the room while I ate. The meal was cold meatloaf, mashed potatoes, and gravy from the restaurant across from our house. So, they had been near us all along. Watching and waiting for the perfect time to kidnap me. Who was this mystery man? Was he as much an idiot as these two?

"Where am I?" I repeated.

"Sure, I'm gonna tell you." He chuckled at the joke.

"Why not? When Cuyler pays I'm going home anyway. So what's the big deal?" I didn't have much appetite, but I ate the food anyway. I had to keep up my strength.

"Cause we ain't runnin the show, little Mama. The man makes

the rules," said Clint.

"And who is he? Someone from around here? A stranger like you two?"

"Ha! You must think I am plain dumb-stupid if you think for one moment I'm gonna tell you that the man in charge is from town. Ha ha."

Yes, I did. Really, Trudy, how could you think old smelly and toothless was ignorant? Oh, somewhere between 'Gee you're a pretty gal' and 'I gets to have her if we gonna kill her' I must have guessed.

When I was finished with my "luscious" meal, Clint untied my feet and retied my hands. I said, "Why do I need to be tied? If you lock the room door; I can't go anywhere."

"Well, I guess that's true. The open window is two floors up, and you'd break your neck trying to crawl out it. But, I cain't untie you."

"Yeah, I know—the man."

"Right."

He took my tray and gave me a serious look. "I didn't knows you was pregnant, Miss. I wouldn't take a pregnant woman. I gotta code about that kinda stuff."

Gee, Clint, how noble and honorable you are you horney little bastard. He wouldn't touch me, but he would kill me. Well, we all must have a code to live by, mustn't we?

He left the room. The closed door left me in darkness. You know how I am about the dark. I tried to relax and lay my head on the foul smelling pillow. The tears started to flow. I wanted my home. I might never see it again. What if the rig flew home leaving the ransom note in a ditch? What if all Milford searches for me on the road thinking I had an accident? The worst thought that entered my mind was, what if the note didn't reach Cuyler? Might he not think that I went "home" like I did during the storm and not look for me at all? These men would kill me if it came to their own survival. I was not convinced these men would let me live even if they *were* paid.

In the movies, they *always* kill the victim after they get the money. Anyone who has ever seen a cop show can tell you that. And, furthermore, they had shown me their faces. I knew *they* were stupid, but what about this man. I could identify them but had no clue as to his identity. Of course, I now knew he lived in town. All I had to do was figure out *which* town.

I fell into an unsettling half sleep with the dreaded thought that I would never watch the sunset with Cuyler again.

Chapter Thirty-One

I awoke after sleeping only a few hours. I tossed and turned uncomfortably on my bed. Fearful thoughts plagued me. Dismal visions of being killed, and or raped, tossed me into a depression. I had been good to people. Why would anyone want to hurt me? I had finally learned what love, and life was all about, and now it was being taken from me.

Then I thought about Cuyler. How could I think of only my own concerns while Cuyler was probably mad with worry? He would not sleep for fear I was gone. If he had the ransom note, he would have to wait until the Milford bank opened tomorrow to withdraw the money. Would he call on the sheriff to help him find me? Would anyone have a clue where I was? Would *I* ever determine where I was? Who was behind this insane attempt to extract money from the kindest man in Otsego County?

I heard some drunken voices from downstairs. Great! If it weren't bad enough to have two half wits kidnap me, now they were going to get drunk on top of everything else. Would they let me go outside to relieve myself? What about water? I was dying for a drink. Would I ever be allowed to get up, move around, wash? I called to my kidnappers.

"Whatdya want?" came the inebriated reply.

"I need to relieve myself."

"Well, get the gun, Clint. We'll have to take her out back. Blindfold her, but untie her hands so's she can feel her way around," Tweed said.

Clint came to the room and did just that. It was wonderful to feel my limbs moving again.

"Look. I won't cause any trouble. I just have to use the Necessary. I've been up here for hours."

"Move!" Clint pushed me to inform me that I should go downstairs. I eased my way cautiously down the wooden stairway. I couldn't see a thing, of course, but I could feel my way into what appeared to be a kitchen.

We walked outside. The summer, evening air was delightful. It only made me more homesick.

I touched the door to an outhouse. "Hurry up," Clint said drunkenly.

I went inside and did what I needed. I also took off the blindfold and tried to see out of the broken side of the shed. I saw some light, a yard, an old tree, but I couldn't see where I was. I *could,* however, hear. I detected Oak Creek. I was somewhere near Toddsville.

I stretched my sore muscles. I put the blindfold back on. Were they dumb or what?

Clint took me back to the house. I heard an owl and then a cry of some animal. From now on, I told myself, I would pay attention to every sound when we traveled because I had to be someplace familiar, someplace near Cooperstown. Then the whole picture spun like a miracle into my head: the creek, a building close enough but deserted, uninhabited, the owl. I could only be in one spot—the ghostly "red house." No one would have the courage to go near it.

I remembered as much as I could about it. A classic two-story, plain, Williamsburg-style building that had been used, perhaps, as a hotel. An addition had been constructed to the left side of the building. There was a front porch. Five pillars. Five windows on the top floor where the peddler had been...murdered. Oh, God, I was going to become the victim in my husband's next *story.*

Clint was just as playful drunk as he had been sober and a little forgetful of his ethics. He sat on the bed next to me, retied me, and took the blindfold away. He let me view his "form."

"You like it, don't you? I can tell, Mama," he said, touching my cheek. "You and your old man ain't been married long, have you? Well, you sure got the body to make a man burn."

He reached over my lap attempting to touch my breasts, and I let him have it between his legs with my knee. He had forgotten my legs weren't tied. Clint doubled over in pain. Then came the crack across my cheek.

"You bitch!" he said.

I reeled from the pain. I thought my jaw had been dislocated.

"I oughta kill you right now."

Tweed called to us. His voice was sluggish and slurred. "Whatcha doin up there, Clint? I told you to leave her alone."

"The bitch kicked me."

It was mandatory for Tweed to intervene. I heard his footsteps on the planks of wood.

"Whatdya do to her?" Tweed said.

"Nothin'. She hauls off and kicks me in the crotch."

Tweed inspected me and then turned around quickly, smacked Clint, and sent him flying to the other end of the room.

"*I told you to leave her alone.* You just *had* to try her. Whatdya think she's gonna do to you? She's expecting a baby. She ain't gonna let you get near her. Then you haul off and bruise her. Look at this."

He inspected my swollen jaw.

"What am I gonna tell the man when he sees this? He might just haul off and shoot your stupid ass."

I wasn't too sure how intelligent Clint's ass was, but the rest of him was none to bright. Tweed's voice softened. "There, there, little Mama." He touched the bruise on my face. My baby blues pleaded for sympathy. "I'll just go and get you a washcloth and clean this up," he said.

As he walked passed the wounded jerk, he said, "You asshole," and kicked Clint in the stomach.

He brought me a cool cloth and untied my hands to allow me to wipe my face. It really hurt, but I think my jaw must have jerked back in place, or else he had hit me higher. I'd have a nasty red welt on my cheek.

The wounded warrior groaned in pain from two different areas. He turned into a total coward when Tweed came on the scene.

"Now you get your fat ass downstairs." Clint did as Tweed said. Tweed turned towards me. He smelled of liquor.

"Sorry, sugar," he said. "He can get a little rowdy when he's drunk. Now you just lie down. We should hear something from the man soon." He retied my hands and feet.

I cried myself to sleep.

Chapter Thirty-Two

I awoke to the sun streaming through my window. I heard birds chirping in the nearby tree. I smelled breakfast, at least I think that's what it was.

When the meal was finished, Tweed redid the routine of blindfolding me and walking me to the outhouse. We were more cautious this time as we no longer had night's cloak to shield us.

I pulled the blindfold from my eyes. I could make out the "red house" for certain now. I prayed that someone would drive their rig passed the house and notice the sudden habitation.

I checked my clothing for any small object that I could accidentally on purpose drop on the ground as we walked into the house. If I played my cards right, I could deposit something close to the kitchen door which was near the road.

I couldn't bear to part with my wedding ring or any jewelry that I might never recover. It had to be a small object too, so that Tweed would not notice it in my hand or falling from it. There was a cluster of pink rosettes on my corset. Strangely enough, I was wearing the corset that I'd worn on my wedding day. Some lace and roses would seem very odd on this muddy yard. I ripped open the rest of the blouse and took the lace from the top of the corset. With a good tug, it came off. I hated to destroy the memories associated with this particular corset, but it meant my life now. I crumpled it into my hand.

When I emerged from the toilet, Tweed pushed me in the direction of the kitchen. I suspected he had the gun under his jacket or shirt. As we neared what I thought was the kitchen door, I let the lace and pink rosette embroidery fall from my hand. Smooth, I was so...smooth. He never suspected a thing. Oh, would I like to see the Carr men run their horses all over these two—especially Ralph.

I guess the bruise looked pretty awful because when I returned to my room I was not tied; I had gained some pity. I could move about the room freely. It was a kind of freedom, but still a jail. The window was locked, and the door bolted behind the man when he left.

I found a cracked mirror on an old bureau and inspected my ravaged face. He had done a number on it; it was crimson. I sat on the bed and devised escape plans. I could look out of the window, but I might get punched for that. Best to try to contrive a way to relay the news that I was the poor peddler about to be murdered in the top floor of the "red house."

It came in a flash. The bed had a sheet. I quickly took it and put the filthy cover back on the bed. I ripped the sheet until I had strips. I tied them together. Then I took my most colorful petticoat and tied it to one end of the rope.

Now what? If I threw it out of the rear window, the thugs would notice it as soon as I went back to the outhouse. If I threw it out of the front window, they might not notice, but it was a risky bet. When the man came along, I would have to bring it back in. The chances of him coming by in broad daylight were slim. He apparently had more intelligence than these two dimwits if he had formulated a plan where they took all the risks, and he stayed anonymous.

I eased the window open an inch and slid the sheet rope out, letting the petticoat dangle a bit. It lay on the lower, smaller roof line that rested over the porch. I would not allow it to go further and hazard the chance of my first floor friends noticing it.

Then I sat down to rest my cheek, my cracked and bleeding wrists, my weary muscles—which had been cramped into a pretzel design for so many hours—and my nerves.

I was in this innocent state when lunch was served. They never saw the sheet rope because the curtain covered the small space from which the rope trailed.

As I ate my lunch, I heard it. I knew instantly what it was. A jingle and a tingle and a flippity flap. It was Clarence riding his bike to Toddsville. Oh, please look up! I prayed he wouldn't be crafting a poem right now. No one else, that I knew of, had that distinctive little bell on a bicycle.

There was a knock on the door. My ears strained to hear the voice.

The door opened.

"Yeah? What do you want?" said Clint.

"Excuse me, sir," said Clarence. "I was unaware that this home had been purchased, or that anyone inhabited this locale."

Please don't mention the petticoat, Clarence.

The other man came to the door. "What do you want, Sonny?

We don't like to be disturbed."

"Yes, I can see that you are otherwise engaged," said Clarence.

Clint said, "Huh?"

Tweed said, "He means; we look busy."

"Oh."

I wished that I could see Clarence or signal to him that I was there.

"I was wondering if you might donate some money to my sister's Epworth League. They're in great need of finances as they have been doing quite a bit of charity work lately."

Tweed said, "Give him some money, Clint, and get him the hell out of here."

"How much?" he said. "Here. Is that enough?"

"Oh, yes, sir. That's most generous. I shall inform my sister, Sally, of your generous donation."

"Just don't come back for anymore," said Tweed.

"Oh, no, sir. Thank you, sir."

The door slammed shut. Jingle-tingle, flippity-flap. Jingle-tingle, flippity-flap. Clarence was gone.

I reached for the rope of sheets and my petticoat and pulled them back into the room. I arranged the slip under my dress and pushed the rope under my bed. I no longer needed them. Clarence had given me a signal. He had been told of my kidnapping. It meant Cuyler had spread the word to all to be on the lookout. He would know that I was there.

Clarence had no sister, and Sally's name mentioned meant that my friends would be informed of where I was. They, in turn, would tell Cuyler. He also knew how many thugs were guarding me. Clarence Peaslee was one *cool* agent.

I rested easier now that I knew someone was aware of my prison's location. I was able to sleep after my dinner and my restroom break. I wasn't as nervous because I knew that Cuyler and the other Carr's would not let me down. As I snoozed, I kept hearing that charming and wonderful bell on Clarence's bike.

I did not sleep for long. THE MAN came to the "red house." I heard the door bang open and slam shut. I heard the drunken men shuffle to greet him, and I detected a certain amount of fear in their voices. Well, clearly it was Al Pacino or Robert Duvall because who else could instill such mortal terror into these two beasts.

"Everything working as planned? She all right?" It couldn't be Pacino.

"Mostly," Tweed said. "Clint tried to get close, and she kneed him just like you told us she might. He hit her, and now she's got a welt on the side of her face as red as this house."

"Damn! You imbecile!" Clint was slapped down hard by Mr. Big whose voice was sounding more and more familiar to me. "I told you that no harm was to come to the lady. Do you want every Carr chasing you halfway across New York State? Those men are relentless. How could you be such a dunce?"

"I'm sorry," said Clint in a pathetic whimper.

"She probably deserved it with that mouth of hers. I've received information from Cuyler. I took my buggy to Milford and found the store closed at noon."

Ellis? It was Ellis!

"Then he's got the money, and we meet him at the bridge—or rather we wait at the bridge until he drops the money. Then we grab the bag."

"That's right. Place this envelope under a rock in the middle of the bridge and keep an eye on it to make sure it's there when he drops the bag. Be careful that he never sees you. The note will tell him where to find his wife. Do not leave the area until you are sure he has left. I'll take Gertrude, to the place Cuyler will find her, in my own buggy."

Oh, shit! That last sentence, so oddly phrased, frightened me. I wondered at its subtext.

"Now, when you are quite sure he's departed, I want you to meet me at old Doc Almy's tomb."

"Why there?" Tweed said, with the sound of distaste for the place on the edge of his voice.

"The brook will disguise our voices, and it will most definitely be deserted after midnight. It's far too ugly a place for anyone to visit. I'll meet you inside. We'll divide the money equally among ourselves, and then I want you to high tail yourselves out of this county. I don't ever want to see you here again."

Clint said, "You don't have to worry about that. We don't want no trouble. Where you gonna put the woman?"

"You let me handle that. I don't want her to recognize me so, before you leave at 11:30, I'd like you to chloroform her and tie her for me. Remember, I'll be alone, and it'll be much easier for me if she's docile. I told you what she was like."

Clint said, "You're afraid of her, ain't you? Lordy, how I'd love to get my hands on that woman."

He was slapped by someone.

"Enough. I have my own plans for her. Just see that Carr gets the note. No, don't open it, you ass. It's sealed. It'll take him a while to find her. That should give all of us time to get to the vault and divide the money. Do you understand? I'll be back at 11:30. I have to attend the prayer meeting at the Union Church with my mother and then take her home. Do you have any questions?"

Silence.

"Good. See that you make no mistake about any of our plans. Has she had dinner?"

"Yeah."

"Very good. Make sure she takes a respite at 11:15 so that I have no worries on that score. Cuyler has the cash, and we're going to have a great deal of money when this little affair is over. The bitch owes it to me. She has made me the butt of public ridicule all over Otsego County. Besides," there was a low laugh, "I have another reason for wanting to avenge myself on her. She made Cuyler and his mother, two of my biggest accounts, withdraw their money from my bank. She must learn never to put me in a temper again."

"Right," said Tweed, sounding slightly amused. I was beginning to think Tweed was redeemable.

"See you at 11:30, and make sure she's chloroformed with this."

The door slammed. I was in deep shit. I would be with Ellis for some time wherever he was taking me, and even Tweed and Clint would not know where that was. Neither would my pint sized hero, Clarence, or my wonderful warrior, Cuyler.

I tried to fall asleep but ugly pictures of Ellis, with my helplessly blindfolded and chloroformed body, kept running through my mind.

Tweed came to take me to the restroom, and I suddenly lost every ounce of courage. I realized that this was it—show time. My palms were sweaty, and my heart was in my throat. I was shaking involuntarily. I stumbled on the last step.

"What's wrong with you? You ain't holding onto the banister. Got good news for you. Your old man came through with the money. You'll be home in no time. The man came by while you was sleeping."

I touched the door to the outhouse with a shaking hand and went inside. I stripped the signal petticoat off this time and shoved it out of the crack in the broken plank behind the closet. I wasn't coming back here.

He took me back to my room. Then Clint came in grinning. He had the extra ropes and the gag. He had the bottle of chloroform and a piece of cotton. He pulled my feet together and tied them. I was oddly relieved about that. Then he rolled me over onto my stomach and pulled my hands behind me tying them tightly. Then he blindfolded me.

I heard him laugh. "You sure is one pretty gal. I'm gonna miss you, sugar. The man will take you to your husband." He leaned over my body and kissed me hard on the lips.

"Mmmm, sweet." He licked his cracked tooth again. "Oh, yeah, so sweet. Too bad we never got better acquainted, eh, sugar?" Then he placed the gag on my mouth and tied it. I was totally helpless. Just then I heard the door open and in walked Ellis, or I missed my guess.

"She out?" Ellis asked.

"Clint's with her now," Tweed said.

I heard him walking up the steps. He was coming to the room. I smelled that the jar was opened because of the bitter chemical scent Clint sloshed onto the cloth.

"I told you to have her out when I came."

"Sorry, Mr. Ellis, I was just having some fun."

Silence. My heart was beating faster than the pedals on Clarence's bike.

"Are you a complete asshole?"

Clint must have realized his mistake. "Oh, Lord. I *am* sorry, Mr. Ellis."

I heard the footsteps advance to my bed.

I could smell the cologne he had over-indulged himself with that evening.

"Well, now you leave me no alternative," Ellis said.

A quivering sound in Clint's voice. "Whadya mean, Mr. Ellis?"

I heard Tweed's feet rushing up the steps.

He demanded an explanation to the hold up and mentioned the time.

"Your idiot assistant just spoke my name in front of the woman."

"Shit," Tweed said.

Ellis lowered his eyelashes and smacked his thigh with his right hand. He said, "Can't be helped."

Tweed said, "No!"

"I can't have her screaming all over the county that I was the one who kidnapped her. The whole town has become her friend and ally."

"I'll not be a party to murder after the husband has paid," said Tweed.

I heard a slap across someone's face.

"If she can identify me to the constabulary how long do you think it will be until you're involved? She has seen both of your faces."

"Shit! Clint, you *are* an ass."

Clint might be an ass, but he had just ended my life. Now I knew that my time had come in Toddsville, not Brooklyn, and that my fans would never know what happened to their favorite romance author. One of these men would kill me tonight. I didn't think Ellis had the guts, Tweed the true conviction, but Clint could manage in a pinch.

"Go and meet Carr and give him the message. Then meet me as prearranged at the vault. I should think it a perfect locale for what has to be done, don't you think?"

Clint growled and wiped his hands on his sleeve, "Makes sense. Who'd look there? You're smart, Mr. Ellis."

"Here, give me the chloroform. You best be on your way. And make sure you leave nothing behind in this house. I'll meet you at Doc Almy's vault in one hour. Now hurry."

I heard them run down the stairs and burst out of the door.

Ellis moved onto the bed. I could feel his presence.

He undid the gag. "Well, well, well, Gertrude. Did you hear all that? Right on schedule and just as I'd planned. I knew that Clint was far too stupid to keep anything secret. I'll not need their help tonight."

"You won't get away with this," I said.

"Maybe not," he said, with a wry smile in his voice, "but you won't be around to find out. They'll never find your body. How will they know you're dead? I'll have the money, and Cuyler will have lost his beautiful wife. The pretty, but stubbornly violent, Gertrude. She appeared from nowhere one June day in Cooperstown, and she'll disappear just as oddly."

I had an hour to live I guessed. Please Cuyler find me. But, he would be searching for me in the "red house," and I would be in the house of the dead.

"The note I gave Cuyler states that we have placed you in your own apartment in Milford. He'll drive his rig home and discover he was lied to. He'll panic. Where can she be? By that time, my dear, you'll be dead. I knew those imbeciles would never agree to my plan if I told them how it would end. They had to believe that they could escape killing a woman if her husband paid the ransom. I've chosen a very nice cherry coffin for you, and it'll blend in nicely with the others in the tomb. The Carr made ones, of course. Nothing but the best for you, my dear. I took it down there myself a week ago, in the late hours, lest someone notice my carriage. I'll admit it wasn't easy to get it down the hill and into the vault by myself, but I was inspired. Now, just a little chloroform to make you docile."

I struggled, but it was useless. The aroma soon put me to sleep.

Chapter Thirty-Three

I awoke on the floor of old Doc Almy's vault. As soon as I could focus, I saw Ellis with a revolver and some tools. He was humming a song and appeared completely mad to my way of thinking.

The floor was dank, cold, and damp from the creek. It smelled moldy. I was still tied, but my blindfold and gag were gone.

"Well, Gertrude," he said, glancing at my movements. "I see that you've awakened. Good. I'd like you to meet old Doc Almy." He pointed to the one tomb on the right." And his daughter," he pointed to the one on the left. "The area you shall inhabit was originally Mrs. Almy's, but, as Cuyler has surely told you by now, she was moved to another internment."

Like a maniac he pulled me up to stand beside him and glared into my eyes. "Such a pretty woman you are."

I rested against some object. My hand touched its smooth finish. I looked down at it and gasped.

"That's right. All for you. I spared no expense. After all, you deserve the best for ruining my reputation in Cooperstown. Now, you'll fade as a mere memory might, a blur. There'll be stories told about the woman married to Cuyler E. Carr for only three months in the summer, who disappeared one night, and was never seen or heard of again. Cuyler will be the romantic hero who'll become part of the legends of Toddsville—aimlessly walking up and down the streets of Milford with no will to live. Losing his wife and father in the same month only one year apart. Such a brief happiness they shared. Wherever did she go? Why did she suddenly leave? Rumor has it that she was kidnapped; Cuyler paid the ransom; but she was never returned. No doubt, murdered by the crooks who kidnapped her. And, *they* were never found either." Ellis chuckled at this one.

"Now, my dear, we have some unfinished business to take care of," he said seductively.

He dropped the tool he had in his hand and placed both hands on my breasts. It hurt. Smiling that insane grin—with the space between his teeth widening—he ripped my blouse from my body. He opened the corset's top button and gazed.

"Such a beauty. I didn't realize. My, my, Gertrude. This *will* be fun," Ellis said.

He placed his hands under my hips and lifted my body onto the top of the coffin. He untied my feet. They dangled helplessly over the cherry coffin. Then he moved his dirty hands up my legs.

God? *Hello!* If You are there, now would be a real good time to start an earthquake or something. INTERVENE! I don't want to tell You what to do, of course, but I think we're in real peril here. Rape. Adultery. Murder. Help!

He pulled my hips to the edge of the coffin then moved closer to me and grinned.

"At last. The moment I've waited two months for."

First, he surveyed my exposed flesh. I closed my eyes. I was hoping my impotent theory of his virility would prove accurate, but by the look on his face, I doubted that would be a problem.

"Don't scream, Gertrude. I know that's what's crossing your mind. Take it, and keep that mouth of yours quiet, or I'll make your final moment slow and painful. It makes me feel rather important to know that I shall be the last man to give you pleasure."

His eyes never left mine. He leaned me back just a bit, slid my hips further towards the edge of the coffin, and came close to my abdomen. I closed my eyes and braced myself for the assault.

"Oh, relax, my dear. You might enjoy it, after all."

The voice said, "Mr. Ellis?"

It was Clint and Tweed.

Thank you, God!

"What is it?" His face was scarlet with anger. "Can't you see I'm busy?"

Clint saw all right, and his face brightened like a Christmas tree.

"I see what you had in mind all along." He smiled and licked his cracked lips. He stroked his genitals. "Well, I want her too."

"I think you should first tell me if you have the money," Ellis said.

"Here," said Tweed, who seemed disgusted with the whole set up. He regarded the new coffin.

"Carr was right on time and alone. He left the money, read the note, and raced to the 'red house,' I guess. We waited for a few minutes until we were sure he was gone and then high tailed it here. New coffin? You were planning this all along, weren't you?" Tweed said.

"Why, no, I told you..."

"Don't *lie* to me. You told us she would be allowed to live if her old man came up with the dough. *He did.*"

"Yes, I see that," Ellis said, "but she'll tell who kidnapped her, and if a jail cell is where you wish to spend your final days, so be it. Of course, the Carrs could come, search you out, and put and end to your misery if you want them to. You touched one of theirs. You caused the favored son grief—a loss of money. Do you want her to tell them who masterminded the whole scheme? Or how about Clint's hand on her cheek here, or who pointed a gun to her belly when she used the facilities?"

Surprisingly, Clint intervened, "But she's pregnant. If you kill her; you kill the baby too."

"She told you that?" Ellis said. "And you believed her? Hell, they've only been married a month. Even if she *were* pregnant, she wouldn't know yet. Where's your brain?"

"I never thought of that," said Tweed.

"She lied to us," said Clint.

"And you want to hand her over to her husband who probably is in a severe state, unable to think straight, and ready to kill any man who has dared to touch his wife."

There was a deadly silence. My heart burned a hole in my chest. I was so scared I no longer felt the nerves in my body. I wanted to live. I wanted my husband.

Tweed condemned me. "All right, I guess we have to. But, I'm not the one who's gonna do it."

"Not to worry," said Ellis. "I shall take care of everything. But, I'm the only one who'll touch her, understand. I have taken the greatest risk of all. I'm a reputable banker who drives his mother to church three times a week and has invested money in every church in the area."

"Yeah," said Tweed, "and everyone knows what a low-down shiftless skunk you are too."

Tweed tried to avoid my eyes and focus anywhere but on my face and form. I was already dead in his eyes, and he had begun to like me. He would not lift a hand to save me, but he couldn't bear to look at the face of the woman Ellis was going to murder.

He did add one thing. "If you're gonna do it, hurry up, and forget the other stuff. Get it over with so that we can get outa here."

He turned his back on me.

"Tweed?" I cried to him for his help.

Ellis slapped me. "Shut up!"

Even reeling from pain, I could see Tweed's neck stiffen. Then he started to walk out of the vault.

"Just one second, Tweed. I need a weapon. You don't expect that I have one, do you?"

I remembered the gun lying on the floor. Tweed reached into his pocket and pulled out a hunting knife. "Here. Make it quick and quiet. Come on, Clint. Let's count the money."

Clint rubbed the stubble on his chin and stared at me.

Ellis motioned him away. Then he turned to me. Rapidly, he stuffed the cloth back into my mouth and retied my feet. "You aren't going anywhere, Gertrude. I can't have you screaming your fool head off, but I have some unfinished business to attend to. I don't want interrupted again."

In an instant, I knew what he was going to do and cried out behind the gag. Ellis glared at me and then smiled. The two men would only think that my cries were my own as he was finishing me off and not be alerted to their own danger. I watched as Ellis unsheathed the knife. He then picked up the gun and turned it in his hand so that the butt could be used as a blunt instrument.

I strained to hear. Maybe they would get wise to Ellis and turn on him. Maybe they were gone, run off with the money, leaving him penniless and alone.

I heard a thump and a groan.

"What the...you son of a bitch!" It was Tweed's voice. It conveyed the physical tension of a man springing into action. I heard what sounded like a short fight.

Then I heard the gurgling sound of bloody death as Tweed's neck was cut open. I heard no more, but assumed Clint had been knocked out so that he could kill the smarter man first. No doubt, Ellis had sliced Clint's throat, as well, and I discovered the truth all too soon when Ellis dragged their lifeless bodies into the vault.

Ellis was out of breath. Clint was too large for Ellis to move, and it took every bit of his strength to do it. Opening the caskets was a chore too. Ellis pushed away the lids of the coffins of the two interred persons, heaved the thugs dead weight over the sides of the caskets, and lowered the two men into their final beds.

I screamed behind the gag. If this were what he would do to his partners, what horrible death had he in store for me?

It took him some time to execute this disgusting deed. How could he desecrate the two corpses like that? He had to be insane. He carefully placed the covers back and nailed them into place.

He lit an oil lamp and pulled the door to the vault only slightly closed. Just enough to shade the light, or cut off any sounds, but not enough to lock us in. I was trembling with fear. I could smell death all around me. My lips were quivering as I tried to appear calm and retain my usual attitude with Ellis. My heart was beating far too quickly. I felt dizzy and nauseous from what I'd just witnessed. I couldn't black out now. I had to think of a way out of this.

"Now, Gertrude, the money's all mine. Your two guardians of the gate lie dead at your feet. I'm going to take the gag off your mouth now, but don't scream. I already warned you that a long and torturous death awaited you afterwards if you caused me trouble. Do you want your final moments to be worse than they have to be?" The gag was removed.

"Ellis. You can't do this. I deflated your masculine ego, that's all. That's hardly a reason to take someone's life."

"Isn't it? My mother has heard the rumors that I'm in trouble for forcing myself on women. Women I had under my thumb are now telling me they no longer wish to supply me with their sexual charms and would rather go bankrupt than sleep with me. You see, I have this room at the Fenimore Hotel. When the woman finally realizes there's no other way, I give her the key, and we spend a few pleasant hours together. She loses all hope of reclaiming her reputation, but has paid me for her home and can feed her children or protect her ailing parents. I had been doing nicely, entertaining as many as three women a week. Now they want to slap my face because Gertrude Carr's story has filtered all over town. I can't show my face anywhere without feeling everyone's eyes burning into my back. I'm losing client's daily. Even those who have never been approached are withdrawing their funds and moving across the street to the First National Bank."

"So you're going to add kidnapping, rape, and murder to your other sins?" I said.

"Oh," he let his fingers stroke my long legs as he undid the rope on my feet, "they'll never know. You'll disappear just like the drunks in those caskets. They'll assume that they, not I, have absconded with you hence doing mischief to you. No one will look here, especially in the caskets. When they see these three, they'll assume they were always here, and the story of the removal of Mrs. Almy's body simply a silly tale."

He leaned over to my face. "I'm sorry for slapping you." He kissed my cheek and then my lips. "Now, we shan't be disturbed," he said with a grin.

A mother's boy controller...think quickly, Trudy. Psychology 201.

"You bastard," I said.

I'm sure that wasn't in the chapter on how to deter maniacs, but I was going crazy. I wasn't following any of the rules the F.B.I. told you to adhere to when faced with a lunatic.

I screamed. I mean, I screamed bloody murder, hysterically, loud, and for a very long time. So much for cool headed Trudy.

"All right. Have it your own way," he said. "Scream your pretty head off. No one will hear you with the vault door closed, and the creek making its splashing sounds."

"Go to hell!"

He laughed. "What colorful language, Gertrude. I rather like it though. I find it titillating. Unfortunately, these interruptions," he motioned to the dead men in their perspective caskets, "have caused us to run out of time. Don't play with me, Gertrude. You won't be the first woman who threatened my business and reputation and mysteriously disappeared."

I was silent. I stared at him.

He chuckled at my reaction. "That's right," he said with this arrogant expression on his face—proud of what he had done. "One young lady was going to tell her father that I was bothering her. I tried to persuade her not to talk and to give me what I wanted. She refused my advances. They found her corpse in the lake. No one could understand how such a strong and healthy young girl could have drowned, or why she had gone so far away from land to swim." He laughed at his brilliance.

"You're a filthy, low-down, scum bastard, aren't you?" I said

"I'd say I was a survivor, Gertrude. Just doing what I have to do to get by. Enough talking."

He kissed me again and looked at my cleavage. "Pity there isn't more time." Then pushed me rudely off the coffin.

He opened the coffin. "Get in," he said.

"What?" My voice quivered. My nightmares were coming true. I was to be placed in a dark, enclosed space by a psychotic killer.

"You won't mind a little darkness will you, Gertrude? That shouldn't frighten an intrepid girl like you." The gun emerged from nowhere. "I *said* get into the coffin!"

I placed my hips onto the rim of the coffin but moved no further. It was awkward with my hands tied behind my back. I felt a horrid, sinking feeling of impending doom. I knew I had insulted him, and there was no way he would let me go. I had nothing to bargain with now. Just a lot of attitude that had placed me in a great deal of trouble with him.

He pushed me, and I flopped into the soft, satin-lined coffin. My wrists ached. I grimaced.

"Perfect." He arranged my clothes and buttoned my blouse—what was left of it—almost as if he cared how I looked in the afterlife. He fixed the curls of my hair around my face and forehead. Took his hanky and wiped my face. He retied my hands in front of my waist, thereby diminishing the aching pain they'd suffered while being tied behind my back. He manacled my ankles with a strap of the rope, but he didn't bind my mouth. The thought of why he hadn't sent shivers up my spine. His finger caressed my lips gently.

"There now, don't you look nice." He leaned over the rim of the coffin positioning himself above my body and gently kissed my lips. "Goodbye, Mrs. Carr."

"Wait! No! What are you going to do?" The lid began to close, and my tied hands raised in a useless attempt to stop it from dropping on me. I screamed and then began sobbing. My cries were stifled as the lid of the coffin was securely fastened over my face. I went beyond hysteria. I was numb with fright. I pounded on the satin roof of the lid. Then bit at my wrist bonds. In a matter of seconds, I was free from the ropes, but I couldn't reach my feet.

I heard his voice beyond my cherry prison. "I told you that if you made me angry, I'd make your last moments slow and painful. I should think it will take some time for you to suffocate to death in there. Hours. Maybe days. Couldn't say."

Then I heard the first screw as it was inserted into the side of the coffin and heard the tool anchor it into place. I cried for help and slapped against the lid until my hands were numb from the initial pain.

"Go ahead and bellow all you want, Gertrude. Scream your lovely head off if you like. It'll capture all the air in your tiny closet."

Now I really went into a frenzy. Darkness, enclosed space, being left alone, slow suffocation, death. No more love. No more Cuyler. No more joy or life. I had found happiness and lost it in a matter of two months.

I wanted my husband. I wanted my little apartment in Milford. I thought of my mother and father, Jennifer, Wainwright, Clarence, Sam and Jim. No one could be so cruel as to kill a person in this manner. I almost wished he had killed me with the gun or the blade...anything but this. These were the last thoughts I would ever have. Seconds of life were left for I could already feel the loss of breath inside the tomb. Life would ebb from me in less than an hour, and the horror of it would be that I would know I was dying for no reason at all. Just the ego stroke of a crazy jerk like Ellis.

I was counting the screws as he fitted them into their proper place. He was finished with the back side of the coffin. He moved to the right side and worked his way around to the front. It was not taking long for him to seal my fate.

I had reached that point where I would beg for mercy, say that I would smile while he took his pleasure with me, anything to save my life, when I heard his voice. He had concluded his task.

He patted the coffin lid. I replied by kicking it with my feet. "How I wish we had had more time together tonight, Gertrude. But, with three murders under my belt, I don't think I should risk staying long in old Doc's final resting place. Farewell, Gertrude. We could have had such fun."

"No, Ellis, my God, you can't do this."

"Oh, yes, I can. I just have. And when I seal the door to the monument, even *I* won't be able to hear your cries for help. But, I will remember them. Forever. They will be the blissful lullaby that shall put me to sleep every night. To know the real truth about Doc Almy's tomb. What a powerful secret it shall be to carry with me every day of my life."

"What do you think you're doing, Ellis?" A voice seemed to come from nowhere. I heard the tool that Ellis had dropped to the floor. I screamed to the voice.

"I ought to kill you," said the voice. Then I heard a tussle, a smack, a groan, and a thud. Ellis was K.O.'d I hoped, but who was there?

The screws were quickly removed, and the lid of the coffin opened. I sat up. There was Cuyler reflected in the shadow of an oil lamp holding a gun that he must have used to clobber Ellis.

"Gertrude, thank God, I've found you," he said.

I threw my arms around his neck, and he lifted me from my promised death.

"Cuyler? Where were you? I was so scared. He almost raped me—killed me. Well, two men almost raped me. They're dead."

"Whoa, one thing at a time. Are you all right?" Cuyler looked at my face. "Who did this to you?" He held me close to keep me from going into shock.

"There were two men who kidnapped me; Tweed in that coffin," I said pointing, "and Clint in that one. Ellis murdered them so that he could take our money and kill me. Some revenge idea. *Oh, I am so glad to see you.* I was so frightened that I'd never see you again." I tried not to cry, as if there were any tears left inside me, but I couldn't stop the flow.

"I've been worried sick that they would killed you," he said. "When I found your rig and the note, I rode all over the county and told everyone to be on the lookout for any signs of foul play. I told the sheriff, and he advised me to pay the money."

"They always do in the movies," I said.

"What?" Cuyler said.

"Never mind. Go on."

"Then little Clarence told us about the 'red house' and your petticoat, so I closed the shop to indicate that I would pay. We thought you were in the Toddsville ghost house. Sally and Mrs. Sloat told us that they'd seen two vagrants talking to Ellis a few days before your abduction. We began to see a connection between your disappearance and Ellis. So, while I delivered the money; Daniel and the sheriff watched the 'red house' tonight. When I came back to the house, obviously disregarding the note under the stone, we realized Ellis must have taken you elsewhere. Then I recalled Nathan saying that he had seen someone down at old Doc Almy's tomb late one night a week ago. He'd been taking his girl home after an Epworth League party and noticed the light. He thought it was odd. He said it looked like someone was working down there. So, in my panic, I thought it might be significant enough to be examined."

Just then the sheriff and Daniel walked into the vault.

I stated for the record that Ellis had masterminded the kidnapping plot and killed the two men in the Almy's coffins. He had thrown Cuyler's money on the floor by the door. I told them that Ellis had also admitted the murder of a young girl previously—the incident appearing to be a drowning accident at the time. Ellis had tried to suffocate me, after attempting to rape me, by sealing me inside this new coffin. Murder, premeditated murder, and attempted murder. I told them that I'd been ill-treated and unmercifully tortured by being tied and gagged for hours at a time, sexually assaulted but not raped, and beaten. If that wasn't enough to hang old Ellis, I didn't know what was.

The look on Cuyler's face must have resembled the expression his ancestor Ralph might have worn when he heard that the British had raped and killed his wife. I was actually afraid he might just kill Ellis on the spot. The gun was in his hand, it was loaded, and I heard the cylinder click waiting for the order to fire...and it was pointed at Ellis's head.

Daniel intervened. He took the gun from Cuyler's frozen hand and released the pressure on the bolt. "Now, Cuyler, let the sheriff do his job. You get Trudy home. She needs a doctor. Take her to the homestead tonight. It's closer than Milford. Let Johanna and your mother take care of her while we take care of Ellis."

The sheriff reassured us with the snap of the handcuffs around Ellis's wrists. Other deputized men came running in and started assessing the damage.

The sheriff spoke directly to me. "We'll need you to sign a report and testify."

How was I going to testify if I were back in 1997?

"If something comes up, and I can't be present, will my sworn testimony be enough."

Cuyler helped as always. "We've had news that her sister in

Brooklyn is doing poorly."

"I see," said the sheriff. "Well, I suppose that'll have to do. I should think justice will be swift with this one. He'll be before the judge by next week. We have an eyewitness to the other men's murder. We have the money, their corpses, the two notes, and Clarence's description of the men in the Toddsville house. That should do it. We may just investigate the other case too. Don't worry, Mr. and Mrs. Carr. Old Ellis will hang for this."

Hang? The death penalty. No more women would experience the fate that young girl and I had endured by his hand. No more women would lower themselves to have sex with this disgusting maggot to save their families and homes again. So, this was part of my fate and part of the reason for my trip into the past. I had changed the dismal history of Ellis's sexual harassment escapades. Because I'd come to Toddsville, I'd played a part in the grand plan to stop the abusive treatment of hundreds of women in Otsego County, simply by stepping into the River of Time.

But, right now I needed to save Cuyler from his ancestral urges to obliterate Ellis. I pretended to faint. I know. How Victorian of me.

I heard Daniel say, "Cuyler, look out. Trudy."

My husband caught me in his arms.

Cuyler said, "You're correct, Daniel. I need to get my wife away from this house of death."

He carried my helpless body to the road above the creek and lifted me into his rig. I heard the clip-clop-sounds Samuel makes as he gallops on dry turf.

I was alive. The valiant Warrior of Toddsville had saved my life again. Any reason left in your mind why I love this guy? I cuddled into his protective arms. He curled his arm around me, clasping me securely into his side for protection. I heard him whisper, "Thank God you're alive. I was so frightened I'd be too late." Then he kissed my hair.

I was treated like a princess for several days by my mother-in-law and Johanna. Sally and Mrs. Sloat visited me the next day, and Daniel brought pink roses. Clarence furnished some hard candy in a bag, and I kissed him on the cheek for helping me.

Cuyler had to work at the store, so I stayed put for a few days and rested from my travail. I was exhausted, dehydrated, and hungry. The doctor cleansed my wounds and found me only in need of tender loving care.

In three days, Cuyler came to take me home. I wanted my little apartment, my bed, and my man.

As soon as we rode into town, all of our neighbors hurried to the store to greet me. I was about to tell the story for the hundredth time, when Cuyler told everyone I needed rest.

Mrs. Bates brought meals for three days solid. She said it was no bother since her recipes fed five at a time, and she always had leftovers.

In the calming dusk of our first night together since the kidnapping, we talked.

"Cuyler? You know I don't want to leave." My eyes filled with tears. "I thought I was going to die in that vault, and when I realized that I might never see you again, I panicked. What are we going to do?"

"I had the same reaction to the situation," my love said. "It was odd. I never once thought you had flashed back to 1997. It never even crossed my mind. Life has become so domestic, so average, normal; I'm not sure how to describe it. But, it feels so right to come home to you, that I forgot that you're going to leave me. It isn't as if we haven't talked about this, but the reality of the situation was made clearer when I thought that you might be gone forever."

"We have to think of a story. I can't hurt the ones I love. I can't let little Clarence think I deserted him. I can't have your mother thinking that I'm a horrible wife for leaving you when you need me most. Of course, we cannot tell them the truth, and I hate lying to everyone," I said.

"I must admit that I too regret falsifying your departure for the same reason. I don't want others to think that we've had some sort of falling out, and that you've left me."

"The setup comes with no rules and no backup plan. I wonder how others have handled it. Sam just tells Abby that he's trapping fur."

I snuggled my head onto my husband's lap.

"I've been thinking of a plan," he said, then brushed my brown hair with his fingers.

"We say I've joined a mission in South Africa."

"Nice try, Gertrude. No, we'll say that you've heard from your sister, and that she's ill, or depressed, or something. You have to leave to be with her, and you are unsure when you can return. After all, you're her only living relative"

I looked up and regarded his eyes. "We've made her so real. It seems we talk about her as if she really is in Brooklyn waiting for me."

Then I reached my hand to his face and kissed him on the lips. "You've saved my life twice. I'll do whatever you wish to support whatever story you decide is best. You can even tell them you've received letters from me. If I don't make it back to you in December, say that I tried to get away, but my sister had a nervous breakdown or something." I put my arms around his waist and listened to his heart's rhythm against my cheek.

He raised my chin with his two fingers and gazed into my eyes.

"It's going to happen to us, isn't it?"

"I'm afraid so," I said, and touched his lips with my index finger then let it outline his chin almost as if I were etching it into my memory.

"I'll have the new house ready for your return," he said.

"I promise to search every conceivable avenue until I find the answers we need. *I will make it back*. Whether it's in December or June, I'll return to you, because without you I have no reason to live."

"Gertrude." He hugged me and kissed the tousled brown curls on my head.

We made love in our warm, comfortable bed. I snuggled in his arms all night long, but I didn't sleep. I wanted to find the answers, and I didn't know where I could research such a topic.

Chapter Thirty-Four

A melancholy atmosphere pervaded our daily activities for a few days after that conversation. Saturday afternoon came with our weekly trip to the baseball game. The old routine made us feel as if life had regained its normality. The Richfields even won.

It was "fair week" before you could blink an eyelash. Though Cuyler didn't want to close the store daily, I insisted on shorter hours so that we could be at the fair grounds by one in the afternoon.

I helped Johanna and Mother Carr set up their displays, and it was obvious they would both win in their categories. No one had anything to match Johanna's pies and cakes, and Mother Carr's jams and jellies were far superior to anything I tasted. But, what I was eagerly waiting for were the writing awards.

We screamed with exhilaration at the horse races, listened to the band, eyed the acrobats, ate outlandish delicacies, and went home tired each evening.

Wednesday trailed into focus. The day the winners of the James Fenimore Cooper Award would be announced. The day I had to tell Cuyler he was a contender for a prize and publication. I regarded his every expression, each laugh, each comment, waiting for the moment I could spring my news on him.

We sipped lemonade as we toured the stands for the fiftieth time.

"Really, Gertrude, I don't see why I had to close the shop for the third day in a row. Mother's preserves have already won first prize. I'm not that interested in any of the other exhibits. You've made me examine every horse in the county, I think. I've already made my bid on four. Now you want me to decipher the snouts of pigs and the eyes of cows. I'm exhausted. Let's go home."

"We can't!" I said anxiously. I searched the grandstand and saw the judges climbing the steps. It was four o'clock. The moment of truth in the prose and poetry contest. It was time to tell him.

"Ah, Cuyler, dear. I need to tell you something."

He placed his arms around my waist and smiled into my face.

"What?"

I took a deep breath, looked sweetly into his eyes, and forged ahead. "You've entered the prose writing contest."

He laughed. "Oh, Gertrude, you're so funny," he said, with the cutest grin. "I can't be in a contest like that. I haven't written anything. Really, darling, you can be so clever."

"Yes, you did. Your histories have been entered into the novel writing contest. From your 'red house' story to Daniel Spencer's last shot. I compiled them into an interesting little novel, typed them, entitled them *Reflections of Toddsville,* and said that you were the author, which for my money you are. You don't credit the secretary, and that's all that I did ultimately."

His visage froze with the smile he had worn earlier, as if he were in some state of shock.

"You didn't. Gertrude, say that you didn't." His voice quivered. "This is just a joke."

"It's no joke. I entered my poem and Clarence's in the poetry category; you have entered the novel writing contest. If you win the award, the Orison B. Curpier Co, Inc. Publishing House will purchase your book and place it on every bookstore shelf in all Otsego County. You'll have attained what you have always wanted but never asked for—wanted in your heart of hearts, that is. You are the storyteller, the historian, the creator of wonderful folk tales. You pass the stories on like the Indians who once lived in these hills—like Jim Cooper told me. Not just the telling of the tales either, Cuyler. You add your own brand of suspense, your own style. They're your stories, and you deserve to be praised for them. I've been writing this book since the first week I came here. I was going to give you the manuscript when I left as my own labor of love gift to you. That's why I've been taking notes on every legend you've told me since the day I arrived. Please don't be angry. I did it because I love you."

"I don't know what to say."

"Just say you aren't angry, and that you love me."

The old man said with a grin as wide as a half moon, "And the winner of the James Fenimore Cooper novel writing award is Cuyler E. Carr for *Reflections of Toddsville.*"

The crowd went wild with applause.

He gazed into my face. I was so proud; I cried. "Go get your prize!"

"Gertrude..." For the first time he was speechless.

"You're not angry? Listen to that applause. Go and get your prize." I brushed my tears away with the back of my hand as I joined their applause.

Cuyler crushed me in his arms and kissed me which only made the crowd explode with continued adulation.

"I did it because I love you!" I said. The tears ran down my cheeks; I could not hold them back. "Now you know why I needed the typewriter; why the apartment was a mess for a week; and why your dinner was served cold. I had to have it typed by the middle of the month. The day I went to town to deliver our work, was the day I was kidnapped."

"I love you, Mrs. Carr."

"Go get your prize before they change their minds." I pushed him towards the grandstand.

He walked to the stage amid a crowd of adoring citizens who would never forget their love for him. At last, he had that gut-wonderful feeling of being praised for his work, for his ideas. No one would ever be able to take this moment away from him.

I watched proudly as he received his prize. Clarence came to my side, smiled, and we hugged each other. It was like having my own family.

"Speech!" someone cried, and Clarence and I picked up the chant. It was the greatest moment in my life. You might think it would pale in comparison with my own first publishing award, but it was far superior. You cannot imagine how wonderful it is to help another person become recognized for the work they've done. Every moment I strained my back typing his manuscript was repaid when I looked at the smile on his face as he received the handshakes, the loving cup, and the certificate. Speech, indeed, my dearest love!

"Well, this is such a surprise!" he said, and shot a look at me, shook his head in disbelief, and smiled a good honest grin from ear to ear. They handed him the manuscript, and he leafed through it. It was his turn to follow my storyline.

"I must tell you that I never expected to win this great honor." Wasn't that the truth!

Then he motioned for me to join him on the stand. I declined. Clarence pushed me and giggled.

I walked up the stairs and joined him on the stage, modestly hoping to hide behind his jacket.

"This woman here, this wife of mine, helped me by typing my work."

Thank you, Cuyler, for claiming it's yours for it is.

"And I can't tell you how proud I am to receive this wonderful prize." The audience applauded again.

He waved his hands for silence. "Oh, I'm pleased with the James Fenimore Cooper Award, but the prize I was referring to was this one." He hugged me and kissed me right there on the grandstand. "Was there ever such a wife?" His eyes adored my face.

Everyone whistled and cheered, and I noticed a surprised and happy Mother Carr and Johanna rushing to join the throng in front of the grandstand. The expression on their faces said it all. They knew full well who had polished the manuscript—especially Johanna who had purchased typing paper for me so often. Mother Carr recognized the sudden need to move the typewriter to Milford as the answer to this mystery.

The Orison B. Curpier publishing company signed him to their contract as soon as I gave Cuyler the all clear which really confused them. How should Gertrude Johnson Carr know about publishing contracts, and why would her husband trust her instincts on something like this? I wasn't about to see my hard work harmed in any way. But, not to worry...standard contract. Publishing in one year. Jennifer would be proud of me.

We left the stage. I had almost forgotten about my own poetry when I heard them announce the winner of this contest.

"And the winner of the James Fenimore Cooper Award for the best poem is...Clarence Peaslee for 'In Otsego.' "

Clarence squealed, and his mother and new father exclaimed their delight. Manfully, he walked to the stage. He received his award humbly.

"I just want to tell everyone that without the support of Mrs. Carr I would never have entered this contest. Her own poem is quite wonderful, and I would like to share this award with her. I'm honored that you have chosen me for this award."

Everyone applauded. He ambled down the steps from the stage. Then suddenly ran to me. He grabbed me around my waist and cried, "You're the *best*, Gertrude. *I love you.*"

Well, folks, that caught me off guard. Cuyler watched as I

knelt to the boy. "You won the prize, Clarence. I told you it was wonderful. I had nothing to do with it."

"I would never have entered the contest on my own. It had to be typed. You typed it for me. You filled out the application and took it to the newspaper office for me. I shall always love you. Please be my friend forever."

I was so touched by his words; I hugged him close to my heart. Cuyler made that sound in his voice when he is pretending not to cry. "Why, Clarence, I'll always be your friend," I said.

I heard his mother say to Cuyler, "Well, you've got a natural mother there, Cuyler." When I looked at her, she was touching her swollen abdomen and smiling down at me.

"Thank you, Gertrude," she said. "Clarence needed this. He's been writing poetry for years, ever since he could read. I appreciate all you've done to bring him out of his shell."

"Shell?" She must be kidding. The imitation Cuyler who had sauntered up to me at the dance and into my heart.

"Oh, yes, he's been quite a recluse on the farm for some time—writing, never making friends, except his little girlfriend. We had to force him to attend the sociable the night he met you. You treated him as if he were your equal and took the time to speak with him. He's been talking of nothing else for months. You and Cuyler have been a real help to my son. I can't thank you enough."

An expression of joy mixed with foreboding fell over both our faces.

"You go and show that little girlfriend of yours your wonderful prize, all right. I'm sure I saw her and her parents buying fudge at the candy tent. Go along," I said to Clarence.

"Promise you won't leave without saying goodbye to me. You and Cuyler...promise," Clarence said.

I stood and looked down at him. "No," I said solemnly, "I won't leave without saying goodbye, Clarence."

He dashed away to show his award to his girl. Cuyler took my hand in his and squeezed reassurance into it.

"Oh, God." My voice trembled, and I wiped the tears from my eyes.

"Don't, Gertrude, don't do this to yourself. It isn't your fault that you have to leave. But, I think tomorrow we best spend the day preparing everyone for your departure to Brooklyn."

He was correct. Today was Wednesday, the twenty-second of September. On Sunday, September twenty-sixth, after church and dinner at the homestead, I would say goodbye to my apartment in Milford, and, wearing the clothes and adornments I wished to take home with me, be driven by my husband in our little rig pulled by Samuel, to the cabin overlooking Canadarago Lake in Richfield Springs. We would spend our last few remaining hours making love and holding onto each other until two o'clock. That's when I would leave him. It would be the night of the autumn equinox.

The last few days were tangled in a web of opposing emotions. Trying to be mature, realistic, and stay sane, we distanced ourselves during the day with never ending chores. I organized my apartment as though I could keep it that way for nine months. I cooked food, even preserved it, attempting the new recipes his mother had given me, as if I could provide for my husband while I was gone.

We didn't tell the others anything. The moment we opened our mouths to speak of it, someone cut us off with some trivial comment or amusing anecdote they thought Cuyler might want to hear. Finally, Cuyler told me that he would handle the discussions—answer the questions—after I was gone.

My husband spent his daily hours tending to his clients' needs but found occasion to run up the side stairs to see me once in a while.

And at night...at night we unleashed fathoms of pleasure, enjoying our physical love too such extreme, touching upon an ecstasy we were sure no other couple had ever experienced.

Chapter Thirty-Five

I regarded the construction sight of our new home and stepped into Cuyler's carriage for my final trip that Sunday. I had my tapestry bag filled with objects I wanted to take home with me: my notebook, my cameo, my ruby jewelry, and, of course, my Tartan scarf.

As calm as he could be, Cuyler hummed his favorite Irish ballad and waved to all he knew as we approached our church and the homestead for dinner. To all who watched us journey through Cooperstown and Toddsville, it appeared that Cuyler and Gertrude were on a lovely, autumn trip to the cabins at Richfield Springs.

The weather was cooler now, and the leaves on the trees were just beginning to change color. How I wished I could see what it would look like in October and November. But, then I could, couldn't I? I suppose trees don't withstand the season any differently in 1997 than they did in 1897. This notion helped me resolve the plan I had been formulating in my mind for days. I would sell my condo and move to Cooperstown. I would investigate the possibility of buying or renting a nice, old home in the area as soon as I returned. Sorry, Jennifer, but my heart is in Otsego County like Clarence's poem suggested. I had to be able to travel to the cabin quickly for my expeditions to and from the past. There was little point in telling Cuyler about my plans. I mean, it wasn't as if he could e-mail me at my new address.

I suppose that's the oddest thing of all. Separation is not such a big deal in my time period. Husbands and wives constantly run in and out of the house these days. But, to not be able to communicate at all. I couldn't phone him to see how he was doing. I couldn't fax him or write him a letter. If, however, there was a psychic bond between two people, we would always be as close as our hearts would allow us.

I could feel Cuyler's distance that last day. Emotionally, he was falling away from me. Not wanting to digress into a moodiness and lose the charming scamp with the light heart whom I'd fallen in love with, Cuyler "pretended" to notice everyone and everything on our trip and commented non-stop. There was barely a moment's tranquility. For in that stillness came reality—a reality a man needed to face rationally. I'm sure he just planned to give me a kiss and head homeward. This made it more difficult for me. Being forever romantic, I wanted him to hold me reluctantly saying goodbye, and prove that he loved me by warmly supporting me as I flew home.

"Well, it's a lovely day, Gertrude, isn't it?" he said to the top of the trees.

"Yes, Cuyler," I said. "Perhaps we could have one last ride in the 'Trudy'?" I said.

"Splendid idea." He slapped the reins and urged Sam up the last section of the hill. "Well, there's Isaac just in time to give you those items he mentioned he wanted you to take home to his sons," Cuyler said.

Isaac waved and hurried to take the horse and carriage.

"It'll be a good journey tonight, Gertrude," Isaac said. "The sky is clear—no troublesome clouds." I was glad something would go well.

"I suppose you know best, Isaac. Do you have the items for Jim and Sam? I'm quite loaded down as you can see, but I'm sure we can fit some more things into my bag."

He inspected my visage. "You don't have to pretend with me, Gertrude," he said for my ears only. "I know you don't want to leave." He touched my shoulder lovingly, and I remembered another similar occasion with a different Cooper. I thought the dejá vu experience amusing.

"I had some entertaining moments in Granny's attic," he said. "Here's a journal for Sam that I didn't know existed. It's the oldest known record of time traveling I've ever seen in our family. And here's an ornate chain I found that used to adorn rich men's velvet tunics in the 1300s for Jim. I also found a woman's diary from 1589. I can hardly understand it, the ink is almost undetectable, but you may have it if you wish. I didn't want to ruin it by turning the pages, but in your time period you may have more sophisticated methods of reading old manuscripts. My eyes hurt when I try to make out the words. I'd never have seen these if you hadn't asked me to do more research. I thank you, Gertrude. Those sons of mine will too."

I looked at the lady's handwriting. "Why, this is from England."

"Yes, of course, the Coopers go back, just as other families do, to European roots. I believe she was an educated woman, so you should be able to understand the language she uses."

I hugged him. "Thanks so much."

"Well, if anyone can find the answers you can. You're the most determined young woman I've ever met. Who knows, when you come back next time, you might have new information for me, as well. By the way, I heard what you did for Cuyler at the fair, the award—the book."

"Oh, that was nothing." I averted my eyes from his and blushed.

"And I also heard about Ellis," he said.

"I won't be around for the hanging, but I'm sure Cuyler will be there." The court case had been over in a matter of days. Court T.V. would have been out of luck. The evidence was weighty, and the Carrs had many friends, some of whom had been injured in the same way. The little girl Ellis had drowned had been a Todd.

Cuyler steadied the boat, with one foot on the dock and one foot in the boat, and called for me to hurry on board. I placed the objects and the bag on the tulip quilt and hurried down the hill.

The water was cold. We rode to the center of the lake as was our custom. Chatty on all subjects except the one most obvious, I decided to let Cuyler endure this whole thing in his own male way.

We ate a nice, picnic-style dinner—salad, apple pie, and cooled tea-by the hammock from which he had fallen just two months earlier. As darkness came, we silently sat on the porch and watched the sunset in each other's arms. I could sense the agitation and fear growing inside him.

About ten o'clock, we moved into the cabin and prepared for bed. I wasn't in the mood for another story, but Cuyler was cheerful. I was glad that I'd have some support from Sam and Jim when I awoke in the cabin tomorrow, but Cuyler would just put together his rig with the horse and drive home. *Goodbye, Toddsville.*

"Shall we sleep or just sit and talk until it's time?" he said. His attitude was domestic and held the easy manner of a man simply deciding whether to make popcorn and watch the second rental video. "We could make love, and then you could put your clothing back on as it nears two in the morning. You'll want to arrive in decent clothing, I should think, instead of some flimsy, floral..." That was it. He broke.

I held him in my arms kissing his face lightly. "I want you to make love to me," I said. "Now. I brought your favorite nightgown, the one from our first night when Lord Cuyler of Toddsville robbed me of my innocence."

He made a chuckling noise in his throat—the memory vivid in his mind. "Yes, Lady Gertrude. Well do I remember that night. But, no stories this time, all right." His eyes feasted upon mine.

"All right," I said. He picked me up in his strong arms, kissed my lips, smiled as he had on our honeymoon night, and carried me into the bedroom. He kicked my bag onto the floor with a sweep of his foot.

We undressed each other as we had done so often before and kissed each escaping piece of flesh with a bittersweet tenderness. My husband had learned how to arouse me rapidly, and I soon moaned in his muscular arms. Little did I know then that he had quite a surprise planned for me.

I remembered another time in our Milford apartment, and said, "I want to please you! I want to make you happy. Anything you want I shall do for you. Anything at all."

"Never leave my side!" The pain shot into his eyes like lightening.

"I'll be working on that," I said.

There was no need to speak now as communication of a different, more glorious type was altering my passive physique, transforming it into a state of ecstasy.

I arched my back and let him find his way. His rhythm, his timing, his pace, his happiness. My body existed to give him joy. He was animalistic in his passion tonight, and I simply complied, for he never showed that he wanted any movement or caress from me.

I toyed with his hair and ran my finger over his mustache when he kissed me. I warmed my hands in the dark curls on his chest. I allowed my tongue to taste his skin and tried to remember it all. As if some sexual computer in my mind had to 'save' every few seconds if it were to hold these memories for months.

There was no quickness about his loving tonight. My emotions were inflamed. The fire between us burned hotter and was far from what I'd ever experienced in my lifetime. I exhaled his name into his ear as I reached the true zenith of my delight. He became even more insatiable. He whispered into my ear, "You will *never* leave me!"

"No, oh, no," I said, sighing next to him.

"I'll be waiting for you in December; I'll find you in June, but you *must* come back to me. You must never forget me. I'll die without you. Do you understand?"

The tears stung my eyes. "Oh, God, Cuyler, I feel the same loss. I could never forget you. I'll come home. Nothing will stop me."

His suffocating kiss, filled with blazing hot devotion, helped me see his plan. He amazed me. And when he let me breathe again, my passion reached another apex, and I was rapidly losing my very will to breathe. I gasped for air as I sighed his name.

"I love you so."

Such delicious loss of reason overcame my entire countenance. He wanted more from me tonight than a superficial submission to his masculine dominance. I weakened into a deathlike surrender in his arms. My lips quivered next to his. I felt his fever when I touched his skin.

He was the master of my life. I could die in his embrace, culminate my existence with a total loss of will. For he had control of my soul as well as my quivering body, and the tears came swiftly as my lover continued. He could change his cadence from unrelenting abandon to a tender sweetness only the kindhearted man I had married could create.

"Do I make you happy, Gertrude?" He expected an answer? A coherent answer now? He smothered my lips with his. My mind exploded into another detonation of delight that I'd only imagined I'd accomplished.

We were beyond fleshly joy now. Emotional wantonness, mindless acquiescence, and an almost spiritual energy force fused our bodies into one unit.

I beheld his face above me. I whimpered, "Of course."

"There can be no other for you?" His voice was raspy and deep.

I pressed my lips against his cheek and cried, "Never. You know that."

"I have fears too, Gertrude. How do I know that when you go back to your modern world, those who love you might convince you that *I* was just a dream? That this life of ours was a mere fantasy. That some other man may convince you to break your vow to me. You are so beautiful. I'm sure there are those who desire you as a wife. After all, how can you explain marriage to a man they can't see?"

"You have nothing to fear. I'll be a nun in spiritual retreat thinking only of you."

"Will you then?" he said.

"You know I will," I said.

"Then I shall leave you with this." He bent down to my face and kissed me as he reached his own zenith and consummated our love.

With a womanliness I had never felt before, I held him in my arms until he could move his body to his side of the bed and hold me in his arms. Quietly, he said, "I love you." And then, he fell asleep; his face cuddled in the brown curls of my head. I stared at his handsome face and cried for a long time. Those were the last words he would speak to me until we met again.

I didn't want to leave his side, but I needed to dress. Moving about with quiet grace was a problem. Soon, I had my clothes on and the filled tapestry bag in my hands. I placed myself next to my husband, kissed his lips farewell and slept in the same blissful security that he had given me the first night I lay in his lap.

Chapter Thirty-Six

Sam kissed me good morning. His hand rested on my right breast. He thought I was Abby; I thought he was Cuyler.

"How's my little mother this morning?" He patted my abdomen.

I said, "Sam? Sam! Get your hands off my tummy."

"Oh! Trudy!" He sat up and rumpled his hair until he was aware of his surroundings.

"You're back in the cabin, Sam," I said. "I traveled too. I went to Cooperstown 1897, and I'm married. I understand you are too. Jim told me everything when I flashed back during a storm. I'll fill you in on my story later."

I looked at the bed as if I might see Cuyler there. Of course, he wasn't. I had my bag, my Victorian clothes, clutching them fiercely as if they could magically bring him to me.

Sam leaped out of bed.

"I'm sorry, Trudy. I thought you were my Abby. Damn, I hated to leave. We're expecting our fourth child. I wanted to be there for its birth this time. That's a laugh, isn't it? I've never seen one of my kids come into the world."

A veil of grief, which I had a feeling would not lift for months, camouflaged my eyes. "I'm beginning to think none of this is very funny, unless you're Jim. I'm married to a wonderful man, and I had to leave him sleeping beside me. He knows the time travel business, but I can just imagine what he's thinking right now as he rises to face a lonely morning. How's he going to tell his mother that his wife has left him?"

"We have a lot to talk about, but let's see whether Jim has made us some coffee." Sam had regained his earthy logic quicker than I had.

Jim had rolls and coffee on the table for our arrival. My eyes took a quick inventory of my new surroundings: microwave, toaster, coffee maker, electric light. And what did it all matter in the final analysis. I didn't care about modern technology. I just wanted my husband. I did, however, sip the hot coffee Sam handed me.

"Nice outfit," Sam said, smiling at my Gibson girl frills.

I regarded his leather breeches and tunic with fringe and

smiled. "Daniel Shipman," I said.

"What?" he said.

"Never mind—private joke. How does Abby handle all this?"

"I'm at a lost to explain it to her." He shook his sleepy head.

"Why don't you tell her the truth? Who knows, she might believe you. Cuyler did."

"Ah, she'd think I had another woman and was lying to her." His eyes filled with emotion, and he changed the subject. "Gosh, it's good to see you. You look great! Your hair is longer, isn't it? And you've put on a little weight too. It looks good on you. Your cheeks and eyes are glowing."

I had to laugh at that one. I knew all to well why my eyes were sparkling and my cheeks crimson. Cuyler had made six months worth of love to me last night.

"Shit! This sucks!" My real voice came back to me with a vengeance.

"Well, that's something I never expected to hear from a Gibson girl."

"I guess I'd better change." I went into the bedroom, closed the door, and changed into a pair of jeans and a sweatshirt. I felt stifled in the jeans. I thought I would be sick with the heavy fabric so close to my body. How had I ever managed before? Of course, the no bra—no corset sweatshirt look was comfortable.

I inspected one of my bras. It looked painful to me. Then I slipped on my warm socks and running shoes. I carefully hung up my shirt waist blouse and skirt in the closet. Looking at the closet and the cabin reminded me that I was past the allotted time for my reservation. I had overstayed my welcome by 26 days.

When I came out of the room, Jim was there. It was a relief to see him.

He was too chipper for me though. "Well, how's our little traveler?"

"Her attitude sucks," I said.

"I can well imagine. Oh, something came from NYSHA for you a month ago," Jim said.

I knew what it was before I even saw it. It was Cuyler's photo. I opened it slowly and gasped when I saw him.

"Oh, God, thank you for this," I said.

"What is it, Trudy?" Jim said.

I showed him. Sam took a look as well.

"It's Cuyler!" I said.

"This is just what he looked like when I visited in 1890," Jim said.

"He's a little older now," I said smiling, "but the attitude is the same." I held my hand over my eyes to hide my tears, but my trembling shoulders gave away my sorrow.

Sam and Jim picked me up from the chair in which I'd collapsed, and held me like two wonderful brothers.

"I have an old silver frame I just polished. I'll let you have it for the picture. It should be just the right size."

"Thanks, Jim, but you've already been too kind."

"Nonsense, we have to stick together," said Sam.

"But, I was only to stay until August," I said.

"It has been a slow season. Don't worry about it. Stay as long as you want," Jim said.

"Do you mean that?"

"Hey, it's *our* cabin now, right?" Sam said.

"Oh, I have something for you in my bag."

It was like Christmas. I rushed to the bedroom and brought back my tapestry purse. "It's from your great-grandfather."

I showed Sam the journal, and he touched it as if it were a new born infant. I gave the gold chain to Jim who immediately saw the great value it held for him. Then I showed them the diary. There was silence in the room. I wasn't sure why.

"Do you realize what that is?" Sam said.

"The only history book of your family's women travelers," I said.

"Yes, and it could be our salvation," said Sam.

"Because Elizabeth Cooper's marriage and death are not mentioned on the family tree. We have no idea what happened to her after her twentieth birthday. As far as we know, she never married or had children. But, she also never died for we have no account of her burial. It's always been a family puzzle. If Isaac had this, it means there may be a way."

Jim illustrated his lengthy summer computer job, which he had finally completed in late August, to his brother. The small globe held hundreds of colorful flags.

"There are portals all over the world. Many in the Western part of the United States."

I have to admit; I didn't hear much of what he was saying. I was obsessed with my husband's likeness. My heart had broken five minutes ago, and I had no will to go on.

"This journal may hold answers too," Jim said.

"If the diary, or journal, held important information, why didn't Isaac tell me when I asked him about the women travelers?" I said.

"He might not have felt comfortable speaking about family matters with you. He might have wanted you to return with it so that we could all view it together. He knew what the journals were, but they aren't the easiest to decipher," said Sam.

Jim cooked a grander breakfast for us of eggs, toast, and bacon. I consumed it quickly and then ran for the woods and was sick to my stomach. I suppose that's what happens to you after a time traveling flight.

When I was sure my stomach wouldn't overturn again, I ambled back to the cabin.

Sam and Jim framed the door with their backs to the rim, and their arms folded casually across their chests. They had the oddest expressions on their faces.

"Trudy Carr," said Jim. They were both grinning.

"What? What's wrong with you two? I just felt nauseous from the trip. It happens during storms remember," I said.

Sam eyed me in an older brother way. "Definitely, or I miss my bet. I'm seldom wrong about things like that."

"Well, *you* should know." Jim said.

I placed my hands on my hips. "Are you going to fill me in on your private joke?"

"What were you doing last night just before you went into the tunnel?"

I remembered and blushed. "That's personal." They waited. "Well, what do you think I was doing? A woman who won't see her husband for almost a year with a few hours to kill."

"Do you think it's possible?" Sam asked Jim.

"Speeded the process, I'll bet," Jim said.

"What are you both talking about?"

"You're going to be a Mom, Mrs. Carr. Congratulations," said Sam.

I did a slow take and then started to laugh. "Don't be absurd."

"Never question a man who has three children and one on the way. I know a little something about women remember. I have a wife. You've the look of a woman with child."

I fainted. I guess it took them some time to get me inside the house.

"Didn't you take any precautions?" Jim said.

"In 1897, we don't have the pill."

"No, but there are other things. Trust me on this one." I remembered the beach bunnies and his summer excursion. I went all soft and helpless inside.

"I didn't care if I became pregnant! I... I...are you sure about this?"

Jim laughed. "Cuyler's going to be a Papa."

"Oh, my God. We've got to find a way for me to stay with him. What has your e-mail survey found?"

"Not much on the bulletin board under my heading 'Time Traveler's Questions'."

I laughed. "Well, I guess." I gently brushed my stomach with the tips of my fingers. I was pregnant? Oh my, Cuyler, will I have a surprise for you when I see you again.

"Wainwright's finally stopped driving me nuts, but his silence is scary. It's kinda like he's the Energizer bunny who suddenly stops mid thump-ah, if you know what I mean?" said Jim.

"I want to move here," I said.

"Into the cabin? Well, if you really must," said Jim.

"No, I mean to Cooperstown. To an old house preferably."

"To the Carr homestead?" said Jim.

I felt a stabbing pain in my chest. It took me a second to catch my breath. I regarded his expression. "What have you done?"

Sam touched my shoulder with empathy. "What he couldn't do for me. He's gone to the NYSHA files and found you. My time period was not noted for backwood's newspapers. We've yet to find Abby. I gather there's a Gertrude Johnson now, eh, Jim? Is she filling a slot?"

"Yes, and what's really fascinating is that she's changing history as she goes along."

"That comes with the territory, doesn't it?" I said.

"Yeah, but it's still neat to watch. Cuyler never had any children; he never married. You should see the changes. None passed today however. *The Freeman's Journal* now mentions the fair and the literature prizes. I knew you had a hand in that one."

I smiled. "And I suppose he never built a beautiful, Victorian mansion for his wife," I said.

"Not at all. I have all the information you need to this date. I followed your progress up to last Saturday. Then—zap—nothing except what happened to those around you; things you might not want to know about. So, when you've decided what you want to hear, ask away."

I knew what he meant. "Is the Carr homestead still standing?"

He said, "Yes, but it's owned by someone else now. Who knows? When Cuyler II comes along that may change as well."

Sam had been introspective for some time and then asked, "What about that house just down from Tunnicliff's, Jim? The stone Federalist building was for sell when I left."

Jim's eyes sparkled. "No one has purchased it, and it'd be perfect, Trudy. If you really mean you want to move from Brooklyn?"

"Yes, and I'll need some help. If what Sam says is true, I'd better not waste any time. First, I think I'll phone my parents, chat with Jennifer, and find Wainwright. After that's all done, I can do some house hunting, and by winter be moved into my new address. Just one other thing I need to do in the next nine months."

I touched my note pad inside that tapestry bag of mine. "I need to write a book." No, not Cuyler's book of historical anecdotes, although I would mention them. I needed to start on this novel—the explanation of what happened—the 'what-I-did-on-my-summer-vacation' one. Explain why I won't be back. At least, I won't be returning to Brooklyn anyway. Then I think I had better get myself a doctor.

So, Cuyler, that was what you had in mind last night, wasn't it? I hope you have a list of mid-wives, because I'm going to need one.

After the three of us washed and put on more respectable clothing, we went to Cooperstown. My eyes were glued to every nook and cranny. My heart took away all speech by jumping into my throat periodically. I hadn't really examined the town the first two times, but now my eyes savored everything. I was glad

I had made the decision to stay here.

We looked at the house near Tunnicliff's restaurant, and I copied the phone number from the 'For Rent' sign. It would be perfect and close to *our* restaurant. If I'd been alone, I might have had a cup of coffee in the restaurant and dreamed a bit, but I had more to accomplish that day.

The Coopers knew the real estate broker, so we just went over to her office and talked. I was given an appointment and asked to meet her at the house at two in the afternoon.

Then I started to survey the surroundings—comparing the old to the new. There was the horse trough Samuel used to drink from on those hot, Saturday afternoons. The First National Bank looked just as it had one hundred years ago. The Mohican Club was still in business, but the Fenimore Hotel was gone. That saddened me a great deal as it had been so beautiful—so grand. There was, however, an annex to the old hotel across the street that had originally been used for summer cabins. It was now known as the *Inn at Cooperstown.* Someday I would ask to see inside the hotel, but not today.

There was the Otesaga Hotel—on the beach of the lake—that hadn't even been built when Clarence had read his poem to me on the park bench. The building was beautiful. *The Cooper's Inn* took visitors, but I only remembered it as a private home when we went to the 'musicales' at the Fenimore.

Putt's little camera shop was now two shops that sold magazines and souvenirs. Ellis's bank was still in the town, but it had been purchased by a new family—the name had been changed. A store called Mickey's Place had once housed Mrs. Sloat's dress shop, and the Carr Hotel was now a furniture and interior home decoration store. I was dying to see whether it still had the room upstairs where Cuyler and I had danced. The publishers who were to print Cuyler's book but had no home must have obtained one. They were on the Phinney and Augur block corner and still doing business. No doubt funded by Cuyler's splendid book sales.

The First National Bank was now a souvenir store, but still proudly waved its green awnings at me as we passed. My little lingerie shop looked the same but now housed baseball paraphenlia. The Glimmerglass Lake was just as lovely as before. The statue looked just as it had on the day it was first placed in the park. Even the bench where I had first met Ellis still existed.

And the boats. Oh, how I wanted Daniel and his boat. A sailboat was flying across the water in the sun. It was the one owned by the dark haired man I had first noticed before my trip. He reminded me so much of my friend that I had to stop myself from waving a greeting to the man. I wanted to trail my toes over the rim of the sailboat listening to Cuyler tell his stories or his gentle snoring as he slept on Daniel's ornate pillow.

Of course, the older hotels, that had been there a century before Cuyler was even born, still stood. There were so many new houses, and a real street upon which to walk and drive now.

Jim and Sam had no trouble giving me a new tour. Then we proceeded to Milford, and I held my breath. The house, whose existence had not been recorded yet, was not there, but our store and what used to be our bank were. I was thrilled and demanded to see inside my apartment, but whoever owned it now was not present. The real Milford Bank had a new stone building across from Jim's home. The Milford Church and its cemetary were still there. Even some of our familiar restaurant was still standing. I didn't want to leave.

We perused the railroad station, and I remembered how Cuyler promised that he would take me for a trip to Brooklyn on the train one day. Ás much as I scanned the area, I could see nothing that remotely looked like it might have been our home.

With a touch of nostalgia, I instructed them to take me home. To Toddsville. This wasn't going to be an easy trip. We were headed for the homestead. I felt initial dislike for anyone who lived in *my* house, well, Mother Carr's house. It was the house where I enjoyed my wedding day reception, typed a manuscript, enjoyed three meals a day cooked lovingly by Johanna, conversed with Clarence while sipping lemonade, and stole kisses from my fiancé in my bedroom.

I entertained the men with my own tour...all right Cuyler's tour. We passed the original Todd homestead, but the vast majority of Toddsville's shops were gone. I pointed to all the "haunted" sights on the road, shivered as I told them what had happened to the peddler and myself in the "red house," and almost became nauseous all over again when I saw Doc Almy's tomb by the creek. I pointed to Clarence's farm.

I sensed when we were close. I ceased chattering and held onto the door handle of Sam's truck for support.

It was still there! All the Carr houses were still standing in their spots. I didn't see the large barn we had used for the horses and cows, though Cuyler's carriage barn was still there. Of course, the beautiful carriages and tack were gone. A mixture of sadness and delight took a hold of me. The house needed a paint job and some TLC but hadn't been altered one bit. The chimney was wrong however. Johanna had cooked in the back of the house, but the chimney was now on the right side. I couldn't remember one being there before. The whiskey bottle and the glass beneath it were still wedged in the stones between the north windows. The center stone indicating the family name Carr and the date 1825 was there too. There was no sign of our white picket fence however.

I could look at each window and tell whose room it had been. Mother Carr must have replaced the front porch with my money, but her huge flower garden was gone. The perennials still bloomed near the stone facade though. She must have used her money to fix the interior, but I didn't want to bother the owner. I couldn't stand to see it now...see it with someone else's curtains, furnishings, family photos, personality.

He let me inspect our homestead by driving passed it twice. Then he parked on the side road—the Indian Trail Cuyler had loved so much—and I scanned the side and back of the house. It wasn't Cuyler's anymore—nor mine. And the pain of that thought stung my heart while suppressed tears burned my eyes.

I closed my eyes and heard the music the band had played on our wedding day. If I could stay in Cuyler's time, I would see to it that I always kept the homestead in the Carr family. I would plant and weed her garden and paint the exterior religiously. I would see that there would be something of our family's life together to pass on to this child—soon to be born in 1898 —whenever I died.

I asked no questions as we passed the various old cemeteries. The family cemetery was close to the road, and he hesitated to see if I wanted to walk up the short hill. I shook my head from left to right. It was all the comunication I could handle. I didn't want to see what I knew in my heart Jim could have shown me.

As we drove through Fly Creek, I marveled at how nothing had changed. A century had weathered the houses. The road returning to Cooperstown took us passed all Cuyler's favorite farms, and nothing seemed different to me but the asphalt road and the cars whizzing passed us.

Before we went to my appointment with the real estate lady, I asked for one more visitation—The First Presbyterian Church of Cooperstown.

I could have taken a picture of Cuyler and me in front of the very same door on our wedding day and shown it to you. You would marvel that the church hadn't been refashioned much at all over the years. The historic marker was still in the front yard. I almost expected to see Reverend McBride yelling hello to me.

I wanted to see inside, but it was closed. It didn't matter, next Sunday I would be in our pew pretending Cuyler and his mother were next to me and the knitting lady two pews in front. The Carrs would be to the front left, and the Todds to the far right, and I would be home again if only in my dreams.

I can't pretend that I was oblivious to the depression that took control of my soul. Everything seemed too similar. The houses and shops had been restored to their original colors, as I mentioned previously. This made the need to see Mrs. Sloat and Sally scurry out of one of the doorways more desperate. The old baseball park was still there, and I wanted to see Clarence and Cuyler in the stands, munching popcorn, forgetting time while watching the game. I wondered if the Cubans or the Athletics were there today. I expected to see Cuyler's pals smoking and discussing the newspaper on the corner by the Mohican Club while I bought clothes in the stores or took out money from the Cooper's account. I turned my head hoping to spy "Samuel" and the rig by the hotel waiting for us to head homeward. The jewelry store, where I had purchased the watch, was still there. Everything was as it was in 1897, except for one important detail—the people were gone. This transition of being home, but not home, was an emotional low for me.

Chapter Thirty-Seven

I met the chubby lady with the too-tight suit and the two inch heeled shoes at two o'clock. The house had many similarities to our homestead: the old fashioned windows, the arched doorway, the sun porch, a few missing side windows sealed by new stone, and the same stone frame—stones no doubt from Abram Van Horne's quarry—just as the Carr's home. I rented it on the spot. I handed her my check for the first month's payment and signed the necessary papers.

I called my real estate agent in Brooklyn, who had helped me purchase my condo, and told her to sell it. I'd be down to Brooklyn next week to pack. She laughed, but I convinced her that I was moving. I told her that I would have my place empty in two weeks. My new house was void of furniture, but soon I would have everything moved into my Cooperstown home. I promised myself to indulge in purchasing some Victorian antiques for the Federalist-style house.

With that done, I bought us dinner at Tunnicliff's restaurant. When we were finished, we headed for the cabins. Sam, Jim, and Trudy had work to do—time traveling research.

We'd decided to split into two cabins and dive into the journals. Jim would redo the old ones; Sam the new journal—which was meant for him anyway—and the lady's diary was all mine. We agreed not to disturb each other for at least one full day.

There were no more summer guests, a chill was in the air, the harvest apples had been pressed for sweet cider at the Fly Creek cider mill, and the trees were gorgeous rainbows.

I cuddled inside the cabin, on the couch, and began to read the Lady's story. It was too chilly to sit outside on the porch, and I didn't want to watch the sunset without my husband. I was going through a mourning process. The bedroom held warm and happy memories for me not sad ones. I pretended that Cuyler was there in the spirit if not in the flesh. This was the first real day of our separation. When I thought of it, I touched his baby growing inside me and smiled. Finding a doctor had been the only neglected item on the busy day's agenda, but I didn't need a physician to tell me what my woman's heart knew.

Another item on tomorrow's schedule would be to tell Jennifer my new address. I would close all my accounts in my Brooklyn bank and open my new bank account in the First National Bank of Cooperstown tomorrow with the last check I had received from Jennifer.

I realized how beneficial it had been to play the miser for so many years. Now that I had a real need for money, my accounts and my credit proved what a conservative spender and conscientious creditor I was. Now I wanted to splurge.

My task was to decode the diary, and I set upon the labor with enthusiasm. The handwriting was elegant but hurried and difficult to decipher. The dates were blotched, and the pages stuck together. I had to become accustomed to Elizabeth Cooper's ancient terminology, but I got the impression she was simply noting various time traveling incidents as her life progressed.

She had been to Rome and Egypt and didn't seem embarrassed about telling all that she'd done there. I chuckled at her language, rearranging it into my own words.

I thought I should copy the journal onto a disk with footnotes on the language and save it. For this book would not last long unless I could place it in a glass case with the precise temperature needed to keep it safe. The attic heat had probably been sufficient, but Otsego County's winter dampness could finish it.

The amorous lady had undertaken many affairs with kings and conquerors. She was passed eighteen by a few years when writing this diary, I supposed, but apparently not married. The Lady Elizabeth was very rich and had no need of a husband. Her life was full of adventure as it was. One season she made love to Alexander the Great, and the next Caesar—pick your favorite—she traveled extensively. She was Cleopatra's favorite party friend on those hot Egyptian nights where the two of them partook of even hotter male servants. She had a close call in the 1000s with a brutal, masculine monster who tried to rape her. But, a summer in Rome, finding ecstasy in Mark Anthony's arms, helped her regain her gentle nature. Apparently, she never told Cleo about her romance with Mark. She couldn't resist all the handsome men, and who could blame her. Brief assignations were much easier when you were never going to see the man again. How she kept from getting pregnant is beyond me, for the girl was certainly athletic.

Then the book drifts to an unusual time. She must have been

twenty or twenty-one. The writing becomes shorter, lacking the notoriety of the first chapters. Apparently, the Lady Elizabeth had found her spot in time and I read:

It is beyond my comprehension how I should have fallen so afflicted by his charms. I have earnestly endeavored to resist him, but have circumvented to his precious words of love and his promise of marriage. I have tried, in vain, to teach my heart not to beat at such a rapid pace when he is near. But, 'tis all in vain! I sense he is the proper man for me. Alas, I shall have to leave him as I have left the others. My mind will be on him for all eternity. My fondest wish is that I might stay here with him and marry him. To be his wife is my soul's passion. What shall become of my darling? What shall become of me?

She must have traveled with the diary, for she writes in a voice that speaks of the present, and then relates the past as if she were there while she is writing it. The next notation reads as if she were back in her own time:

It is no use. Sister speaks with such wisdom, but my heart cannot learn her words to forget him. I have been entertaining the notion of fleeing to him on the next solstice, forgetting all other plans. If I cannot be with him for all time, then I can at least be with him twice a year. Oh, my darling, what you must think of me leaving you thus—without reason or cause. I love you, and if I must die to be with you, I shall.

Her plan seemed a bit drastic, but, clearly, the lady was in love. There the diary concludes. I suppose, when I piece this together, it'll make sense to me. Women can travel the same way men do. They obviously can reproduce; my pregnancy is living proof of that. You can return to the same world as often as you want. Was she filling her spot or just in love?

I stared at the journal entries while I pondered all I'd learned. A thunderbolt of a tenet hit me. The book was the clue. Either she didn't take it on her last trip, chose not to write anymore, or died. The closer I got to the right questions—the further I got from the right answers.

The night of our group's meeting came, and we all gathered to discuss everybody's research. Sam wasn't happy. The journal he had was from Sam Cooper the great-great-great grandfather of our Sam Cooper and for whom he had been named. His forefather never traveled except to research his ancestors. He'd done this by taking over the body of one of his own ancestors to find out about the 1500s. My Coopers hadn't been aware of this possibility. The original Sam had done this before his marriage—to Abigail. This meant that our Sam had *not* found his spot. He had transferred to his ancestor's body and lived that man's life not his own. The disappointment and heartbreak were obvious on his face. The new research had not helped but destroyed him.

"Then," I said, "Abby is never alone. That's good new, isn't it?"

"To learn that the woman you adore is your great-great-great grandmother isn't such a great discovery, Trudy," he said.

He was right. Reeks of Oedipus. That was why Isaac had raised his eyebrows when I'd mentioned his great-grandson Sam's travels to Abby, and why he'd suddenly "found" this lost journal. We'd learned a new wrinkle in the time traveling guidebook however. You could transfer to your own relative's time slot to see what life for him or her was really like. You could cruise as Jim had and simply enjoy yourself without fear of complete involvement in any way. You could have been born to go back to your true spot in another historic existence. We hadn't learned much about staying in the past or traveling into the future. Critical bits of information for me.

Jim told us that he'd poured over all the previously seen journals and had found Lady Elizabeth Cooper. I told them what I had learned first so that he could blend it with his own data.

Jim explained that she had been a time traveler who had disappeared. The diary had been found near the portal one year after her disappearance. They presumed she had died, or been kidnapped, or run away. The later seemed farfetched as she had tons of money.

We viewed each others' homework as we sipped tea or beer. Suddenly, there was a knock at the door. We examined each others' expressions. No one was expected. I cautiously moved to the door and opened it.

"Where the *hell* have you been, Trudy?"

It was Wainwright! I was happy to see him, but the countenance he bore resembled a certain amount of ownership that I didn't appreciate. "Wainwright, how nice to see you too," I said.

He burst through the door and glared at the two men who were silly with beer.

"Oh, I see," Wainwright said. "A regular party. Menagé et trois. What's all that on the floor?" Only Bruce could get jealous of his lady boss and two men reading *historical journals* together.

I folded my arms across my chest. "Research books. Do come in, Bruce, don't stand on protocol."

"We're having a research party," said Jim, "and you're more than welcome to join us. You're Bruce Wainwright, aren't you? I'm Jim Cooper, and this is my brother, Sam. Don't mind him, he isn't feeling much like himself tonight. Why don't you pull up a piece of wood planking and make yourself comfortable?" Jim had a way of lightening the atmosphere that was tense to say the least. I could see fire in Bruce's bloodshot eyes. Must have taken the red eye flight again.

He softened when he saw that we were all friends, and that two of the "dwarves" were related. My attitude towards them was informal, not appearing to be romantic in nature.

"Would you like something to drink?" I said.

"You're having rum, so will I, I guess." He sat down on the floor.

"I'm not having rum, Bruce, but you're more than welcome to some if you wish."

"Not drinking? Let me guess, you've become the quiet tea and crumpet type," he said sarcastically

"Yes and no. I've never had a crumpet, but I do love tea." I made him a *stiff* rum and Coke. He would need it.

"So, what's going on? I've been trying like mad to get in touch with you," he said.

I did a quick double take in Jim's direction. He nodded that he had been speaking with him on the computer.

"I've e-mailed you," I said.

"Well, of course," Wainwright said, "but hiking trips and camping doesn't sound like you. I was worried."

"You needn't have been, dear Bruce." I let the Victorian language sweep into my voice.

"Are you all right, Trudy? You seem different." He removed his glasses and said, "You look beautiful."

"Well, thanks, Bruce."

"I have a wonderful idea for your new novel," he said, looking at the two men just to make sure it was all right to speak of a plot idea in front of them. "I'm going to need you to travel back to England with me next summer though." Jim gave his spy smirk and shook his head. "I've found some interesting information on the conqueror days of the 1000s. However, I am not at...ah..liberty to bring it to the states."

Jim winked and pointed his finger behind Bruce's head. "Right!" he said almost inaudibly, "I'll just bet you have."

"Well, that's a very kind offer, but I must tell you that I won't be able to travel with you next summer. I've plans to...ah...return to the cabin next summer."

"Why?" he said in disgust, which probably offended Jim and Sam.

"I like it here. It's very relaxing. Besides, my next book will be...ah...more personal, and I plan on using the Victorian Era again."

"I thought you'd exhausted all possible subjects in that genre." He sipped some more of his drink and loosened up a bit.

"Well, let me just relax from my air trip," he said. "You go ahead and continue whatever it was you were doing." He stretched his lean body on the floor and propped himself up with his elbow.

Well, of course, we couldn't.

Jim said, "Hey, Wainwright, why don't you tell us about your vacation to England? I'm sure it's far more exciting than camping around dull, old Cooperstown," he said it so slyly it went unnoticed as sarcasm.

"I told Trudy that I'd discovered many old and informative manuscripts in the churches and libraries both in London and in the other cities to which I've traveled."

"That's amazing." Jim smiled, and lifted his right eyebrow. "How did you find the time to contact Trudy during all of your adventures? I wasn't aware that you could reach a computer that quickly in the countryside towns of England."

"You'd be surprised. I had to hunt them down in libraries mostly. But, once I found one, all I had to do was call 'Sleeping Beauty' here, who sent the sketchiest information, sparsely transferred because of her sudden interest in hiking, etcetera." He sipped more of the rum drink.

I looked at Jim, and he sneered. Sam looked at both of us as if we were doing a hidden agenda thing without him.

"But, I did write to you didn't I, 'Prince Charming'? "

"And it's a good thing you did too," Wainwright said.

"I must have disturbed your fun sending you," I looked quickly at the catcher who threw four low fingers to the floor for me, "*four* messages a day."

"I didn't mind, Trudy. You know how I worry about you."

"It was a relief to hear from you," I said, looking again at the catcher who motioned four more strikes heading the batter's way, "four times a day too. Do you mean you stopped everything just to contact me?"

"Of course, you must know how crazy I am about you. If anything were to happen to you, well, I couldn't live with myself."

"No, I suppose not. And yet with *eight* messages a day to send and answer, your heightened degree of concern and undying adulation, you somehow forgot that my screen name is 'Snow White' not 'Sleeping Beauty'. "

Bruce resembled a man who had just swallowed a fur ball.

Jim laughed. "Oh, how I'd love to know who I've been talking to."

"What're you two talking about?" The picture on Wainwright's face said it all.

I said, "You've been speaking with Jim all summer. With whom has Jim been communicating, dear? Want to tell us what's going on?"

Sheepishly the man—my friend—told us. "Well, I have a friend who does all my mail. I told him all about you, Trudy, all about the cabin and the vacation. But, I was never near a computer all summer."

Sam slammed the journal onto the table next to him and swore, "Damn!"

Bruce inspected the discarded book. "It can't be?" he said in awe.

"What?" I said, prepared to cover the truth.

"That's a time traveling journal, isn't it?" Wainwright said.

We all did a triple glance to each other.

"What do you know about it, Wainwright?" said Sam.

"I've been a time traveler for years. That's why I know so much about history. Don't tell me you are too, Trudy.. I've *dreamed* that it would happen. I always thought...hoped...that you were the sort who could travel. I mean, your respect for history and all. It just seemed natural. I leave in the summer and return in the fall. I make up lies about summer vacations, and my time traveling friend, who's a winter traveler, covers for me."

"Well, Jim has been doing the same thing all summer for me. I traveled rather unexpectedly to 1897 Cooperstown from this portal—the cabin."

"That's great! I traveled from a castle just outside London this time. I like to fly by jet to the departure spot and then flash back. Less risky and tiresome on the body."

Jim said, "Tell me about it."

Wainwright was beside himself with glee. "You travel too?"

"We all do. Although he's a bit upset today about the whole thing. Hey, come over here and have a look at my globe," Jim said.

Wainwright did. I was still astonished that someone I knew so well did this wonderful thing and had kept it a secret from me for so long. I had never suspected. Why would I?

"Yes," Wainwright said, "that's a good likeness of the holes. I don't think anyone has done a graphic depiction like this since Leonardo Da Vinci."

"Leonardo Da...? Are you serious? He traveled too?" Jim said.

"He was one of those 'slot people.' Came from the future and popped into the past."

I said, "Ah, yeah? Well, my-my, I'd like to hear more about that."

"How could he have known as much as he did? I mean, in those days. Stands to reason. Some of history's greatest inventors were time travelers from the future and went to the past to help."

"I'm a General Transfer myself, which means I cruise from one time to the next."

Jim brightened. "So do I. I'm an antique dealer. I like to research the time period and bring home items to sell. Keeps me ahead of the competition."

"I'll bet," Wainwright said and laughed.

Sam said, *"Stop it will you. Enough!"*

Wainwright lowered his voice. "What's wrong with your brother?"

Jim told him about the disoriented husband.

"Oh, I see, a Genealogical Traveler." We looked at him with interest.

"There's a lot of different ways to travel. I usually cruise. Had an interesting time in the Middle Ages this time. That's why I told my friend to type that to you—the sword and sex idea. You can also do past life transfer or what we call Reincarnation Transfers. You have to do research for those two transfers. You can even get costumes, read old letters, things like that."

"What's a Genelogical Transfer? We have no records of that in our journals," Jim said.

"Well, if you Genealogically Transfer, it means you swap lives with a real ancestor. You can do research and get costumes for that too. They're collectively called Selective Transfers and you need the Gemini Effect for them, and that means you become one body with them and live their life for three months."

I handed him another rum and Coke. Keep talking, Wainwright. This guy was worth every penny I paid him.

"A Reincarnation Transfer is different because you're not traveling to a blood relative. You are traveling to a...ah...karma relative, so to speak. You want to go back into the past to learn about a past life—to see what mistakes you've made—triumphs—whatever. I've never done it myself, but I've known others who have."

"So, Sam here has Genelogically Transfered?" I asked.

"Probably. Don't feel bad. Except for a small conveyance of your own personality traits, no one recognizes that there's another soul inside your relative."

"But, Trudy spontaneously transferred," said Sam defensively.

"That can happen. As a matter of fact, it happens quite often. Spontaneous Transfers happen in two ways: Death Transfers and Slot Transfers. Death Transfers are unusual. A person who looks vaguely like the one about to die fills the life void of one who has passed over. Rather like a near-death experience. If someone is near the portal at the time a soul passes out of it, another drops unexpectedly into their body. Everyone thinks the dead person has been revived. The new person is so close in appearance, no one ever notices. You can stay if you want, but if you leave that's it; you can't do it again. The person is presumed to be dead, and you can't play that game more than once. It would be too grim, you know."

"I see. And the Slot Transfer?" I was praying he would say the sweet words I longed to hear.

"Oh, a Slot Transfer must be a person who was born to fill a slot like Leonardo Da Vinci. This person never existed until Leonardo, who was born in 1801, transferred to that time. Actually, the funny part was that Leonardo was an actual artist but a lousy scientist. Thank God he stayed, huh?" Wainwright said.

"Did he *stay* in that time?" I said, getting miffed he was taking so long.

"After the year?" he said.

"After the year," I said.

"Yeah. In Slot Transfers, you have one year after the initial transfer to settle your modern business. Then you can return and stay forever."

Thank you, Lord!

"Actually, it would be cruel if you didn't because you're meant to be there. You can travel back to the present time for short flash back periods, during storms and such, but most Slot Transfers like to stay put. I have heard of cases where they come back and leave messages, letters, diaries, and such. Usually, they fall in love, marry, or achieve fame or fortune, or just enjoy the great feeling they get from helping someone else discover things."

Sam held me in his arms for a second and said, "Thanks, Wainwright. That's just what we wanted to hear, huh, Trudy?"

"I don't get it," Wainwright said.

Jim handed him another drink and said, "You will soon enough, and you're not going to like it."

I tried to be gentle. "Bruce, when I traveled in June, I awoke in this cabin's bed next to the man I used for Hemingway. I *mean* the man who posed for the Smith and Telfer photo I used for Hemingway."

I ran to find the book I'd purchased; the one I'd planned to give Bruce. I handed it to him. "This is your copy of the book. I bought an extra one." I folded the book to the page where Cuyler's picture lay.

Bruce smirked trying to understand what the problem was. "Oh yeah, the guy with the mustache reading the newspaper and smoking the cigar. The well-dressed Victorian *dude*."

I was offended by the smug comment. "Yes, that's right."

"Says here his name was Carr. I bet he freaked when he saw you in his bed."

"He did just that, and then he asked me to marry him to save our reputations."

Bruce sobered. "Hey, he didn't take advantage of you, did he?"

I remembered a morning at the homestead when I had curled my finger seductively in his direction, motioning for him to follow me into my bedroom. "Ah, no, he was a perfect gentleman all the time, but I was meant to be his wife, and we fell in love. Turns out he was...ah...is...a natural storyteller. To make a long story short, we wrote a book together. I left one behind for him to publish and brought my notes back for another book—a more romantic type for my fans in 1997." I noticed but ignored the disappointed and jealous expression on Wainwright's face.

"I learned to give up my reclusive ways and made friends—a whole three towns full of friends. I had neighbors who comforted me when I was sick..." He stopped me.

"Sick? *When* were you sick?" he asked.

"When the sexual harasser tried to rape and kill me by burying me alive in an old tomb; I got a little sick."

Even the Coopers were in awe.

"What? Trudy, I forbid you to return to that time period, slot filler or not."

"Relax. I'm okay. I'm more than okay. I'm in love. My life has a new, more powerful meaning for me. I have Mother Carr and Johanna who love me. There's my good friend Mrs. Sloat who would cut her right arm off for me. Then there's precious Sally and her beau. Oh, and Clarence, he's worth going back to see. Nathan and his fiancé. I must not exclude Mrs. Bates. And I couldn't forget my pastor, Reverend McBride, of the First Presbyterian Church of Cooperstown. And last, but certainly not least, Daniel, whose boat the 'Trudy,' a wedding gift to Cuyler and me, is still docked on this lake."

Jim Cooper lowered his eyes and shook his head. "I had no idea that this experience had been so spiritually awakening for you."

I touched his arm. "You said that I was searching for the thing that I'd already found but hadn't recognized. That was Cuyler. The bonus was a revival of my soul; that gave me a life-giving force; that resurrected me and made me *want* to live. I have someone special waiting for me. I want to bring happiness to those people who love him and there are quite a few. Do you understand?"

Sam said, "I do. You should return anyway, even if you weren't pregnant."

"Pregnant?" said Wainwright. "What the...? You *can't* be pregnant."

"Sam thinks I am. I need a doctor's opinion first, but my heart is telling me it's true. It's rather personal though, and I'd rather not go into the details, if you don't mind. I'm moving to Cooperstown in two weeks with Sam's and Jim's help."

Wainwright put his empty glass on the table. "Congratulations," he said halfheartedly. "I'd always hoped you and I would time travel together. Once I had the nerve to tell you that is."

I hugged my friend. "You'll always be my friend, Bruce. You can visit us in Milford any time you want. Although, I must tell you that Cuyler can get very jealous."

Jim smiled, "Wouldn't you if you were married to Trudy?"

I was surprised by the comment and smiled. "Thank you."

"I told you, when I first met you, that you had an inner glow, a special beauty all your own, a spiritual energy force. When a man finds that sort of woman he needs to hold fast to her. Cuyler's no idiot. He knows what he's got, and he intends to hold onto it forever. I guess he was smart enough to figure out how to do that."

My maternal eyes sparkled. "And I know what I have too." I turned to Wainwright. "Bruce, be happy for me. For once, I am living my own love story."

Wainwright said, "If he ever troubles you or gets mean just come home."

"I don't think that's likely to happen. He's building a mansion for us in Milford. I have finances enough to see that we get through all the depressions and wars that will come soon enough, and see to it that he and I live a happy life."

Sam consoled Bruce. "Jim and I would love to go cruising with you. It's clear I can't return to Abby. I thought she was alone all this time. I guess she believed my fur trapping story because it was true. Now that I know, well, I can't go back. I don't have to worry about the kids; I know how *we'll* turn out."

We laughed. It was good to hear the jovial tone in Sam's voice return.

We spent the rest of the evening trading stories. I told Bruce about Cooperstown, and he told me about merry old England. We agreed that I'd continue to write books and flash them back to the cabin. Bruce would send them to Jennifer and keep my bank account for me. I'd tell my parents and Jennifer that I'd not be reached; that I was married and pregnant.

I'd correspond by letters which Bruce would mail for me when he could. He would also write me important messages and leave them during big storms in the hopes that I'd read them. He, Jim, and Sam even promised to sit in the cabin from time to time when the Weather Channel spoke of severe summer storms.

Of course, they had plans of their own and chatted happily about the summer solstice and where they might want to go for vacations. They had so many ideas, I was sure it would take days for them to figure it all out. I took my picture, in the silver frame Jim had given me, and clasping it to my breast, fell asleep on *our* bed.

Chapter Thirty-Eight

The next month was hectic. I moved from Brooklyn, said goodbye to my neighbor, collected all of my junk, had lunch with Jennifer, and planned Christmas with my parents. I purchased Victorian furniture and mentioned that Bruce was welcome to the antiques and furniture if he wanted to rent the place when I vacated. Soon enough, he would become the lord of my manor, paying bills in my name, and generally playing Gertrude Johnson.

I visited NYSHA and asked if I could see the entire Smith and Telfer collection of photos. They agreed and chatted amiably about how nice it was to have a famous author living in Cooperstown, and how I could research there anytime.

I found it! I was looking to see if Gertrude Johnson's photo, that she had taken on her first day in the Cooperstown circa 1897, was there. It was. With my short hair, my new clothes, and my even newer smile; Putt's picture of me was just as clear and vivid as the day Cuyler and I brought it home to Mother Carr.

Jennifer was not thrilled with the long distance setup because she wanted me to make appearances and go to book signings. I told her about my wonderful reclusive husband, and she said she understood.

The last time I saw her, I cried a little and hugged her. "Thanks for being my best friend. And thank you for the photo book and the cabin in Richfield Springs. You know, maybe you and Sydney should have some kids of your own."

"We are," she said, beaming with joy.

At last, the two college friends had made good in all ways.

I went to the nearest Cooperstown gynecologist. I knew that this visit would be rather tricky. He declared me undeniably pregnant. I would give birth at the close of June or the start of July. If I were lucky, I might stretch the waiting period to July tenth. What a first wedding anniversary present that would be, but even if *he* were born at the solstice, a sort of anniversary wish would be granted. I'd wanted a baby ever since I thought we shouldn't. I hoped Cuyler would be happy he had an heir to the Carr estate.

Anyway, the baby was healthy, and my plan to give birth naturally was received with optimism and pamphlets. I promised the Doc I'd go to the classes, but my husband couldn't as he was out of town. When he gave me a list of good mid-wives and discussed the possibility of a hospital delivery, I smiled and said I'd look at all the options.

Jim told me that in his research of the history of Milford, he'd read about a famous and much loved mid-wife who had helped in the delivery of all the town's kids at the turn of the century. Her name was Mrs. Bates, and she had lived over the Milford bank. I laughed. Could anything be more perfect? PATIENCE! Well, I guess.

I started writing this novel which caused me to relive the happy and sad moments all over again and listen once again to Cuyler's stories. It was as if he and I were sitting next to each other in our carriage and traveling to Toddsville. The book progressed, and the emotions returned vividly. I was loving him as every page was written, which was a comfort to me in my loneliness.

It was not an easy Christmas for many reasons. I struggled through a bittersweet celebration with my parents knowing it would be our last one together. Sensing that Cuyler was waiting for my winter return to the cabin's bedroom, hoping to enjoy our first Christmas together, only added to my maudlin disposition. The solstice had returned, but I had not.

Before I close, I would like to tell you about an incident which occurred one February night—Valentine's Day to be exact.

I was feeling fat, ugly, "blue," and cranky. A horrendous winter blizzard—I had discovered what everyone meant by horrible Cooperstown's weather—was giving me a case of cabin fever. So, I walked out of my warm home, with the cozy fireplace ever alive in its hearth, and went to Tunnicliff's restaurant. I decided that since I was without my man on Valentine's Day, they'd just have to make a special meal for me so that I could celebrate on my own. I wanted to indulge my crying spree.

You remember how Cuyler and I said that we'd try to sense the other's presence by going to Tunnicliff's restaurant because it existed in both our times. Well, I sat down determined to have a feast, maybe drink a little wine and feel really sorry for myself. The room was quiet—no—reverent would be a better word. An eerie spiritual cognizance pervaded the room. There was a hot fire in the fireplace. There was only one other person, a man seated at a far table who was deep into some novel.

The music began.

I smiled at the waitress who took my order for chicken breasts, and decided to placate my mood with a nice glass of White Zinnfadel. Just after she left to get my wine, the restaurant's background music began to play ever so softly over the speakers. I was intuitively aware of the orchestral piece. The melody entranced my soul, but I couldn't place the song's title, or where I'd heard it. I thought it was a love theme from a movie, but I couldn't identify the film.

Then I held my breath, forcing myself to stop trembling and inhale normally. I had seen the movie. I *had* watched that long-forgotten video which had collected dust on my kitchen table. The one which had cost me a fortune to return. The movie had been *Somewhere in Time.* The restaurant was playing the movie's haunting theme from a taped soundtrack, and it seemed as if some supernatural force knew the effect the music would have on me.

I couldn't swallow; I couldn't speak; and the tears came to my eyes quickly. I was afraid the man in the corner would notice.

I dabbed at my eyes with a tissue from my purse and tried to remain cool by sipping water, but, the music held me in each stanza and told me that Cuyler was *here.* Forced to stay in Tunnicliff's restaurant by the 1897 version of this blizzard, he was with me if only in spirit.

The waitress brought my wine, looked at me quizzically, as if she knew the spell I was under, and smiled. With this interesting expression on her face, she moved to the wall's light switch and turned the lighting down. A romantic mood enveloped the dining room.

Now get this, the restaurant played the whole soundtrack from the movie—EVERY SONG—twice. Try to eat and not choke when you want to cry your eyes out with grief and joy. I just knew he was with me—thinking about me over dinner.

Want to add the real corker? As soon as the soundtrack was finished for the *second* time, the waitress started to *hum* the love theme from the movie as she hovered over me with my food and kept smiling into my eyes as if she wanted to give me a secret message. I even asked her for her name. I think it was Becky, Betty, Betsy, or something like that. I tried to read the little name card on her uniform.

Since I was alone, she decided to tell me about the restaurant, how old it was, and how I could walk around the building freely, and look at everything if I wanted.

I contained my emotions. Then the man in the corner turned towards me.

"I don't mean to be bold, but we do seem to be the only two customers in the restaurant, and it seems rather stupid not to share some conversation. What do you say? Share coffee with me?"

"All right," I said. I motioned for him to come to my table. "My name is Trudy, and I write historic fiction-romance novels," I said, as he took the seat.

He told me that he was a doctor, an obstetrician, and if I needed a good baby doctor for the little one, he was fresh out of medical school and looking for clients.

I laughed. "Oh, I'll be all right. I'm new to the area. My baby won't be delivered in Cooperstown. I'm going home for the delivery. Have you lived here all your life?" I said.

"Well, yes, in a manner of speaking. My family has lived in this area for years—Cooperstown, Milford, Toddsville."

"Really? I know some people in the area. Who was your...ah," be careful, Trudy, "forefather?"

"Well, my family line goes way back for many generations, but my great-grandfather was Cuyler E. Carr. In fact, I was named after him."

I stammered, my hands fluttered, and I tried to swallow the coffee. My heart was beating rapidly, the baby kicked gently, and my mind whirled.

"But, I don't suppose you'd have ever heard of my great-grandparents if you just moved here," he said smiling. "Still, the name of Gertrude and Cuyler Carr continues to bring smiles to the faces of the people who live in Otsego County. My forefather was some kinda guy I guess." He chuckled. He had Cuyler's looks without the mustache, the soulful brown eyes, the dark hair, the mischievous twinkle in his eyes, and the smile—oh yes—the smile.

I whispered. "*Yes, he was.*"

"I guess he wrote a history book or something. It won first prize at the fair in 1897, I think—The James Fenimore Cooper Award for prose. You can still find copies of it on the bookshelves of the local Cooperstown bookstores. He owned a store and was a businessman of some fame in those old times."

And you are proud of him, aren't you? I can see it in your eyes.

"Well, it sounds like he was quite a guy." The tears were filling the rims of my eyes, and I was glad the subdued lighting would conceal it.

"Ah, he was *great. Everyone loved him.* Hey, look at the storm." He opened the curtain beside us further to look at the snow. "I'd better get back to my apartment before it blows away. Do you need a ride home?"

The wheels of change had turned again. The baby's growth had reached a pivotal moment in time. There would be an heir to the homestead—the one in Toddsville and the one in Milford. I had someone to leave my possessions to, as well. Wouldn't he be surprised that the author he had entertained one evening at Tunnicliff's restaurant had left him a fortune? I still had one more piece of literature left to write—a will.

He apologized for leaving so soon, but he had enjoyed our talk.

He reminded me, with his business card, where I could reach him if I changed my mind about a baby doctor. He promised that he knew a lot of history if I wanted to know more about the area for my books. His address was all I needed to put my plan into action.

I said goodbye to him, looked at the doctor's card which said: Dr. Cuyler E. Carr obys/gyn/ped., Cooperstown, New York. I sat as rigid as stone for some time.

I must finish the book and be ready to leave. I must return to my time period—our time period—for love was there. Life was there.

As I retrieved my wallet, to get money to pay the bill, and slipped Cuyler Junior's card into the credit card part of it, a new song filled the room from the hidden player.

I knew right away what it was—*I'll Take You Home Again, Kathleen.* Only a murmur in my ear at first, the enchanting Irish ballad floated to me as if it were a spirit itself—meant for my ears alone to hear.

I left extra money for the waitress and put my black wool coat on to leave. But, I couldn't leave. I was drawn by some supernatural power to stay with him until he was ready to go. Stay for a moment more, Gertrude, the spirit seemed to say.

I hummed a few bars of the song he loved, closed my eyes, and smiled. I pretended he was here with me in the restaurant. I imagined he was holding out his arms, motioning for me to come to him, to dance our wedding day waltz with him. He wanted to kiss me and tell me he loved me.

In my vision, he held me close to his heart and embraced me. "I love you, Cuyler," I whispered to the spirit in the room.

"You'll take me home this June, won't you, Cuyler, my love? To Toddsville. To our new home in Milford. Home for all time. Our time. And I cannot wait, my dearest love!"

The End

Author's Note

The story you have just read is true—save some fictionalizing on my part. Cuyler E. Carr and Gertrude Johnson Carr were real people. Clarence Peaslee really wrote his poem and published it in the local newspaper. Mrs. Bates ran a boardinghouse in Milford, New York where Cuyler and Gertrude lived the first few years of their married life. Mrs. Sloat's real name was Mrs. Van Horne, so I changed it. McBride was the real pastor of the church then. Mother Carr was an amiable woman with a beautiful face; Chester Carr was just as handsome as his son. Yes, indeed, much of this story has been fictionalized to add to the reader's amusement, and the characters' adventures in this book are the product of the author's *imagination.*

The "red house" is now a "blue house," and I have a photo of it with an actual ghost coming right out of the right corner window. Doc Almy's tomb still sits by the creek, but you can't see the vault very well anymore because of the green vegetation that covers the door. You should have seen the scratches on my legs trying to get to it! I mean, there are snakes in there! The Indian Trail can be traveled by car, but I wouldn't advise it unless you're filled with rum and Coke. Alas, vandals have harmed the Carr Cemetery, but Cuyler isn't buried there. No...*not* there! The church looks exactly as it used to. The old Carr Hotel in Toddsville was going to be torn down, but a kind soul purchased it and turned it into an apartment building. You can still see the Toddsville general store at the Farmers' Museum. You can also see Governor Dick's carriage there too. The old carriage is quite lovely and in perfect shape because that was how Cuyler was about historical things he owned. Almost everything he cherished belongs to NYSHA now, and I am supremely happy about that because they are diligent in keeping things preserved for all time. The Carr/Todd family reunion photos are there. Well, a few *are* missing, but there are those who have original copies. Cuyler's photos are safe in the file, but not just anyone can see them. In fact, you can see one of his photos on a hospital wall in Cooperstown, as well as several family reunion pictures at the Otesaga Hotel and at other locations in Cooperstown. No one has forgotten Cuyler.

Ellis's bank still stands. The baseball stadium is a tourist attraction now. The cabin is wonderful, and I go there often. As a matter of fact, I visit Cuyler's home, and the sweet lady who lives there, as much as I can. She loves to hear about Cuyler. There are many facts in this book, however, that did not have to be researched; and there is no one "living" in Cooperstown, Toddsville, or Milford who can tell you why I know them and others do not. Only Sam, Jim, and Wainwright know the truth as to why the song "Somewhere in Time" played in Tunnicliff's that night, and why the book and I are here, but Cuyler is not!

Love and Laughter in the Now and Hereafter,

Hollie Van Horne

Printed in the United States
63846LVS00002B/185